Murder in an

Carlene O'Connor comes from a long line of Irish storytellers. Her great-grandmother emigrated from Ireland to America during the Troubles, and the stories have been flowing ever since. Of all the places across the pond she's wandered, she fell most in love with a walled town in County Limerick and was inspired to create the town of Kilbane, County Cork. Carlene currently divides her time between New York and the Emerald Isle.

Also by Carlene O'Connor

An Irish Village Mystery

Murder in an Irish Village
Murder at an Irish Wedding
Murder in an Irish Churchyard
Murder in an Irish Pub
Murder in an Irish Cottage
Murder at an Irish Christmas
Murder in an Irish Bookshop

Murder
IN AN
Irish Churchyard

CARLENE O'CONNOR

CANELO

First published in the USA in 2018 by Kensington Publishing Corporation

This edition published in the United Kingdom in 2022 by

Canelo
Unit 9, 5th Floor
Cargo Works, 1–2 Hatfields
London, SE1 9PG
United Kingdom

Copyright © Mary Carter 2018

The moral right of Mary Carter writing as Carlene O'Connor to be identified as the creator of this work has been asserted in accordance with the Copyright, Designs and Patents Act, 1988.

All rights reserved. No part of this publication may be reproduced or transmitted in any form or by any means, electronic or mechanical, including photocopy, recording, or any information storage and retrieval system, without permission in writing from the publisher.

A CIP catalogue record for this book is available from the British Library.

Print ISBN 978 1 80032 689 7
Ebook ISBN 978 1 80032 688 0

This book is a work of fiction. Names, characters, businesses, organizations, places and events are either the product of the author's imagination or are used fictitiously. Any resemblance to actual persons, living or dead, events or locales is entirely coincidental.

Look for more great books at www.canelo.co

Printed and bound in Great Britain by Clays Ltd, Elcograf S.p.A.

2

This book is dedicated to:

My mother, Pat Carter. My favorite fan and source of inspiration. Thank you for the idea for this one, including the title!

I can't leave out my other favorite fan, my father, Carl Carter. He buys out all the copies of my books from his local grocery store. Thanks, Dad.

From a headstone in Ireland:

Death leaves a heartache no one can heal,
Love leaves a memory no one can steal

Chapter 1

Siobhán O'Sullivan was up at the wee hours of the morning, combing through her new employee handbook, when Father Kearney discovered a dead man in the cemetery. And unlike the rest of the poor souls in Saint Mary's Churchyard, this one didn't belong there.

When a loud rap sounded on the door to Naomi's Bistro, Siobhán jumped, scattering the *An Garda Síochána* papers across the bistro floor. She scrambled to pick up her mess, and glanced at the large round clock behind the counter. It was the type of clock that might be seen in a railroad station: sturdy iron hands, a beautiful green patina, and large numbers that could be read from a great distance. It gave Siobhán a jolt of unexpected excitement whenever she glanced at it, but this day all she felt was dread. It was half one in the morning. Whoever was at her door at this ungodly hour would not be bearing good news, and her heart began to dance in her chest. She should be in bed, fast asleep. What was she thinking? In a few hours it would be her first day as a guard at the Kilbane Gardai Station. Folks depended on their local guards to be well-rested, not sleep-deprived and as jumpy as a rabbit. She would deal with whoever was at the door with great haste, and then it would be straight to bed.

On her way to the door she nearly tripped over Trigger, their Jack Russell terrier, who was curled up in a ball on top of the mat. He looked up at her through one glaring eye. "Some guard dog, that," she chided him. He yawned and tucked his head back into his body. Siobhán pulled her robe tightly around her, tried to straighten her mass of long red hair, and peeked out the curtain.

Father Kearney stood under a flickering bulb above their door. She'd meant to change it ages ago. There were too many things to keep track of these days. As she opened the door and gazed out, she was surprised to see gorgeous white flakes swirling around the iron street lamps situated up and down Sarsfield Street. The snow they had been predicting for weeks had finally arrived. She would have cried out with glee, had it not been for the priest's deeply troubled expression. She motioned for him to step inside as the cold air came rushing in.

"Hurry," he said, stamping snow onto the floor mat. "There's a dead man in the churchyard."

Siobhán regarded him through a sleep-deprived haze. "I'd say there's more than one, Father."

Father Kearney arched an eyebrow. "This one is lying aboveground." His full cheeks were bright red from the cold and his voice was laced with panic.

"I don't understand." She couldn't possibly have heard him correctly.

"There's a man lying in the cemetery. Aboveground. I'm quite sure he's dead."

Her hearing was fine; it was her brain that was slow to compute. "Who is he?"

Father Kearney shook his head. "That's the other odd bit. I've never seen him before in my life."

A shiver ran through her. Kilbane was a small village, where everybody knew everyone and their business. It was one of the things she loved about home. It was one of the things she hated about home. "Could he be passed out from drink?" A lad or even lass passing out from too many pints was not uncommon around Ireland. She threw a silent prayer of gratitude to the heavens that her older brother, James, had been out of alcohol's grip for over three years now.

Father Kearney shook his head and then glanced around, as if he were afraid someone would overhear. "I heard a gunshot." His voice was a low whisper, but it hit Siobhán as if he'd been shouting. "There's a lot of blood."

"Gunshot?" And this bit of news delivered a second jolt. He must be mistaken. Firearms were unheard of in Kilbane. Rare in most of Ireland, thanks be to God. The guards didn't even carry them. Her baton and a stern look were her only sanctioned weapons, and thanks to a hand mirror and hours of practicing, more often than not the look was enough to do the trick. Although it was quite possible she'd perfected her penetrating gaze by raising her siblings. Four younger ones and a sometimes-troubled older brother had been some training, alright. It was grand when you could funnel your life skills into your professional life. If she could just learn to bring down criminals with her brown bread, she'd be sorted.

"Hurry." Father Kearney gestured to her robe.

"I have to call it in. The man might need to be taken to hospital."

Siobhán turned to find her mobile phone when Father Kearney's hand reached out and gently squeezed her arm. "It's too late, pet," he said. "I checked. The poor creature has passed." Father Kearney crossed himself. "God rest his soul."

"Was it self-inflicted?" Suicides, sadly, were common. Siobhán ached for those who were in so much pain that they couldn't see any other way out.

"It's possible. Although…" His eyes darted around again.

"'Although'?"

"I could have sworn I saw a figure running away from the cemetery." He rubbed his eyes as if to erase the image.

"Father. Why didn't you just call 999?"

"I told you. He's passed."

"You know what I mean. Why didn't you call the station?"

"Why do you think *Garda* O'Sullivan?"

A tingle rushed through her: *Garda O'Sullivan. Garda Siobhán. Garda Siobhán O'Sullivan.* She'd been doodling a variety of combinations for her new title, just like lasses did with men they wanted to marry. And hers was more than a crazy daydream, for it was the new reality. Would she ever get used to it? Now that she was on the other side of it, it felt as if her two years at Templemore Garda College had come and gone in the time it took a carousel to go around. But so much had changed in two years. Here she was on the brink of a new career. She never imagined it would be off to such an auspicious start. She immediately felt ashamed. A man was dead. Possibly murdered.

Common sense washed over her. "I can't just assign myself to a case, Father. I must call it in."

Father Kearney frowned. "How do you know what you're calling in unless you give it a look-see first?" There was a message in his eyes. He wanted her to be the first to check out the scene. If she called it in, they wouldn't let a rookie like her anywhere near it. She was the newest member of the guards, so she would be given grunt work, not murder probes.

She definitely should call it in.

However…

This desperate early-morning plea was coming from a priest. Surely, one must listen closely to a man of the cloth. Father Kearney was well-loved in Kilbane. He'd baptized her, presided over her First Communion, heard her confessions, and, most important, hadn't lectured her on her dwindling attendance. Would her superiors really blame her for following his very pointed request?

Furthermore, he had an excellent point. How could she call it in when she didn't even know what exactly she was calling in? Perhaps the man lying in the cemetery was passed out from drink after all. Or someone could be having a laugh, acting the maggot. Perhaps it was fake blood. Shenanigans abounded in the village. Lads got up to no good when boredom set in. Snow made everyone a little mischievous, just like a full moon.

It was settled. She would quickly check out the scene and then call it in. She glanced down at her robe, pajamas, and slippers. "I should change."

He shook his head. "I don't think the company in the cemetery will mind how you're dressed. The dead wait for no man, pet. Hurry."

"Actually, Father, I think that's exactly what they do. Wait. For a long time, like." His frown deepened. "But point taken." She threw her winter coat on over her robe and pajamas, flipped off her slippers, shoved on her snow boots, and finally donned her brand-new garda cap before stepping out the door with the priest.

–

Heads bowed against the snow, they made their way to the churchyard. Her village hushed in the winter, like a television on mute. The wash of pinks, blues, and greens, on the facades of homes and businesses that dotted Sarsfield Street, took on a grayish hue against the winter Irish sky, and even the artistic murals splashed on the sides of pubs—grinning lads holding up giant pints, colorful Guinness advertisements showcasing imbibing animals, and welcoming local business signs—all shrunk under the dome of January. Christmas had passed along with New Year's, and now they were midway through the month. The end couldn't come soon enough for Siobhán; January was her least favorite month. A flash of guilt rose in her as she thought of the man lying in the cemetery. If he had indeed passed, for him the end had most assuredly come too soon.

Surrounded by a medieval stone wall, steeped in history, Siobhán O'Sullivan felt both protected and claustrophobic in Kilbane. The four original entrance gates to the town were posted like friendly sentinels at even intervals. She drank in the sight of the Bally Gate entrance as they neared the churchyard. The wind rattled through them, chilling Siobhán to the bone, and forcing her more than once to grab onto her garda cap to prevent it from flying away. The cap, with its golden shield, was her favorite part of the uniform.

"Why don't you start from the beginning?" Siobhán asked. "Tell me everything you remember." Father Kearney began his tale again. At approximately one in the morning he had been in a deep slumber when he was rudely awoken by a loud bang. "Could it have been a door slamming? Or a motor backfiring?"

"The sound came from the cemetery. I'm sure of it. And then there's the matter of the man lying on the ground."

"Right." If he was correct on all accounts, then they already knew the approximate time of death. And if it was indeed a murder, that would be a big problem. For at one in the morning all potential suspects would point an accusing finger at the same alibi: *the Sandman.* "And then what did you do?"

"I dressed and ran down to the churchyard immediately. That's when I made the gruesome discovery."

An involuntary shudder ripped through her. "Don't worry, Father," Siobhán said, hoping to calm her own nerves. "We'll get to the bottom of this."

Father Kearney pulled his coat up and lowered himself into it as he fought the wind. "There's only two people I trust in this village to properly investigate a crime scene. And one of them is a right fool who tripped off to Dublin because he was terrified of you making changes." Father Kearney glanced at the gold shield on her cap. "Changes you should be very proud of, by the by."

Siobhán tucked the compliment away for later. "Tell me about the figure you saw running away from the scene."

"I'm afraid there's not much to tell, pet. He was wearing dark clothing, and I only saw him from my window high above. A blur going by."

"It was definitely a man?"

"It was a person. I assumed it was a man, but a blur has no gender. Either sex is capable of evil." He shuddered.

"That they are," Siobhán lamented.

They picked up the pace, as if trying to outrun the cold and the snow. Hearing him talk about Macdara

Flannery filled her with the longing of *What-Could-Have-Been*. He *had* been a fool. Browned off that she enrolled in garda college. He was the one who told her she'd make a good investigator. He'd made changes of his own the past few years. He was Detective Sergeant Flannery now, stationed in Dublin. She hadn't seen him since she enrolled in college. Maybe it was for the best. He deserved the promotion, maybe even deserved to get out of this small village. But she'd never imagined life turning out this way. She was the one who was supposed to fly away, explore the great world beyond; he was supposed to be the homebody, begging her to stay. Did life ever work out the way one dreamed?

Siobhán gripped the torch and forced herself to focus. "How many shots did you hear?"

"Just one."

"One's enough."

"'Tis."

The snow was thickening, limiting their vision. What horrible timing. Every single flake would be covering up precious evidence. And she would not be able to do anything but observe. No one would be allowed to touch the body until the state pathologist arrived from Dublin to officially declare it a crime scene. Still, there was great benefit to observing an unspoiled crime scene. Time was of the essence. "Do you mind if I run ahead, Father?"

"Go on then. Be careful. He's lying near the headstones in the back. The oldest section." Siobhán nodded and began to run. She paced herself so she wouldn't slip on the icy ground. Minutes later she was maneuvering along the stone wall that wound around the cemetery like a protective maze. She knew the yard well. Her parents, whose lives were cut short by a drunk driver three years past, were buried in the cemetery, but she turned the torch on, anyway, aiming the beam toward the back, where the oldest headstones could be found. They were her favorite. There was something so awe-inspiring about looking at a link to someone who lived hundreds of years ago. Reading the names and the epitaphs on their tombstones and wondering who they were and what they were like. Did they live life to the fullest? Were they loved? Did they love? A link to history, a testament to the past. So many lost lives, so many buried secrets.

She slipped past towering Celtic crosses and statues of angels, stone hands clasped in prayer. The air held the sharp scent of falling snow. Inscriptions leapt out at her as the light bounced over them: *Beloved Mother. Loving Husband. Our Darling Angel.*

Her heart raced as she continued through the hallowed ground. When she reached the last row, she aimed the light, and there, six graves in, a man was prone on the ground with nary a twitch. He was lying on his side, his right arm stretched out, his index finger protruding. Was he pointing? If so, at what?

She dropped to her knees beside him. Father Kearney was correct; death had come to him. Blue eyes, open and glassy, stared out through snowflake-dotted lashes, and his thin mouth was parted as if he'd died midspeak. *Poor, poor soul.* Just over a fortnight into the brand-new year. Was the killer nearby? Watching?

Siobhán studied the dead man's face. From his generous wrinkles, spotted hands, and full head of white hair, she pegged him to be in his mid to late seventies. There was something so utterly tragic about making it into old age, and then meeting a violent end. *Outrageously unfair.* It took a special kind of evil to purposefully harm an elderly person.

He was wearing a brown trench coat, gray pants, and pointy black shoes. The shades were a horrible match. Perhaps he was color-blind, or simply a man who didn't give two figs about fashion. His tweed cap had fallen off and thick black spectacles had slipped down his long nose. She swung the light over his chest once more. There was no weapon that she could see, bolstering the theory that he did not shoot himself.

A pool of red soaked the stranger's chest and seeped into the ground around him. Partial footprints surrounded the body. Most likely, Father Kearney's prints, but she snapped photos with her mobile before the snow could obliterate their existence.

This was personal. The thought struck her hard and fast. Close range. Perhaps one shot to the heart. A passion kill. She would have to keep her opinions out of the report, as her college advisors often reminded her: "Your opinions, Ms. O'Sullivan, are to stay out of your reports. They're going to get you in trouble one day, if you're not careful."

She bit her lip. *Conjecture frowned upon? What kind of training was that?* Her instincts had served her well in the past. And even if she wasn't going to put them into the report, her opinions began to flood in. *The killer didn't just bump into his victim. He or she most likely* lured *the poor soul here. Who wandered into a cemetery at this hour of the morning?* There was another possibility, one that prickled the hairs on the back of her neck. *Someone might have* chased *this poor man into the cemetery.*

She found herself wanting to apologize to the corpse, to console him. Another bit that had been frowned upon in her training: Do not get emotionally involved with a case, let alone a corpse. There was sense to that, of course. One must keep all possibilities alive while investigating. An open mind was an investigator's most precious tool. Let the facts guide you to a conclusion. Do not come to a conclusion and then try and force the facts to fit. Stay flexible but sharp. Professionalism above all else.

But really, would a quick prayer kill anyone? She silently offered one and then picked up her mobile and called it in.

Chapter 2

Siobhán was about to leave the crime scene and wait for the guards when a glint of a medal on the dead man's lapel caught her eye. She edged closer. It was a pin of an American flag. Was he an American tourist? She swiveled the light on the ground. A piece of cream-colored paper was partially covered in snow. A small corner was visible, but all Siobhán could make out was a smear of black ink and what appeared to be the letter A. She sighed and took a photo. She was dying to pick it up. If only she had the authority and knowledge to do everything herself.

There was nothing else to see on the ground, for the snow was already covering up the crime with its soft blanket. If there were bullet casings, or a gun, or any other clues, they would remain buried until the state pathologist arrived. She glanced at his protruding finger once more. His right hand. The rest of the fingers were curled in tight, and the index finger stretched forward. His finger was slightly crooked at the end, as if his hands had been stricken with arthritis. She followed the trajectory of his finger to the closest headstone:

JOHN MALLON
1828–1903

There was a puzzling inscription on the headstone:

The very bottom of the headstone was faded with time and Siobhán could only make out the vowels *E, U,* and *A,* with too many spaces in between. She had never been one for crossword puzzles. Her dear mam had loved them. Her slim figure was always hunched over a puzzle, solving it with a Biro no less. Siobhán would have needed pencils and a stack of erasers. If only she could turn to her mam now for a little help. In lieu of that, perhaps they would be able to find something in the church burial records. She made a note to speak to Father Kearney about it, then snapped photos as quickly as she could.

Was he pointing at the name *John*? The surname *Mallon*? Something about the dates? "*Out to the field.*" That was a nice way of describing the great beyond. She hoped everyone was in a gorgeous field, filled with love and peace.

The victim had used the last few moments of his life trying to communicate, desperate to tell her something about his killer. If only she knew what he'd been trying to say. "I'll do everything I can to find the person who did this to you," she said softly to the stranger on the ground. "I promise ye that." The man wore a gold wedding band. If this were a robbery, wouldn't he, she, or they have taken it? She wished she could search the body for a wallet. She had no patience for waiting, but, of course, everything had to be done properly. A detective sergeant would have to be assigned to the case. Would it be Macdara? A shiver ran through her at the thought of seeing him again. In the distance a wail of sirens penetrated the silent night. Siobhán clenched her fists. Why were they running their sirens? She'd made it crystal clear when she called it in that the poor fella was dead. The sirens would wake up the insatiable curiosity of the townsfolk. Should she mention this to her superiors? Too late now. Besides, it was probably best to wait until *after* her first official day before doling out sound advice. The guards were here. Time to step back.

–

Siobhán stood on the church steps with Father Kearney as the guards trekked back to the crime scene, fat rolls of yellow tape clutched in their gloved hands. "Our victim appeared to be pointing at a nearby headstone. John Mallon." She showed him that photograph. "Can you look into Saint Mary's burial records?"

"Whatever would you gain from that?"

Siobhán shrugged. "Sometimes you don't know until you see it."

The priest sighed. "Of course. But don't expect a quick turnaround. Records of that age may not be easy to locate."

"I'd appreciate whatever you can do." Next she showed Father Kearney the pictures of the victim, just to make sure he had never seen the man before. He stared at them and then shook his head. "Poor fella." He crossed himself. "On holy grounds no less." His voice was thick with sadness.

"Have you seen anything unusual lately?" Siobhán asked. "Anything at all?"

He looked as if he thought of something, then shook his head. "It's probably nothing."

"Go on."

"I have seen an old lady wandering the churchyard the past week."

Siobhán nodded to show she was listening, but that was hardly alarming. In addition to the regular visits from the folks of Kilbane, cemeteries were a popular tourist destination. They even had a name for them: Tombstone Tourists. "Not a local then?" Siobhán asked. Could this old woman be related to the victim? His wife?

"I'd say not. She was nearly six foot tall. And she left indentations in the ground!" Father Kearney's hands flew off his ample belly and gestured wildly as spittle flew from his mouth. He was very protective of his churchyard.

"Indentations?"

"Stabbing around my churchyard in heels. Why does an elderly lady need high heels when she's already up to the clouds?" He folded his arms across his belly and harrumphed his displeasure.

Siobhán, nearly up to the clouds herself, took a deep breath and held her tongue. "Tell me exactly what you saw."

"Twice I spotted her from my window." He gestured toward his living quarters that loomed over the churchyard. "She was pacing back and forth along the back row."

"The same row where our victim was found?"

Father Kearney gasped. "The very same."

That could be significant. "Go on."

"She was frantic. Mad as a bag of cats, I tell ye. Both times I ran down." He looked around.

"And?" As much as Siobhán loved the anticipation that came with great stories, she was eager for him to spit it out.

"Gone. Poof. Vanished." He rubbed his chin. "I thought maybe it was me. Getting senile. Seeing things in my old age."

Siobhán felt a shiver, and knew the weather wasn't to blame. If anyone else had been telling this story, she would have marked it down to foolishness or tall tales. But Father Kearney was a somber man, even in the best of times. Who was this old woman, and why had she been pacing in the cemetery? Did she have anything to do with the murder?

Siobhán pulled out her notepad. "And you're sure she wasn't from Kilbane?"

"Never seen her before in me life."

"I'd like a full description, please."

"Well, I've only seen her from high above. She was a tall one. Like you. She was wearing a long coat and a small hat."

Siobhán frowned. At Templemore they had been taught the importance of clear descriptions. The tiniest detail could crack a case wide open. But if she went around Kilbane asking after an elderly woman in a long coat and a small hat, she'd be laughed out of the village. Tall, elderly ladies were a rarity in Kilbane. Most of them were petite, even shrinking with age.

"How do you know it was a woman?"

Father Kearney tilted his head. "She had long gray hair. Like a witch."

Siobhán wrote down the description, once again biting her tongue. Her silence was a disappointment to women with long gray hair, feminists, and witches everywhere. "Anything else?" Father Kearney shook his head. "Do you remember the color of the hat or the cap?"

He started to shake his head again. Then thrust his index finger up. "Red!"

"The cap or the coat?"

He frowned. "The cap. No wait. Or was it the coat?"

She sighed as she made a note and added a question mark. Eyewitness accounts were notoriously flawed and had to be taken with a grain of salt. Siobhán took out her mobile again and swiped through the photos. Their victim looked tall. "Is there any chance it wasn't a woman you saw, but this man instead?"

"Unlikely," Father Kearney said with another harrumph. "Unless you found a long gray wig on him and high heels, then I'm sure your training didn't encourage you to play guessing games."

His words stung, but she didn't let it show. "Then is it possible that the figure you saw running away from the churchyard is this mysterious old lady?"

"Possible? Why anything is possible. A blur, I said. *A blur!*"

Siobhán took a deep breath. Murder had a way of tilting everyone on edge. She'd struck a nerve in the priest. Maybe he felt she was accusing him of not paying enough attention. He'd been squinting lately too. It occurred to her that he was having problems with his eyesight and didn't want to admit it. *Most likely at war with growing older. He's a priest, but human first.* Siobhán didn't inquire any further into the sighting of the old lady. That could wait.

Siobhán put her notepad away and looked up to see Garda O'Reilly making a beeline for her. Her favorite guard, Sergeant O'Brien, had retired last year, and Garda O'Reilly was nowhere near as jovial. He was a bullet of a man, with all gun and no powder. He had protruding red ears and a constant look of irritation on his pale face.

He glared at Siobhán. "You came straight here, instead of calling it in?"

"I begged her to come," Father Kearney broke in. "I thought it was a vandal."

Garda O'Reilly tipped his cap to the priest. "I'm not angry with you, Father. But this one knows better. She should have called the station." He squared off with her.

"I called it in the minute I saw the body. Like Father said—"

Garda O'Reilly held up his hand. "Go home."

"I took as many photographs of the crime scene as I could."

"I said go home."

"But I thought you would like to see them."

O'Reilly's eyes traveled over her. "Are you wearing your pajamas?"

There was no way around it. "I am indeed."

The red in Garda O'Reilly's ears spread to his face. "One more word and I'll be putting your first warning into your file," he sputtered. "And I'm reporting this to the detective sergeant assigned to this case."

Siobhán's lips moved, wanting to ask who that might be, but she was smart enough to know when to shut her gob. She nodded to the priest and the senior guard; then she left without another word, heading back down Sarsfield Street to her bistro as the wind and snow swirled around her. *A verbal warning.* She hadn't officially begun her first day and she had already been issued a verbal warning. What if becoming a guard had been a colossal mistake? She'd sacrificed two years for this. Commuting back and forth every single weekend, and never feeling like she was giving enough to either endeavor. She'd lost out on the social relationships cultivated between students on the weekends—parties, study groups, and dates—and lost precious time with her siblings during the weekdays. She'd lost the affections of Macdara Flannery just a year into their blossoming romance. She'd placed a high burden on her brother James, who took on the running of the bistro and the care of the young ones so that she could become a guard. It had been exhausting. On all of them. But it had been for a reason, a purpose. How could she have been so foolish? She would make up for it, do whatever it took to get back in O'Reilly's good graces.

She pulled her coat around her and picked up her pace, as if trying to outrun her thoughts. Her father's voice came into her head like a gentle touch. "*Those who know better do better, petal.*" And she would. From now on, she was going to do better. She was going to do absolutely everything by the book.

Chapter 3

Gráinne O'Sullivan draped herself over the counter at Naomi's Bistro and blew out a puff of air, sending her black fringe temporarily airborne. "Elise yelled at me twice. In my own bistro, like." She lifted her pale hands in an approximation of strangling someone. "Don't ye just want to?"

Siobhán threw a look of warning at her younger sister, then glanced at the kitchen door, behind which the subject of Gráinne's consternation was lurking. Most likely listening. There was something very sneaky about James's new love, but saying that to him would amount to disaster. Her older brother had been smiling so much, she was starting to worry about his jaw, and that was worth something. Even if Elise was like a tiny fly *zizzing* around, driving you mental. Making you want to squash her.

Monday morning had engulfed them and Naomi's Bistro would open in a little under an hour. The comforting smells of Irish rashers, the black and the white pudding, soft-boiled eggs, brown bread, and coffee mingled in the air, and Siobhán clung to them like miniature life rafts. It was one thing to say that it was the little things that made life worth living, but you had to actually stop once in a while and smell them.

"Why are ye sniffing?" Gráinne said. "If you're getting sick, stay away from me."

"I love the smell of brekkie in the morning, I'm taking it all in," Siobhán said, exaggerating the sniff this time, given that it was irritating her sister.

Gráinne shook her head and drummed her painted nails on the counter.

Blue! What will customers think when they get a look at her long blue nails? Siobhán didn't have the energy to lecture her about it. She hadn't slept since returning from the cemetery. She was to wait here until the guards contacted her. *Torture.* Were they going to suspend her? Write her up? Who was the poor man in the cemetery, and where was his killer at this exact moment?

She hadn't breathed a word of the dead man in the cemetery to her siblings, and keeping that big of a secret was clawing a hole in her stomach. She thought changing into her running clothes and charging up and down the stairs would calm her down. Instead, she was just as anxious, and now perspiring on top of it. *Cheer up*, her Da used to say. *Things will get worse.* She had a feeling that saying would bear out today. Her siblings, not to mention the entire town, would hear soon enough, and then gossip would rage through the village like an uncontrolled and unstoppable wildfire. They would pour in, hoping to hear Siobhán's firsthand account of the crime scene. She wouldn't say a word, of course, but it would be good for business. Folks would gather around heaping plates of comfort food and mugs of Barry's tea, just to turn over every tidbit as the case unfolded.

She couldn't stop thinking about the victim. Somewhere somebody was missing him. Most likely, calling his mobile over and over again. Worrying. Waiting. She prayed the guards would identify him as quickly as possible. There was nothing worse than worrying and waiting.

Not to mention there was a killer nearby. Had he or she fled Kilbane, or were they weaving in and out with the locals? It had been snowing steadily since the early hours of the morning. It stopped just short of a foot. She hoped the guards would change their minds and want to examine the photographs she'd taken of the scene.

"Are you listening to me?" Gráinne barked, her dark eyes fixed on Siobhán. "Or do you just want to sniff some more?"

"Sorry. What are you on about?"

Gráinne's pretty eyes narrowed into slits. "What is the matter with you this morning?"

"It's my first day at work."

"So what are you still doing here?"

"Never mind. I'll be going in soon enough." *I can only hope.* "What are you on about?"

"Elise!" Gráinne said.

"She makes James happy," Siobhán said, lowering her voice. "And I need him here."

The sound of *thunking*, like a body being dragged, diverted their attention past the French doors leading into the bistro and to the stairs. Like a lot of families who owned businesses on Sarsfield Street, the O'Sullivan Six (as they were known about Kilbane) lived above the bistro. The youngest O'Sullivan girl, Ann, was on the descent, huffing and dragging her camogie equipment down the steps. When she reached the foyer, she let out a whoop of relief, abandoned her equipment bag where it lay, and bounded into the dining room.

Siobhán sighed. "How many times have I told ye you can't leave your bag in the middle of the floor for someone to trip over?"

Ann looked up and at first Siobhán thought she was rolling her eyes, but she was only counting. "This makes twenty-three."

Siobhán couldn't help but laugh, and Ann's cheerful laugh came bouncing back at her. Since none of the lads had ever joined the hurling team, it was a surprise when Ann took to the stick-and-ball game like she'd been born hoisting up the winning trophy. Almost identical to hurling, camogie was an all-female sport. And their sweet, shy little Ann was a raging tiger on the field. Her siblings never ceased to fill Siobhán with wonder.

"Can't believe you've turned into a jock," Gráinne said, eyeing her younger sister. "That's mad." Ever since Gráinne had come home from New York City, she'd been observing Ann like she was from another planet. Gráinne was most certainly a wee bit jealous. Ann wasn't a child anymore, and her days of following Gráinne around like she was the queen of Kilbane were quickly becoming a thing of the past.

"'Jock,'" Ann said with a shake of her head. "What a misogynistic thing to say."

"What are ye on about?" Gráinne said.

"America is rubbing off on you," Ann said. "And not in a good way."

America. Most likely where the dead man was from. Why else would he be wearing a pin of the American flag?

"Don't be cheeky," Gráinne said.

Is his family here with him, or had he been traveling on his own?

"'Cheeky' is another diminutive word." Ann put her hand on her hips. Gráinne's mouth literally dropped open and this time she glared openly at Siobhán. Siobhán stared out the window, replaying the crime scene.

"I have no idea what we're talking about anymore," Gráinne said. "Just forget it." She swiped her latest fashion magazine off the counter and headed over to an armchair near the fire. She dangled her lean legs over the armrest and buried her face in the pages.

"'Jock' is a misogynistic thing to say, because it implies that girls aren't supposed to get into sports or be any good at them." Ann stood over Gráinne, with hands on hip.

"Whatever," Gráinne said without looking up.

"And 'cheeky' applies to a naughty child, instead of a young woman."

"Are ye listening to yer one?" Gráinne said to Siobhán, jerking her thumb at Ann.

"Yes," Siobhán said. "And I want to go and happily squeeze her teachers and coaches to death."

Ann grinned. Her pale blond hair was cut short and framed her face beautifully. She'd nearly shot up to Siobhán's height of five-nine, missing it by an inch.

"But be careful," Siobhán said to Ann with a wink. "'Pride goeth before the fall.'"

This time both girls' mouths dropped open. Siobhán had imitated their late mother, Naomi O'Sullivan, perfectly, down to the pursed mouth and fist planted on her slim hip. The three soon dissolved into laughter, and the earlier tension dissipated. What a sigh of relief. Siobhán worried about those girls nearly every hour of the day. As much as she supported their independence, and was proud of all her siblings, she equally loathed how everyone was changing, and changing fast. She was guilty of it herself; only five years from thirty, now wasn't that just completely out of control?

"Are ye coming to my game on Saturday?" Ann asked.

"I'll be there with bells on," Siobhán said. *Unless they assign me weekend work as punishment.* She would find out soon enough.

"I meant Gráinne," Ann said. "But I don't mind if ye come too."

"You warm the cockles of my heart," Siobhán said. Ann cocked her head and squinted in confusion. Siobhán sighed, turned to her beautiful machine on the counter, and set about making herself a cappuccino. Some days the heavenly concoction was her only comfort.

"God, I miss New York," Gráinne announced, her voice rising over the *hissing* and *gurgling* of the machine as Siobhán frothed the milk. "The only hurling that goes on there is after a long night of drink." She threw her head back and laughed. Then lifted it and sighed. "Yanks really can't hold their drink."

Siobhán and Ann exchanged a look. Since moving to New York City last year, Gráinne acted as if Kilbane (and most likely all of Ireland) wasn't class enough for the likes of her. If that's what the Big Apple did to folks, Siobhán didn't even want a bite. And to think, Siobhán had been so happy to see her a month ago, just in time for Christmas. Siobhán thought she'd go back right after the New Year, but a fortnight had passed and Gráinne was still hanging around. Even so, Siobhán wanted her to stay. She'd begged her to enroll in college, but Gráinne insisted she wanted a year off. Who in her right mind would think waitressing in Queens, New York, was better than going to college? Siobhán had no idea how her parents would have handled it, but all her attempts at persuading Gráinne to choose a different path had failed miserably.

"Why haven't you headed back if it's so perfect?" Ann asked.

"She'll have to wait until the snow melts now," Siobhán said. Their little village would be practically shut down.

Ann frowned, then bounced to the front windows overlooking Sarsfield Street. "Goodness!" she exclaimed. "It's really coming down." She turned her face, beaming. "School will be canceled."

"Most likely," Siobhán agreed. Which meant when the news of the murder hit, everyone would be snowed in and stir crazy. Not a good combination.

"You won't have a game on Saturday," Gráinne said.

"There's loads of time until Saturday," Siobhán said to Ann's worried face.

"New York wouldn't shut down after a few measly flakes," Gráinne bragged.

Her constant praise of the city was getting to Siobhán. Last night she dreamed she was competing with the Statue of Liberty for Macdara Flannery's attention. "He likes a girl who can stay in one place," the Statue of Liberty said, hoisting her torch.

"I am in one place," Siobhán said.

"I'm tall," the statue said.

"I'm tall," Siobhán said.

"I'm green," the statue said. "And I never change."

She woke up in a sweat.

After they squabbled some more, Ann and Gráinne buried their heads in their smartphones, disappearing into their electronic worlds so thoroughly Siobhán had an urge to push them to see if they'd topple over like stones. Apparently, limiting their exposure to mobile phones and iPads as young ones had done nothing to quell their addiction. Perhaps denial had made things worse. One never knew whether one's parenting skills were effective, no matter how well-intentioned. It was a thankless job. "Are the lads still sleeping?" Siobhán asked. Neither of her sisters looked up.

As if on cue James burst out of the kitchen door. "I'm awake. Been a slave to the cooker since dawn." His dark hair was mussed and there was a spot of bright red lipstick on his cheek.

"Have ye?" Siobhán said, staring at the lipstick.

His eyes narrowed. "Rashers are on, eggs are at-the-ready, brown bread cooling on the rack."

"Thank you."

He shook his head. "No need to thank me. We all do our part." He glanced toward the kitchen. "But you might want to thank Elise."

"Right," Siobhán said. "Not a bother."

"She's a little sensitive," he said.

"Understood."

"She thinks you don't like her."

Gráinne made a strangling noise, and Siobhán shot her a look. She smiled at her older brother. James was as handsome as ever. He so strongly resembled pictures of their da when he was the same age, that it brought a pang to Siobhán every time she looked at him. And although he could change moods like the weather, when James was good, he was very, very good. And these past two years that she had been studying to become a guard, commuting from Templemore, he had been an absolute saint. "Schools are officially closed for the day," he announced with a grin. Even though it meant the young ones would be home and underfoot, James always did like a good snow day.

Gráinne looked up. "Lipstick on you. At this hour of the morning?" She flicked her eyes to Siobhán. "How do you like his 'missus' now?"

The thought of Elise actually being married to James made Siobhán cringe. James didn't appreciate the tease either. He narrowed his eyes, then turned to Siobhán, as if daring her to answer. Siobhán twirled a strand of her long auburn hair around her finger and flashed what she hoped would be mistaken for a genuine smile.

The kitchen door swung open again and Elise darted out like a young deer. Big brown eyes, long fawn-colored hair, and all bounce. Just like Bambi. If Bambi had grown up to be an evil dictator.

Siobhán cleared her throat as James stared at her. "Good morning, Elise," she said. Elise squinted as if trying to puzzle out Siobhán's meaning. "Thank you for getting up so early to start the breakfast. It smells wonderful."

Elise scanned the room, eyes narrowing in disapproval. "Did anyone hear sirens screaming in the middle of the night?"

"I thought that was the two of you," Gráinne said without looking up from her magazine.

"Do you need any help with the breakfast?" Siobhán said, wanting to change the subject.

Elise frowned. "James and I have it sorted. It's all prepped, except for the brown bread."

"James said the brown bread was cooling on the rack." Siobhán kept her voice even. Elise was so confounding.

"But you prepared the batter. All I did was pour it into pans and slide them into the oven." Her voice was on a pitch slightly higher than everyone else's and twice as loud.

"That's right," Siobhán said for the umpteenth time. "I'm the one who makes the brown bread." Siobhán's brown bread was well-loved around Kilbane, and the minute Elise got wind of that, she'd been trying to insert herself into the game. That wasn't happening—even if James smiled so much, he'd need his jaw wired shut.

"Yes, Queen Bee." Elise curtsied. "Or should I call you *Garda* Bee now?"

Siobhán clenched her jaw. "Siobhán will do."

"Siobhán 'will do' what?" Elise said. Her eyes sparkled and her teeth gleamed as she bared them. She was thoroughly enjoying herself.

Siobhán flashed a pained smile in return. The lass had been curtsying and coming up with cheeky little sayings ever since Siobhán had made it clear that she was the only one in the bistro who made the brown bread. Siobhán felt her fists curl at her sides. Elise continued. "The kettle is on the cooker, and the pots and pans are soaking. Bridie is three minutes late." Elise scanned the bistro as if Bridie might pop out from underneath a table. "I'm docking her pay."

Bridie was a neighbor, a dear friend, and a part-time employee. She'd been with Siobhán through thick and thin. She was an energetic and kind woman, and the fact that Elise had taken an instant dislike to her just confirmed Siobhán's suspicions that there was something seriously off about Elise. But for James's sake she kept her gob shut.

"You don't handle anyone's pay," Siobhán said. "And with this weather she's entitled to be late." Elise had apparently spent the night. She wished James wouldn't do that with the younger ones still at home, but he was a grown man and it wasn't her place to lecture.

Was it?

"You should let me handle the pay." Elise brightened. "It would save you time and trouble."

"What on earth would I do with myself without time and trouble?" Siobhán replied with a smile, hoping it would elicit a smile in return.

Elise frowned. "You should at least let me make the brown bread. It's not magic, you know."

"*Never*," Siobhán said.

Elise frowned and began to hum. Or was she making a buzzing noise?

"Why can't you both make brown bread?" James said. Ann and Gráinne gasped from their respective corners.

"Elise is free to make whatever she wants in her own kitchen," Siobhán said. "But we are running a business. You know they love my brown bread." Revered it, worshipped it, craved it. Even during her two years at Templemore, she'd come home on the weekends and double up on the batches so that all James had to do was slide the batter into the pans, and the pans in the oven, during the week. She was doing her best to be kind to Elise, but she was never going to let someone else make the brown bread. Besides, no one knew the secret ingredient, although many tried to guess.

Elise curtsied. "Yes, Queen Bee." Siobhán bit her lip. *Just one little punch. Maybe two.* Instead she entered the hallway and dragged Ann's camogie bag to the wall alongside the front door.

"Something was definitely going on last night," Elise said, following her into the hall. "There were loads of sirens."

As Siobhán ignored Elise's implied question and turned to make her way back into the dining room, a loud rap came upon the door, sending her heart crashing in her chest. What would garda college think of her if they knew a simple knock on the door could startle her so?

Probably take away her credentials, make her do the past two years at Templemore College all over again. She glanced at her certificate framed on the wall, and had half a mind to take it down, just in case anyone wanted it back. Siobhán edged toward the curtains and lifted the end for a peek.

Garda O'Reilly was planted on her stoop, with his face pressed to the glass. His cheeks were ruddy, his hair hidden under his cap, large ears poking out like antennas. He jerked back when he saw Siobhán staring at him, then jabbed a stubby finger at her. Siobhán pointed to the front door and he nodded. Were they going to skip formalities and let her go straightaway? Or was he here because he wanted her help? She couldn't get the dead man out of her mind. And she couldn't think of him without being reminded that there was a killer out there.

"Who is it?" James asked.

"Work," Siobhán said. She hurried and opened the front door, wishing she had changed out of her running clothes. She smiled and stepped back to let him in. He did not smile back and remained on the footpath.

"Garda O'Sullivan," he said, then took her in from head to toe. The good news, she was no longer in her pajamas. Nonetheless, his look still seemed disapproving. Maybe it was just his default expression. Siobhán could feel herself blush. She reprimanded herself. Members of *An Garda Síochána* should not blush.

He thrust a piece of paper at her. "What's this?" she asked as she glanced at it. On it was an address.

"George Dunne. Called to report a break-in."

Chapter 4

A break-in? Siobhán's fingers tingled. George Dunne was an elderly man who had moved to Kilbane last year from Limerick. He kept mostly to himself in a small stone house at the end of Sarsfield Street, behind what used to be Kelly's pub. There were too many abandoned businesses these days.

A break-in right after a murder. Could it have been the killer? Searching for a place to hide, or maybe looking for money or a weapon to escape? Riding out the snowstorm while he or she spied on the investigation?

She was dying to ask Garda O'Reilly what was going on since she'd left the churchyard, but she resisted. Besides, nothing more would happen until the pathologist arrived. "I'm not suspended?" she whispered.

Garda O'Reilly narrowed his eyes and wagged his finger at her. "Don't gloat. Detective Sergeant Flannery said he'd handle it. You'll stay out of trouble until then."

She was right. Macdara Flannery was returning to Kilbane to lead the murder probe. Feelings began to spark inside her as images of Macdara played out in her mind, starting with his rain-soaked body holding her close after he delivered the news of her parents' death, to his contagious laugh, messy hair, lopsided smile, and killer blue eyes. That tall, good-looking, whip-smart man. Who once only had eyes for her. His touch, his desire, his solid

32

dependable frame—all of that was something she thought she'd be able to count on for a long time to come. Life was what happened to you when you were busy making other plans. She hated when clichés panned out.

Garda O'Reilly snapped his fingers.

Siobhán nodded. "I'll be right down in uniform. Shall we go from here?"

A smile crept over his face. "It's just you."

"Just me?" She narrowed her eyes. She knew for a fact they were supposed to work in pairs. "Shouldn't I have a team?"

Garda O'Reilly belted out a laugh. "You weren't asking for a team last night when you scurried into the cemetery all by your lonesome, now were you?"

Siobhán flushed. "I'm very sorry."

"If you ask me, you and your imagination would be better off in the Yank's comic-book store."

He was speaking of Chris Gordon, the only American in town who did, in fact, own a comic-book store. Siobhán wondered if the guards had yet to suss out if the victim was American. She supposed it would be rather silly to ask Chris if he knew of any visiting or missing Americans. The rest of the world was not as cozy (nosy) as Kilbane.

"I'm happy to go on my own, if you'd like," she said.

"It's not a matter of what I like," O'Reilly said. "It's a matter of what I say." She had no idea what that meant, so she just nodded and smiled. "Take thorough notes and report straight back to the office." His lips were twitching. Was he trying to keep from laughing? If so, why?

"Got it." He was gone before she could thank him, doing his best to stride off despite his boots struggling in the deep snow.

"Your first case?" The question came from James, but she turned to find her five siblings staring at her, including Eoin, who was sitting on the bottom steps shoving on his trainers, signature baseball cap on backward, and the youngest, Ciarán, hanging on the bannister, red hair radioactive as usual. Now that he was thirteen, he rarely let her smooth it down. She wanted to freeze him in time, stick him in a bottle, and put him on the shelf. He had shot up in the past two years, he'd be taller than her any day now. But to her, he was still a little boy. Every time she looked at him, her mam's saying came hurtling into her head: "*A face without freckles is like a sky without stars.*" Ciarán's lovely face was filled with stars. He loathed whenever she mentioned it, and she did her best to honor his wishes.

"School is canceled," Ann informed the lads. A cheer rang out. This was Eoin's last year of school. Then he would get his Leaving Certificate and hopefully go to college. Siobhán had one year left to wear him down. So far he was insisting he wanted to be a chef, and that his training would be "da school of life." She was going to give him the school of life, alright, he just didn't know it yet.

Ciarán tripped down the remaining steps and practically hurled himself at the nearest window.

"Snow!" he shouted. "Can we go sledding?"

"I don't think we have a sled," James said.

"We can buy one," Ciarán said.

Eoin strolled to the window. "Deadly." He flashed a grin and turned to Ciarán. "We don't need a sled. We'll just sit you down on your arse at the top of a hill and I'll give you a shove."

Ciarán frowned.

"He's just joking ye," James said. "We can buy a sled." He turned to Siobhán. "So what's the case?"

She took a breath. "A break-in."

"Sounds horrible," Elise said. She blinked her Bambi eyes. "How can ye stand your job?"

"It's my first day," Siobhán said. Elise just blinked.

James glanced at the door. "Aren't you supposed to work in teams?"

Siobhán shrugged. "They trust me to handle it." Her brood frowned. "Better get me legs under me." Siobhán headed for the stairs and tripped right over Ann's hurling bag, her nose smacking on the stone tiles as she went down.

Elise stood over her, hands on hips. "That would have never been left there if I was in charge."

"Sorry!" Ann cried out. "Need to mind my sticks and balls. That was a 'dumb blonde' thing to do."

Gráinne let out a victorious cry. "Who's the 'cheeky misogynist' now?"

—

Siobhán gripped her notepad, and held her breath as she stood in George Dunne's messy kitchen, hoping a show of professional concern would put a damper on his outrage. So far it was backfiring, for the longer she stood before him, the redder his face grew. He was a bony old man, with wispy gray hair that sprouted from his nose and popped up in random patches on his head in a manner that made her want to applaud his follicles for the effort. He wore a red jumper with holes in it, and the only thing keeping his tan trousers from hitting the floor was a thin piece of rope tightly cinched around his waist.

Despite the cold bite of winter outside, she was dying to open a window. The odor of unwashed feet and stale cigarette smoke strangled her as a nearby cuckoo clock ticked away precious moments of her life. The cup of tea he'd given her tasted as if the milk had come from his great-grandfather's cow. She clinked the cup down on the table, praying she wouldn't have a tummyache and mentally counted the seconds until she was out the door.

"Next time your wooly socks go missing, you should go to the shops and buy some more, instead of calling the guards," she said firmly. Did that come out too harsh? Her training hadn't prepared her for this. She wanted her tuition back. There was a dead man lying in the cemetery and she was investigating an old man and his missing dirty socks. The world was cruel.

George Dunne cried out, shaking his fist, spraying her with spittle. "You think stealing an old man's socks in the middle of winter isn't a crime? Shame on ye. I've got frostbite. They're going to have to sever me big toe." He stuck his right foot up, and pointed to his gnarled toes. They were red and pinched, the most abused little piggies she had ever had the displeasure to lay eyes on. He had a crooked index finger to match. Old age was certainly demolishing his digits. She was sure, in that moment, that all the lads back at the Kilbane Gardai Station were busting a gut laughing. Macdara wasn't going to let them suspend her, so they were going to find other ways to torture her. "Where's the detective sergeant? I demanded to see him, not some rookie."

"I assure you I will take your problem back to the station." *And dump it on them.*

They knew. They knew George Dunne was missing a few pairs of wooly socks and they'd wound her up and shoved her off like a right eejit. Humiliation washed over her. It was bad enough that they'd ordered her uniform a half size too small. She could barely breathe or bend over.

She intended to hold her head high when she got back to the station, have a right laugh, even though she'd love nothing more than to line them up and give out a series of hard slaps. *The case of the missing socks... Jaysus.* Siobhán suddenly couldn't remember why she thought spending two years of her life to become a guard was a good idea. She could be in the bistro right now, cozying up to the fire and making herself a nice cuppa. Still, a case was a case. She took a shallow breath.

George jabbed his crooked finger at her. "I want to see a senior guard."

"I'll let them know."

"Give them a bell right now."

"I can't do that, sir."

George Dunne shook his head. "No time for an old man? Why?" He leaned in closer. "Something to do with those sirens screaming last night?"

Siobhán ignored his question. "How do you dry your socks?"

His brow furled. "How do ye mean?"

"Do ye put them in a drying machine, or do ye hang them somewhere to air-dry?" It wasn't the weather to be hanging anything on the clothesline, so she imagined George draped his socks over chairs and windowsills. They had probably slipped to the floor, and with the state of his place, you'd never notice. Stacks of mail were piled in the corner on top of a heap of old newspapers. Books spilled out of their shelves. Dirty dishes rose from the sink like a porcelain mountain. Even the cuckoo looked terrified to peek his head out of the clock. Maybe the old fella didn't wash his socks at all. That could explain the odor.

"I wash them in the basin and hang them around so," he said. "What was it?" George asked, his filmy eyes bulging with curiosity. "Did somebody get taken to hospital? It's not Father Kearney, is it? The commotion was at the church."

So he didn't just hear the sirens, he went out and had a look. The gossip had already begun no doubt. "Father Kearney is fine." She looked around. On the wall hung a painting of Saint Vincent de Paul, the patron saint of charities. It seemed incongruous, his calm, saintly face hanging directly above a scowling George Dunne. She had the urge to tell him that one should be charitable in word and deed, a practice that would keep on giving long after a donation had been spent. However, she wasn't here to lecture the man on how to be a decent human being, so she turned her attention back to the case. "Have you carefully searched the floor and underneath furniture?" As she spoke, she bent down and peeked underneath the kitchen table. It had succumbed to crumbs, and dust, and yesterday's dreams. *Top of my class at Templemore Garda College. Yay, me.* There was a discarded business card with a tree logo wedged underneath a dining chair. She was reaching for it, when the old man poked her with something hard. She turned to find him wielding a broomstick.

"Hey," she said. "Don't even think about doing that again."

"I didn't give you permission to go snooping around."

She stood tall and crossed her arms. "Socks can be very slippery. I can help you look." As long as she didn't have to do any deep knee bends. She'd been keeping up with her running and she was lean. They had definitely ordered her the wrong-size uniform.

"Someone took them out of me hot press."

Siobhán raised an eyebrow and wrote *hot press* on her notepad, then drew a little sock puppet with a scowly face. If he was telling the truth, then someone was probably messing with the old man, having a right old laugh.

"Maybe I should have a look at the hot press."

"It's in me bedroom. I'm not letting a colleen in my bedroom rooting around me drawers." He stared at her breasts as if they were unwelcome intruders.

Siobhán drew a noose around the sock puppet's neck. "And they've not taken anything else? Just your wooly socks?"

He slammed his fist on the table and a mess of sour tea splashed out of her cup and crashed onto the worn surface. She watched it seep into the cracks in the wood and disappear, along with the last of her pride. "I said so, didn't I?"

"Have you seen anyone lurking around?" Her eyes landed on a black-and-white photograph of a somber young man, framed and hanging askew on the wall next to a calendar that was a decade old. It looked like George Dunne as a young man. Better-looking, but the exact same scowl. It was fascinating to her that moods could be genetic.

"What happened at the cemetery last night? Catch a lurker, did ye?"

Siobhán started to think this business about his socks was a ruse to get the dirty details. Since he brought it up, she figured it couldn't hurt to continue the conversation. "Have you run into any Americans in town?"

"The lurker is a Yank?" Excitement rang from his voice.

Siobhán bit her lip. She was skirting the edge. She wasn't here to inquire about the dead man. But she had to ask. "Or tall old ladies?"

"'Tall old ladies'?" He shuddered. This appeared to offend him even more than Yanks, and his face went nightmarishly still.

Siobhán took a step forward. "Anything unusual at all?"

He scratched his chin. "Just me missing socks! And I want the bastard caught and punished to the fullest extent of the law."

"Right, so. Until we do that, may I suggest you buy a few pairs and find a new hiding place for them?" Siobhán took a deep breath and tried, but failed, not to look at them. "Like, say, on your feet."

He squinted hard, stared forlornly at his ruined toes, and then eyed her garda uniform. As she slipped out the door, his parting comment rang after her long after she was gone. "Went to college for this, did ye?"

Chapter 5

Siobhán entered the Kilbane Gardai Station, wedged herself into the hard seat at her wobbly desk, and began to fill out a lifetime of paperwork about missing wooly socks. Several guards were huddled in a clump, just a few feet away, no doubt sharing information about the murder. She sighed. She was dying to be a part of it.

To make matters worse, someone had hung a framed photograph of Macdara Flannery where she would be forced to look at his handsome face every day. Even though she hadn't attended, she could tell it was taken at his going-away party. He was standing in front of a banner that read: CONGRATULATIONS!

Yes. Well-played, Macdara. Get out of Kilbane as fast as you can.

–

At least it was nearing her lunch break. If she just happened to ask a few questions, or overhear gossip by the locals while she was out and about, no one could fault her for that, could they? By now the news of the murder had surely spread. She wanted to find out if anyone had run into tourists in town lately. The thought of doing some real investigating lit a fire in her. She grabbed her coat and was out the door before anyone could stop her.

O'Rourke's pub was at the end of the street, several blocks past Naomi's. Before entering, Siobhán stood on the footpath and stamped snow off her boots. The one snowplow Kilbane owned hadn't been used in ages, and clearing the streets would be slow-going. The people of Kilbane were taking advantage of it: Children were sledding and sliding down the streets; snowmen sprouted up on footpaths; a line snaked out of the hardware store as folks swarmed in for salt, gloves, and shovels. Their village was magical under the soft blanket of snow, and for a moment Siobhán allowed herself to enjoy it.

A snowball whizzed by, narrowly missing her head, and exploded onto the window of the pub. She glared at the culprit, a chubby boy with bright red cheeks. She shook her head at him and he roared with laughter before bending down and gathering more snow in his oversized mitts.

"Oh, no, you don't!" Siobhán bent down, as best she could in her tight uniform, and gathered up a ball of her own. But the youth was faster, and before she could let it fly, his icy weapon hit her directly in the chest. She threw hers at him, aiming for his sleeve.

He ducked and pointed at her chest. "You're dead!"

"You got me." She stamped snow off her boots again and stepped into the pub before his third snowball could hit her in the arse. Her best friend, Maria, was wiping down the counter, chatting easily with a man at the end of the bar as she rotated the cloth. She was a short girl with long, dark hair and a strong body, like a gymnast. Hers was a loud cheerful voice, and it warmed Siobhán at once. Just recently, Maria had returned from a few years at Trinity College in Dublin. Homesickness, mostly for a lad, got the best of her, and she returned without getting her degree.

Siobhán approached the bar. Due to the snow and the drama, every stool was filled, forcing Siobhán to lean at the end of the bar while she watched Maria serve a row of lads without missing a breath or a beat. Declan O'Rourke must have been fetching ice or taking a break.

When Maria finished serving her patrons, she headed for Siobhán. She took one look at her in uniform and brought her a mineral, instead of asking if she'd like a pint.

"Thank you."

Maria leaned in. "What's the story? Who found him?"

Siobhán sighed. She was here to get the gossip, not give it. "I'm sure you know more than me. Has anyone seen an older American man around here recently?"

Maria pointed at Siobhán. "I see what you're doing."

Siobhán blinked. Declan waltzed in with a bucket of ice and grinned. "Hi, petal." He passed her and dumped the ice into the bin. He was bigger than life, as round as he was tall. An institution in Kilbane, he was a Renaissance man, who loved everything from the opera to old Westerns, as evidenced by the posters on the walls. This was his pub and he was respected and adored. He could also strike fear in any lad who decided to get cheeky.

"Hi, Declan."

"Snow and a murder probe," he said, flipping a rag over his shoulder. "'Tis a terrible way to start the year."

"Aye."

"I heard the dead man was a Yank," Declan said. "Is it true?"

"I can't comment just yet," Siobhán said. "It's an ongoing investigation."

"Of course, pet," Declan said. "Why don't you just nod your head if I'm right?"

Siobhán offered a little smile. "Nice try."

He chuckled and ambled over to the other side of the bar. "If he's not an American, then why did I hear you asking Maria if she'd seen any Americans in town?"

Darn it. She bit her bottom lip. She'd have an easier go of it if the folks in this town didn't all consider themselves amateur investigators. The other patrons in the pub, mostly older men, buried their heads into their pints or remained glued to the televisions overhead running sports and horse races. That was odd. Normally they would say hello, and chat about most anything and everything. Maria caught her frown. "They're not used to it," she said with a nod to Siobhán's cap and uniform.

Siobhán sighed. It had been easier getting information out of people when she wasn't a guard. "It's me lunch hour." She leaned in. "What have you heard?"

Maria leaned on the counter and lowered her voice. "A few heads say that an American tourist had been spotted in Houlihan's the past week. I heard he was a nosy fella."

"'Nosy'?" Houlihan's was a pub a few blocks away from Sarsfield Street. It had a younger crowd. They even drew lads as far away as Cork City on the weekends. They had musicians most nights of the week. Siobhán couldn't remember the last time she'd gone out socially and she took a moment to bathe in self-pity.

"Asked a lot of questions, took a lot of notes." Maria glanced at the Biro and pad of paper in Siobhán's hands and frowned. "Like you."

"What kind of questions?" Was there a notebook inside the dead man's trench coat? It wasn't fair that they couldn't investigate straightaway. It was a wonderful thing that murders were so rare in Ireland that they didn't have the authority or resources to deal with it within the village; but all the more frustrating when waiting for the proper channels could compromise a case. It was literally easier to get away with murder here.

Maria shrugged. "I don't have the slightest idea."

Siobhán nodded. "I'll head over."

"Now?"

"They only give me thirty minutes. I'm pretty sure everyone else takes an hour."

Maria's frown deepened. "Where's your lunch?"

"Who has time to eat?"

"I'm making you a ham-and-cheese toastie."

"I have to get to Houlihan's."

"We'll go tonight. When you're finished with work. And you are not wearing that." Maria gestured vaguely around Siobhán's entire body.

"Yes, I am. The lads can keep their dirty paws to themselves."

Maria leaned in with a grin. "Do you also want them keeping their dirty secrets to themselves?"

–

Siobhán stepped into Houlihan's, hoping to keep her winter coat on, but Maria quickly slipped it off her shoulders, insisting Siobhán would have better luck getting lads to talk if she showed a little of the goods and flirted. Her denims and black top were respectable enough, but Maria had insisted on blowing out Siobhán's long hair, and had gone a little heavy on the makeup. But some ideas were timeless, and unlike the heads-in-sand reaction she got when in uniform, here the lads were

45

indeed drawing closer and closer to Siobhán and Maria as the evening wore on. Maria was barely five-two, and although not as classically pretty as Siobhán, her sharp wit and outgoing personality attracted plenty of attention. Maria was a natural-born flirt. When they had most of the lads hovering in their orbit, vying for who could make the women laugh, Siobhán waited until there was a short lull in the conversation and then deftly cut in.

"I heard there was an American man hanging around this pub lately," she said, disgusted with herself for fluttering her eyelashes. "I'm dying to hear the story."

"There was some Yank in here, alright," a lad to her left said. "Old guy. Said he was 'Irish.'" He made air quotes with his hands. "He was here researching his family tree."

Siobhán straightened up. "When was this?"

The lad shrugged. "Friday week."

"What was his name?"

Out came another shrug. "I was half in the bag."

Siobhán sighed. This was turning out to be a waste of cleavage. She was dying to put on a jumper.

"Jimmy might remember." One of the lads yelled across the pub, and a few seconds later a man, presumably Jimmy, ambled over. He was in his thirties with pale hair and an easygoing grin. "Yer man there, Friday week," the lad who called him over said. "Tell us the story."

"The two Yanks?" Jimmy said. His eyes gleamed. He was ready to entertain.

This was news. Siobhán straightened up. "There were two?" She was dying to take out her notebook, but couldn't run the risk that they'd clam up at the sight of it. Lads were strange creatures. They loved a girl who would hang on every word, but they'd get twitchy if you started recording those words.

Lads shook their heads, claiming there was only one.

"I said there were two," Jimmy insisted as he swayed side to side. "Peter, Peter, and Pumpkin Eater." He threw back his head and roared with laughter.

"Were they together, or did you encounter two separately?" Siobhán asked, her impatience growing. She was dying to grab his shoulders and steady him. He was making her dizzy.

"What?" Jimmy shook his head as if her question was too complicated.

"You said there were two lads—"

"He was probably seeing double," one of the men cut in. Rowdy laughter followed.

"You're gorgeous," Jimmy said, sliding Siobhán a drunken grin.

"Were there two men?" Siobhán asked again.

Jimmy was still grinning. "I might have been seeing double." His wide mouth revealed gaps in his teeth.

Lovely.

"Do you have a story for us, or not?" Maria barked. She shoved a stool under him. Jimmy plunked down.

"I remember one thing for sure," Jimmy said, his voice taking on a somber tone. "Young or old, one or two, this one thing I remember."

"Yes?" Siobhán said, clenching her fists and resisting the urge to kick his stool out from under him.

"I'll never forget what he said."

"Spit it out," Maria said.

Jimmy pointed at the bar. "He sat right up there, lifted his pint, and announced that he had come to Ireland to 'right a great wrong.'"

The following day Siobhán was at her desk an hour early. She had typed up every comment she and Maria had gleaned in the pub the other night, although they hardly added up to anything. Most of the witnesses described seeing an older American man in and out of the pub the past week. Several said his first name was Peter, he was staying in Cork City, and that he was here researching his family tree. A few others said they didn't remember his name but they were quite sure it wasn't Peter. One or two lads said the man in question mentioned something about a big television event. Several swore they heard the old man talking about his brother. She looked at all the tidbits she gathered:

Name: Peter... ???
Staying in Cork City
Researching Irish heritage
Possible television show... ?
Brother
One man or two?
Young or old?
"Right a great wrong."

Most of the accounts matched. The ones who thought the man was younger could have been mistaken. Or they had met a different man than the others. It was within the realm of possibility to have more than one American tourist in town. Perhaps Peter had come to Kilbane with someone or met him here.

She had also asked if any of them had seen any tall, strange old ladies about town, and as she had feared, that had elicited a comedy hour rather than any real answers.

Macdara and the state pathologist from Dublin were expected to arrive at the station sometime today. Siobhán hadn't slept a wink.

She took out her photos—she'd had them enlarged and printed—and began taping them up on her wall. She stood back to look at them, paying special attention to the headstone. *John Mallon*. She didn't know anyone in Kilbane with the surname Mallon. Next she glanced at the photo of the poor old man lying on the cold, hard ground. "Are you Peter?" Was there a wife or children staying in Cork City wondering where he was? If so, what had brought him from Cork to Kilbane?

She stared at her notes. Family tree. Something wiggled in the back of her mind, a memory, a reminder, but she couldn't catch it. She took some deep breaths and tried to think calming thoughts. Gorgeous snowflakes. Cappuccinos. Crackling fires. The rolling green hills of Ireland. Fluffy sheep. She'd read somewhere that the subconscious mind cooperated best when it was relaxed and under no pressure. But before she could figure out what was nibbling at the back of her mind, she heard a man clear his throat. She whirled around and there he was, Detective Sergeant Macdara Flannery, his tall frame leaning in the doorway, his brown hair soft and messy as always, his beautiful blue eyes watching her. The sight of him hit her like a gut punch. She let out a little gasp.

"How ya?" he said softly.

Two years had gone by since she'd spoken to him. Two years. She had to fight the urge to throw herself in his arms, and then pummel his chest with her fists. And then kiss him. And then slap him. And then start all over again. "Detective Sergeant." Her voice was barely a whisper. She chided herself, wishing she had the chance to say hello again. Louder this time, a confident hello, as if the pieces of her broken heart weren't rattling around in her chest attempting to put themselves back together at the very sight of him.

He nodded. "Garda O'Sullivan." He broke out in a grin.

They both laughed. She'd been so worried about seeing him again, and now it all melted away with one goofy smile. He, too, seemed to relax, and stepped into her space. "Your first few days on the job and we've got a murder probe," he said. "Now, why doesn't that surprise me?" He sat on the edge of her desk. *We?* Was he going to have her work the case? He folded his arms against his chest and studied her. "You were the first guard on the scene?"

"Yes." She handed him the folder with her notes and gestured to the photographs on the wall. "I know I should have called it in—"

Macdara held up his hand. "I've already spoken with Garda O'Reilly and Father Kearney. I'm going to assume that the next time anything like this happens, your first action will be to call the station."

She prayed he couldn't hear the *thump, thump, thump,* of her heart. "Absolutely."

"A verbal reprimand was issued and went in your file. From now on, O'Sullivan, every step you make must be by the book."

"Yes. I swear to God." She held up her hand.

He gestured to the photos. "Let's have a look." He stood and they stepped up to study them. "The snow was a bit of bad luck," Macdara said. "You were smart to take these."

"Thank you." She pointed to the photo that showed footprints barely visible. "I suspect these are Father Kearney's prints. But perhaps we should compare them to his shoes."

"Indeed." He fixed his eyes on her. "I understand the murder took place just before the snow began to fall?"

"Just before," Siobhán confirmed. "Father Kearney heard a single gunshot at one in the morning. He looked out his window and saw a figure running away. Just a blur, he couldn't even be sure if it was a man or a woman. He dressed, ran down to the churchyard, and discovered our victim. By the time he arrived at my house at half one, the snow had just begun to fall. Our killer caught a lucky break."

"Or..." Macdara said, starting to pace in the tiny cubicle. He stopped. She saw him take in the few items she'd brought to make herself at home. A picture of her siblings taken at her graduation from Templemore, proud grins on their faces, a picture of her at her graduation, a photograph of her parents, and a small lovebird she had whittled for her parents' fortieth wedding anniversary. Whittling was something she used to love to do. It kept her hands busy and her temper in check. She hadn't had time to whittle lately. "Or," Macdara said as he started to pace again, "our killer was paying attention to the weather forecast."

Siobhán hadn't thought of that. *What a rookie mistake! Of course. A premeditated murder.* The killer had learned it was going to snow. A rare event, one that could send the village screeching to a halt. There would be chaos. It would be harder to travel. And, most important, the killer knew it would cover up precious evidence. He or she bided his or her time. But how had he or she lured the victim to the cemetery at that hour of the night?

Once again she wondered if the victim had been chased into the cemetery, and she could imagine it too clearly: the adrenaline, the running in the dark in a strange country, the pursuit, the heart-thumping fear. She had no idea what happened, so it was no use torturing herself thus. She discussed both scenarios with Macdara.

"There's a third possibility," Macdara said.

"Go on."

"Our victim could have entered the cemetery for reasons of his own and *then* our killer enters, taking him by surprise."

"Or the killer could have been taken by surprise. The killer could have *already* been in the cemetery."

"Numerous possibilities," Macdara said. "Our task will be to try and eliminate as many as possible."

"Everyone knows that weather predictions are often wrong," Siobhán said. "How did he or she time it so exact?"

"True," Macdara said. "A bit of luck then, and some educated guessing?"

"So many questions." She filled him in on the mysterious old lady Father Kearney had reported as "stabbing around" his cemetery the week before, and the possibility that there were two American tourists in town. Lastly she pointed to the victim's outstretched hand, his arthritic pointing finger, and the nearest headstone.

"Pointing to something," Macdara mused. "Or reaching for something?"

"Looks like pointing to me."

"Yes, but we can't rule out reaching." Macdara's voice was that of a teacher. He probably didn't need some fresh graduate stomping on his experience, or his new position. He stared at the headstone. "John Mallon." He turned to Siobhán. "Researching his family tree?"

Siobhán grabbed her notes. "Yes. Several witnesses said the American man told them he was here researching his family tree. Also something about 'righting a great wrong.'"

"Mallon," Macdara said. "I don't know any Mallons in town, do you?"

"No," Siobhán said.

Macdara's eyes roamed over the tiny space and the uniform she was squeezed into. Then he looked behind him and saw the photograph of himself hanging just beyond her desk. He looked at her. "Take your hour for lunch. There will be a few changes when you get back."

An hour for lunch. She knew it.

–

When she returned from her lunch break, she found a new uniform hanging on the back of her office door, boxes and files had been cleared out to give her more room, the wobble in the desk was fixed, and the photograph of Macdara had come down and was replaced with a photo of the Cliffs of Moher. As soon as she finished changing into her new uniform, one that fit perfectly, she came out to find Macdara waiting for her.

"Come on," he said. "The Cork City Gardai Station just called. They've got an American family that just filed a missing person's inquiry."

"Finally." Siobhán felt an equal sense of relief and dread.

"There's more." Siobhán held eyes with Macdara. He pointed to the name *Mallon* on the headstone.

"No," she said.

"Yes," he said. "Our victim's name is Peter Mallon."

Chapter 6

It was both thrilling and strange to be back in a car with Macdara, headed for Cork City. Despite this, her nerves were on edge for the family. So far all they knew was that their loved one was missing. They were most likely holding out hope that Peter Mallon would walk in the door at any moment. She wished that were the case, and loathed the burden of delivering the life-shattering news. She wouldn't want anyone other than Macdara Flannery by her side for such a sensitive task.

It was slow-going with the ice and snow, but Macdara was a careful driver. The fields were luminous, covered in a blanket of white, and the Ballyhoura Mountains were stark and gorgeous in the background. Every time Siobhán gazed out, she could feel her heart swell with pride. This gorgeous land was home. She felt sorry for the Mallon family, having tragedy strike when they were so far from where they lived. Siobhán supported the spirit of traveling, but she prayed that when she passed, it would be in this land that she loved.

The state pathologist was examining the body as they spoke; she would call in as soon as there was any news. In the meantime they'd learned from the Cork City Gardai that one Peter Mallon had been missing since the prior afternoon. His family had been calling, but his mobile was going straight to voice mail. Now the voice mailbox was full. Siobhán wondered if the state pathologist would find his mobile phone in his pocket. She was relieved that someone was finally examining the crime scene.

The car began to slide and Macdara eased off the accelerator. Macdara fiddled with the radio, but when a love song came on, he snapped it off. Siobhán turned her attention away from the scenery. "Should we mention the headstone bearing the Mallon name?"

"Not yet," Macdara said. "We're going to get information first. Not give it."

"As I thought." Still, they might have knowledge of it that could help their case. "Will we show them the photos of our victim?"

"I don't know. Leave that to me."

She didn't see the point in drawing the suspense out any longer, but she kept her gob shut. He was the lead investigator.

As they entered Cork City, Siobhán gazed at the snow-covered bridge over the river and the flash of pastel buildings lining the street. Cork was a lively city and she always perked up whenever she was here. Had she not been on official business, she would be shopping, or taking a stroll, or hitting one of the pubs. Just like in Kilbane, the folks who were out and about seemed to be enjoying the snow day; and because there weren't very many cars on the road, they had made good time. Macdara found a parking spot and after checking the address and map, they began the walk to the flat, their boots crunching in the snow. The Mallons had rented their vacation stay online, and were staying in a downtown flat. It would have been easier if it had been a hotel; they could have checked out camera footage of everyone coming and going.

"We should check the CCTV footage from Kilbane for the day and night of the murder."

"I've already requested them," Macdara said. "Although there won't be any footage near the churchyard."

"Hopefully, we'll spot Peter Mallon on some footage and at least see if he's alone or with someone."

Macdara stopped in front of a plain three-story building with brown siding. "This is it." He turned to look at her. The hum of attraction between them flowed stronger than ever, and hope lurched within her.

He fixed his gaze on a spot just above her head. She held her breath. "I'm only going to say this once. I can't tell you how good it is to see you. I know I shouldn't have just stopped talking to ye. I just…" The curtain of silence fell again.

"It's okay," Siobhán said softly. It wasn't, not really. It was far from okay. He'd hurt her deeply, just as she had hurt him with her big announcement that she had been accepted at Templemore Garda College. But she didn't want him to suffer, and he looked as if he was doing just that. The urge to throw her arms around him was strong, so she clenched her fists at her side and waited for him to speak again.

"It's not. None of this is okay with me." His face darkened. "And you should have told me how they were treating you back at the station."

Siobhán straightened up. "I can take care of myself."

"I know ye can. You take care of everyone, and nobody could do a better job of it. And you were right to go to garda college. I should have made that clear a lot earlier. And you're hands down the best person I could have on this case with me." He finally met her eyes. Her heart lurched again. He was chewing on something.

"But?"

He gave a soft smile and a nod, acknowledging that she picked up on the undercurrent. "You and me? We're strictly business. I can't talk about the past, about us, and work alongside you at the same time. I knew it the minute you said you wanted to become a guard. That's why I was so conflicted. I won't mix business and pleasure. If there's anything you need to say to me about anything outside of work. Just. Don't." His voice was thick and he was so close, she swore she could feel his heartbeat.

Pain gnawed at her insides. "One question," she said. Her heart thundered in her chest.

"One." He did not seem happy to grant it.

"Why didn't you tell me?"

"Tell you what?"

"That if I chose becoming a guard, I would lose you."

He fixed his eyes on her. "You didn't start a discussion with me," he said. "You announced you were going to become a guard."

He was right. She did. "I thought you'd be happy for me." *I thought we would make it work.*

"I am. Truly, I am." He looked away, shifted. It was apparent he had no more to say on the matter.

"I see."

He nodded. "Are we good?"

"We're good," Siobhán said. And by "good" she meant she wanted to pull him in close, kiss him, and then gut-punch him.

–

Macdara pushed the buzzer and instantly they heard a click and they were in. It was a three-flight trudge to the flat. The door was flung open just as they reached the landing. In front of them stood a beautiful woman with platinum blond hair and intense green eyes. She was just a few inches shorter than Siobhán, and extremely shapely. She was probably in her forties, but could pass for younger. Siobhán couldn't help but think of an American Barbie. The woman searched their faces. "Is it Father? Have you found him?"

"We'd like to come in," Macdara said. "Take this one step at a time."

She let out a little gasp and her hand rose to her mouth in horror, even before Siobhán could say, "I'm so sorry." Her nails were painted a pale pink and a diamond tennis bracelet dangled from her wrist. "I told you!" she shouted to someone inside as Macdara and Siobhán used the entrance mat to stamp snow off their boots. "I told you!"

Two men stepped up to the doorway as the elegant woman stumbled back. To the right was a tall, older man with a shiny bald head. To the left was a shorter but much younger one, with dark blond hair and the same penetrating green eyes as the woman, only his were extremely bloodshot. Definitely siblings. From his hungover state Siobhán deduced she was looking at the black sheep of the family. Macdara and Siobhán placed their caps respectfully over their hearts and introduced themselves.

"I'm Tracy Mallon," the blond woman said. "Peter's daughter." She turned to the younger man who shared her likeness. "This is my brother, Brandon, and my uncle Frank." The men nodded. Macdara gestured to the sofa. Soon the trio was seated, staring at them expectantly.

Tracy suddenly grabbed her brother's hand and she must have squeezed, for he grimaced and yanked his hand away. He was nursing a sore head. She knew the look well. Truthfully, it wouldn't hurt if he had a nip out of a bottle. The hair of the dog. But she wasn't here to give hangover advice, nor did she agree with that particular cure. Suffering was nature's way of teaching one a lesson. Siobhán wished the Irish hostess was home to offer tea; she had an urge to make it herself. It seemed impossible to deliver such news without a little mug of comfort.

Macdara cleared his throat. "In the early hours of the morning, we discovered a man lying dead in our local cemetery. We have reason to believe it's your loved one, Peter Mallon."

"Oh, my God," Brandon said. "Oh, my God." He hung his head, then grabbed handfuls of his hair with both fists.

"In a cemetery?" Tracy said. "You found him dead in a cemetery?" She looked around, trying to see if anyone else saw the irony.

"Yes," Siobhán said. "He was lying on the ground near some of the oldest tombstones in the back of the yard." She felt a kick to her boots and scooched away from Macdara.

"This can't be," Frank said. "It can't be." There was something about shock that made one repeat him – or herself. Siobhán had seen and experienced it before. The human brain was a remarkable organ, one that always tried to protect itself. Repetition was a way of slowly taking it in, absorbing the horrific news little by little.

Tracy Mallon rose from the sofa. "Wait. Did you say you had 'reason to believe'? You mean you're not sure if it's our father?"

Siobhán reached for her mobile to show them the photos of the victim, then stopped, remembering Macdara's request.

Macdara cleared his throat. "The state pathologist is with the body now. She'll contact me as soon as she has any more information."

"We're so sorry," Siobhán added.

"Did you find his wallet?" Tracy pressed as if Siobhán hadn't spoken. "Was there any identification on him?"

"We're not allowed to touch the body until the state pathologist examines him," Siobhán explained. "If she finds a wallet, we'll know straightaway."

"What about a leather satchel?" Brandon asked, leaning in eagerly.

A wallet? A leather satchel? Peter Mallon's grown children just learned their father is dead and the first things they're asking after are wallets and satchels? How peculiar. And sad.

Siobhán knew there had been no satchel at the scene. She made a note of it. "Is this satchel something you think he would have carried with him?"

"Of course," Brandon said. "It was practically attached to his body."

"What was in it?"

Brandon wrung his hands. They trembled. She wondered how much he'd had to drink the previous night. "Does this mean you didn't find it?"

"No," Macdara said quickly. "These are just routine questions."

"Correct," Siobhán replied. "Nothing we say means anything at all."

Macdara threw a look of warning at Siobhán as the American faces scrunched in confusion. She kept her face still.

Tracy leapt from the sofa. "But if there was no ID, how can you be sure it's our father?"

"He had a pin of an American flag on a brown trench coat…" Siobhán thought of the photo. His unblinking eyes, eyelashes and brows brushed with recent snow.

Tracy cried out and sank back into the sofa. It squeaked beneath her. "He must have changed his mind. It's him then. Oh, God. It's really him."

Siobhán's ears perked up. "'Changed his mind'?"

"The pin," Tracy said. "He made a big fuss, saying he wasn't going to wear it anymore."

"I don't understand," Siobhán said.

"We all have them," Frank said, pointing to a pin on his suit jacket. Indeed it was a pin of an American flag. "Jay gave them to us."

"'Jay'?" Siobhán said. "Who is 'Jay'?"

"He's our employee," Brandon said. "Jay Shepard. We're making a documentary. We *were* making a documentary."

One of the locals had heard Peter talk about a big television event. He must have been referring to this documentary. "Why didn't he want to wear the pin anymore?"

Tracy shook her head. "Our father hadn't been making much sense lately. I fear he was losing it."

"Nonsense," Frank said. "Your father was perfectly fine."

"I'm sorry if the truth is hard to hear," Tracy said. "But he was *not* perfectly fine."

"Not now," Brandon said.

Siobhán wanted to keep asking questions, but it was better to just let them go at each other and see what spilled out. She was slightly fascinated by these rude Americans; it was a little like watching wild animals plotting their escape from a zoo.

"How did he die?" Frank asked. "Heart attack?"

Siobhán cleared her throat. "I'm afraid not. It brings me terrible pain to tell you that the gentleman we found in the cemetery most likely died of a gunshot wound."

"'Most likely'?" Frank said. He angled his bald head as his gaze swung from Macdara to Siobhán. "What kind of a ragtag investigation is this?"

"It will be a very thorough one," Macdara said. "There are procedures."

Frank rubbed his bald head, then narrowed his eyes at the pair of them. "How long have you two been on the force?"

"He shot himself?" Brandon interrupted, his voice rising to a panicked pitch. "Where did he get a gun?"

Interesting, Siobhán thought. *Brandon immediately assumes it's suicide. Or, if he's the murderer, he's pretending.*

The same went for Frank Mallon asking if it was a heart attack. For a murderer lies slid off the tongue, although even the best of liars let the truth slip now and again.

Had Peter Mallon been depressed? She leaned in. "Did your father own a firearm?"

"He abhorred guns," Brandon said. "He was against violence in all forms."

"He owned guns as a younger man," Frank interjected. "He definitely knew his way around a gun." Tracy and Brandon swiveled in his direction at the same time, clearly peeved. Frank shrugged. "He liked target shooting when he was a teenager. He was quite good."

"He certainly wasn't target shooting here," Tracy said.

"Are you quite certain?" Brandon said. "Our father? Guns?"

Frank sighed. "That's the worst part about getting older. Everyone thinks they know everything about you. Your father had his secrets, just like everybody else."

"'Secrets'?" Siobhán said.

Frank look startled, as if he regretted his words. "I don't mean anything sinister about it. Just that he once liked guns. Brandon is right. He hadn't touched them in ages."

"This is crazy," Tracy said. "Guns or no guns. Our father wouldn't shoot himself. He wouldn't."

"We don't believe he did," Macdara said.

"You just said he died of a gunshot," Brandon said. The three family members glared at them, waiting for an explanation.

"I'm sorry," Siobhán said. "We believe your father was murdered."

As three stunned faces stared at them from the sofa, a male voice rang out from the front door. "No way!"

Siobhán was momentarily stunned. *Who shouted "No way" like an excited schoolboy over the announcement of a murder?* She whirled around to find a tall young man in the doorway—maybe five years of age on her—holding a video camera up and scanning the room with it.

"Turn that off!" Tracy shrieked.

"That's Jay Shepard," Frank said. "He gave us the pins."

"'Pins'?" Jay said, moving the camera away from his face to look at Frank. "What about pins?" He was a classically handsome man, but his gregarious personality was out of synch with the grief in the room.

"'Murdered'?" A woman stepped out from behind the man with the camera. She was in her midthirties, plain with thick dark glasses, her figure swallowed under an assortment of baggy clothes topped off with a thick cardigan. "Not my Peter?"

"This is Greta Mallon," Frank said, bowing his head slightly toward Greta. "Peter's wife."

"Third wife," Tracy said with an eye roll.

"Why must you always say that?" Greta said, waving Tracy off with a dainty hand. "And what is going on here?" The anxious woman standing before them was definitely in her thirties. Not exactly a trophy wife—more the librarian variety—the kind given a certificate of participation and a clap on the back instead. The fact that she wasn't a raving beauty made Siobhán like Peter Mallon even more.

The man with the video camera set it down and stepped forward with his arm extended. "I'm Jay Shepard. The director." He grinned, flashing white-picket-fence teeth. He was tan, too, such a contrast to the pale Irish folk.

"You're filming a documentary?" Siobhán asked politely. She much preferred fictionalized television dramas. Real-life stories often depressed her for weeks at a time.

He grinned and stood taller. "Yes, I am. Maybe you've seen some of my work? I did a piece on an Irish dancer. *Dancing Irish?*" He seemed to be waiting for Siobhán to respond.

"No," she said. "I've never heard of it."

Jay kept talking. "You will. As soon as I can get it on Netflix. Do you have Netflix here?"

"No," Siobhán said. "We have a man on a pony who brings us the mail and tales from the big, big world beyond." Macdara cleared his throat, almost a choking sound. Jay frowned. "Yes," Siobhán said. "We have Netflix here."

"She was born in the United States, but her parents were from Galway," Jay said. It was Siobhán's turn to frown. "The dancer. Maybe I can scare up a copy." He held up his hands. "Don't worry, I won't ask if you have a DVD player."

Siobhán just stared. *Why is this documentary filmmaker so cheery? Did he not just hear a man has been murdered?*

Chapter 7

As Siobhán turned away from the filmmaker, she saw a flash of pink and realized there was yet another woman hiding in the doorway. She was a petite girl in her twenties, with lush brunette hair. The flash of pink was from a scarf wrapped around her neck. Her eyes were wide, showed no signs of grief or even shock. She looked like one of those lasses on a reality television show where she has three days to pick the man she wanted to marry.

The girl must have felt Siobhán's gaze, for she stepped up and held out her hand like she was on a job interview. "Hannah Stripes."

"Hannah is our father's nurse," Tracy said. Her voice rang with sarcasm. *Jealousy?* More likely, she was annoyed that her father had employed such a pretty young nurse. Siobhán was reconsidering her assessment of Peter Mallon. He may not have picked the stereotype of the younger wife, but he'd hit it out of the park with this femme fatale nurse.

"Nurse?" Siobhán said. "Was he ill?"

Tracy sighed. "He has a tendency to get too excited."

"'Too excited'?" Siobhán asked.

"He has high blood pressure," Hannah chimed in. "*Had* high blood pressure. Oh, my God. He's gone. We have to say 'had.'" Hannah covered her face with her hands.

Greta began to blink rapidly. "Is it hot in here? I feel hot."

"You're not hot," Hannah said. Greta pulled a face. "I mean. It's not hot in here." Tracy stared at Hannah as if trying to figure her out. Hannah simply stared, open-mouthed at Siobhán and Macdara.

Siobhán rose and slowly approached Greta. She looked as if the slightest wind would knock her down. "Maybe you'd like to sit down? Have a nice cuppa tea?"

Greta shook her head. "What's 'cuppa tea'?"

"A mug of tea?" Siobhán said.

"Oh," Greta said. She shook her head as if Siobhán had suggested something distasteful. "No."

"We need something much stronger," Tracy said, heading over to the makeshift bar by the wall. She held up a bottle of whiskey. "This is more our cup of tea."

"Are you rehearsing something?" Greta said. She threw a hopeful look to Jay. "Is this part of the film?" Everyone stared at her. "Is this part of the film?" she shrieked.

"No," Jay said. "No. I swear."

"Sit, sit," Macdara said, gently guiding Greta by the shoulder and easing her into an armchair. She sank into it and it seemed to swallow her whole.

Macdara knelt next to her and repeated the story. "We found him in our local cemetery last night. We believe he died of a single gunshot. We'll know more soon."

"This can't be," Greta said, clutching Macdara's arm. "This simply cannot be."

"Maybe someone should put the kettle on," Siobhán said.

"'Kettle'?" Tracy said.

Uncomprehending eyes bore into Siobhán. *How can they not want tea at a time like this?*

"I can make tea," Hannah said, as if she had just discovered a hidden talent.

"Good girl," Siobhán said. Hannah flung off her winter coat, threw it on a nearby chair, revealing a very tight pink dress. She hurried into the kitchen. Siobhán was dying to ask why Peter's nurse was dressed like she was going out clubbing, but that would have to wait.

"When was the last time any of you saw or heard from Peter?" Macdara asked. Siobhán poised her Biro above her notepad as they waited for someone to speak first.

"We were all at the Titanic Experience yesterday morning," Tracy said.

"In Cobh?" Siobhán added. One by one, heads began to nod. Cobh was on the south side of Great Island in Cork Harbour. It was a popular tourist destination, a busy port from which the ill-fated *Titanic* had set sail. The museum was geared all around the *Titanic*, but also featured many other ships that had carried Irishmen off to new destinations.

Greta spoke up. "Peter was hoping to find a ship's manifest listing his great-grandfather."

Frank bobbed his head in agreement. "Our great-grandfather emigrated to America with his wife, Ann, in 1853. He was a Limerick man, so it's very likely he departed from here."

"We took a tour of the museum while Peter was making inquiries," Greta added.

"And I was hoping to gather every prop I could for the film," Jay said. "I guess you could call me the writer, director, and executive producer all rolled into one."

"There you go again about the film," Frank said. "Not everything is about the film." He rubbed his bald head, then pointed to Siobhán and Macdara. "They are not here about your stupid film!" He shook his head in disgust.

"I'm a passionate man," Jay said, puffing out his chest. "It takes an artist to understand an artist."

"Takes a few stiff drinks as well," Frank said, joining Tracy at the bar.

"Genealogy was Peter's passion," Greta said, her eyes lighting up. "It's how we met."

"Can we get back to the last time you saw Peter?" Macdara said. His tone was polite but impatient.

Brandon stepped in. "An hour into the guided tour Father left abruptly."

Siobhán felt a tingle up her spine. "What happened?"

"He said he had an excited stomach," Brandon said.

"He didn't tell me he had an 'excited stomach,'" Greta said. "He was constantly checking his phone. I thought one of his inquiries was contacting him."

"You didn't ask him?" Siobhán pressed.

Greta sighed. "I couldn't keep up. He's been like a man possessed ever since we arrived. Chasing down every lead he could."

"What did I tell you?" Tracy said, lifting a shot glass. "Does obsessed sound like a healthy man to you?"

"Where exactly was he making inquiries?" Macdara said.

"Courthouses, libraries, genealogists, locals. You name it," Greta said. "He was in research heaven."

"If you have the names of specific places he visited," Macdara said, nudging Siobhán to write them down.

Greta shook her head and threw a glance at the director. "Jay, didn't you have his itinerary?"

"For the filming, of course," Jay said, holding up his hands. "But Peter made it very clear he did not want a shadow the rest of the time." He stared at the floor. "I shouldn't have listened. He might be alive now if I had insisted on accompanying him."

"Stop it," Tracy said. Tears streamed down her face. "It might not be him."

"What do you mean 'it might not be him'?" Greta screeched.

Tracy whirled on Jay. "Did you give that stupid American flag pin to anyone else in Ireland? Did you?"

Jay started to stammer. "W-why are you asking?"

Tracy jabbed her finger at him. "Answer me. Did you give that pin to anyone else?"

"I don't think so." Jay looked around the room, like a man trying to figure out if he was awake or dreaming. "What does that have to do with anything?"

"The dead man was wearing one," Tracy said. "Did you give it to anyone else or not?"

"I don't think so," Jay said.

"You 'don't *think* so'?" Tracy said to Jay. "It could mean life or death!"

Jay retreated to his camera, as if he wanted to hide behind it. He was intimidated by Tracy Mallon, and she seemed quite comfortable with that reaction.

"Is it or is it not Peter?" Greta said, her voice rising to a panicked pitch.

"That's why I asked Jay if he gave the pin to anyone else," Tracy said.

"I only gave them to family members," Jay said. He turned to Macdara and Siobhán. "I thought it would be a nice way of tying them all together. I planned on pinning an Irish flag on them at the final scene."

Greta shook her fist. "I am going to scream at the top of my lungs if someone does not explain what Tracy meant by 'It might not be him.'"

Macdara caught Siobhán's eye. "We have photographs of the victim," he said. "We can settle this now."

"No," Tracy said, turning away from Siobhán's smartphone.

"I can identify him," Jay said.

"You're not family," Brandon said. "Show me." Even though he was a short man, he was strong and muscular, and led with his chest. Siobhán had been fascinated by the brief study they'd done in college of body language. People had different centers from which they led when they walked. The groin, the head, or the chest. Brandon led with his chest—that usually denoted a special attention and awareness to one's body. An athlete might lead with his chest, whereas an intellectual often led with his or her head. Frank, she noted, led with his head. And, of course, leading from the groin was often a sign of a person who was in touch with his or her sexuality and the power it could yield. Tracy Mallon led with her groin. Greta led with her head. Siobhán kept these observations to herself. Sometimes the biggest mystery she faced was what to do with all the random thoughts ping-ponging through her mind.

Greta hauled herself out of the chair and lurched forward. "He's my husband. I want to see."

Siobhán reached for the widow. "Why don't you sit down."

Greta jerked away, even though Siobhán wasn't even close to touching her. "I'll stand." Siobhán sighed, then showed her the photo of Peter lying in the cemetery. Greta cried out, then sank back into the chair, tears streaming down her face. "It's him. It's my Peter."

"There you have it," Brandon said, throwing a dirty look to his sister. "Satisfied?"

"Would you rather not know?" Tracy shot back. "Denial is your thing after all." She stormed back to the bar. "More tea?" she said, pouring herself another shot of whiskey. She raised the glass at no one in particular and then downed it.

"Pour me one," Brandon said. "Or two."

"You're swimming in alcohol as it is," Tracy said. "You reek of it."

Brandon's face flushed red. "I'm entitled to a night out."

"Out partying while our father is getting shot in a cemetery." Tracy's beautiful face was marred with an angry line cutting across her forehead.

"I couldn't have known," Brandon said. "How could I have known?"

"Where were you last night?" Siobhán asked.

"Pubs," Brandon said. "I was in and out of pubs."

"You were in pubs," Tracy said. "Until you were thrown out."

"I'm very sorry to all of you for your loss," Siobhán reiterated. She stopped short of lecturing them that alcohol was just going to make things worse. Much more time in their squabbling company and she'd be taking a nip off the old bottle herself.

"My brother was a good man," Frank said. "His life's mission was to continue our great-grandfather's legacy of feeding the poor." He shook his fist. "You'd better catch the bastard who did this, before I do."

Macdara put his hand on Frank's arm. "I understand how you feel. Believe me. But I cannot have you threatening to interfere with an active investigation."

Frank turned to Macdara. "What is your title again?"

"I'm Detective Sergeant Flannery." He nodded to Siobhán. "This is Garda O'Sullivan."

"How long have you been on the job?"

"Why do you ask?" Siobhán said.

"Because my brother is dead. I need to be sure this investigation is being handled by the best." He crossed his arms against his chest. "How long?" When neither of them answered, Frank reached into his jacket and pulled out his mobile. "I'll call the police station." He stared at the phone and then looked up. "How do you place a call in Ireland?"

Seriously? These Yankee Doodle Dandies are high-maintenance. Siobhán pointed at his mobile. "You push those little numbers in the correct order, and if you do it right, you'll hear ring-ring." He stared at her. "And then most folks say 'Hello.'"

Macdara gently shoved her out of the way as Frank glared. "I was promoted to Detective Sergeant a year ago. I've been a guard for ten years." He nodded to Siobhán. "This is her first day."

"'Her first day'?" Frank sputtered. "And she's assigned to my brother's case?"

Macdara held up his hand. "She was the first guard on the scene, and as such is in the best position to assist. She graduated at the top of her class, and I will be supervising her every move."

Siobhán was dying to tell them she'd unofficially solved previous murder probes, but she had a feeling it would elicit another kick from Macdara. She didn't realize that

Macdara knew she'd graduated at the top of her class. He certainly didn't hear it from her.

"I'd like to request more experienced officers," Frank said.

"You just did," Macdara answered. "Request denied."

"I'll go above your heads."

Macdara gave a curt nod. "Do whatever you have to do. I assure you we're committed to solving this case."

Siobhán glanced toward the kitchen, where the young nurse in the tight pink dress was apparently still making tea. "Eventually we'll need to know everything you can remember about your trip here so far," Siobhán announced to the group. "It might help to write it down while it's fresh in your minds."

Eyewitnesses were the trickiest part about an investigation, and the most unreliable: from faulty memories to little white lies or even out-and-out subterfuge. Still, if everyone was forced to write down his or her accounts, it was easier to track where the stories started to change. Sometimes the best way to solve a crime was to pull on a thread and unravel a ball of lies.

"I could film everyone's account," Jay said.

"That's not a bad idea," Macdara said. "If everyone is willing, that is."

He glanced around the room, but nobody acknowledged the request. Tracy stared at a spot on the wall. Brandon folded his muscular arms against his chest; Frank rubbed his head; Greta slouched in her chair.

"I'll take care of it," Jay announced. "I'll even include myself."

"How big of you," Tracy drawled from the bar.

Hannah returned with a tray of tea. As she walked, the cups rattled on the tray like chattering teeth, momentarily distracting everyone. Unlike the rest of them, Hannah's center of movement seemed practiced. She stood tall, and moved gracefully. Everyone accepted a cup, but then stood around staring at it, as if they weren't quite sure what to do with it. *Jaysus.*

Macdara cleared his throat. "We'll need to take statements from all of you, one by one, but for now we just came to deliver the news. How long had you planned on staying in Cork?"

"We're supposed to check out of the flat today," Tracy said. "I have to call the owner and see if we can extend."

"I have a better idea," Siobhán said. "Why don't you all relocate to Kilbane?"

"I second that," Macdara said. "It will be easier to keep you abreast of any developments. And once the state pathologist is finished, we can arrange for a local undertaker to help you with arrangements."

"Yes," Greta said. "I want to be near my Peter."

"Stop calling him *your* Peter," Tracy said. "I can't bear it."

"I'm sorry," Greta said. "I don't mean to lessen your grief."

"Whatever," Tracy said. "Fine. Let's go to Kilbane. I want to see my father." Brandon and Frank nodded. Jay and Hannah looked as if they were mentally digging a tunnel to far, far away.

"Whatever needs to be done," Jay said at last.

"Am I still getting paid?" Hannah asked. It took her a moment, but she finally registered the shocked expressions on those around her. "I just w-wondered," she stammered. "B-because with him gone. He no longer needs a nurse. Right?" Hannah continued to blink as the group stared at her. With her fluffy hair, big eyes, and wide mouth, she reminded Siobhán of a pretty, young owl, obliviously hooting from the nest.

"We'll arrange for the lodging," Macdara said. "You have transportation?"

"We have a rental car," Jay said. Macdara wrote down directions to Kilbane and took Jay's mobile number.

"We'll call as soon as we have lodging," Siobhán said. "It won't be long."

They took their leave and walked back to the car in silence. On the way Siobhán turned over everything she had just seen and heard, cataloguing her first impressions, and wondering which one of the Americans might be a cold-blooded killer.

Chapter 8

Siobhán waited until she and Macdara were halfway down the street, about to cross over Patrick's Bridge, when Siobhán whirled around and faced him. "That was a mistake."

Macdara cocked his head. "You'll learn."

"Excuse me?"

"You're new at this. Don't worry. You'll learn."

"What are you talking about?"

His eyes narrowed. "What are *you* talking about?"

"You. You should have never told that man it was my first day on the job, and you less than a year."

"Why ever not?"

"It made us look like neophytes."

"He would have found out on his own. He seemed determined."

"I've solved murders in the past."

"Not as a guard you didn't."

"He's inferring that we don't know what we're doing."

"Only amateurs think they know what they're doing. Professionals admit that half the time they don't have a clue." He turned his blue eyes intently on her. "Since when do you give two figs what other people think?"

Siobhán shook her head. "Frank knows something, but he's holding back because he doesn't trust us."

"You got all that from a brief chat?"

"I did."

At the sound of someone sloshing through the snow, they turned to find Greta Mallon running full tilt toward them, her thick glasses bouncing on her nose, no coat on her frail, shivering body. "I just remembered!" Macdara and Siobhán came to such an abrupt halt that Siobhán started to slip on the footpath and suddenly Macdara's arms were around her waist, holding her up. She wondered if his hands were lingering longer than necessary, but then, as if he could read her secret thoughts, they dropped to his side.

"What's the story?" he said to Greta, his voice husky.

Greta clasped her hands as if in prayer. "Peter had been especially interested in visiting memorials for The Great Hunger. Does Kilbane have one?"

The Irish referred to it as *An Gorta Mór*, but this was no time for a history lesson. "Of course," Siobhán said. "We have a grand famine memorial."

Greta nodded. "Peter would have definitely paid a visit."

Siobhán doubted there would be any clues to find, but the widow was grieving and trying to help. Or she was a killer and she wanted them to think she was grieving and trying to help. In either scenario, a nod and a smile was the required response, so that's what she gave.

"Thank you," Macdara said. "Anything else?" Greta looked behind her, her eyes wide and frightened. "Go on."

"I think I know why Peter wasn't quite himself these last few days." She looked around again, as if worried someone was listening.

"We're alone," Siobhán assured her.

"I told him he was being ridiculous." She dropped her voice and leaned in closer. "He was convinced Tracy was conspiring against him."

Macdara stepped forward and lowered his voice. "'Conspiring against him' how?"

"He said she was trying to have him declared mentally incompetent."

Siobhán did her best not to react. It was a potential game changer. "What made him think this?"

She shook her head. "We never had time to get into the details. But he changed his will so that I'm the beneficiary. You must know that I didn't want him to. I loved Peter. I'm not a gold digger. Research is my passion."

Siobhán noticed that she did not exactly answer her question. "Why did Peter think Tracy was conspiring against him?"

Greta threw her arms up in exasperation. "I don't know. He just did." A bitterness crept into her voice, she was annoyed that Siobhán had pressed the question. "I don't want his money. What would I do with all that money?"

"Most folks could think of a few things," Macdara said.

"I had a good life," Greta said. "All I wanted was Peter. Not everyone has dollar signs in their eyes."

Macdara was right. Siobhán could think of a lot of things she'd do with extra money. Buy their building, instead of just renting. Pay off college debt. Start saving for her siblings to go to college. Travel. Oh, how she would travel.

Greta interrupted Siobhán's daydream. "Tracy and Brandon don't know about the new will. At least I don't think they do." She took a few tentative steps. "When they find out, they're going to accuse me of murder!"

"Is it at all possible that one of them found out?" Siobhán asked. *Or both of them.*

"I don't know," Greta said. Her eyes widened in shock. "I guess it's possible."

"Thank you for telling us," Macdara said, holding up his hand and throwing a warning glance to Siobhán. "Let us know if you think of anything else."

Greta wrapped her cardigan around her and started back for the house. Siobhán called after her. "Where were you and Jay and Hannah when we arrived?"

"Pardon?" Greta said, turning. She looked like a student who had just been presented with a surprise test.

"You, Jay, and Hannah came in the door shortly after we arrived. Just wondering where you were?"

"We had to get out of that flat. Tracy and Brandon were at each other's throats. Tracy accused Brandon of gambling again."

"'Gambling'?" Macdara asked.

Greta nodded and pursed her lips. "He's an addict. She thought Peter found out and that's why he hadn't come home."

"I'm not sure I understand," Siobhán said.

"Before the trip Peter told Brandon if he ever so much as laid a dollar down on a bet that he would be out of the will. And he meant it. Peter was a wonderful man. But he was also a man of his word. Tracy and Brandon, born with silver spoons in their mouths. I know that sounds unkind, but it's true. Everything they have has been handed to them. You'd think they'd be grateful." Her voice shook with rage. "He was a good man," she said. "Not perfect. But good. He didn't deserve this. No matter what."

She turned and was walking away before Siobhán could ask what she meant. "*No matter what.*" She raised an eyebrow at Macdara and he gave a nod. He'd heard it too.

-

The back roads of Ireland were filled with dangerous curves, and many lads took them at equally dangerous speeds. Siobhán was grateful Macdara wasn't one of them. He kept an even pace, which, besides affording them the luxury to look at the scenery, also gave them time to mull over the information Greta had given them. The revelations certainly put Tracy and Brandon in a suspicious light. One child trying to have him declared mentally incompetent, the other warned he would be cut out of the will if he didn't stop his addiction. With betting shops on every corner, Ireland wasn't the best place for gamblers trying to quit. And Siobhán couldn't help but think about the first questions the children asked upon learning he was dead. Did they find his wallet? Did they find his leather satchel? When she found out her parents had been killed in a car accident, money or possessions were the furthest things from her mind. All she wanted was one more day with them, one more conversation, one more precious touch. She'd developed an instant bias toward the Mallon children, she didn't like them at all, and she'd have to keep that feeling in check. Greta was certainly forthcoming. *Too forthcoming?* The more she'd tried to convince them she wasn't interested in money, the less believable she became.

And even if Peter did visit the famine memorial, so what? Unless he left a secret note there identifying his killer, what could they possibly hope to find? Especially when any possible evidence would be buried under inches of fresh snow. There was no CCTV footage at the memorial. But maybe they could make use of it somehow.

"We could gather the group at the memorial," Siobhán said. "See what happens when we force them to interact."

"You've been trained well," Macdara said with a wink. They decided as soon as the Mallons arrived and had settled into their accommodations, not to mention have a spot of lunch at Naomi's, they would take them all to the memorial, see if anything shook loose.

"We should ask Jay Shepard to turn over everything he's filmed so far," Siobhán said.

Macdara nodded. "That's an excellent idea."

"He was an odd one, don't you think?"

"They were all odd," Siobhán said. "Even for Americans."

Macdara gave a nod of his head. "But yer man, Jay. Don't you think he was a bit too exuberant about the news?"

Siobhán nodded. "Very out of place. Same with Florence Nightingale."

Macdara laughed. "Very pretty, that one," he said lightly.

"Too pretty to be a killer?" Siobhán said, hoping the depth of sarcasm showed.

He laughed again, and Siobhán shook her head. She thought Macdara was just going to drop her off at Naomi's, but instead he accepted her offer to come in and have a mug of tea. The lunch shift had just ended and the CLOSED sign hung on the door. Breakfast and lunch were all they served; dinner was family time. Siobhán was thrilled to find the fire still going. She put the kettle on the cooker and in no time they were settled in front of the fire with brown bread with butter and jam, and mugs of Barry's tea, Siobhán with her notebook in her lap.

"More initial impressions?" Macdara asked.

"Hannah Stripes was awfully sophisticated for a nurse. At the same time she seems a bit immature." Siobhán fluttered her eyelashes. "Pretty as she may be."

"Agreed." He shrugged. "But she's young. And American."

"But where's the respect for the dead man and the family? And she certainly wasn't dressed like a nurse."

Macdara grinned. "She was dressed like lads imagine nurses dressing," he quipped. Siobhán resisted the urge to lob her tea bag at his head. Macdara dropped the teasing. "People can be clueless, even heartless, inappropriately dressed, yet still innocent of murder."

Siobhán sighed. He had a point there. Or did he see a young, pretty girl and refuse to think she could be a killer? Siobhán wasn't that much older than Hannah, but she felt ancient in comparison. "We have a lot more to learn."

"Indeed."

"Something caused Peter Mallon to abruptly leave the museum tour. We need to figure out what that *something* was."

"Hopefully, the pathologist will find his mobile phone. We can also pull CCTV footage from Cork City— especially around the museum. We'll talk to the tour guides there as well. We'll canvass anyone who might have come across him."

"He could have even come into the bistro. I'll have to ask James. Or Elise," she said with a growl. Macdara raised his eyebrow. "James has a new girlfriend." Siobhán forced a positive tone. "Her name is Elise."

Macdara registered the news in silence. He had warned her not to talk about anything personal, but they had to have some conversation, didn't they?

"I can't imagine anyone visiting Kilbane without coming to Naomi's," Macdara said with a wink.

Siobhán sighed in relief and smiled back. She hated how different things were between them now. If she could turn back time, go back and do it over, would she have chosen a different path?

There probably wasn't a soul alive who hadn't wondered the same thing. And what a woeful dilemma; nobody ever got a do-over. Her father used to say, "*If wishes were horses, how Siobhán would ride.*" He was right. She wanted it all: the job and the man. Garda Siobhán O'Sullivan. She did the right thing. Why couldn't *he* see that?

"Tracy certainly doesn't like her stepmother," Macdara said. "And it seems the animosity is mutual."

"'Tis only a stepmother would blame you,'" Siobhán quipped. Her mam used to love that saying as well. Naomi O'Sullivan had a million of them, and Siobhán missed hearing every single one, delivered in her mam's soft lilt with a tilt of her head and a gleam in her eye.

Macdara winked and twirled his teacup on the plate. "Greta certainly went out of her way to let us know she isn't after Peter's money."

"She doth protest too much?"

Macdara tossed his head. "It crossed my mind."

"Me too." She jotted down a few notes. "What were your impressions of Brandon and Frank?"

"Brandon looked like a coil ready to spring. Could be that gambling addiction Greta was on about. Maybe he's

85

jumpy from withdrawal. Or his own urges. Frank was very reserved. Hard to get a bead on that one."

"Except for the fact that he rubs the top of his head when he's nervous," Siobhán said. "We also can't ignore the fact that Brandon was out all night."

"Agreed. It's an odd group. Interesting days ahead."

"When are we going to tell them about the headstone bearing their surname?"

"When it's no longer a crime scene, we'll take them to the churchyard and show them. See what kind of reaction it stirs up." Macdara finished his tea and stood. "I have to get back to the station and meet with the state pathologist."

"Shall I come back to the office with ye?" Siobhán asked. She was dying to hear firsthand what the pathologist had to say.

"Why don't you start in town? See if anyone met the poor fella and remembers anything that might help."

Darn. He wasn't going to let her. She already canvassed the town and he knew that. Was he purposefully keeping her at arm's length? "Will do."

Macdara tipped his cap and was off. She watched him from the window until he was out of sight.

–

Siobhán found Bridie Sheedy coming out of Courtney's gift shop. She was a petite woman with bouncy chestnut curls and an abundance of energy.

"How ya," she called brightly to Siobhán.

"Grand, grand, you?"

"Not a bother."

Bridie began to walk and Siobhán took up alongside her. "I was wondering if you'd seen an American man in the bistro the past week?"

"I was wondering when you were going to ask me that," Bridie said. "He came into the bistro, alright."

Siobhán came to full attention, and touched Bridie's arm. "Tell me everything."

"Not a bother, pet, but you'll have to come with me to spinning class. If you're late, the instructor makes you turn up the resistance to ten." She shuddered.

"Why don't you skip the workout today?" Siobhán said, having no desire to injure her lady parts on a hard bicycle seat.

"Are you joking me? After working all week with Elise, I'll go mental if I don't get in my workout. I wouldn't have imagined James with such a sour little puss, in all me life."

"Why don't we go shopping instead?" Siobhán suggested. "That's good for stress."

"I'm going spinning," Bridie said. "With or without ye."

Siobhán preferred a good run outside, but since that wasn't wise with all the ice and snow, she acquiesced. After having spent the day with Macdara, she could stand to burn off some extra energy as well.

Soon they were both in the gym, pedaling like mad, in a room full of other women pedaling like mad, but none getting anywhere. Not to mention that it hurt. Not just the drill sergeant commands from a tiny woman with a bouncing ponytail, and a set of lungs like a bullhorn, but Siobhán found she had to pedal standing up, or face the torture of sitting down and risk not being able to walk a straight line for a solid week. How Bridie could pedal and talk at the same time was one of life's little mysteries, but soon she began to fill Siobhán in on her encounter with Peter Mallon.

"He was a tall, skinny fella. Older. Dressed like a color-blind professor." Bridie's curls bounced as she pedaled.

Siobhán sucked in air. "That sounds like him. What else?"

"He ordered the Irish breakfast."

Eggs over easy, rashers, black pudding, white pudding, sausages, potatoes, brown bread slathered in butter, and Barry's tea. Siobhán hoped he had liked it. It was sad to realize it had been one of his last meals. At least he had chosen something delicious and hearty. Every second of life counted in the end. Every meal should be savored. "Did he talk about why he was in Kilbane?"

"Said they were doing a show on telly about tracing his Irish ancestry. Said his great-grandfather emigrated to America just after an Gorta Mór. A friend in America helped his great grandparents start a pub and restaurant, and a hearty portion of the profits were donated to local organizations to feed the poor. They never wanted anyone to experience the horror of starvation. A grand tribute to Ireland I'd say. Peter Mallon dropped the pub, can ye imagine that, but continued with the restaurant, and feeding the poor. Said there were six franchises all over the States, and all of them were required to be just as generous with donations to local food kitchens. But he also winked and said Naomi's was better. He wanted to speak with you."

"Me?" Siobhán said. This was news.

"He wanted to know if we'd be willing to share any of our recipes."

"Sweet." He sounded like a nice man. Not that they would have given him any recipes, but who would want to harm a nice older man whose mission was to feed the hungry? She was eager to learn more about these restaurants from the Mallon family. Maybe she could adopt a similar model with the bistro. She was ashamed she hadn't thought of it. "Anything else?" Siobhán panted as sweat dripped down her face.

Bridie started pedaling faster. "He said something about family being both a blessing and a curse. And then he did ask me a strange question."

Siobhán wished she weren't so out of breath. "Go on."

"He asked if I thought you could ever know someone. Like *really know* them."

Was he talking about Tracy? Was she trying to have him declared incompetent? "Anything else?"

"No." She was flying it now, pumping away. "Wait. One more thing. He asked if there were any living Mallons in Kilbane."

Siobhán thought of the headstone. Apparently, there used to be. "I don't know of any, do you?"

Bridie shook her head. Siobhán had to duck to keep sweat from pelting her. "Could be in someone's maternal line."

Siobhán hadn't thought of that. Maybe she would have to check in with the church records. "Thanks," Siobhán said, hopping off the bike.

"The class isn't over," Bridie said, horrified.

"It is for me," Siobhán said, hobbling away. "I intend on having children of me own someday."

Chapter 9

Chris Gordon, the only American living in Kilbane, and the owner of Gordon's Comics, had recently purchased the flats above it, and rented them out through Airbnb. Siobhán secured enough rooms for their group from Cork City. She also asked Chris to report anything odd. She stood in his store and watched as he stocked the shelves with violent and glossy-covered comics.

"You mean I'm like a spy?" he said with a grin. He was a very good-looking lad, the dimpled kind featured on soap operas on telly, yet, despite attracting tons of attention from a variety of local ladies, he had always had a crush on Siobhán. Chris Gordon was definitely a man who led from his groin.

"Not 'like a spy,'" Siobhán said. "Just alert me if there's anything suspicious or worrisome."

"Like a spy," he repeated, eyes shining with excitement.

"I just want to keep everyone safe," she said.

"Wait. Are you saying that a murderer will be living up there?" He sounded more hopeful than worried.

"I'm saying no such thing."

"Right," he said with an exaggerated nod and a wink. "Do you want me to put cameras in the rooms?"

"No!" Siobhán said. "Don't even joke about that."

"Sorry." Chris promised he'd behave, but the grin didn't leave his face. "First snow and now a murder, with the suspects living right above." He looked around his empty little shop. "Business is going to be booming."

Siobhán nodded, although she knew very well it was his trust fund—and not business—that kept the shop open so that he would have an excuse to read comic books all day. At least she'd found their guests a place to stay, and who better to put up with Americans than one of their own?

"They'll be checking in soon. If everything's ready?"

"For you?" he said, treating her to a slow grin. "It's always ready."

Siobhán frowned. "But for them?"

His grinned disappeared. "The rooms are ready. They'll actually be my first guests."

"Good on ye," Siobhán said. She stopped before leaving the shop. "Did an American man come in here last week?"

"You mean the victim? Peter Mallon?"

She sighed. The entire town knew everything by now. "Yes. Did Peter Mallon come into the shop?"

Chris shook his head. "No. He did not come into the shop."

Siobhán nodded. She thought as much. A man here to see Irish history wasn't about to waste his time in a comic-book shop. She realized she was still staring at Chris. He winked at her. She hightailed it out the door before he started flexing his biceps.

–

To Siobhán's surprise, the group wanted to gather at the famine memorial before checking into their rooms or having a spot of lunch. They gathered in the park in front of a somber stone pillar and dedicated plaque that read:

*Let us remember the famine victims lying here in
unmarked graves and without anger or reproach
dedicate ourselves to ensuring that nobody will
ever again die in want in this bountiful land that
God gave to us.*

It tugged at Siobhán's heart every time she read it. The
fields surrounding them took on a high glow as the sun
bounced off the snow. A quiet stillness always came over
her whenever she was here. Countless victims were buried
beneath them in unmarked graves. It was both a somber
place for reflection and a gathering place for family and
children. The Americans gathered around, and Siobhán
was surprised to see Jay was filming.

"Peter would have wanted us to continue making the
documentary," Greta said, catching Siobhán's glance at the
recorder. "We all agreed."

"Not all of us," Tracy said, crossing her arms tightly
across her chest. "I think it's morbid." Her coat looked
like the latest fashion trend and her blond hair spilled out
of a stylish cap. Greta, on the other hand, had a knit cap
pulled over her head and a winter coat that was so bulky,
she all but disappeared in it. Brandon wasn't wearing a coat
at all, and Siobhán didn't know whether he was trying to
be masculine or was just immune to the cold. But every
time she looked at him, she had an urge to wrap him in
a blanket. He gave off the air of a man trying to appear
more confident than he felt, which was probably true of
all men and women, but with Brandon it was easy to spot
the forced bravado.

"I hope Peter made it here," Greta said, clasping her
hands and looking around. "I think he must have."

"He would have felt a connection here," Frank agreed. "This is where our mission started." He unfolded his arms as if they were wings. His trench coat was similar to the one they'd found his brother in. Although unlike Peter Mallon's mismatched attire, Frank's outfit was made up of complementary shades of black and gray. He stood tall and exuded the air of a distinguished gentleman.

"*Your* mission?" Brandon said. His shoulders were hunched against the cold.

Frank looked startled, then shoved his hands in his pockets and stared at the ground. "Your father deserves the credit."

"Damn right he does," Brandon said, chest thrust forward, eyes flashing.

"That's enough," Greta said. "Your uncle has been on board for many years now. Let it go."

Siobhán and Macdara's eyes flitted around the group, taking it all in. Once again she noticed Brandon shivering. "Don't you have a winter coat?"

Brandon looked startled, then shrugged. "I had no idea it got so cold in Ireland."

Tracy sidled up to him. "What happened to your black coat?"

Brandon shrugged. "I think I left it on the plane."

"No, you didn't," Tracy said. She brought out her mobile and swiped through it. She then faced the screen to Brandon. "You were wearing it at the Titanic Experience."

Brandon glanced at the photo. "So I was," he said. His gaze shifted to Siobhán. "We tried to get father to get in the picture. He wouldn't do it. It would have been the last photograph we'd had of him."

"You're right," Tracy said. Fresh grief appeared on her face. Siobhán knew exactly what they were going through. Grief was a thief, stealing bits of you like a vulture, pecking anew when you least expected it.

"I went to the restroom after we took the photo," Brandon said, snapping his fingers. "I bet I left my coat there."

"I'm sure if you call the museum, they'll have a lost and found," Siobhán said. People were always leaving items behind in the bistro. Umbrellas, sunglasses, jackets, scarves. If they weren't so honest, they could open a thrift store out the back.

Frank came up behind Tracy to look at the photograph. In it, even though they were on opposite sides, he appeared to be looking at Greta.

"I'm sure Peter would have posed for the picture if he had known how much all of you would have treasured it," Siobhán said gently.

Frank turned to her. "I didn't support all of Peter's business decisions in the beginning," he said. "I was reluctant to turn our family restaurant into a chain. We fought bitterly. I wish I could take it all back."

"That's an understatement," Brandon said.

"You, of all people, casting stones?" Frank lashed out. This time it was Brandon who turned red.

"I got on board, though," Frank said. "I helped build the chain into what it is today." Jay moved in with his camera. Frank's eyes narrowed as the lens approached. "It was all going perfectly until this documentary business started."

Jay lowered his camera and stepped closer to Frank. "You're so closed off to progress," he said. "I'm an artist. This is my passion."

"There's something funny about you," Frank said. "I don't like this filming business one bit." Jay laughed. Frank glared. "Is something funny?"

"You just admitted you were wrong about the family business. So the fact that you don't like 'this filming business'"—Jay stopped to make air quotes—"means it's going to be wildly successful."

Frank turned to Macdara and Siobhán with a slight bow. "I stand by my conviction. I hope you thoroughly investigate the man behind the camera."

"I'd love that," Jay said, turning his camera on the pair of them. "I'd love to show you my work."

"Excellent," Macdara said. "Because we'll be needing all of your footage from the very beginning of this project." Jay lowered the camera and frowned. "Will that be a problem?" Macdara asked, his voice dropping into a lower octave.

"I guess not. It's just. Not finished yet."

"Good. Deliver it to Kilbane Gardai Station by tomorrow noon. Every scrap of footage."

"Or what?" Jay's tone was playful but challenging.

"Or I'll arrest you for interfering with an investigation," Macdara said.

Siobhán was pretty sure he could do no such thing, but Jay seemed to take the threat seriously.

"Tomorrow at noon it is."

Would he mess with any of the footage? Delete anything?

"Unless you want to come back with me now," Macdara said. He had probably just had the same thought. The less time they gave Jay, the better.

"As soon as I get to my room with my laptop and I can e-mail you all the digital files."

"I also want all e-mails you ever sent anyone regarding this project."

"Why?"

"'Why?'" Macdara repeated, sounding as if he couldn't believe Jay had just asked that.

"I'm willing to cooperate, but you seem to be picking on me."

"We're going to pick on everyone eventually," Siobhán said. "Just so happens you're first in the rotation." She smiled. He cocked his head.

"There's something interesting about you," he said, pointing at Siobhán. "Besides your classic beauty. There's something simmering beneath your surface. I'd love to film you."

Siobhán shook her head. "All my simmering takes place above surface," she said. "What you see is what you get."

Macdara cleared his throat, once again making it impossible for Siobhán to ascertain if he was laughing or choking.

Jay scanned the group with the camera. "Everyone, notice I'm cooperating. Let's all cooperate. Help find Peter's killer. We know it's not one of us, so just let these people do their jobs."

Hannah stepped forward. She was wearing a black coat with a fur collar. It didn't look fake. Did she not get the memo that real fur was out? "I remembered something last night," she said. "Should I say it in front of everybody?" She stroked her collar. "I don't want anyone to think I'm keeping secrets."

The outburst seemed to startle everyone and they turned to the pretty brunette and waited. "Just before he left the Titanic Experience, Peter told me he made a possible new discovery about his great-grandfather. He said it was explosive." Her long eyelashes began to blink.

Tracy was the first to turn on her. "You're asking us to believe that just slipped your mind?"

"Nonsense," Frank said. "I hardly think anything he learned could be 'explosive.'" Macdara caught Siobhán's eye. She wondered if he was thinking of the headstone too.

"What was your great-grandfather's first name?" Macdara asked.

"John," Frank answered. "John Mallon."

Despite a feeling that this was where it was going, Siobhán still felt a shiver. Peter found his great-grandfather's grave right here in Kilbane. That must have been quite a pleasant shock. It was rare though, that a relative be returned home for a burial. Most who left were buried in America. He must have made his wishes quite clear, or perhaps the man himself had returned to Ireland to die. Ireland was definitely where Siobhán intended to be buried. Anywhere else was unthinkable. But it bothered her. It would have been so difficult back then to arrange travel home. Siobhán looked up to find Macdara staring at her. Tracy suddenly pointed between Macdara and Siobhán. "You two keep looking at each other. Why?"

Macdara held up his hand. "When it's no longer a crime scene, we want to take you to the cemetery where Peter was found. We have some idea what he discovered."

"'Explosive' pretty much covers it," Siobhán added.

"Keeping us in suspense," Jay said. "Film thrives on suspense."

"If you're going to keep filming, you must stop making such heartless comments," Greta said. "This isn't a celebration."

"I'm sorry," Jay said. "I just get excited. Like Peter."

"Nothing like Peter," Greta said. "There was nobody like Peter."

"It was an expression," Jay said. He let out a heavy sigh.

Exhaustion was pinned on their faces. And whereas being tired to the point of delirium might cause one of them to slip up and say something revealing, most of them were not killers. And they deserved a little rest.

"Your rooms are ready," Siobhán said. "Shall I take you there?"

Chapter 10

True to his word Chris Gordon had the rooms ready, and either the accommodations were lovely, or the guests were too weary to complain. Frank lingered in the comic-book store, and just as Siobhán and Macdara were leaving, he cleared his throat. Siobhán and Macdara stood and waited.

"I loved my brother," he said. "But we quarreled a lot. I guess it's in our Irish blood." He flashed a grin that disappeared as quickly as it came.

"I have plenty of siblings," Siobhán said. "I'm well-aware."

Frank looked grateful. "Greta is a wonderful woman," he said. "I think they would have been very happy." Siobhán could sense he was leading up to something, so she made appropriate nods and murmurs.

When he didn't offer anything more, Siobhán stepped up. "Did you know Peter was going to change his will?"

Frank's deep brown eyes darted to the right. "You'll have to speak with Greta. Peter didn't discuss his will with me."

"That wasn't what she asked you," Macdara said.

Frank lifted an eyebrow. "Pardon?"

"She asked if you knew Peter was thinking about changing his will."

He sighed. "I know what you're thinking. Tracy and Brandon can be difficult. Petulant at best, both of them.

But they have their reasons. Imagine, my old-fashioned brother a playboy."

"A 'playboy'?" Siobhán echoed. An image of his mismatched outfit came to mind, his wrinkled skin, his gnarled finger.

"Hard to picture," Frank said. "But true. Greta was his third wife, and who knows how many women were on the side?"

"Are you suggesting he had a mistress?" Macdara asked.

Like his nurse? Siobhán thought.

"Of course not," Frank said. "Peter stopped his philandering when he met Greta."

"Then what are you trying to say?" Siobhán asked.

Frank sighed. "One shouldn't expect Tracy and Brandon to love and trust their father's women. Even one as gentle and sweet as Greta." His voice thickened and he immediately looked away. Macdara made eye contact with her. Frank hadn't directly answered the question, but he had just revealed something he hadn't intended, maybe something he hadn't even admitted to himself. Frank was obviously in love with his brother's wife.

Siobhán put that aside for now and tried once more. "Did Tracy and Brandon know Peter was going to change his will?"

"They suspected it. Did Peter actually do it?" Frank's voice was calm, as if he hardly cared about the answer. But when Siobhán looked down, she could see him twisting his handkerchief into a knot.

"That's under investigation," Macdara said. "What's of concern to us is whether or not Tracy and Brandon knew."

Frank shook his head. "It doesn't make them murderers."

"Money is the strongest motive there is," Macdara said. "And sadly, the most common."

"Even if he changed his will, there's still plenty of money," Frank said. "I told them that. I told them not to get so worked up."

"About the will?" Siobhán asked.

"No. I m-meant," Frank stammered, "worked up over Greta. They aren't nice to her. She doesn't deserve their wrath. Peter would be so ashamed!"

"What about his first two wives?" Siobhán asked.

Once again Frank looked startled. "What about them?"

"Just wondering if they are still in the picture?"

Frank shook his head no. "Tracy and Brandon's mother died when they were small. Breast cancer. Peter was a very busy man. We had just started to franchise. He married again quickly. A waitress. I think he did it for the children. She was very nurturing. She lasted a few years. They divorced quietly, with a big settlement. We've never heard from her again."

"So he was single for a while before he met Greta?"

"Correct. He said he'd never marry again. He went out with a lot of women. Seemed happiest that way. Until three years ago. He met Greta, and well. I guess he was a changed man." A bitter look crossed Frank's face. Yes, without a doubt, he was coveting his brother's wife. That must have been such a hard secret to keep. Living and working so close to her as he did.

Was it motive enough to kill his brother? After all, Greta is now free. "How much of the family business do you own?" Siobhán asked.

"Twenty-five percent. I'm not looking for more." He used his handkerchief to wipe the excessive sweat off his brow.

Both Frank and Greta had gone out of their way to declare they weren't interested in money. Siobhán wasn't sure she bought it. "What did you do all afternoon and evening the day of the murder?"

"I parted ways with the group. I'm not young anymore. These bones get tired. I got a bite to eat and then went back to the apartment to read a good book and settle in for the night."

"Lovely," Siobhán said. "What was it?"

"Pardon?"

"The book."

Frank scrunched his nose. "A paperback from the airport."

Siobhán edged forward. "A thriller? Mystery? Love story?"

"Yes, yes," Frank said, waving his hands. "It's one of those. Will you excuse me?" He strode to the counter, his coattails flapping. Chris Gordon handed him his room key. The door chimed as he exited in a huff.

Siobhán nodded to Macdara. "A book with no name or plot."

"Noted," Macdara said. "Meanwhile our real-life mystery seems to be thickening."

Siobhán and Macdara had just stepped onto the footpath when Macdara's mobile rang. He spoke quietly and then hung up and turned to Siobhán. "One of my mates spotted one of our Americans in Paddy Power."

Siobhán glanced down the street, to where the popular betting shop was located. "Brandon?"

Macdara nodded. "That's my guess."

Siobhán looked up at the flats above. "I thought he was upstairs."

"I have a feeling quite a few folks in our little group aren't always where we think they are."

"Or reading the books they say they're reading," Siobhán said. She glanced down the street in the direction of the chipper. "Are you going?"

Macdara looked away. "Why don't you take this? I'll stay here in case anyone else in this little group wants to have a private chat." He glanced up at the bank of windows where the Americans were staying.

An irrational jealousy overtook Siobhán as an image of Tracy putting the moves on Macdara swarmed in her mind. Would he fall for the grieving daughter? No, he was a professional. He wouldn't take up with a suspect. Was he dating anyone back in Dublin? "Why? What are you doing?"

"I just told you. I'm going to start with this group upstairs."

Siobhán heard a scraping sound and glanced up to see one of the windows open. Tracy Mallon leaned out, smoking a cigarette, her ample cleavage on full display. "Brandon's going to be defensive," Macdara said, his eyes on Tracy. "I think you'll have better luck with him than me."

"I see," Siobhán said. She knew her tone was clipped.

Macdara's head swiveled to Siobhán. "Something wrong, boss?"

God, those blue eyes. That sneaky smile. He knew she was jealous and he was enjoying it. "Not a thing."

"Good luck," he said. "I'll see you at Naomi's later." The entire group had been invited to Naomi's for an early supper. It was an extra shift, but Elise had stepped up and said she didn't mind hosting the Americans. Siobhán hated to owe her, but was thankful for the favor. She headed off to the betting shop with a nod to Macdara, sans the smile.

–

Paddy Power was at the end of the street, across from the chipper. It was easy enough to spot Brandon Mallon. He was still standing underneath one of the mounted televisions that played horse races all day long. And when there wasn't a real race on, lads could bet on cartoon dog races. It was madness. Brandon Mallon was situated in a corner, with a betting slip in his hand, right leg bouncing. The small shop was filled with twitching, sweaty lads. It smelled of money and desperation. Siobhán hated it. She approached Brandon from the side, but he was too engrossed in the television to notice her.

"I heard you were here," Siobhán said. He jumped, then turned around, his eyes wild and searching.

"Oh," he said, running a hand through his hair. Sweat dappled his forehead. "Oh. Hello."

"I thought you were settling into your room."

For a second he looked as if he was going to lie or make an excuse, and then his shoulders slumped in defeat. "I'm a gambler," he said. "But they all think I quit."

"I see." Whereas some people had no tolerance for the addictions of others, Siobhán had great empathy. Was there any worse torture than being imprisoned within your own desires?

"I know how this must look."

Siobhán tilted her head. "How does it look?"

Brandon swallowed. Tears pooled in his eyes. "Like I don't care that my father has been murdered."

"I wasn't thinking that," Siobhán said softly. "Would you like to get out of here?"

He glanced at the telly, where the results of the latest race were scrolling across the screen. "Lost again," he said.

"A basket of curried chips might cheer you up," Siobhán said. "Does the trick for me."

He stared longingly at the betting screen, then shook his head, as if trying to knock the urge out of his head. "I'm in."

They ventured out into the cold and the snow, and Siobhán led him across the street to the chipper. Only after they were seated, each with a basket of curried chips— such a sweet, sweet basket—did she speak again. "How long have you been addicted to gambling?"

He slumped in the booth. "I stopped for two years. My father would be so disappointed." He pawed in his jacket pocket, as if looking for something, then sighed. "God, I quit smoking too. I'd kill for one. Just one." He glanced at her.

"I don't smoke."

He sighed. "Good for you. You're probably perfect. An angel without faults."

Siobhán threw her head back and laughed. "I might have a few wee ones."

Brandon laughed and then a curtain of sadness fell across his face again. "The old man would not be proud."

"I'd like to think they aren't judging us after they pass," Siobhán said. "I'd like to think it's only our well-being they worry about."

He sniffed. "That's a nice thought," he said. "I'll take it."

"Why do you think you like gambling so much?" Siobhán was genuinely curious. Her parents had always stressed the importance of earning one's way. "*There's no pleasure in being handed something*," Naomi would say. "*But when you earn something because of this*"—she'd tap her head. "*Or these*"—she'd hold out her hands. "*No feeling like it in the world*." Once her mother won a gift basket from a local raffle and she immediately marched it over to the nuns and handed it over, despite the O'Sullivan Six whining for just a few wee bites of the chocolate biscuits. Whenever Siobhán ran into the nuns, she still wondered if they enjoyed the basket of sweets, and still felt just a twinge of resentment.

Brandon straightened up. "There's nothing like placing a bet. The rush. The adrenaline. When I win?" He patted his heart. "There's no feeling like it in the world."

Siobhán nodded. "And when you lose?"

His eyes watered with shame. "There's no feeling like it in the world." He looked up as if he hadn't meant to become vulnerable, his face stricken. "Please," he said. "Please don't tell the others."

She mimed zipping her lips shut and tossing the key. "Where were you the afternoon and evening your father was murdered?"

He reached into his trousers, pulled out a stash of betting slips, and tossed them on the table. "The races. I'm ashamed to say I was there most of the day and evening. Then I took my meager winnings and drank in a pub."

"Which one?"

"'Which one?'"

"Which pub?"

Brandon looked perplexed. "I have no idea. They all look alike."

Siobhán sighed and reached for the betting slips. "May I?"

He shrugged. "I don't need them."

Then why did you keep them? The question flashed in her mind, but she kept it to herself. He was open and personable. She wanted to keep that going. "Do you know of anyone in your group who would want to harm your father?"

He put his head in his hands. "No. No. I would hate to think that."

"But if you were forced to think that?"

"Frank and my father have been arguing this entire trip. And Greta! I don't believe that 'I didn't marry for money' act for a second. I think she's a gold digger through and through. Thank God she's not inheriting the estate."

The last comment seemed genuine. Either he didn't know his father had been thinking about changing his will, or he was putting on a good act. Was now a good time to stir the pot?

She hesitated as Macdara's words came back at her: "*From now on, everything by the book.*" Certainly, a little harmless conversation couldn't hurt. "It has been brought to our attention that your father was actually going to change his will."

Brandon's head snapped up. "Excuse me?"

Siobhán put her hands up. "I don't want to start rumors. But it's possible Greta might be inheriting more than you think."

Brandon pounded his fist on the table. *A temper.* "Lies! My father wouldn't have done that. He knew how we felt about Greta."

"She seems alright to me."

Brandon groaned. "You don't have to live with her."

"You don't live on your own?" Siobhán kept her voice as light as possible. *A grown man living under his father's roof and complaining about it.*

"We have a very large house. We all run the family business."

"Of course." *And it's hard to pay rent if you gamble it away.*

"I'm going to have Tracy contact our attorney. We'll need to have his will read as soon as possible."

"I'd be so grateful if you didn't repeat what I've told you to anyone." She smiled. "Just like I won't tell them about your gambling."

He nodded, sweat gathering on his forehead.

If Brandon truly didn't know about the will changing, he would either run straight to Tracy and blab, or try and contact the attorneys about the will. Hopefully, they could monitor what he did next. If he had killed his father and removed the original will, he wouldn't need to check on it. They'd never be able to get his mobile records quickly enough. If only she could somehow sneak a peek at it in a few hours. Find out if he immediately called anyone or not. But stealing someone's mobile was hardly playing by the book. Policies and procedures! So inhibiting to an investigation.

She leaned in and lowered her voice as if they were the best of friends. After all, they were now sharing each other's secret confidences. It wasn't exactly a technique she learned in college, but it was a nifty skill. "Have you seen any of them with a firearm?"

"Of course not." He shifted in his chair. "However..."

"Yes?"

"Frank owns them. All that talk about my father. He's the one who knows how to shoot."

"He said he and your father learned as young lads."

"'Young lads,'" Brandon said. "I love your accent." This time his eyes traveled over her face, and down to her chest.

Siobhán took note of it. "Do you have a girlfriend back home?"

Brandon continued staring. "I'm available," he said. "And I quite like it here."

Great. All I need. Another American stalker. "What about Jay Shepard?"

"You're interested in him, are you?" Disgust rang through his voice. "Join the club. Hannah definitely drools over him. I daresay Tracy does too."

"Actually, I was just wondering if he knew his way around a firearm."

Brandon shrugged. "You'll have to ask him. I know so little about him."

"Hannah?"

Brandon laughed. "My father's nurse, with a gun? Are you crazy?"

"Because she's a woman?"

"Because she's Hannah. The poor thing looks frightened all the time. Watch her sometime. She's tensed up as if bracing herself for someone to jump out at her and yell 'boo.'"

"And who hired her?"

"I assume it was Greta. Anytime you ask who did anything, the answer will usually be Greta. She's a librarian through and through. My father was way too trusting of her."

"And you're not?"

He scoffed. "Tell me what a woman her age is doing with a man my father's age?"

"If he's made her the beneficiary of his will, that must make you very angry." Siobhán had to tread lightly. Riling up a possible murderer could have grave consequences. A gear in her mind jammed as she replayed that thought. *Grave consequences. Pun not intended.* She was grateful no one could read her mind, unintended or not; the danger was too serious for puns. An angry killer might not just come after her, but the bistro, and her family could be possible targets as well. She had to always be mindful of that, and protect them every step of the way.

Brandon's boyish demeanor vanished, as a hard look came into his eyes. "Our father fell for women too easy. Made him an easy target. The second one left him heart-broken and vulnerable. I know what you're getting at—his greedy, grown children—but that's not the case. We were only trying to protect him."

By making sure you kept the family fortune. Siobhán gently laid her hand on his arm. "Our job will be to check into all angles. I'm trying to find your father's killer."

"Well, you can rule me out, and you can rule out Tracy. We've sacrificed everything to make him happy."

"I see."

"I'm serious. You're wasting your time investigating us."

"Just doing my job."

He stood. "Please. You must not tell them where you found me."

"You're a grown man. Why would it bother you so much?"

He sighed, as if she were a child constantly asking why, and he the weary parent, tired of coming up with an answer. "I made a promise. Let's just leave it at that." Now would have been the perfect time for him to confess that his father had threatened to cut him out of the will if he was caught gambling again. Instead he stuffed one last curried chip in his mouth and strode for the door.

Siobhán wrote a single word next to his name in her notebook: *Defensive.* "I'll see you at the bistro," she called after him.

He turned, his eyes like lasers bearing into her. "Does that mean you're not going to tell?"

"I'll keep your secrets if you keep mine." They held eye contact. He broke it with a curt nod, and exited, the door slamming shut behind him. She watched through the window until he was out of sight.

He wouldn't keep her "secrets," of course. He'd leak like a sieve. And that's exactly what she was counting on.

Chapter 11

Early that evening every member of the American group showed up at the bistro for a spot of dinner. Elise had made shepherd's pie, which Siobhán reluctantly admitted was terrific. The crust was just the right amount of crisp, the lamb savory, the vegetables fresh, and the potatoes fluffy. Siobhán wanted to go back for a second helping, but couldn't run the risk that Elise would use the revelation to negotiate her way into making the brown bread.

Besides, Siobhán had work to do. She was most interested in seeing who paired up with whom. Tracy, Frank, and Brandon sat together; Jay and Hannah huddled across from each other at a table near the window; Greta was left on her own. Siobhán felt a stab of sadness for the "widow non grata" and soon joined her.

"I hope your room is alright."

Greta nodded. "It's fine." Worry poured from her voice.

"Is something wrong?"

Greta glanced over at Tracy and Brandon, then dropped her voice to a whisper. "If Peter did change his will, they're going to use it against me." She wrung her hands. "I begged him not to do it. I swear."

"You've tried speaking with his attorneys?"

"Yes. They want to wait until we're all back in the States to read the will."

"I'll need their phone numbers," Siobhán said. Maybe Macdara could get them to talk. It sure would help to know whether or not the will had been officially changed. Or maybe they could get the attorneys to come to Ireland for the reading of the will.

"How did this whole documentary business come up again?" Siobhán asked.

Greta frowned, pushed her glasses up, and sniffed. "How do you mean?"

"How did the idea first come up?"

"I don't remember. I think Peter saw *Dancing Irish*. He was very impressed with Jay's work. Yes. I believe that's how he came up with the idea."

"So it was Peter's idea?"

"Yes. Peter came to me after seeing the documentary. I'm sure of it."

Siobhán wasn't even sure where she was going with the line of questioning. But she couldn't help feeling like Peter Mallon had been lured to Ireland. Was it possible the entire documentary was just a smoke screen? "I'd like to find out how much Jay is getting paid to make this documentary."

Greta's mouth pursed. "Funny you say that."

Siobhán sat up straight. "Oh?"

"Peter refused to tell me. I was so angry. It was the only time he had ever done that. Kept secrets from me."

The only time he was caught. "You have no idea how much Jay is being paid?"

"None whatsoever," Greta said. She glanced at Jay and so did Siobhán. He and Hannah were laughing, heads bowed close together. "He certainly didn't come cheap," she said as they watched them. She drew her attention back to Siobhán. "But Peter had his own bank accounts. We weren't a young couple. We didn't share everything."

"I see." Even though Greta was in her thirties, she behaved like a much older woman. She seemed most attracted to older men. *Is she aware of Frank's crush on her? Does she have a crush on him?* Greta's hand trembled. "Would you like a cup of tea?" Greta shook her head no. Siobhán would never understand these people. "How about a coffee?"

Greta looked hopeful. "I didn't know you served that here. There's not even a Starbucks in this town." She looked forlorn. "It's hard to trust a town without a Star-bucks."

"Coffee it is." Siobhán nodded and headed for her machine, trying not to imagine serving it by pouring it over her head. While the machine worked its magic, she glanced over at Jay Shepard. He was apparently getting paid quite handsomely. Exactly how much? And if he was getting paid either way, and so obviously loved his calling... why on earth would he want Peter Mallon dead? It bothered her when suspects had strong motives, but it bothered her even more when they didn't.

–

It was late and the Kilbane Gardai Station was empty of everyone but herself and Macdara. Siobhán had blown up a photo of each of their suspects, and had taped them to the wall with a photo of Peter below them. From the left to right, she scanned each face: Tracy Mallon. Brandon Mallon. Greta Mallon. Frank Mallon. Jay Shepard. Hannah Stripes. Her eye landed on Peter's photo. "*No matter what anyone else says,*" one of her instructors had told her during her training, "*you work for the victim.*" Siobhán was determined not to forget that. Peter Mallon deserved justice, and it was their job to deliver it.

She turned to Macdara. "Do you have a few sheets of paper?"

He raised his eyebrow, but turned to a nearby shelf. "How many?"

"Two will do the trick." He handed her the paper. She stared at them. He stared at her. "And a Biro. Please."

He shook his head, but reached over to a nearby desk to hand her a pen.

On one sheet of paper she hastily sketched her best rendition of an elderly woman and underneath wrote: *OLD LADY.* She pinned it up near their suspects. On the next sheet of paper she drew a blank face and in the middle put a question mark. Underneath she wrote: *UNKNOWN.*

Macdara folded his arms across his chest as his eyes traveled through all the options. "We've certainly covered all bases."

Underneath the photographs they combined their notes, everything they'd learned so far about their suspects. Siobhán tapped the piece of paper that read *OLD LADY.* "Father Kearney hasn't spotted her since the murder."

"Right. But the cemetery has been cordoned off."

"True." She hated when he hit her with logic. "So where did she go?" There weren't many places to hide in Kilbane.

"And who is she?"

Siobhán sighed. She lifted the pile of family tree information dropped off to the station by Greta. "I don't know how to sort through all of this."

Macdara grinned. "Nobody warned you about all the grunt work?"

"I was a bit naive." She laughed. "Did Jay Shepard turn over everything he's filmed?"

"Yes. That's what I'll be slogging through."

"Including recording our suspects' accounts of that day?"

Macdara nodded. "I've watched them once. Some of them are more camera shy than others, but given the time of the murder, they either claimed to be in bed or in the pubs."

"Let me guess. Brandon was in the pub."

"And Tracy. But not in the same pub."

She sighed. Definitely not a close brother-sister relationship. She couldn't imagine going on holiday with her siblings and then avoiding them. "I'll watch the rest of the films if you want to read through the family tree."

"Nice try."

"Peter Mallon seems like he was a good man. They all agree on that."

Macdara looked thoughtful. "People don't like speaking ill of the dead."

"So you think Peter might have been stirring up trouble?"

"Somebody stirred something up. And nobody's perfect."

"True," Siobhán said. "Not a single one of us."

"Some of us come closer than others," Macdara said with a smile.

"Do they?" Siobhán said. They held eye contact. *Is he flirting? Breaking his own rule?* She forced herself to concentrate and glanced at the photographs of the suspects again. Her eyes lingered on the *UNKNOWN* face with a question mark.

Macdara followed her gaze. "What's the story?"

"Isn't it possible the suspect isn't somebody he knew?"

"What are you thinking?"

"It was widely reported that Peter Mallon had been nosing around town. What if he angered someone local?" She could think of a few locals who weren't big fans of Americans.

"Angry enough to kill him?"

"It's not probable, but isn't it possible?"

"At this point all possibilities are on the table. But my gut tells me he was killed by one of his group." They sat in silence for a moment; then their eyes met again, and stayed locked on each other for another few moments. Macdara cleared his throat and stood. "I'll try rattling the attorneys. Any day I get to rattle a solicitor is a good day." He grinned.

Siobhán looked away. "Any news on the state pathologist?"

Macdara brightened. "There's a bit of good news."

"Tell me."

Macdara grabbed his cap. "Better yet, first thing in the morning, she's going to tell you."

"Why don't you just tell me now, and in the morning she can tell me again, and I'll pretend it's the first time I'm hearing it."

"No."

"Really, I can act surprised. Watch." She flashed him her best expression of surprise.

"Impressive. Still no."

"What's wrong with telling me right now?"

"Nothing." He grinned. "Consider it a lesson in patience." She wished she could give him a lesson in face slaps. He chuckled, knowing he had gotten under her skin. "Come on. I'll walk you home."

–

Jeanie Brady, the state pathologist, was a short, round woman with intelligent hazel eyes and a mad pistachio addiction. In between filling them in on her findings, she was cracking nuts into her mouth, and spitting the shells to the ground. It was wildly distracting. She wasn't sharing to boot. Siobhán and Macdara stood with her just outside the churchyard. Although Peter Mallon's wallet was missing, along with his satchel, and the snow had obliterated any chance of finding major evidence, she did have a few tidbits to share. A bullet had been found underneath the body and Jeanie said she'd never seen anything like it.

"It's an antique bullet!" she exclaimed, holding up the plastic bag that contained it.

"'Antique'?" Siobhán repeated.

"It only fits an old-time revolver. Most likely, a British Army revolver from way back. I can't even imagine where the killer got one."

Siobhán and Macdara looked at each other. "The Kilbane Museum," they said at the same time. It had a collection of revolvers dating back to the earliest gun conflicts in Ireland. Most of the revolvers would have been from the British Army.

"Show her the note," Macdara said to the pathologist. Jeanie Brady held up a second plastic bag. Inside was the remains of the letter Siobhán had spotted on the ground.

My Dearest Ann,

*How could you? I used to believe the truth shall
set you free. However, I am a prisoner.*

"What on earth?" Siobhán said. "That's it?"

"That's all that survived," Jeanie said. "We found
matches on the ground. It appears someone attempted to
burn the note at the churchyard."

"Did you find a matchbook?"

"No. Just discarded matches."

Siobhán sighed. "We've basically got nothing."

"We know that Ann is the name of John Mallon's wife,"
Macdara said. "Peter's great-grandmother."

Jeanie spit another pistachio shell onto the snow-
covered ground. She was going to torture the poor squir-
rels. "There's more," she said, her eyes lighting up. "I've
been able to date the paper and the letter. It's from the
nineteenth century."

Siobhán whistled. Macdara nodded. "So we've got an
antique letter and revolver," Siobhán said. "Found near
headstones from the same time period."

"It's intriguing," the pathologist said. "I almost envy
you."

Siobhán groaned. "I wonder if Peter had the letter in
his satchel?"

"Meaning someone killed Peter first and burned the
letter second?" He shook his head. "That doesn't fit."

Siobhán gazed out at the cemetery. What would bring
a man like Peter here at this hour? Something irresistible.
"Maybe Peter was at the churchyard to purchase the letters
from the killer."

"So we're assuming this letter was written by Peter's
great-grandfather?" Macdara said.

Siobhán nodded. "John Mallon. We'll need to find other examples of John Mallon's handwriting to prove it, but it would explain why Peter agreed to meet someone at that hour."

"In that scenario, it's the killer who suggests the time."

"Of course. What man in his right mind wants to be in a cemetery in the middle of the night?"

"Okay," Macdara said. "So why burn the letter?"

Siobhán shrugged. "The deal went bad?"

"Peter had money. If he wanted the letter so bad that he agreed to the time and place of the meeting, I don't see how the deal could have gone bad."

"Maybe the killer demanded more money. Everyone has pride. A point of no return. Maybe Peter was pushed to the edge." Siobhan could imagine it so clearly. Poor Peter, finally grasps the letter in his hand when—

"Or maybe the killer never intended for anyone else to see the letters," Macdara said, interupting her imaginings. "It wasn't about money at all. It was all a ploy to lure Peter Mallon to his death."

"I said that already," Siobhán said. *Hadn't she?* Maybe she'd just thought it. Macdara always had been a bit of a mind-reader. Siobhán shuddered. Jeanie was watching them wide-eyed, her bag of pistachios nearly gone.

"Maybe a third person came on the scene?" Jeanie ventured. She stared at her nearly-empty bag of nuts with what could only be described as grief.

"Did you find evidence of a third person?" Siobhán asked.

Jeanie reddened. "No. But the snow and time lapse made it very difficult."

"We need to find the satchel," Macdara said. "Along with Peter's mobile phone and wallet."

"And the revolver," Siobhán said.

Jeanie cleared her throat. "'Envy' might have been too strong a word. You two certainly have your work cut out for you." She balled up her empty bag of pistachios and shoved it into her coat pocket.

Siobhán pulled up her photograph of the headstone. She pointed to the letters at the bottom: $E\_\ \_u\ \_A\_\_$. "What if the last word on here is Ann?"

Macdara nodded. "Good catch." He stared at it. "So what's the rest?"

"I solved one," Siobhán said, wishing she knew the rest. "Can't I just take a second to bask in my glory?"

Macdara raised his eyebrow. "Bask away. Will you let me know when you're finished?"

"You've already ruined it," Siobhán said. "I couldn't bask now if I wanted to."

"I'll leave you to it," Jeanie said, looking totally lost now that her nuts were gone.

They thanked her and hurried to the museum.

–

The Kilbane Museum was a small affair—a one-room museum with an attic loft, but it held treasures going back to the fourteenth century and was adored and protected by the locals, who kept it afloat by volunteering for shifts. Siobhán even manned the desk once in a while. Today their neighbor Pio Mahoney stood there, grinning at them as they walked in. He and his wife, Sheila, lived across the street. Sheila ran a hair salon and Pio was a gifted musician. "Ah, a bit of company," he said. "A fella can go mad in here surrounded by all these artifacts."

They said their hellos and got straight to business. Macdara asked if any of the revolvers had gone missing.

"Not that I'm aware," Pio said. "But let's have a look." He went straight to a glass case on the back wall. Mounted behind it was the collection of revolvers. Third from the right was a blank spot. A faint outline of a revolver, etched in dust.

"I'll be damned," Pio said. "There's one missing, alright. How on earth did I not notice?"

Siobhán felt a tingle. This was it. The murder weapon. How did someone get into the glass case without breaking it?

"How does this open?" Macdara asked. Pio pointed to a hook on the wall where a key hung. "You keep the key right there?"

Pio looked frightened for a moment, as if the blame was going to fall squarely on him. He held up a mess of keys. "That's just a spare. Some volunteers don't like carrying this around in their pocket. Doesn't bother me."

"You leave a spare key hanging in plain sight?" She leaned closer. At least the key wasn't labeled. There was no sign above it that screamed: KEY TO GUN CABINET. A stranger coming into the shop would probably never even notice it. Unless, of course, they were desperate for a gun.

"Never had reason to think anyone would take it. With so many volunteers it seemed safer than making multiple copies."

Siobhán scanned the room. It was filled to the brim with books, and objects, and photographs. "Is it possible the revolver is lying around here still?"

"Let me give a look." Pio slowly looked around the shop. Macdara and Siobhán joined in, combing through shelves and boxes. They came up empty.

Macdara sighed. "Since you didn't know it was missing, I don't suppose you've any idea when it was taken?"

"This is my first shift in ages. Nobody mentioned it, and I wasn't really looking."

"Do you have the schedule book?" Siobhán asked. All the volunteers were required to sign in and out of their shifts.

"Sure." Pio dipped into the shelf behind the counter and handed Macdara the schedule book. Macdara tucked it under his arm.

"You're keeping it?" Pio asked, alarmed.

"Just going to photocopy the last few weeks," Macdara said. "I'll have a guard drop it off as soon as I'm finished."

"What about bullets?" Siobhán said. "Are there any here for that revolver?"

"As a matter of fact, that's the only one that has bullets. We keep 'em in a jar in this cupboard." Pio knelt and unlocked another cupboard. "That can't be!" he exclaimed.

"They're gone," Siobhán said.

"They're gone," Pio said.

Siobhán pointed to the hanging key. "Don't tell me they open with the same key?" Pio's bright red face provided the answer they needed.

"Someone has a flare for the dramatic," Macdara said, staring at the empty spot where the antique revolver once rested.

"And a lot more bullets," Siobhán said.

Chapter 12

Lough Gur, just a short drive away in County Limerick, was a local historic park defined by a horseshoe-shaped lake banked by a short trail where swans and cows alike came to drink, swim, and bathe. It was the site of megalithic remains, stones that remained from prehistoric dwellings. Behind the lake towered Knockadoon Hill. Humans had lived here since 3000 B.C., making it an important and rare archaeological site.

Siobhán always felt a deep sense of appreciation and awe whenever she was here, and today was no exception. Part of her wanted to show the Americans the magnificent site, and the other part of her selfishly wanted to keep it a secret. The largest Grange Stone Circle in Ireland was located near the lake, as well as an ancient dolmen. In addition, the remains of three artificial islands, called crannogs, were present, as well as Stone Age houses, ring forts, and, last, a hill fort overlooking the lake. In another life Siobhán wanted to be an archaeologist, spend her days unearthing secrets from the past, and preserving treasures for generations to come. She never wanted to lose the link between the past and the present, the strong bonds that were literally etched in stone. She loved walking along the lake, although today the snow was covering most of the treasures. It was still a fresh and stunning sight. It was here Siobhán and Macdara agreed to go over the case while away from the prying eyes of the Americans. That was his official excuse. Siobhán expected the truth was somewhat different. The office was stifling. They were forced to sit in close quarters and stare at each other. Here, they could gaze into the distance and not be confronted by accusations in each other's eyes. Siobhán suspected that was the real reason Macdara had driven them out here, but she wasn't going to complain. She would rather be outdoors even if the chill could take off her toes.

In addition to the visitor's center there was a castle at the entrance of the car park, named Bourchier's Castle, but it was on private farmland, and inaccessible to the public. That didn't stop the farmer's collies from trotting into the park to check out visitors, three scraggly-looking dogs that eyed Macdara and Siobhán from a safe distance, ears back and tails tucked between their legs.

As they strolled along the path by the lake and inhaled the fresh scent of the earth and water, Macdara handed Siobhán the volunteer log from the museum. It didn't take her long to find it. "George Dunne," she exclaimed. "He volunteered a few days before his socks went missing."

A gleam shone in Macdara's eye. "You have good instincts. But the socks just aren't speaking to me."

"Maybe if you put one on your hand and move it like a puppet, it will," Siobhán said, doing her best demonstration.

He threw his head back and laughed. It filled her with joy. "Regardless," he said when he'd recovered. "If you have an instinct about it, then I agree that we need to speak with him."

"There's no 'we,'" Siobhán said, staring at the lone cow who had made its way through ice and snow to poke at the lake.

Macdara stopped. "Boss?"

"It's all you. He hates me. You'll have to go it alone."

"I'll do me best," Macdara said. She could feel him watching her as she watched the cow. She grew tired of looking at the cow, who was chewing extremely slowly, but she never grew tired of Macdara watching her, so she remained staring at the bovine as if fascinated. When she could take it no more, she flicked her eyes to Macdara and tried not to notice how blue his eyes looked against the gray Irish skies. "We'll have to speak with everyone who has volunteered at the museum in the past week," he said.

Siobhán shivered. "If the missing revolver is indeed our murder weapon, then that means this was premeditated."

"That is pretty much a foregone conclusion."

"Right. Who accidentally shoots someone in a cemetery at one in the morning?"

"Unless they went there for another reason, then fought, struggled, and the gun went off."

"That letter has to be what brought Peter to the churchyard. If only we could read more of it."

"And find Peter's wallet and satchel."

"The killer certainly isn't making this easy on us," Siobhán said with a sigh. "Do you think that particular gun holds any significance? The fact that it's an antique?"

"You mean the killer was sending some kind of message?"

"Yes." They started walking again. In the distance the cow lifted her head from the water and studied them for a second before turning around and showing them her large arse. Siobhán couldn't help but think it was on purpose.

"My guess?" Macdara said. "Someone in the museum mentioned it was the only one that had bullets."

"How would one of the Americans know not only about the gun, but where to find the bullets?"

Macdara let out a laugh. "The Kilbane Museum isn't exactly Fort Knox. The key to the guns and the bullets was hanging in plain sight. Anyone who stood there long enough chatting with a volunteer could have put it together."

Siobhán sighed. "We Irish do love to chat."

"In their defense… you can't blame the volunteers for not looking at every tourist as if they were possible murderers. Even if they were Yanks."

"So no significance that the gun is antique?"

Macdara shook his head. "I think it was about access and bullets."

"We're going to have to round up all the volunteers and see who opened his or her piehole." Macdara nodded. "Still. We've got an antique revolver and a family paying homage to an ancestor."

"Your point?"

"We also have to dig into the Mallon family tree."

Macdara grinned. "You have the files from Greta. You should get started."

She gave him a look and he laughed, but the truth was she didn't mind. Paperwork didn't lie, or sidestep, or insult. She'd take a stack of papers over a shifty eyewitness any day. "Bridie suggested that Mallon could be a surname for someone's maternal line in Kilbane." Macdara's face went still. He looked so stern. Siobhán felt her stomach twist. "Something wrong?"

"You've been discussing private details of this case with Bridie?" He turned and headed back to the car. Instead of the leisurely pace they had been enjoying, Macdara was speed-walking now. She had to jog to keep up, his words feeling like a slap to the face. Even the collies turned tail as Macdara strode by, then tucked and hustled up the hill back to their farmhouse and private castle. For a second she was jealous of them, jealous of scraggly farm dogs. She hadn't been *discussing* the case with Bridie. She had been asking questions. Just enough to get her talking.

"I was gathering information, not giving it," Siobhán said to the back of Macdara's head. "And she met Peter Mallon shortly before he was murdered. Of course she needed to talk about that."

"What did you learn?" Macdara asked while still walking ahead.

Infuriated, Siobhán kept up with his pace. "Peter asked her if she was aware of any Mallons living in town."

Macdara stopped. Stared at her. "And?"

"And what?"

"Are there? Any Mallons living in town?"

"Only time I've seen the surname in Kilbane is that tombstone."

"And you're sure Bridie doesn't know anything more about the case?"

"I'm sure."

"You need to be more careful." He started walking again.

Siobhán crossed her arms. He was so stubborn. She took a deep breath. This wasn't about them. There was a murderer out there. Siobhán softened her voice. "Even if we find a long-lost relative, why on earth would they want Peter Mallon dead?"

"I don't know. But somebody certainly did. And he was pointing to one of the graves in the cemetery."

"Or 'he was reaching for something,'" Siobhán said, echoing Macdara's words back at him.

"Reaching for what?" Macdara said.

Seriously, did he not remember saying that? "The gun?" Siobhán said. "Maybe there was a struggle and it dropped."

"Number one rule. Do not make up facts and then try and get the evidence to fit. Follow the evidence and see where it wants to fit."

"I'm keeping an open mind while throwing out possibilities. The evidence, at best, is vague."

"Then we keep digging until it becomes clear."

"Yes, sir," she said, a bit more sarcastically than she'd intended.

If he picked up on it, he didn't let on. "I'll arrange for the group to go to the cemetery. It should be quite a surprise for all of them."

They got in the car. The heat inside was undone by the coolness that had risen between them. Macdara hesitated before starting it up. "I'm going to set up a time for all of us to meet at the cemetery. Continue watching Jay's footage."

Siobhán nodded. "And I'll look over the family tree."

"You could," Macdara said. His voice suggested he had a better idea.

"Or?" Siobhán said.

"There's another name on the volunteer list I found interesting."

"Who?"

Macdara handed her the notebook again as he started up the car and headed out. She looked through it, saw the name, and cursed.

Chapter 13

Siobhán shivered as she waited for the heater to crank up in the guard car, wishing it were warm enough to take her scooter. She stared at the name in the schedule book: *Chris Gordon*. He'd volunteered at the museum a few days before Peter was murdered. Had Peter come into the museum then? Surely, if Peter had come into the museum, Chris would have mentioned it. Wouldn't he?

She had to ask him if he remembered seeing the revolver while on his shift. But she couldn't help but think back to how he answered one of her previous questions. She had asked him if he had seen Peter Mallon in the comic shop. She remembered his answer sounded very stilted, rehearsed even. Something along the lines of: "*No, I did not see Peter Mallon in the comic-book shop.*" Was there more to that? Possibly, "*But I did see him in the museum…*"

If that was the case, she was going to throttle him. It was one thing to have one of the American strangers lie to her—or all of them—but it was a worse betrayal coming from a man who had decided to call Kilbane home.

Siobhán thought she'd find him at the comic-book store, but was instead greeted by a surly young lad who barely looked up from his werewolf comic to mumble that Chris was doing some work back at his house. She wanted to roll up the comic and smack him across the head with it; instead she thanked him and walked out.

Chris lived in a farmhouse just outside of town. Given that the lad who killed her parents in a drunk-driving accident used to live in that house, Siobhán wasn't thrilled to go. And with the snow making it difficult to drive, well, she was tempted not to go at all. But if she was right, someone stole that revolver right out from under his nose, and any information she could glean might just help their case.

She found Chris shoveling his driveway. A snowman was built next to it. She felt a moment of guilt. She should have made a snowman with Ann and Ciarán. She should have bought a sled and found a hill to careen down, or started a snowball fight. There simply hadn't been any time.

Chris looked alarmed when her car pulled up; then he smiled when he saw Siobhán step out.

"How ya?" she said. It took all her control not to lunge at him.

"Better now," he said, leaning on the shovel with a grin. "To what do I owe the pleasure?"

"Do you mind if we step into the house for a chat?" She blinked rapidly, hoping it passed as flirting. He looked alarmed. "It's a bit nippy out here," she added. "I could use a mug of tea."

"Did I do something?"

"Did you?" She smiled sweetly. Her stomach turned.

He sighed and tossed his shovel down. "Is this about Peter Mallon?"

"It is, yeah."

He held her gaze, then abruptly broke it off. "I'm out of Barry's tea. I only have instant coffee."

She sighed. It would be nothing like the liquid heaven her cappuccino machine spit out. "That'll do."

The last time she had stepped into the house, it had been dark and smelled of cigarette smoke. She had to hand it to Chris Gordon, the change was outstanding. He'd given it a fresh coat of paint, and everything was tidy. She wondered if the place had had a woman's touch. Chris had no shortage of suitors. Girls were constantly hanging around in his shop, and Siobhán knew it wasn't for the gory comics.

He hummed as he set about making the coffee, and for a few seconds she felt as if she were on an awkward first date. When he set his coffee down in front of her, she could smell his cologne, or aftershave, and she had to admit it wasn't entirely unpleasant. She immediately thought of Macdara, and felt a flush of shame, then irritation for his intrusion into her thoughts. She was a grown woman, fully capable of smelling any man she wanted to.

"Everything okay?" Chris said, flashing his dimple.

She sat up straight, pulled out her notebook, and slammed it on his table. "You volunteered at the Kilbane Museum the week Peter was in town."

"Oh, my God," he said. "You're right. He did come into the museum."

She stood. Her anger flaring. "Don't give me that."

He concentrated on stirring heaps of sugar into his coffee. "So you are mad at me."

"Of course I'm mad at you. How could you keep this from me? I should arrest you right now for interfering with an investigation." She sank back into her seat, mainly because her feet were tired and she didn't want to stand.

Chris held his arms out. "I panicked."

"Explain."

"I'm working in the museum. Some fellow American man comes in and starts telling me this magnificent story... Really it was so cool—"

"Wait. Peter Mallon told you his great-grandfather's story?" She clenched her fists, wishing once again that she could dole out punishment for deception and/or stupidity. "Why didn't you tell me?"

Chris's eyes widened. "I didn't think it was relevant."

She pinched the bridge of her nose, having read somewhere that it helped to induce a calm state. It did not.

"Are you okay?"

She pointed at him. "From now on, you don't think. I'll do the thinking for you."

"Yes, ma'am."

"Don't ever call me that again."

"Sorry. Garda."

She drummed her fingers on the table, imagining Peter in the museum, a glint in his eye as he spoke of his great-grandfather. For some reason she was jealous that Chris had heard Peter Mallon's story firsthand. She hoped she wasn't getting too emotionally involved with the victim. "Tell me everything Mr. Mallon said."

"He told me a love story." Chris held eye contact with her.

She squinted at him. "A love story."

"John and Ann Mallon."

Siobhán felt a tingle up her spine. "Go on."

"They were young and in love during The Great Hunger. Stole away on a ship called the *Swan*."

Siobhán sat up straight. "The *Swan*. Are you sure?"

"That's what he said. It sailed from Cork to New York."

At least he'd been paying attention. She had a new nugget of information. The *Swan*. It was a lovely name for a sailing ship. She would have to do some further research.

Chris shrugged. "There was a friend in America waiting to help the young couple. They started a restaurant to feed the poor, while going on to have a beautiful family. Made a fortune and gave back to the people. It's the quintessential American story. You know. Via Ireland."

Siobhán frowned. "While regaling you with the love story, Peter Mallon may have stolen an antique revolver and bullets right out from under your nose."

Chris almost fell out of his chair. "What?" His shock was genuine. Siobhán almost relished delivering the news.

"Do you know the antique revolvers that hang in the glass case at the museum?"

"Of course."

"One of them is missing."

"Which one?"

Siobhán was flummoxed. "What does that matter?"

"I'm just trying to picture the case."

"The third one from the left."

"Are you sure?"

"Yes. There's nothing there."

"My God." He held up his hands. "I didn't take it."

"Could Peter Mallon have taken it while regaling you with this love story?"

"If he did… that would make me look like a freaking idiot."

Siobhán sighed. He was only thinking of himself. "No one is worried about that. Think back. What was that day like? Is it possible Peter Mallon took the gun from the case?" If Peter brought the gun, it means the killer wrestled it from him. Perhaps there was a quarrel. Maybe the killer shot in self-defense. She couldn't discount the fact that Peter had been in the museum in close proximity to the murder weapon. She had to leave room for all the possibilities. But why would Peter bring a gun in the first place? He could have felt uneasy about the meeting. Spooked even. Imagine. Killed with the very gun you stole to protect yourself. How was that for the luck of the Irish?

Chris poured more sugar into his coffee. Then stirred. Then poured some more. "I didn't see him do it, but it had to be him. Right?"

Siobhán moved the sugar out of his way, just in case he was thinking about diving in headfirst. "You're positive you didn't see him do it?"

"I swear. I would have told you."

"Was your back ever to him?"

Chris looked up and to the right. "I would have said no. But it had to have been, right? For him to steal it?"

"Unless you think you wouldn't have noticed if he did it right in front of you," Siobhán said, unable to stop the sarcasm this time.

"And he had been asking about the gun."

Siobhán felt a jolt. "He did?" Her fists curled in. Why on earth did she have to squeeze information out of people? There was seriously something wrong with human beings. "Why didn't you lead with that?"

He shrugged. "You're the detective. I don't know what matters and what doesn't."

Siobhán took a deep breath that wasn't at all cleansing and drummed her fingers on the table. "What did he ask you about the antique revolvers?"

Chris rubbed his chin. "I don't remember."

"You have to. This is important."

Chris looked up and to the right, then snapped his fingers. "I don't think he was very happy with his wife."

"What?"

"I said that was a great love story. His reaction was odd."

"Go on."

"He said you never know what's behind someone's love story. He said you never really know someone at all."

It was very similar to the strange comment he made to Bridie. Didn't he say something to her about never really knowing somebody? Obviously, things had not been so perfect between Greta and Peter. Did this have anything to do with Frank and Greta? Maybe Peter found out his brother was in love with his wife. Or maybe he was speaking of his daughter, Tracy, trying to have him declared mentally unfit. Or maybe it was about Brandon gambling. Siobhán almost groaned out loud. So many options. She urged Chris to go on. "And then he asked about the guns?"

"Yes. I didn't think he was planning on shooting anyone. Not with antiques."

"Meaning you showed him the case of revolvers."

"Yes."

"Did he touch them?"

"Of course not."

"Did you open the case?"

"Nope."

"Did he say anything about them?"

Chris shook his head. "He looked at them closely, then shook his head as if he was disappointed."

"'Disappointed'?"

"He made some comment... What was it... oh. He said this was all a waste of time. That there was no need to get dramatic."

"*No need to get dramatic.*"

Did that mean he took the gun, or did he leave the gun?

"Are you sure all of the revolvers were there the entire time you volunteered?"

"I'm sure. I mean I wouldn't have been sure... but he asked about the revolvers, remember?" Chris hesitated.

"Did you think of something?"

"We had a large donation that day." He snapped his fingers again. Siobhán wanted to bite them off. She wondered if these mini-thoughts of violence were normal this early in her garda career. "That's right! When I came in, boxes were piled on the counter. They blocked the view of the case." He exhaled and crossed his arms. A satisfied grin spread across his face. "Peter could have taken the gun right in front of me without me noticing."

Siobhán let that sit for a moment. "Who donated boxes?"

He frowned. "I think Bridie did. Some of her hand-made scarves. And George Dunne."

Siobhán nearly spilled her coffee. "Were there any wooly socks in his boxes?"

Chris nodded. "How did you know?"

This time Siobhán spit out her coffee and began to choke. Chris sprang up from his seat and pounded her on the back. When she could breathe again, his hands remained, and he gently started massaging her. She tossed his hands off. "Are you joking me?"

"A box full of socks," Chris said, going back to his seat with a swagger and a smile. "I thought he was crazy and threw them out."

"Oh, no," she groaned. "He's reported them missing."

"He what?"

"He's been railing about those missing socks."

Chris was the one who almost choked this time. "Dude is losing it. Poor man. I don't ever want to get that old."

"The alternative isn't much better. So, did you throw out the socks?"

"I was going to."

"But you didn't?"

"I did."

"You're not making any sense."

Chris shook his head. "Someone took them."

"What? Who?" That's all she needed. Who knew that George Dunne's socks really had been stolen.

"It was the strangest thing."

"Go on."

"I had just set the box outside the door. I was just temporarily putting them there to load into my car. I was going to take them to one of the travelers' camps. I know you Irish don't like them, but that doesn't mean they should have cold feet in the winter, now does it? And they were perfectly good socks. But I had to pop back into the museum to shut off the lights and lock up. That's when I saw a figure go by the door and bend down near where I had placed the box."

"A figure?"

"A tall old lady. Long gray hair—"

"With a tan coat and a red cap?"

Chris's eyes widened. "You know her?"

"Go on." *This has to be the same old lady Father Kearney encountered in his churchyard.*

"That's it. By the time I got outside, she was gone. And so was the box."

"Did she look homeless?"

"I'm sorry, it was just a glimpse."

"You don't know for sure if the revolver was still in the case?"

"Correct. The other boxes were piled up, blocking my view."

Siobhán tried to think through it. What if the person who stole the gun, placed it in the box of socks, perhaps to hide it? Maybe it was a freak, random event that some crazy old lady who had already been wandering the cemetery winds up with a loaded gun. Then one night here comes poor Peter Mallon into the cemetery for a prearranged meeting, and he startles the crazy old woman, pacing back and forth, this time with the gun…

No. She was making things up again. *Just the facts. See where the facts lead.* All she knew was that this was another confirmed sighting of a tall old lady. That, and she'd solved the mystery of George Dunne and his missing wooly socks. This was getting her nowhere. It was looking like Peter Mallon had taken the gun. And maybe it wasn't because he was spooked, wasn't meant for self-defense. Maybe he had much more sinister plans for the gun.

"It's been a while since I've volunteered at the museum," Siobhán said. "Are donations just on certain days?"

"Yes," Chris said. "Saturday mornings only." *Two days before the murder.*

So someone could have known that boxes would be donated that day. She wished visitors were required to sign in. "Who else besides Peter Mallon came in that day?"

"You can't possibly ask me to remember that," Chris said.

She sighed. Peter might not have stolen the gun; actually, it could have been anyone. She pushed her lousy instant coffee away and stood up. "If you think of anything else, please let me know."

Chris saw her to the door. "Now that you're no longer dating that guard." Chris let it hang. He knew Macdara and it was disrespectful to call him "that guard."

"Detective Sergeant Flannery, you mean."

"Is he?" He raised his eyebrow. Siobhán knew he knew that too. "Good for him. Dublin must be an exciting city."

"I'd better go."

"I messed that up. I would love to take you out sometime."

"I'm pretty busy. New job and all." She gave him a wave and headed off the porch and to the car.

"Of course. It must be hard on you. Given whom he's dating and all."

Siobhán came to a stop. She felt her insides go cold. She turned around. "Pardon?"

Chris leaned against his porch rail. "I mean she's one of your best friends, isn't she?"

Don't fall for it. Don't fall for it. "Who?" She barely had any breath in her chest.

"Aisling. Your friend who lives in Dublin? And Detective Sergeant Flannery, who now lives in Dublin?"

"What about them?"

"I heard they were dating."

The skies were low and gray and seemed to sink into Siobhán's chest. "You're lying."

His eyes widened. He straightened up. "Oh, God. You really didn't know. I'm so sorry."

"Who told you that?"

"Maria was in the store the other day. Talking on her mobile. She's not exactly quiet."

Siobhán couldn't help but picture it as he spoke, couldn't help but get reeled in. "And what exactly did she say?"

"She said she was tired of keeping it a secret. 'Aisling, you have to tell her about you and Macdara, or I will.'"

Maria. If it's true, Maria is betraying me too. All of them.

Was this why Macdara had forbidden her to talk about anything personal? Make her think it was too painful for him to talk about them? "I have to go." She tripped down the porch steps and hesitated at the snowman. She wanted to scream at him and punch him, and kick him to the ground. Maybe it was a good thing she hadn't built one with the young ones.

"I'm really sorry," Chris called from the porch. "I just assumed they told you. What jerks."

She jumped in the car, started it up, and careened out of the driveway. And tried to convince herself it was all about the ice and the snow.

Chapter 14

On the drive back to the station to return the car, Siobhán lectured herself. She wasn't going to believe a word Chris Gordon had to say. She wasn't even going to dignify it with another thought. *Aisling wouldn't date Macdara, would she? Isn't she dating a Scottish lad?*

They'd lost touch lately. Siobhán assumed Aisling was just wrapped up in her busy life, as was she. But maybe there was another reason she'd been avoiding her.

Siobhán sent a *Hey There!* text to Aisling. She stared at her phone, waiting for a response. None came. That didn't mean a thing. If Siobhán lived in Dublin, she would be too busy to answer texts as well.

Maria, on the other hand. Maria couldn't avoid Siobhán. Her best friend. Whatever was going on, Maria knew the story and she hadn't said a word. Siobhán wanted to find her right now, shake her down, but she'd learned not to react when her temper was this high. Chris Gordon might be making the whole thing up. Maybe he misheard the conversation.

She could not let this distract her. She was new to this job and could not blow it. She parked her car in the correct spot behind the gardai station and headed home. She had put in a long day, and didn't want to risk going into the station and running into Macdara. She had to sit with the news, process it first. She took deep breaths as she walked down Sarsfield Street. She waved at Annmarie who was manning the counter at Courtney's, her move to Spain hadn't lasted more than a month and she was back. Kilbane had a way of wrapping you in its cocoon, making it hard to leave. Siobhán hoped that was what was happening with Gráinne. Maybe she would stay, instead of returning to New York.

She popped into the chipper and bought a basket of curried chips, then went back to the counter and ordered a second helping. Some folks might comfort themselves with ice cream during times of stress, but Siobhán would take the curried chips any day. She'd make sure to go for a long run as soon as possible. She was just passing the hardware shop when she saw a sled propped up near the front door. She popped in and purchased it. The snow would melt soon, it never lingered long in Ireland, but Siobhán would be prepared for the next one. She would make snowmen, and throw snowballs, and wave at Ciáran as he careened down a hill.

No matter what was going on, *she* wasn't dating Macdara anymore. He was a free man. She was a free woman. The fact that anger coursed through her, along with the thought, was her problem, not his. She would put it out of her mind. There was a murder to solve. From now on, she was all about this case and nothing else. When it was over, she would confront all of them: Maria, Aisling, and Macdara. They had no right to keep this from her. But right now she had more important things to worry about. Chris Gordon's pronouncement had thrown her off, but she'd also learned some important clues. She had the name of a ship for one. The *Swan* sailing out of Cork Harbour. Peter Mallon was at the museum, lamenting about never really knowing someone, and may have stolen the gun. Or one of the volunteers may have placed the gun in a box of wooly socks and set it outside the door for someone else to pick up. She also had a second confirmed sighting of their mysterious, tall old lady.

Siobhán leaned the sled against the bistro as she stamped snow off her boots. She was desperate for a mug of tea and a biscuit, not to mention she needed to pitch in at the bistro, but just as she was preparing to enter, someone grabbed her arm and yanked her away from the door. She almost screamed when she turned around and saw Tracy Mallon, blond hair flying behind her, pouty lips flapping, and eyes flashing.

She was so pretty. Yet, there was something about her that equally repelled Siobhán. It was as if she was wearing a hard armor. "Sorry. Wanted to grab you before you went in."

"You managed," Siobhán said. She was grateful they hadn't tipped over.

"Can we go somewhere and talk?"

Siobhán pointed to the door. "There's a perfectly nice somewhere in here." It was freezing and she just wanted to put her feet up and have a nice cuppa tea. Just one.

"The others are there. I need to speak with you privately."

Siobhán nodded. "We could go to a pub, or the shops, or for a stroll, although it's mighty cold out here…" She shivered for good measure. Tracy either didn't pick up on it, or didn't care.

"A stroll would be great. I love the fresh air." *Brilliant. One of* those. Siobhán ached to go inside. "Let's go." They started to walk, with Siobhán in the lead. She headed in the direction of the abbey. If it was privacy Tracy wanted, that was the place to go. The ruined monastery looked absolutely gorgeous when the field was covered in snow.

Tracy appropriately gasped when she saw it. The ruined abbey stood majestically at the end of the white-blanketed field. The little creek running behind it was frozen over. Icicles hanging over the five-light window gleamed in the sun. "You have this in your backyard? You're so lucky! The only castle we have back home is a White Castle."

"A White Castle?" *What an odd color for a castle.* Siobhán had never heard of it.

Tracy laughed. "It's a hamburger joint."

"Oh." *Stranger yet.*

"Rat burgers, some call them."

Siobhán frowned. Thank goodness her job wasn't to understand Americans. That was one mystery she wasn't likely to solve. "This isn't a castle. It's a ruined abbey. The castle is back in the town square."

Tracy laughed and grabbed Siobhán's hands. "See? You're so lucky!"

They began to walk around the remains of the abbey. Calmness spread through Siobhán as it always did whenever she was near this magnificent structure. She often pictured the monks moving about, stirring the fire in the kitchen, brewing beer by the river, standing in the tower, gazing out over the green fields. Did they ever wonder what the future would look like?

Tracy pulled out her phone and began taking pictures. "I wonder if my father got to see this."

"I'm sure he did," Siobhán said gently. "He was at the Kilbane Museum, which is just on the other side of the field. He wouldn't have been able to miss it."

Tears came to Tracy's eyes. "What did you want to tell me?" Siobhán asked. It was better to keep her mind occupied. Siobhán could say the same thing for herself.

"Has Brandon been gambling again? I need to know."

"I'm only here to listen to information," Siobhán said. "Not supply it."

"He is. I know he is."

"You sound angry."

"Father would have been furious."

"And how would Brandon have reacted?" Siobhán kept her voice light. *Maybe he found out. Maybe he was furious.*

"I know what you're thinking, and you can forget it."

"Pardon?" Siobhán laid her Irish lilt on a little thicker. When around Americans, the Irish accent was a weaponiz-able trait. She wanted to sound pleasant and innocent.

"Brandon couldn't kill a fly. He's a slave to his own weaknesses. He couldn't look Father in the eye, let alone shoot him." She stuffed her hands in her pockets. "I've been investigating Jay Shepard and Hannah Stripes," she said, coming to a halt and wiping her eyes.

Siobhán almost plowed into her. "Investigating?"

"My father was too trusting. I hired a PI back in the States to do background checks."

"And?"

"He hasn't gotten back to me. Or answered any of my calls. Do you think something could have happened to him?"

Siobhán was having enough trouble finding out what was happening to folks here. She couldn't worry about an investigator back in the States. "What is it you think he'll find?"

"I don't know. But one of them has to be the killer."

"Hannah or Jay?"

"You can't think a member of his own family is guilty?!"

"It does happen."

"Not in this case. I didn't do it, of course, and Brandon didn't do it, and neither did Uncle Frank."

"You left out a family member."

Tracy's face clouded over. "If you're talking about that woman... she is not family."

"So you think Greta is capable of murder?"

Tracy began to pace. "Perhaps. However, what's her motive? Brandon and I are the ones who inherit."

Greta was right. As soon as Tracy and Brandon found out Peter had changed his will, they were going to accuse her of murder. Maybe they already knew and were setting the groundwork to accuse Greta. Could all this have been planned? Kill their father and frame his third wife? Do it somewhere far away. Away from their customers and the American police? "Money is often a strong motive," Siobhán said. "But not the only one."

"I hate to think Frank would do something like this."

"Did your father and Greta seem happy?"

Tracy shrugged. "I guess."

"No fights?"

"Not that I ever heard. But if she was milking him for his money, she wouldn't want to cause trouble, now would she?"

But she must have, if Peter was referring to her with his comments about never really knowing someone. Perhaps they kept their difficulties private as well. With children like Tracy and Brandon, Siobhán couldn't blame him.

"Are you quite sure the documentary was your father's idea?"

Tracy frowned. "I think so. But 'quite sure'? No." Tracy's eyes widened. "Do you think this was a setup from the very beginning? That someone used the documentary to lure us to Ireland? That the killer intended to murder my father?"

"I don't know," Siobhán said. "Please let's not get too ahead of ourselves. Besides, what could your family history have to do with any of this?" It did, however. In her bones Siobhán knew it did. But she was missing something. It seemed like the perfect story. An Irishman makes good in America. Becomes rich. Gives to the poor. Who would take issue with that? It was generations ago. Surely, she was reaching by trying to find any kind of connection.

But he was killed in a cemetery in front of his great-grandfather's headstone. She couldn't just ignore that.

"What can you tell me about Ann Mallon?"

Tracy frowned. "Who?"

"Your great great-grandmother."

Tracy shook her head. "I can't tell you anything. I didn't get into that genealogy stuff. You'll have to ask Greta."

"Got it." Tracy was trying to remain in control of the conversation, regulating her answers, to make it sound as if she didn't care. But Siobhán wasn't quite buying it.

Tracy grabbed Siobhán's arm. She had a strong grip. "Do you think the killer will come after Brandon or me next?"

Siobhán not-so-gently extricated herself. "Why would you say that?"

"I don't know. I don't know anything anymore."

"As soon as you hear back from the investigator, you must let me know if he found anything on Hannah or Jay. Anything at all."

"But he's not answering my calls."

"Why don't you give me his information, I'll see if our detective sergeant can make any headway."

Tracy removed a Biro and paper from her purse and scribbled down the number. Siobhán tucked it in her pocket. Tracy shoved her hands in her pockets. "You need to catch the killer soon. We all need to get back home."

How long could they legally hold them here? Siobhán had no idea. Probably not long. "When your father left the Titanic Experience, are you sure everyone else in your group remained?"

"Immediately after? Yes. But once Father left, there was only a few minutes of the tour remaining. As soon as it was over, we went our separate ways."

"Where did you go?"

Tracy's eyes flicked over Siobhán. "Are you asking for my alibi?"

"Of course."

Tracy closed her eyes. When she opened them, she offered a sad smile. "I went shopping. Then I went barhopping. I never do that. I was barely aware of what time it was, or who was around, when I came back to the flat. I'm afraid I passed out."

They began to walk back to the bistro. If Siobhán was going to confront Tracy, it was now or never. "I heard your father was somewhat upset with you." Siobhán hated rubbing salt in the wound. She could imagine nothing more painful than having unresolved issues with someone who had passed. The time to say "sorry" was always now.

"'Upset' with me?"

149

"Were you speaking with his doctors and lawyers behind his back? Trying to have him declared mentally unfit to handle his finances?"

Tears came into Tracy's eyes and she angrily brushed them away. "I suppose Greta told you."

"So it's true?"

"You don't understand. He wasn't himself. He was forgetful. Angry. And obsessed. I was simply trying to protect him."

"But he didn't see it that way."

"Of course he didn't see it that way. None of us want to admit we're weak. I was really, really worried about him."

Siobhán kept her voice light again. "Have you ever held a firearm?"

Tracy let out a wry laugh. "Never." She shuddered. "And now I absolutely never will."

–

"You wanted to see me?" Siobhán stood just outside Macdara's office. She looked anywhere but at him, fighting with everything she had not to hurl accusations at him, beg him to tell her that everything Chris Gordon said was a lie.

"Yes, yes." Macdara grabbed a stack of receipts off his desk and approached. "The betting slips you got from Brandon?"

"Yes?"

He fanned through the stack in his hands. "They're not recent. Most of them, anyway."

Darn it. Now she had to make eye contact. "What do you mean?"

"The dates are from months ago. He must have dug them out of the rubbish bins."

That sneaky addict. "Show me." He handed her the slips. It took her forever to find the dates. The typeface was so tiny, she practically needed a magnifying glass. Still, she should have paid more attention; she should have looked for the dates. "I'm such a fool."

"We all make mistakes. You won't make it again."

"But why dig betting slips out of the rubbish? Just to lie about his alibi?"

"A lie with props," Macdara said. "He must have counted on you not scrutinizing them."

She bit her lip, hating that he had been right. She wished she weren't so new at this. A rookie mistake. Still, she found it odd. Brandon wasn't exactly proud to be gambling. Even giving her that alibi could cost him his inheritance. Logic dictated that if he was going to lie about anything, it would be about the gambling. And if he wasn't gambling, what was he doing the night of the murder? Following his father around Kilbane? "I'll have another word with him."

"Before you do that." Macdara pulled a betting slip out of his pocket and handed it to her. It was a slip from the Cork Racecourse Mallow, under an hour's drive from Kilbane.

"I don't understand."

"This is the one exception. Look at the date."

Siobhán studied the slip. "The day after the murder," she said. She got the chills. If this slip belonged to Brandon… Who in the world would go to the racetracks the day after it was discovered that their father had been murdered? "Couldn't it just have been a slip someone threw in the trash and our man picked it up with the rest?"

Macdara nodded. "Could be."

But it might not be. "Looks like I'm taking a trip to the races?"

Macdara shook his head. "*We're* taking a trip to the races."

Siobhán tried to ignore the flash of heat that flared inside her at the thought of spending time alone with him. "You think we might find something at the races?"

"That," Macdara said as a slow smile spread across his face, "and I have a hot tip on number fourteen."

Chapter 15

The Cork Racecourse was hopping. On the banks of the River Blackwater in Mallow County Cork, it was known to have the best horse racing in Ireland. A mix of flat racing and jumps, but in the winter it was all jumps. The dirt track was surrounded by a simple fence that allowed viewers to stand "up close and personal" to the horses thundering by. The sun was peeking out from puffy gray clouds, and the crowd was immense and noisy. Large stands surrounded the perimeter, selling food and beverage. There were a total of five public bars at the races, just in case folks got a little thirsty. There was a carvery restaurant, a hot-roast-beef and snack stand, and a fast-food restaurant. Siobhán's mouth watered as soon as the smell of burgers hit her. She couldn't remember the last time she'd eaten. Garda work was the best diet she'd ever tried.

Slightly farther away, bookmakers were lined up with their leather bags stuffed with money resting at their feet. The snow had been thoroughly dealt with, the bits that hadn't melted had been meticulously plowed and the fields were clean. It took a lot more than a little snow to stop an Irishman's love of the ponies. In between races Irish music blared from speakers. Macdara's race was about to begin, so Siobhán and Macdara propped themselves near the fence to watch.

Siobhán had always loved coming to the races, and she felt a familiar thrill swirling inside her. She had to remind herself she was on duty. Number fourteen jumped his little heart out, but he didn't win. Macdara took it with a grin and a shrug. It was time to show Brandon's picture to a few bookmakers and see what they could learn.

They approached the first man they saw, a short barrel of a man with a green cap and a big grin. His smile faded as he took in their garda uniforms and his toe began to tap. "Coming to place a bet, are ye?" His glum tone conveyed he knew otherwise. His eyes shifted, never landing directly on them. This was something they didn't teach you in garda college: how unpopular it would be to wear the uniform.

Macdara turned his mobile to the man to show him a photo of Brandon he'd secretly taken. "Two days ago, did you happen to see this American around here?"

The man frowned, first browned off they weren't going to place a bet, but then he squinted. He removed a pair of eyeglasses from his jacket, put them on, and examined the screen closer. "A Yank, you say?"

"Yes."

"Does this have anything to do with the murder probe in Kilbane?" He looked at them with expectant eyes.

Siobhán groaned. She hated knowing their little village was the center of gossip. "Just answer the question." Macdara obviously didn't like it either. Kilbane was home to him too.

Or is it Dublin now? And Aisling?

The bookmaker shook his head. "Never saw him."

Macdara showed him the photograph again, this time much closer. "You're sure?"

He took his glasses off and looked away. "Didn't come to me."

There were at least twenty bookmakers. This was going to take a while. They thanked him and headed for the next one in the row, a tall, slim man with the same "*c'mere to me*" smile.

Here were a few of the answers they received when they asked each one if they had seen Brandon at the races:

"No."

"No."

"No."

"Could have done. But I can't be sure."

"He's a short man. Looks like everyone else around here. But I don't remember hearing an American accent. They're so loud, you usually can't miss 'em."

"A Yank? We had a few of them in, alright. But they didn't come to me, they went to him." He nodded at a bookmaker across from them, one of the very last ones they needed to speak with.

They approached him. He was younger than most of the middle-aged bookmakers; this was a good-looking lad in his twenties. His leather bag was thinner than the others, and he had it strapped across his body. Macdara showed him the photograph.

His eyes lit up with recognition. "Ah, yes," he said. "Great lad. Very generous."

Macdara and Siobhán shared an excited glance. This could be the breakthrough they needed. "Left you a good tip, did he?" Macdara asked.

"I'd say he did."

Siobhán frowned. "Brandon doesn't strike me as a big tipper. He said he lost money on the races here."

"Aye," the lad said. "He did. He won a few bob at first and tipped generously. Then he got cocky. After two wins most of his picks came in dead last." He laughed and shook his head. "Still tipped me, though."

"Who would tip on a horse that came in dead last?" Siobhán wondered out loud.

"An American?" the bookmaker said cheerfully. He winked. "He thought I'd bring him a bit of luck. I could have sold him a leprechaun. You know yourself."

"Is there anything else you can tell us?" Macdara asked.

The bookmaker said no. Macdara turned to leave. The lad's eyes slid down to his satchel. Siobhán looked at it too.

"I think we're done here," Macdara said, lightly touching her arm. "Let's go confront Brandon."

"I don't think we're quite done, are we?" Siobhán said to the bookmaker. Macdara turned around, his eyebrow arched with curiosity. She eyed the leather bag hanging across his body. "He tipped you with that satchel, didn't he?"

The answer came in the form of bright red splotches that broke out on the lad's cheeks.

"Good catch," Macdara said, admiration in his voice.

"I didn't s-steal it," the bookmaker stuttered as he clung onto it, clearly nervous.

"You didn't tell us about it either, did ye?" Macdara said.

Siobhán had to admit, if only to herself, that there was something quite attractive about Detective Sergeant Macdara Flannery pulling rank. *Aisling probably thinks so too.* "The American man gave it to you?" Macdara asked.

"It was a gift, alright."

"Let's see it," Macdara said.

The lad took it off lightning quick. "Can I remove my things?"

Macdara glared at him. "Was it empty when he gave it to you?"

The lad's head bobbed up and down so fast, Siobhán was afraid it was going to fly off. "He emptied it out himself, sir."

"Where?"

The lad's eyes slid to the left. "It won't do you much good."

"Why do you say that?" Siobhán said, trying to make her voice stern too. It elicited another eyebrow raise from Macdara.

"I saw a few of the papers," the lad said, leaning in and whispering. "Looked like half of them were burned."

"'Burned'?" Macdara said.

"The matches in the cemetery," Siobhán said. The lad's eyes widened and Siobhán clamped her mouth shut before Macdara could give her a kick to the shins.

"Where did he throw out these papers?" Macdara asked.

This time the cheeky lad smiled. "The Dumpsters," he said with a jerk of his head. "Around back of the stands."

"'D-dumpsters,'" Siobhán stammered. "More than one?"

He gave a friendly jerk of his head. "It's a big place." He leaned in, and nodded to the buildings. "Lucky for you I saw which one he used. Last one. The only one you can see from here."

Macdara and Siobhán turned. Sure enough in the distance they could see the Dumpster he was on about.

"Have they been emptied since he was here?" Macdara asked.

157

The lad shrugged. "I'd say the snow delayed the pickup, alright. So you could be in luck!"

"Hear that," Macdara said, turning to Siobhán with a wink. "We 'could be in luck.'"

"Too bad he can't sell us a leprechaun," Siobhán quipped. The lad had the decency to blush. A Dumpster full of rubbish. Luck of the Irish indeed.

—

A mountain of rubbish was more like it. Kilimanjaro. Crisp wrappers, red sauce, half-eaten cheeseburgers, wet newspapers, mineral cans, cigarette butts. Macdara groaned and threw a look to Siobhán, who was standing as far away as she could get. "Didn't plan for this in college, did ye?"

"No. But there's plenty of it in the bistro life." She left out the fact that she usually let the lads handle the rubbish.

Macdara stared at it as if he hated his life. "Might as well dig in." He kept perfectly still.

"We should," Siobhán said. "Anything Brandon threw away is going to be at the bottom, you know." She didn't move. She glanced at her hands. "We'll need gloves." She stared at the enormous container. "And a ladder."

"No need," Macdara said. "I'd be happy to give you a boost up."

"Ah, sure. Then I can pull you in after me."

Macdara laughed. "Ladder it is." He looked in the direction of the beer stand. "And plenty of Guinness."

"We're on duty."

"I don't care."

An hour and a half later, buzzing from a few pints and up to their elbows in trash, Siobhán pulled out a charred piece of paper from the mound of horrors. "This might be something."

"What is it?" Macdara slid close to her and looked over her shoulder. She could smell his cologne, a welcome relief from the smells wafting out of the Dumpster. The desire to turn around and put her arms around him was at an alarmingly high level. Making out with your detective sergeant would most assuredly be frowned upon. She concentrated on the piece of paper, at least what was left of it. The handwriting was the same as the letter the pathologist had found. "This is it. It must be penned by the same person. The 'Dear Ann' letter."

"Guess it's better than a 'Dear John' letter."

"Funny man."

"Sorry. What does it say?"

The handwriting was loopy, and with it halfway burned and smeared with unknown Dumpster substances, it was hard to read. She could make out *Cork*, *America*, and *on the boat*. "It will take some time to decipher. And we're missing half."

Macdara nodded, then looked at the paper. "Why only burn half?"

"Maybe he or she was interrupted?"

"Or maybe they just burned the incriminating parts." Macdara sounded as if he was onto something.

Siobhán shook her head. "I don't agree."

"Why not?"

"One in the morning in a cemetery? Why wouldn't he or she just burn the whole thing?"

"Good point."

Siobhán began to pace. "I think we can safely assume the burning took place before Peter was killed."

"I'll give you that," Macdara said. "Hard to imagine someone sticking around to burn papers after shooting a man in the heart."

"Exactly. The killer had to know that someone might have heard the gunshot. He or she would run."

"Someone trying to provoke him?"

"Someone who didn't want Peter to have these papers?"

"But why?"

Macdara sighed. "If we knew the answer to that, we'd be further along. I'd say Brandon Mallon may be the man to answer our questions."

Siobhán tried to imagine the scene. "Let's go with it. Let's say Brandon met his father in the cemetery."

"Okay," Macdara said. "Why?"

"What if Peter found out Brandon was gambling again? Remember, one more infraction and he would be cut out of his father's will."

"Go on."

"Maybe Brandon discovered the headstone first. Remember some witnesses saw a younger man in town."

"Who said he was here to 'right a great wrong.' What would Brandon have been referring to?"

"His years of disappointing his father by gambling?"

Macdara shrugged. "Keep going."

"Brandon decides to make up for it. What better way to impress Peter Mallon than to show a love for genealogy? Brandon may have purchased the letters or found the letters. But at the cemetery things don't go as planned. Peter doesn't agree to reinstate Brandon into the will. In a fury Brandon starts to burn the letters. Peter could have lunged to stop him. The gun falls out—"

"Who brought the gun and why?"

"Peter definitely could have taken the gun. But not to kill Brandon."

"Then why?"

"I don't have all the answers." She stared at horses in the distance. "Tracy insists her father was failing mentally. It could account for some of his odd behavior. Perhaps he stole the gun because he was becoming increasingly paranoid." She thought of the mysterious old lady, and brought the subject up with Macdara. "Father Kearney said this old woman appeared as 'mad as a bag of cats.'"

"And?"

"And she'd been seen pacing in the cemetery, in the back row where the Mallon headstone was located."

"I'm waiting for your conclusion."

"Peter could have had his own run-ins with her. He could have stolen the gun because he was afraid of her."

Macdara held up his hands. "Speaking as a man, I think you might want to hold off before you go accusing our victim of being afraid of an elderly woman."

"That's sexist."

Macdara gave a nod of his head. "Might be. Advice still stands."

"Chris Gordon admitted that Peter was in the museum asking about the antique revolvers close to when the revolver went missing. A donation blocked his view of the gun case. Peter Mallon would have easily been able to steal the gun. Chris Gordon also confirmed the sighting of our tall old lady. *She* could have taken the gun. Startled Peter."

"One theory at a time. Let's stick with Brandon."

"Right, right." Siobhán began to pace, allowing the fresh air to heal the memories of the Dumpster. "In the cemetery Brandon could have freaked out when he saw the gun. The two of them could have reached for it at the same time. Brandon gets the gun. Either he panics and shoots, or he's so enraged about the will that he kills him."

"Then he has to find a way to get rid of the satchels and the letters. It's a solid theory. Good work."

"It's not completely solid," Siobhán said.

"Correct. There's the gun. What happened to it? What else?"

"Why would Brandon give us the receipt from the races? Why not get rid of that one?"

"It's possible he didn't realize it was mixed in. Or he didn't count on us figuring it out."

Siobhán bit her lip. It was true. Killers made mistakes all the time. Especially when they were under pressure. "Now what?"

"We see if we can find anything else and then get the heck out of here."

Siobhán had been pacing again, when she saw something balled up behind the Dumpster. A swirl of black material with a dark red patch caught her eye. She knelt, and even though she was wearing gloves, she only used two fingers to pull it out. It was a black coat. Covered in blood. "Something like this?"

Macdara stared. "Yes," he said. "Something just like that."

"A black coat," Siobhán said. "Just like the one Brandon was wearing in the photograph at the Titanic exhibition."

"That's right," Macdara said. "I'd forgotten all about that."

With her gloved hand Siobhán held up the bloodied coat. "Guess he didn't leave it in the jax after all."

Chapter 16

Brandon Mallon was back in Paddy Power, twitching under a television alive with cartoon dogs racing. Siobhán wanted to turn it off and drag every lad out of the place by the ear. Instead she gently tapped Brandon on the shoulder. He nearly jumped out of his trousers. When he whirled around, his eyes were bloodshot and glassy. Deep into his addiction, he seemed to take several moments before even registering who they were. When his eyes finally lit with recognition, Siobhán hoisted up Peter Mallon's leather satchel. "Look what we found."

He stared at it as if it were a severed head; then he licked his chapped lips and ran his fingers through his hair. Siobhán wondered when he'd bathed last. They had better solve this mystery before every member of this group had a complete breakdown.

"Hey," he said, his voice cracking, "where did you find it?"

"At the Cork Racecourse," Macdara said. "Fancy that."

"Oh," Brandon said. "I see."

So far he wasn't lying to them, but he wasn't being forthright either. "Why don't we go somewhere and have a little chat," Siobhán said.

"How about I meet you in a little bit?" Brandon said. "I have a race coming up."

163

Macdara glanced at the television in disgust. "Fake Fido will have to wait." He took Brandon by the elbow. "Let's take a stroll to the station."

–

At the station Brandon perched on a wobbly chair and stared at the exit as if biding his time before he could bolt. Beads of sweat dotted his forehead. He was terrified of authority, or maybe after spending all day in the betting shop, he wasn't acclimated to natural light. His knee was bouncing, and his eyes were constantly flicking around. Siobhán wanted to sit on his bouncing knee, kick it, do anything to stop it. She hated watching other people fidget.

"We know you burned the contents of the satchel, then dumped it on a bookie," Siobhán said. "I'm sure you're on CCTV at the races. We can check it." She felt a kick to her shin and stopped short of crying out. Macdara glared at her. She kicked him back and returned the glare. Brandon put his head down. "We spent hours digging through a nasty Dumpster," Siobhán said. "I'm scarred for life. You'd better start talking." She didn't care if Macdara kicked her again; she couldn't get out of her head the horrific image of wet newspapers smeared with red sauce and unidentified slime. It may have killed her appetite forever. Brandon's shoulders started to shake. When he looked up, tears were streaming down his face.

"My father was already dead," Brandon said. "There was nothing I could do."

Macdara and Siobhán exchanged a look.

Siobhán leaned forward. "You were in the cemetery that night?"

Brandon sighed. Macdara reached down and brought up the bloody jacket. They were going to send it for testing, but had decided to present it to Brandon and see his reaction.

Brandon's tears ran down his cheeks, and he buried his face in his hands. "I swear, he was already dead. I checked for a pulse. He was so cold. There was nothing I could do. *Nothing.*"

"You could have called the police," Siobhán said. She felt a flush of shame, knowing the same applied to her.

"Instead you stole his satchel and ran?" Macdara said.

"I wanted to see if his will was in there," Brandon said. "He'd been threatening to cut me out."

"Was it?" Macdara asked. They hadn't found a will in the Dumpster.

"No," Brandon said. "It was more of his genealogy research."

"Which you burned," Siobhán said.

"No," Brandon said. "When I arrived, there were papers all over the ground. Partially burned. I stuffed them back into the satchel. Then I just dumped them out when I realized there was nothing important."

"'Nothing important'?" Siobhán said. "If you weren't the killer, then obviously either your father or his murderer started to burn those papers."

"It must have been my father," Brandon said.

Macdara leaned forward. "Why do you say that?"

"If it was the killer, why didn't he take the satchel with him?" Brandon asked.

"Maybe he did," Siobhán said.

Brandon blinked. "I don't understand."

"She's suggesting *you're* the killer," Macdara said.

"He was already dead!" Brandon's voice rose to a wail, and all heads in the station turned toward him.

"At the least you've destroyed evidence, lied to the police, and hindered an active investigation," Macdara said. "We could charge you right now."

"You're going to need a good attorney," Siobhán added.

"Please," Brandon said. "Do you know the exact time of the murder?"

"Why?" Macdara said.

"Because I was in a pub until ten past one in the morning," Brandon said. "Talk to the bartender. It's that funeral pub."

"Butler's?" Siobhán asked.

"Yes. Butler's Undertaker, Lounge, and Pub. I was there until ten past one. Ask him."

"We can't trust you now," Siobhán said.

Brandon wiped his tears and crossed his arms. The grief was gone, and Siobhán watched as Brandon entered the anger phase. "If he hadn't been so obsessed with the past, he'd be alive right now. Who cares about letters from hundreds of years ago? I hated my father's obsession with his research. Greta's even worse. The past! That's all they care about. The past. And he judged me for my addiction? He was way more of an addict than I was, and unlike mine, his addiction got him killed. I wish we'd never come here!" He pounded his fist on the desk.

"How did you know your father was at the cemetery?" Siobhán asked.

"I followed in his footsteps," Brandon said. "In a way."

"Start from the beginning," Macdara said. "And if we think you're leaving anything out, then these are going to get used." Macdara opened his drawer and pulled out handcuffs. Siobhán resisted the urge to pat him on the back. Props were fun and effective. Brandon's eyes widened with fear.

"The beginning," Macdara said again. "Every single step."

—

Brandon took a moment before he began his account. "I was sitting in a pub in Cork when I saw my father pass by the window. I almost missed him. He was speed-walking, nearly running. I hadn't seen him since he'd abruptly left the museum." He looked up as if he'd just realized something.

"Go on," Macdara said.

"I just thought of something he said to me at the museum. 'Secrets always come out.'"

"'Secrets always come out,'" Siobhán repeated. *Very cryptic.* "Did you ask him what he was referring to?"

Brandon hung his head. "I didn't have to. It was his way of telling me he knew I was gambling again."

Siobhán wasn't convinced that's what Peter meant. Perhaps he was referring to his discovery of his great-grandfather's tombstone. But, of course, Brandon, having a guilty conscience, would have taken it that personal way.

"Let's get back to the story," Macdara said. "You saw him pass by the window. Then what?"

"I ran out after him. Followed him down the street. I was shocked to see him getting into a cab. It was half past eleven. Where was he going?"

"So you got into a cab and followed him?"

"No," Brandon said. "I got into *his* cab."

"What?" This revelation floored Siobhán.

"I practically threw myself in front of it. I don't know why. Maybe I sensed something horrible was going to happen. Just a feeling. I don't know. I'd never thrown myself in front of a moving vehicle before."

Siobhán clenched her fist. So somewhere in Cork was a taxi driver sitting on this information. She wished she could find him and charge him with obstructing an investigation.

"Go on," Macdara said.

"I got in the cab. Started blabbering like a drunken idiot. Apologizing. Asking him where he was going. He tried to tell me everything was fine, tried everything to get me out of his cab. He kept looking at his watch. He finally told the driver to go. I kept blabbering. He stopped me. Told me he knew that I was gambling, but he wasn't going to cut me out of the will. Said he was going to get me help instead. I was flabbergasted. I mean. That was not like my father."

"He was meeting someone," Siobhán said. She allowed herself for a moment to pretend that everything Brandon was saying was the truth. First, to encourage him to keep talking; and second, to see if the sequence of events made sense with the facts they already had.

"He said there were going to be some changes in our family. That we were all going to start being honest, no matter what."

"Did you ask him what he meant?"

Brandon shook his head. "I didn't have to. He was talking about me. About my weaknesses. I was so grateful he wasn't going to take me out of the will. But then I realized we were leaving Cork. I asked him where we were going." Siobhán and Macdara were on the edge of their seats. She nodded for him to continue. "He said he

168

had a contact in a neighboring village. He was meeting someone who had pertinent information about our family history. That's a direct quote. 'Pertinent information.'"

Once again, assuming Brandon was telling the truth, that *someone* was Peter Mallon's killer.

"Did you ask for more information?" Macdara said.

"About this 'pertinent information,'" Siobhán added. Macdara frowned.

Brandon waved the question away. "I told you, I didn't care about that stuff. I did ask him why we were meeting him so late."

"What did he say?" Siobhán asked. Her Biro was poised over her notepad.

Brandon shook his head. "'There's no "we".'"

Macdara frowned and Siobhán stopped taking notes. "Pardon?"

"He looked at me and said, 'There's no "we".'" He told me he would drop me off at a pub and fetch me after his meeting." Brandon shook his head. "'Fetch' me. Like I was a dog." He sniffed. "I'm sure he didn't mean it that way. But I hate that those were the last words my father ever spoke to me."

"Did you try to argue?"

"No," Brandon said. "It was late and cold, and I was losing my buzz. I didn't care about his meeting. I just wanted a pint." Shame filled his voice. Siobhán found herself feeling sorry for him. She took a deep breath and pulled back. He could be a liar. And a murderer.

"So you went to Butler's," Siobhán said.

Brandon hung his head. "Yes. Ask the bartender."

"We will," Macdara said.

Yet another witness who hadn't come forward. John Butler certainly had some explaining to do. If Brandon was lying, they would know straightaway. If he was telling the truth, she was going to see if they could fine or even arrest Butler for not calling the guards. Having an American in one's pub was not a crime, but Butler surely had realized that one of the Americans was in his pub on the night another was murdered.

Macdara pressed on. "What time did you arrive at the pub?"

Brandon sighed. "I only know it was after midnight." He looked up as if listening to something in the distance. "I heard the church bells toll."

Saint Mary's bells did emit a beautiful sound, but Siobhán kept that to herself.

"So how did you end up at the cemetery?" Macdara asked.

"The bartender tried to throw me out at half past twelve. I couldn't believe a pub in Ireland wouldn't stay open longer. I had a full pint in front of me. I managed to delay until ten past one."

"How did you happen to remember the exact time?" Macdara asked.

"Because the bartender yelled, 'It's ten past one! Get out of me pub!' So I did. I was surprised to see it was snowing. I could clearly see my father's footprints in the snow. I followed them to the cemetery."

Siobhán shivered at the thought of Brandon literally following in his father's last footsteps.

"You know the rest," Brandon said, the tears starting again.

"But you only saw your father. No one else? No one fleeing the cemetery, no one at the cemetery, no one on the streets?"

"It was a ghost town," Brandon said. "Beautiful and eerie."

"Did you hear a shot?"

"No," Brandon said. "I swear. I saw no one. I heard nothing." *Is he telling the truth?* "There's only one thing I can tell you. And it doesn't make sense. It's probably nothing."

Those are the best clues. "Go on," Siobhán said.

Brandon sighed, reached into his pocket, and laid two identical pins out on the desk. The American flag. Brandon pushed one forward. "My father wasn't wearing that American flag pin when he left for the cemetery."

Siobhán was on full alert. "How do you know that for sure?"

"Because right before he left the pub, he took it off and gave it to me." Brandon nudged the other pin forward. "One of these is mine." He pointed to the second pin. "The other belongs to my father."

Siobhán and Macdara locked eyes. Somehow this was a very important clue. "Why did he take it off?" Siobhán asked.

"He hadn't been wearing it for a while. He took it out of his breast pocket. Said he was done worshipping the past. Said from now on, he was more about truth than pride."

Macdara shook his head. "You didn't think that was strange? Ask him what he meant?"

"Father had been acting strange ever since this documentary business started. I'm afraid I agreed with Tracy. Our father's mental state was deteriorating. Tracy was right to look after him." He shrugged. "My pint arrived. Father said he'd be right back. Wait." Brandon sat up. His

171

eyes filled with tears. "*Those* are the last words he ever said to me. 'I'll be right back.'"

He looked up at them with grief-stricken eyes. "I'm sorry I lied. It was wrong. But I was afraid. I'm still afraid. Who would want my father dead? Who was he meeting? What if they saw me?"

Macdara leaned back, crossed his arms, and stared at Brandon. "Not a word of this to anyone."

Brandon's head jerked up. "You're letting me go?"

"For now." He pointed at Brandon. "I'm going to assign a guard to follow you until we verify your alibi." Brandon swallowed hard, then nodded. Macdara left the room and returned a few minutes later with a guard by his side. He gave Brandon a warning. "You keep your mouth shut. And I'm not promising there won't be charges filed. And from now on, if we ask you a question, you spill absolutely everything you can think of about the subject."

Brandon continued to nod furiously, reminding Siobhán of a Bobblehead doll. "Go back to your room and get some sleep." Brandon was out of the chair in a flash, racing for the door. The assigned guard had to run to keep up with him. "And see to it that he takes a shower," Macdara called after them.

Chapter 17

Butler's Undertaker, Lounge, and Pub was impossible to miss. Largely due to the huge sign above it that featured an older gentleman lifting a pint. This was the only funeral home in town, so jokes abounded, mainly of the drink-and-die variety. Some said it ought to be named The Last Pint. Today Butler's had a sandwich sign posted outside: CUSTOMERS WANTED. DEAD OR ALIVE! NO EXPERIENCE NECESSARY. APPLY WITHIN.

Siobhán rolled her eyes; Macdara shook his head and laughed. They entered the pub and found John Butler alone behind the bar, wiping down the counter.

"I don't suppose you're here for pints or a viewing," he said in a pinched voice. He was a thin man with slicked-back hair. He dressed theatrically, and today was no exception. He was wearing a white shirt with ruffled sleeves and a red jacket, which resembled a topcoat. His cane was perched behind the bar, as if sitting out this dance and waiting for the next one.

"Do you have any idea why we're here?" Macdara said, the anger in his voice obvious.

John sighed. "Yes, he was here. The young American and his da. The night of the murder."

Macdara slammed his hand on the bar. "Why on earth didn't you say anything?"

John Butler flushed. "Do you have any idea what you're doing to this town?" The question was pointed at Siobhán. Macdara straightened up and took a step forward. Siobhán placed her hand on his chest and shook her head. She could fight her own battles.

"Me?"

"Murder follows you around," he said, pointing a bony finger at her. "You're making this town into some kind of spectacle."

Siobhán thought it was an extremely hypocritical comment coming from the one man in town who profited off death, but she kept the thought to herself. Instead she turned it back on him. "We could wrap this case up a lot faster if the residents of this town did the honest thing and came forward with pertinent information."

"At half twelve I told him he had to go. He didn't stumble out until ten past one, shortly after it began to snow."

Father Kearney heard the shot at one in the morning. Was it possible the priest's clock was a little slow? She glanced at the clock behind the bar. The time matched the one on her mobile. If he was correct in his account, and Father Kearney's clock was correct, then Brandon couldn't be the killer.

"How did he seem while he was here?" Macdara said. "Did you chat about anything?"

"I don't like Americans," John said. "He seemed eager to talk about horse racing. I nodded my head a few times, but that was it."

"Was anyone else in here?" Siobhán asked.

"His father—the dead man—dropped him off. As you know, he didn't come back." For a second he looked abashed. "Well, he's back now. But you know what I mean." Unfortunately, they did know what he meant. Peter Mallon's body was in the basement, awaiting shipment back home.

"How did Peter seem?" Macdara asked.

"Irritated. Like me."

"Did he say anything?" Siobhán prodded.

"Not to me. He might have had a word or two with his son, but I wasn't listening."

Siobhán sighed. "Did you happen to see him hand his son a pin of the American flag?"

John Butler nodded. "As a matter of fact I saw the younger one place two of them on the bar. Self-centered, the Americans. I wouldn't be wearing that if I was them."

"Is there anything else you can tell us?" Macdara said. He looked eager to get out of the dim, depressing pub. Siobhán felt exactly the same.

"If you ask me, the man shot himself. He had that look. I've seen it before."

"We're not asking you to make wild guesses," Siobhán said. "Did you see a gun? Did you hear him say he was going to kill himself?"

John Butler shook his head. "I didn't see or hear a t'ing."

–

Siobhán set the timer on her mobile as she and Macdara walked from the pub to the cemetery. They kept a moderate pace. It had been dark and snowing, and Brandon Mallon had never set foot in Kilbane. By the time they arrived at John Mallon's grave, fifteen minutes had passed.

"If he left at ten past one, and it took him fifteen minutes, then he was here at one twenty-five."

"And you arrived?"

"One forty-five."

Macdara glanced up at Father Kearney's window. "And the shot was heard at one."

"We should make sure Father Kearney's clocks are working," Siobhán said.

"And if they are," Macdara mused, "then Brandon isn't our killer."

"Are you going to charge him with interfering?"

Macdara sighed. "I'm not taking it off the table. But what I really want is to ship them all out the first chance I get."

So they were getting on his nerves too. She hated how happy this made her.

"Come on," he said. "Let's have a look at Father's timepiece."

–

Several hours later, after confirming that Father Kearney's clock was indeed telling the correct time, Siobhán and Macdara found themselves in the churchyard again, this time with all of their suspects. Everyone stood in a semi-circle around John Mallon's headstone. So far none of them had said anything, but eyes were wide and mouths open as they took in John Mallon's grave. Brandon seemed as shocked as everyone else, which meant he hadn't noticed the headstone that evening. Macdara had decided not to tell the rest of the group about Brandon's recent confession. The less they knew, the better. Eventually everyone would find out, and Brandon would have to face up to his lies.

"So you can see what brought Peter to the cemetery," Macdara said at last.

More openmouthed stares.

"He must have been excited to see his great-grandfather's burial place," Siobhán said. The family exchanged looks.

"Oh, you have no idea," Jay said, zooming in on the headstone with his camera. "This is explosive, alright."

"This can't be," Frank said, clearly agitated. "What is going on?" He glared at Jay. "Is this one of your cinematic tricks?"

"I don't practice cinematic tricks," Jay shot back.

"I don't understand," Siobhán said. She expected them to be surprised, but their reactions were very strange indeed.

Brandon pulled out his mobile and swiped through screens. A few minutes later he turned the phone to Macdara and Siobhán. Macdara had to move in close behind Siobhán to look at the photos, and she had to concentrate even harder on what Brandon was trying to show them. It was a picture of a headstone:

John Mallon
1833-1913
A Loving Husband

Siobhán looked up quizzically.

"That's my great-grandfather's burial place," Frank said. "In Dublin, Ohio. John Mallon never returned to Ireland."

Macdara took his cap off and ran his hands through his hair. "You're saying there are two John Mallons?"

Siobhán pointed to the photo on Brandon's phone. "This John Mallon was born five years later, and lived ten years longer."

"And there's no mysterious letters at the base to puzzle out. Just 'A Loving Husband,'" Macdara pointed out.

Frank glanced at the headstone in front of him. "Very strange indeed."

"Isn't John Mallon a common enough name?" Tracy asked.

"I don't like it," Siobhán said.

"Maybe his family here never heard from him again," Hannah ventured. She gestured to the plot. "Maybe it's an empty grave."

"And they just guessed at the date of death?" Siobhán said, hoping her sarcasm was showing. She knew an Irish priest would never allow for an empty grave.

Jay peered in closer. "'Out to the field,'" he read off the tombstone. "Maybe that means America."

"We thought it meant heaven," Siobhán said.

Jay zoomed in with his camera.

"Or maybe the grave in Ohio is empty," Hannah continued.

"What's this mean?" Brandon knelt down to see the bottom of the tombstone where $E_{\_}\_u\,A\_\_\_\_$ was visible.

"I believe the last word is Ann," Siobhán said.

"His wife," Tracy said. "My God."

"What about the rest?" Brandon asked.

"Haven't figured that out," Siobhán said. "All we know is that Peter was found with his arm outstretched and his finger was pointing at this headstone."

"Only the vowels survived," Brandon mused.

"Could it be... Europe, United States of America?" Hannah asked.

Everyone stared at her.

Siobhán tried not to laugh. "I don't think all that would have fit on the tombstone."

"So they abbreviated it," Hannah sulked. She didn't like being wrong.

Greta began to pace. "The murder has something to do with the past. Something in the Mallon family tree."

"That's ridiculous," Tracy said.

"We're wasting our time," Brandon said. "Father may not have even been pointing at the grave."

"If this were any other headstone, I'd be inclined to agree," Siobhán said. "But it's not. It's John Mallon. We simply cannot ignore that fact." She turned to Hannah. "Whether one of the graves is empty or not."

Hannah shrugged and thrust her pretty chin up in defiance.

"It's an exercise in frustration," Frank said. "There's no telling how discovering this grave led to my brother's murder."

Siobhán spoke softly. "A witness in town said he overheard an American man say he had come to Ireland to 'right a great wrong.'"

"'A great wrong,'" Jay repeated. "Can I get you to say that again, only this time look at the camera and speak from your diaphragm?"

"No," Siobhán said.

"Brilliant!" Hannah exclaimed. "The killer is a man."

"How do you figure that?" Brandon snapped.

Hannah pointed at Siobhán. "She just said a witness heard a *man* say he had come here to 'right a great wrong.'"

"Are you saying it was the killer referring to my father?"

"What else?" Hannah asked.

"How about it was my father referring to whatever 'great wrong' it was that he had discovered?" Brandon interjected. His glance flicked to Siobhán and Macdara; then he looked away.

The witness swore the statement had come from a man much younger than Peter. They had assumed it was Brandon. Brandon denied telling anyone he had come to Ireland in order to "right a great wrong." He said the only night he'd been in Kilbane up until now was the night his father was murdered. John Butler didn't recall Brandon saying anything of the sort. Could it have been Jay Shepard? It was a dramatic proclamation, one a filmmaker might make. He was relatively young. Was he bragging about his documentary again? Did he know more about the family saga than he was letting on?

If Peter was meeting someone he already knew, why meet at the cemetery? That had bothered Siobhán. Why not just meet in Cork? But if he was meeting Jay, that would make sense. Jay wanted to capture everything on film. Peter wouldn't have found that odd. And night shots in a cemetery offered up an eerie atmosphere, something that would have been in Jay's wheelhouse.

He merited a much closer look. She hoped Macdara would agree.

Hannah piped up. "It's obvious to me that the killer isn't a woman," she said again. "I'm so relieved." Her eyes lingered on Tracy. "Surprised. But relieved."

Macdara frowned at Hannah, then turned to Greta. "We need you to check all the genealogical records in Cork for John and Ann Mallon. Let's see if we can get to the bottom of this."

Greta's eyes practically glowed. She truly loved this stuff. "Absolutely," she said. "Peter had been gathering records too. Do you have his leather satchel?"

Brandon flushed red. All eyes, except his, pinned on them, awaiting an answer.

"Processing is slow," Macdara said. "I'd prefer to start from scratch."

"Regardless of what Hannah thinks, you're still a suspect," Tracy said to Greta. She glared at Hannah. "And so are you."

"Me?" Hannah said. "Why would I kill the old man?" The venom that came out of her was incongruous with her pretty face. She seemed to realize it and tried to backpedal. "I mean Mr. Mallon."

"We might have some information on that soon," Tracy said, flicking a glance at Siobhán. Macdara picked up on the glance and raised his eyebrow. Siobhán had forgotten all about the private investigator Tracy had hired. She had the number in the pocket of her uniform. She would have to mention it to Macdara as soon as this little soiree ended.

"What do you mean?" Hannah asked. This time her eyes were wide and innocent, her voice that of a frightened child.

"Don't listen to her," Jay said, putting his arm around Hannah.

"Stop it," Greta said. "All of you. I'll thoroughly dig into the past. We'll get to the bottom of this."

"How are we supposed to trust you?" Tracy said. "You could be the killer. You could skew whatever research you find, or bury them in boring facts that make us all wish we were dead."

"I can go with Greta and film everything she finds," Jay said.

Macdara rubbed his hands together. "Perfect. That's settled."

"I don't need a babysitter," Greta said.

Tracy jabbed her finger at Greta. "We disagree."

Greta sighed and glared at Jay's camera. "Just don't bother me with your chatter."

Jay saluted.

They began to file respectfully out of the cemetery. Siobhán walked ahead of Macdara. Father Kearney was standing just outside the churchyard. He appeared to be waiting for them. Siobhán was headed for the priest, when she felt Macdara's hand on her arm. She turned. His blue eyes bore into her. "You okay, boss?"

She bit her lip. "Fine."

"You don't seem fine."

She'd been doing her best not to think about Macdara and Aisling. Throwing herself into the case had helped. And here she was so proud of herself. Yet he still picked up on an undercurrent. She hated how well he knew her. "Just working the case."

He stared at her for a minute. His eyes narrowed. "Does this have anything to do with your visit to Chris Gordon?"

He was like a beacon, aiming in.

"You're asking in an official capacity?" Sarcasm poured out of her. It was taking everything in her not to dwell on the bombshell that Chris Gordon dropped. She wanted to corner Maria first, and see what she could get out of her, but there hadn't been time. Macdara's eyes narrowed even more, he seemed to be chewing on how to respond.

Father Kearney cleared his throat. "May I have a word with you two?"

"Of course," Siobhán said, darting past Macdara and his penetrating gaze. Thank God she'd been saved by the priest.

The minute they stepped inside the church, they were enveloped by warmth, sweet incense, and soft organ music. Siobhán was grateful to get out of the cold, and drank in the dancing shadows on the walls cast by flickering candles. They followed Father Kearney back to his cozy office, where he offered them mugs of tea and biscuits. After they were settled, Father Kearney slid papers across the desk. "Saint Mary's burial records from 1903."

They were copies of the original. At the top it read: *Registry of Internments at Saint Mary's Cemetery in 1903.* That portion was typed. Next to it, written by hand, was the month: *January.* Siobhán shivered at the coincidence; here it was, January once more, well over a century later. She continued to scan the form. The categories were all typed and separated into columns:

DATE. NUMBER. NAME. AGE (further broken down into *Years, Months, Days*). How sad that some wee creatures only lived for days. She continued across the form. LATE RESIDENCE and lastly REMARKS. The columns were all filled in by hand. She scanned down to John Mallon.

> *DATE:* 17
> *NUMBER:* 22
> *NAME:* John Mallon
> *AGE:* 70
> *LATE RESIDENCE:* 32 Fair Lane
> *REMARKS:* Poor ground. Plum tree at rear.

"'Plum tree'?" Siobhán said. The handwriting was hard to read.

"Could have been," Father Kearney said, "the Victoria plum tree. It would have taken some tending."

"It's long gone now," Macdara said.

"Fair Lane doesn't exist any longer either," Siobhán said. "But everything sounded much lovelier back then, didn't it? I wouldn't mind being buried under a plum tree."

"I'll keep that in mind," Macdara said with a wink.

She resisted sticking her tongue out, and turned back to the priest. "We can confirm we have the correct John Mallon," Siobhán said. "Now what?"

Father Kearney folded his hands across his ample belly. "There's a bit more." Siobhán and Macdara leaned in. "I couldn't help but overhear," Father Kearney said slowly, as if he relished drawing it out. "I should have said something earlier."

"Is this about the old woman?" Siobhán asked. "Have you seen her again?"

"No, no. It's about the headstone. I believe you've misinterpreted something."

"Go on," Macdara said.

"'Out to the field.' It's from Genesis. Cain and Abel. Cain said to brother Abel, 'Let us go *out to the field*.'"

Siobhán squirmed in her seat, suddenly wishing she knew her Bible better. Macdara drew in a sharp breath. "What?" she asked.

"And while they were in the field," Macdara continued, "Cain attacked his brother, Abel, and killed him."

Chapter 18

Siobhán and Macdara stood outside the church, staring out at the somber gray sky. "Cain and Abel," Siobhán said. "Was Peter Mallon trying to tell us he was murdered by his brother?"

"It can't be," Macdara said. "Not statistically possible."

"What do you mean?"

"He just happens to be right in front of a tombstone with an epitaph about a brother killing a brother, and he immediately understands the meaning, unlike us? Then points to it with his arthritic finger, just after his brother shoots him, and prays we'll put it all together?"

Siobhán sighed. "When you put it that way." She let the rest go unsaid. *It makes me sound like a right eejit.*

"I do think, however, that Peter was trying to tell us that his murder had something to do with his family tree."

"Me too." Siobhán mulled it over. "And we just learned something significant."

"We did?"

"Of course," Siobhán said. "We learned that John Mallon had a brother."

"Possibly."

"Possibly?" Siobhán sometimes wondered if he just liked arguing with her. "John Mallon obviously went to a lot of trouble to have the quote put on his tombstone.

And I believe the puzzle at the bottom has something to do with his wife, Ann."

"Perhaps the Cain and Abel quote is a reference to a friend—someone *like* a brother."

Siobhán shook her head. "Who's reaching now?"

Macdara sighed. "Hopefully, Greta will come up with something in her research."

"Unless she's the killer and she skews the research," Siobhán pointed out.

"True," Macdara said. "But then we'll have her red-handed."

"Who's going to check her work? You?" She didn't mean for it to come out as snippy as it sounded so she softened it with a smile.

Macdara sighed. "Regardless, it's way in the past. How does any of it help us find Peter's killer?" They started to walk toward the town square.

"A brother. A betrayal. Peter in the museum asking about the revolvers. Peter going around and asking if you ever really know someone. Dropping hints that he didn't have a good marriage."

"Maybe you're right," Macdara said. "Maybe it isn't smart to trust Greta to dig up information."

"Because she could be our killer?" Siobhán said.

"Because she could be our killer," Macdara repeated.

"Then *you're* right."

"Say that again? Louder?"

"We've got the perfect test," Siobhán said, delivering her reply with a soft punch on Macdara's arm.

Macdara cocked his head. "How do you mean?"

"We double-check all the research she comes up with. If we find she's manipulated any of it, we confront her."

"I just said that seconds ago." He punched her back.

"Did you?" She grinned. "I didn't even realize I was listening."

"As long as you're the one doing the double-checking."

Siobhán curtsied. Macdara rolled his eyes. She laughed and stopped short of asking him if he could go for a basket of curried chips.

—

They arrived at the underpass to King John's Castle. The fifteenth-century four-storey tower held court in the middle of the square and had quite the colorful history. Over time it had been an arsenal, a hospital, a depot, and even a blacksmith. Now it was a local treasure. Siobhán and Macdara entered the underpass without breaking stride in their conversation.

"I've been thinking about our mysterious old woman," Siobhán said. Her voice echoed in the passage. Siobhán could only imagine the secrets these stones had been privy to over hundreds of years.

"And?"

"I don't think she's a woman."

"Pardon?"

"I think she might be a man."

Macdara lightly punched her on the arm. Is this what they had become? Would he be pulling her hair next? "I understood what you were saying. Just not *why* you are saying it."

They emerged from the underpass and slowed their pace. The guard station was just ahead, but neither of them seemed eager to go inside. Siobhán would much rather be physically active when working on a case. It helped her think.

Siobhán held up three fingers. "Because of her height. Because she hasn't been seen again. But mostly because no woman I know would walk around a cemetery in high heels. Father Kearney specifically said she was 'stabbing around.' I think it was a man not used to walking in heels."

"Good catch," Macdara said. "So maybe this man—disguised as an old woman—was following Peter Mallon around town as he made his inquiries?"

"Exactly. And it started to spook him. Maybe that's why he stole the gun."

"It still doesn't explain why on earth he would go to the graveyard after midnight. Especially if he was already spooked."

Siobhán sighed. For every high in an investigation, there was an equal but opposite low. Every thread they pulled out made four more stick out of the tapestry. "We're getting closer, though. Don't you think?"

"We do seem to be on the trail," Macdara said. "I'll talk to all the museum volunteers once more. See if we can get CCTV footage from across the street. Maybe we can get a glimpse of our mysterious old woman, just in case the gun was hidden in the box of socks."

"Have you visited George Dunne?" Siobhán said. "Informed him that I solved the case of his missing socks?"

"Slipped my mind," Macdara said. "Besides, then I'd have to tell him the box is still missing."

Siobhán laughed. "Better you than me." They stopped walking, but they didn't make a move for the station. "Oh, I totally forgot!" Siobhán pulled a piece of paper out of her pocket with the name and number of Tracy Mallon's investigator. She handed it to Macdara.

"What's this?"

"Tracy Mallon was having Hannah Stripes and Jay Shepard investigated back in the States. This is the private investigator's number. Tracy said she's been trying to get ahold of him and he's not answering."

Macdara tucked the paper into his trousers. "I'll give him a bell." He turned his gaze on her. It wasn't lost on Siobhán that normally they would have been at the chipper discussing the case over a heavenly basket of curried chips. She missed those days. "Anything else on your mind?" he said. His eyes lingered on her face.

Are you dating one of my best friends? "Not a thing." She curled her fist and dug her fingernails into her palm.

Macdara sighed. "I don't believe you."

"Didn't you tell me we weren't to discuss anything personal?"

He gazed past her. "I did."

"That settles that, then."

"I guess so."

"Right, so. My shift is over. I need to get back to the bistro."

He nodded, then turned and headed for the station, while she turned and headed for home.

–

Siobhán was halfway down Sarsfield Street when her mobile rang. It was Chris Gordon. "You said to call you if I saw anything." He sounded out of breath.

"Yes?"

"It's the young girl. I think she's planning a runner."

"Hannah?"

"The young one," Chris repeated. "Not the librarian or the MILF."

Siobhán sighed. "Why do you say that?"

"Because she's hot and I want to—"

"Why do you think Hannah is doing a runner?" Siobhán cut in.

"I saw her sneaking a suitcase down the stairs. She tucked it behind one of the bookcases. As if I wouldn't notice."

"Why on earth would she be doing a runner?"

She could hear Chris sigh through the phone. "I didn't mean to frighten her."

She was going to kill him. "What did you do?"

"I might have said something about how you will get to the bottom of this. Root out the killer."

"And?"

"And she said something about how she hoped you'd find the guilty party, and I might have said…" There was a pause.

"You might have said?"

"I might have agreed, and really I was just making conversation."

"Spit it out."

"I might have said how terrible it would be if the wrong person was arrested, and thrown in prison, and how challenging it would be to survive prison in a foreign country—and I'm sorry but I find the history of the Kilmainham Gaol in Dublin fascinating, so I might have gone on a bit about the executions that occurred there—"

"You're joking me—"

"But it was clear that I was talking about events from so long ago. Who knew she was so sensitive?"

"Who knew?" Siobhán said through clenched teeth.

"I told her the jail is a museum now, that she'd be more likely to end up in a Cork prison. What more do you want?"

"I want you not to frighten any more of the Americans."

"I've kept her here," Chris said. "Doesn't that count for something?"

"I'm on my way. Don't let her leave."

"How?"

"I don't know. Think of something."

"Like you want me to flirt or something?"

"Sure. Give that a try. See if you can do better than chatting about ancient executions."

"I can totally do that. Do you want me to do that with the MILF too?"

"Stop calling her that."

Chris laughed. "I've already been flirting," he said. "It's my thing."

"I'm chubbed to bits," Siobhán said.

"What?" She could hear Chris's perplexity across the phone lines.

"I'm happy for you," Siobhán translated. "Flirt away. Do your thing. Although I highly recommend you keep your thing to yourself."

—

Siobhán stepped into Gordon's Comics just in time to see Chris Gordon and Hannah playing tug-of-war with her suitcase. "Easy," Siobhán said.

Hannah turned and dropped her end of the suitcase. Chris Gordon stumbled back, knocking a wall of comics to the ground.

Hannah bolted out the door. "You won't get me!" she yelled. "Never, ever, ever."

"Hey!" Chris yelled. Siobhán ran after her. "You're welcome!" Chris shouted after her.

The girl was fast, already a blur in the distance. "Stop!" Siobhán yelled. *Where does she think she can go?* Siobhán was gaining, when she slipped on a patch of ice and landed on her back with a thud. She let out a cry. Hannah stopped, whipped around, brunette hair flying in the wind. Then she turned and ran again as Siobhán struggled to her feet, her back and head throbbing. *How dare that girl!* Anger coursed through her as she moved off the footpath and into the street, where the cars had taken care of all the ice. She ran faster.

Soon she was upon Hannah again. "Stop or I take you to the ground," she said. Hannah took her chances. Siobhán didn't know if she was even allowed to take people to the ground, but she wasn't going to let her get away. When Hannah kept going, Siobhán sidestepped her, wrapping her arms around Hannah's slim waist. Hannah kicked her feet and screamed. Siobhán lost her balance, and the two of them slid left and then right as Siobhán struggled not to fall. "Taking someone to the ground" meant *taking oneself* to the ground as well, a tidbit lost on Siobhán until she was in the middle of it. She managed to keep their balance; but throughout, Hannah continued to scream and kick.

Sheila Mahoney sauntered out of her hair salon and lit a cigarette, watching the struggle with an amused smile. "How ya?" she called.

"Grand, grand," Siobhán said as Hannah squirmed in her arms. "You?"

"Ah, 'tis miserable weather," Sheila said.

"'Tis," Siobhán said.

"Seriously?" Hannah said.

"You're not going anywhere," Siobhán said. "Stop struggling or I'll take you to the station and throw you into a cell." There weren't any cells in Kilbane, just a regular room that they could hold someone in if they were forced to, but Hannah didn't need to know that. Hannah stopped kicking and slumped in Siobhán's arms. "If I have to chase you again, I'm taking you in."

"I heard you the first time," Hannah said. The girl started to sob. Big, heaving cries, which tugged at Siobhán's heart. She set her down.

"Smoke?" Sheila said to the girl, holding out her pack.

"Yes," Hannah said, snatching a cigarette.

"Really?" Siobhán said. "You smoke?" She was always dumbfounded when doctors or nurses smoked.

"What?" Hannah said as she stuck the cigarette in her mouth and lit it. She waited until she had inhaled and exhaled before finishing. "You don't think girls should smoke?"

"I don't think anyone should smoke," Siobhán said. "Especially nurses."

"Oh," Hannah said, blinking furiously. "Well, this one does. I drink too. So there."

Siobhán plucked the cigarette out of her mouth. "Why don't you come have a cup of tea instead."

"There's something seriously wrong with you people," Hannah said, stooping to fetch the cigarette. Siobhán crushed it with her boot.

"Have you ever thought of putting blond streaks in your hair?" Sheila asked, sauntering over and running her hands through Hannah's hair.

"No," Hannah said.

"You should," Sheila said, dropping her hands from Hannah and running a hand through her own platinum locks streaked with hot pink. "You're a bit on the mousy side."

Siobhán almost choked. If Hannah was mousy then what did that make the rest of them? Ratty? She waited for Hannah to set Sheila straight.

"Sure," Hannah said, nervously toying with her gorgeous locks. "Can you do me now?" Even the sexiest of women were insecure about their looks, Siobhán was reminded with a start. How sad. And Sheila sure knew it; she made her living counting on it.

"Of course," Sheila said.

"No," Siobhán said. "She's coming with me." Before Sheila could wrestle Siobhán away from her, Siobhán grabbed Hannah's coat and dragged her across the street to the bistro. "Why were you running?" she asked when they were safely on the other side.

"I'm an American," Hannah said. "I want to go home."

"You're a murder suspect."

"You can't keep me here. I have rights."

"We're doing everything we can to sort this out. You're not helping yourself by doing a runner."

"I'm calling an attorney."

"Why don't you make the call from my bistro," Siobhán said. "We can have a little chat after."

Chapter 19

Siobhán was grateful to be back in her kitchen. She'd missed it. She loved investigating, but the stress of it made her appreciate home and family more than ever. She felt as if she hadn't seen her siblings in a long time. They were such a part of her, like breathing. Even if it was labored breath at times, and holding your breath other times. She would have to make a point of having supper together soon.

Making brown bread was almost a spiritual experience for her. It put her head in a peaceful, floating space, which she needed now more than ever. She cleared Elise out of the bistro, something she knew she'd pay for later, and set Hannah up on a stool as she donned an apron and started pulling the ingredients from the cupboard and refrigerator. Rolled oats, whole-wheat flour, baking soda, a single egg, brown sugar, and, of course, buttermilk. She continued with the rest of the ingredients, including a little secret touch of her own, and set everything on the counter next to a large mixing bowl.

It was her grandmother's recipe, and for all she knew, several generations before that. All this business with the Mallons made her realize that she didn't know much about her ancestors, barring a few stories from her parents about their grandparents. They'd all hailed from Cork and Limerick on her mother's side, but many of her father's relatives had been from the west coast of Ireland: Galway, Connemara, and Donegal. She'd visited a few times as a child, but it had been ages. She loved the west coast, its rugged wild features, soaring cliffs, roaring ocean, and the liveliness of Galway. She would have to make it a point to visit again soon. She was hit with a pang now that she hadn't thought to ask her parents more about generations past. Although it might not have been satisfying, for Siobhán didn't want just names and dates, it was the stories that she would have loved. Stories lost in time.

Hannah forgot all about her phone call and seemed content to swing her feet and watch Siobhán work.

"Jay is nice to me. But the rest of them are mean. Especially Tracy. I hate her." Siobhán mixed, all while nodding and empathizing. "You're a policewoman and you own this bistro?"

"It's really a family business," Siobhán said. Once the mixture was ready to go into the baking pans, she tipped a bit more buttermilk on it for luck, along with a sprinkle of oats, doled the mixture into baking pans, and slid them into the waiting oven. The other thing she loved about making brown bread was that it would be done in less than an hour, filling the bistro with its magical scent. She could use a generous slice herself, slathered in brown butter, with a mug of tea.

"Oh. Like the Mallons' family business," Hannah said.

"Right. Have you been to their restaurants?"

"Totally. I wouldn't say they have the best food around, but I like that they feed the hungry. They never wanted anyone to experience the kind of hunger their Irish ancestors did. You know. Like they did when they ran out of potatoes."

Siobhán bit her tongue at the girl's naive distortion of an Gorta Mor. She wanted to treat her to a thorough history lesson, but right now she needed answers from her, so she continued to press. "Where did you go to nursing school?"

Hannah blinked. "America," she said slowly.

Siobhán laughed. "I figured that." She began to clean up as they talked.

"Oh. Right. Do you know much about Ohio?"

"No."

"Oh. Well, that's where I went to nursing school."

"And you decided to become a private nurse?"

"Are you officially interrogating me?"

"I have to question everyone."

Hannah sat up straight and a smile stole across her face. "Do you think I'm capable of murder?"

Siobhán regarded the cheeky young girl. "Under the right circumstances, I think, many people are capable of murder." She shuddered, hating how true this was.

"Peter didn't deserve this. Do you want to know who I suspect?"

"Of course."

"Tracy. She did it. She was so mean to him."

"How so?" Siobhán rinsed her hands, wiped off the counter, and began washing the mixing bowls.

"She was always putting him down. Lecturing him. Hounding him about his medications."

"Maybe she was worried about him."

"I heard her whispering on the phone the day before he went missing. I heard something about having him declared mentally incomplete."

"Incompetent."

"Hey, I'm just telling you what I heard."

"Wait," Siobhán said. She placed the clean bowls in the drying rack and wiped her hands on a towel. She took off her apron and approached Hannah. "Did that mean Peter heard the same thing? Did he know Tracy was trying to do this behind his back?"

Just when Siobhán didn't think Hannah's eyes could get any wider, they did. She slowly nodded her head.

"When and how did he find this out?"

"I heard him on the phone with his doctor. Tracy had been asking his doctor for all his medical records."

"What else?"

"He said he was going to call his lawyer, change the will. He said she wasn't going to get away with this. I think he meant to cut her out entirely."

"*Cut her out entirely.*" Much more dramatic than simply leaving more to Greta. Was this why Tracy had come to her with her suspicions of Hannah and Jay? Was she trying to distract Siobhán from the truth?

Macdara was going to have to put pressure on these American attorneys and find out whether the will had been changed.

And there was another option to consider. Even Brandon suggested that Tracy's concerns could have been valid. Peter Mallon could have been failing mentally. Maybe he *was* incompetent. Most of his family had described him as worked up lately. Excited. Agitated. He was an older man. What if Tracy saw the signs and was right in taking action?

"What did you think about Peter's mental state?" she asked Hannah. "As a professional?"

Hannah shrugged. "He seemed fine to me. You know. For an old guy."

"That's your professional analysis?"

Hannah cocked her head to the side. "Huh?"

"Never mind."

"If Tracy finds out I told you, she's going to kill me next," Hannah said.

Siobhán studied the girl. "No one is going to be next, if I can help it."

"What are you making?" Hannah asked as the scent of baking bread began to fill the kitchen.

"Brown bread," Siobhán said, her voice ringing with pride.

"Oh," Hannah said. "Yuck."

The kitchen door swung open and Ciarán rushed in. He was sweaty and his red hair was sticking up like a science experiment. It used to drive Siobhán mad, but she'd come to find it endearing. "Do we have any bandages?" He was cradling his bloody finger within his hands.

"What on earth happened?" Siobhán asked.

"Sledding accident," Ciarán said with a grin.

"But the snow has nearly melted," Siobhán said.

"Exactly," Ciarán said with a grin. "That's why I crashed into a wall. It was awesome."

"Let's get you to the jax and get it disinfected," Siobhán said. As she hurried to the bathroom with Ciarán, she heard a thud. She turned around. Hannah Stripes had slid off her stool and fainted dead away.

–

Siobhán was impressed that her mother's old smelling salts still did the trick. Hannah came to immediately, blinking her eyes. "What happened?" She tried to sit up.

"Slowly," Siobhán said. "Here." She handed her some water. "You fainted."

"I did?"

"Let's get you to a comfy chair. Get you a mug of tea and a sandwich. Then you can tell me all about why you've been impersonating a nurse."

Chapter 20

Macdara and Siobhán sat in the dining room of the bistro across from Hannah as she nibbled on her sandwich and eyed her tea. "I am a nurse," Hannah said. "I just don't like blood."

"Remember Tracy Mallon hired a private investigator," Siobhán said. "He'll tell us the truth."

Macdara leaned back in his chair. "It would be much better if it came from you."

Hannah's big blue eyes immediately filled with tears. "That old witch."

Macdara leaned in. "Are you going to make us wait for the official report?"

Hannah sighed. "Okay, okay. I'm not a nurse. But Peter knew that. That's why he hired me."

Siobhán cocked her head. "He wanted to hire a nurse who wasn't a nurse?"

"Exactly," Hannah said, beaming. She pushed her tea away from her.

"We're going to need a bit more of an explanation," Macdara said.

Hannah sighed as if it was a burden to explain the obvious. "He didn't want a nurse at all. He was furious with Tracy for suggesting it." Hannah flipped her hair and stuck her chest out. "I was his revenge."

This meant Peter had known for a while that Tracy was deeply involved in his medical issues. That didn't bode well for Tracy. "How did Peter find you?"

"Through Jay," Hannah said. "I've acted in some of his films."

No wonder Jay seemed so fond of her. "Are you two romantically involved?" Siobhán asked.

"You mean me," Hannah said, "and a dead guy?" Horror was stamped on her faux-nurse face.

"No," Siobhán said. "You and the handsome film-maker."

"Oh," Hannah said, breathing out a sigh of relief, followed by a laugh. She shook her head. Siobhán half-expected cobwebs to come out of her ears. "Jay's only in love with his camera." She turned her gaze to Macdara and flipped her hair. "Besides. I like a man with an accent."

Siobhán laughed, a wry, bitter sound. Macdara pinned his eyes on her and lifted his eyebrow.

"This could be a serious offense," Macdara said. "You should probably get an attorney of your own."

Hannah's eyes widened. "What's a 'serious offense'? *Not dating Jay?*"

"No," Siobhán said. "Your little Florence Nightingale act."

Hannah scrunched up her nose. "Huh?"

"Impersonating a nurse," Macdara said slowly.

"Gotcha." Hannah cocked a finger gun at him, then withdrew it as he stared at her. She folded her arms across her ample chest. "Peter knew I wasn't a nurse. He hired me as his personal assistant. It was my job to annoy Tracy as much as possible." Hannah grinned. "I think I did pretty good, if I do say so myself." She grew somber. "I didn't know she was going to get so mad she'd kill him. Maybe it is all my fault. Oh, God." She put her hands over her face and started to sob. "I want to go home. I just want to go home." Trigger tore over, sat in front of Hannah, and looked up at her. She stopped crying, sniffed, and wiped her eyes. She patted her knees. Trigger jumped up.

"Well, what do you know?" Macdara said. "He's like a therapy dog." Hannah hummed as she continued to stroke Trigger. He was practically purring himself.

Or he's cozying up to a killer, Siobhán thought.

"May I have a word with you in private?" Macdara said.

"Let's go out to the garden," Siobhán said.

–

The back garden, alive with herbs and flowers in the spring and summer, was a bit sad in the winter, but it afforded them some fresh air and privacy. Siobhán spoke first.

"What do you think?"

"I think it fits. From what we've learned of Peter Mallon, hiring Hannah would be the perfect way to get back at Tracy."

"I kind of agree," Siobhán said. "She's a liar and an impersonator, but I just don't see her as our killer."

"Plus the dog likes her." Macdara winked. Trigger used to love everyone but Siobhán. Luckily, that had changed over the years.

"There's no accounting for taste," Siobhán said. "And I don't like how Hannah was working for Jay Shepard. I think we need to take a closer look at him."

"Funny you say that," Macdara said. He reached in his pocket and handed her a business card. It had the logo of a tree on it:

JAY SHEPARD
AWARD-WINNING
DOCUMENTARIES
DON'T JUST RESEARCH YOUR
FAMILY TREE
FILM IS FOREVER

"What awards has he won?" Siobhán wondered out loud.

Macdara cocked his head. "Don't think that's what we should focus on."

"He changed his card," Siobhán said. "The one he gave me has a camera on it."

"Again," Macdara said. "How is that pertinent?"

Siobhán shook her head. "I don't know. But it interests me." She began to pace in the small yard. Something else was dancing at the back of her mind. "I think I've seen this card somewhere."

"Not surprised," Macdara said. "He's been papering the town with them."

She put her hand on the card, covering most everything but the tree. "That's it," she said. "This is the business card I saw under George Dunne's kitchen table."

Macdara raised his eyebrow. "Are you sure?"

Siobhán nodded. "I started reaching for it and he poked me with a broomstick." The memory brought up a flash of rage. *Cheeky old man.*

Macdara let out a laugh before he could stop himself. Siobhán gave him a playful smack before she forgot that they didn't do those kinds of things anymore. She recovered and moved away from him. "Don't you think it's unusual that he had Jay's card?"

Macdara scratched his chin. "He could have picked it up in town."

"Why would he do that?"

Macdara shrugged. "Maybe he wants a documentary of his own."

She could see it now: *My Wooly Socks*, by George Dunne. "I think we should ask him, don't you?"

Macdara took off his cap. "I suppose we should."

Siobhán thought of the cup of tea he had given her, the taste of the curdled milk. "Once again—there's no 'we,'" she said with a smile. "I told ye. You'll get much more out of him if you go it alone."

"Sorry," Macdara said. "O'Reilly called a briefing meeting today. I'm afraid you'll have to visit dear old George on your own."

"It can wait until you're done with your meeting."

"I think you should go now. You're right, it's odd that he would have Jay's card under his table. And either he didn't want you to know that he had it, or he simply liked poking you with a broomstick. Whatever you do, don't let him do that again."

"You're enjoying this, aren't you?"

"And make sure to tell him that we made some progress on his wooly socks."

"You want me to tell him some mysterious old lady stole his entire box of woolies? That will put him right over the edge!"

Macdara laughed again, then tipped his hat. "Perils of the job, m'lady. Perils of the job."

–

Siobhán stood outside George Dunne's house, her eyes trained on the front door. The curtains were closed. Maybe he wasn't home. *Wouldn't it be nice if he wasn't home?*

It was a lovely stone house with a blue door—much more charming than the man inside. She knocked on the door and waited.

A few seconds later it opened and she was greeted by George Dunne's scowling face. "Have ye found me socks?"

Siobhán closed her eyes for a second. "Not exactly," she said, "but we're closer."

"What does that mean?"

"Did you donate a box to the Kilbane Museum recently?"

His eyes narrowed into tiny slits. "What about it?"

"Your socks were in it."

His jaw dropped open. He scratched his chin. "Must have taken the wrong box. So why didn't you bring them?"

"Because someone already took them. I'm sorry. You're probably just going to have to buy more."

"That's outrageous! Those were my socks!"

"You gave them away."

"It was a mistake. I want them back."

"I don't know who has them."

"You came here just to torture me, did ye?"

"No. I need to speak with you about another matter. May I come in?"

"No, you may not."

She sighed. She was dying to see if the business card was still under his kitchen table. She didn't trust him to tell the truth. She had no doubt that George Dunne wouldn't hesitate to lie through his false teeth. Especially to her. But she couldn't force her way into his home, so she took out the business card and held it up.

"What can you tell me about this?"

"Nothing." His eyes flicked away.

"You didn't even look." Siobhán held it closer.

George turned his head. "I don't have me glasses." She shoved it even closer. He squinted and bent down to read it. "Still nothing."

"Funny," she said, "because I saw this exact card under your kitchen table. Maybe it's still there?" She took a step. He blocked her.

He used his hooklike finger to jab at the business card. "That's the filmmaker."

"Yes." Siobhán gritted her teeth. Whoever said people should be kind to the elderly had never met George Dunne. He held up his gnarled finger again, this time to ask her to wait, but then slammed the front door in her face. She sighed. It felt like an eternity before the door opened again. He was holding a DVD in his hand. He held it up: *Dancing Irish*. "The card was attached to this."

Jay Shepard's documentary. "And where did you get that?"

"The museum. Someone donated it."

"I didn't know you were a fan of Irish dancing."

He glared at her, and then to her shock, he broke out in a few dance steps. "I used to be good in me day."

"Impressive."

"T'anks." He shoved the DVD at her.

She took it, at a loss as to what to say next. "When was this donated to the museum?"

He glared. "How should I know?"

"Did you get it before or after the Americans came?"

He scratched his chin. "I'd say well before. I've had it for ages."

This was a surprise. Someone in Kilbane had had a copy of *Dancing Irish* before Jay Shepard came to town. "Are you sure?"

He shrugged. The old man had reached his cooperation limit for the day. "Will that be all?"

"For now."

"*Wunderbar.*" He did a few more dance steps back into his house, flashed a nasty grin, and then slammed the door shut in her face, a second time.

Siobhán headed off the property, and had just passed George Dunne's garden shed when she stopped cold. She'd almost missed him. A man was crouching behind the shed, dressed all in black. She stopped, placed her hand on her baton. Her mobile was in the other pocket, at the ready. "Don't move." She used her sternest voice.

The man's head popped up. It was Jay Shepard.

Chapter 21

"Policewoman," Jay said, coming to a standing position. "Hey." He flashed a smile as if it wasn't unusual at all that he had been crouching behind an old man's shed.

Siobhán released her grip on her baton, then grabbed it again and squeezed. "What are you doing?"

He shrugged and gestured around him. "Just scouting the village for places to film."

"Really? Because it looks to me like you were hiding behind George Dunne's shed. Dressed like a cat burglar."

"All filmmakers wear black."

"And crouch behind sheds, spying on people?"

He sighed. "If you must know, I followed you." He held up his camera.

"Why?"

"To see where you were going. Why else?" He glanced at the DVD in her hand.

"Hey! That's my film."

She took out the business card. "Did you used to have this attached to the DVD?"

"No," he said. "I made those cards especially for Peter."

"What do you mean?"

"I wanted the job, so I tailored my business cards to fit the assignment." He pointed to the tree. "Voila. My other cards have cameras on them."

"Like the one you gave me."

"Exactly."

"But this card must have been attached to the DVD when it was donated to the Kilbane Museum."

"What do you mean 'donated'?" Jay's handsome face was marred by a flash of rage.

"George said he got this copy at the museum. That someone had donated it. Ages before your arrival."

Jay looked petulant for a moment, and Siobhán couldn't figure out why. "Hope they at least watched it before they got rid of it," he said. *Ah, that's why. Because everything is about him.* Jay couldn't imagine someone donating his precious film to the museum. She silently thanked the heavens she wasn't an artist.

"So you're saying you didn't give this DVD to the museum, nor did you leave your business cards there."

"Correct."

"But you just happen to be spying on George Dunne."

"Who?"

She pointed at the house. "The old man who lives there."

"No. I swear. I was following you." He looked around again. "I could have taken this to the other fellow, but I like to consider myself a feminist."

"Excuse me?" She stepped closer. "Taken what to whom?"

He pulled a piece of paper out of his pocket. "I found this lying on top of my camera bag. Just a few hours ago. I followed you so that you could be the first to see it."

Siobhán took the slip of paper. It appeared to be a photocopy of an original:

> *We set sail in the morning. She's a big ship but after months on the ocean I'm sure she'll feel like*

> *a tin can at sea. Michael is worried about getting seasick. As the sun set a brilliant red over the horizon, I drank a pint for the homeland. Hope America shines as bright as they say. Ann too thin. Such a beautiful wife. I will do everything it takes to make good in our new home. But my heart will remain, always, forever, at home, Ireland, my beautiful home.*

Siobhán could feel Jay staring at her as she read it. When she finished, he moved in closer. The handwriting looked as if it matched the note found in the cemetery. If that was the case, this appeared to be copied from John Mallon's journal.

"Is it real?" Jay asked. "Some kind of diary?"

"Tell me exactly where you found this." Siobhán was hoping to avoid his fishing expedition. The less he knew, the better.

He gestured behind him. "I was shooting in the churchyard, getting some B-roll. B-roll is—"

"I know what B-roll is," Siobhán said.

He grinned. "Very well. I had left my camera bag by the wall to get a shot of the headstones. When I returned, the note was lying on top, underneath the handle of my bag, so that it wouldn't blow away."

"And you didn't see anyone?"

"Just you, going by. That's when I hurried after you."

She pictured him hiding behind the shed. Hardly the image he was trying to portray. "Is this the first time anything like this has been left on your camera bag?"

"Yes."

"Don't mention this to anyone else in your group."

"If it's John Mallon's journal, I'm going to want to use it for my film."

She was sure he'd filmed it already or even made a copy of it. "Wait for us to give the all clear. The investigation must take priority."

He held up his hands. "Of course, of course."

The paper was plain, white. No definitive marks. There were probably half-a-dozen photocopying machines in town, and, of course, folks had personal printers as well. Still, Siobhán could check at the shops and see if anyone could remember someone coming in to photocopy a journal. But a smart person would have done so in Cork City or Limerick. Lucky for investigators, people weren't always smart.

If this was authentic, then John Mallon had kept a journal. And someone had it. The handwriting appeared to be a match, and he mentioned his wife, Ann. Who was Michael? More to the point, who had left this for Jay, and why? "Thank you. I must ask you to report to us immediately if you receive anything more."

"Use my camera bag as bait? I love it." He grinned. He was trying to be helpful. Or he was pretending to be helpful. Either way, the outcome was the same. Overly helpful people annoyed Siobhán. Elise, for example, was one of those overly helpful types that didn't mean a word of it.

Siobhán stood tall. "Follow me again and I'll have you arrested."

"Got it." He let out a long sigh. "May I walk with you back to town?"

"Fine." They headed off the property. Siobhán stopped outside the gate to look around. To their right was the churchyard. Straight ahead was the back of Kelly's. It had been abandoned forever, and litter was piled up around the back door. She'd have to enlist her siblings to go in with her on a cleanup day. Just because a business was closed didn't mean you let it fall to disrepair. She hoped she lived long enough to see the Celtic Tiger roar again; she hated seeing so many businesses failing up and down Sarsfield Street.

They walked ahead, passing the churchyard and the pub. When they reached Sarsfield Street, Siobhán stopped. "I thought you were supposed to be with Greta?"

He shook his head. "She gave me the slip."

"How?"

"Told me to meet her at nine o'clock sharp in the lobby of the shop. I was there fifteen minutes early. Only to find out she left at eight A.M."

"Are you sure?"

"Ask Chris Gordon. She took the rental car too."

Why didn't she want Jay Shepard to go with her? Was it really because of his chatter, or was it because she was up to something and she didn't want any witnesses?

But Greta would have to wait. She had a few more questions for Mr. Fancy Filmmaker. "Want to continue walking about town with me?" Siobhán said. "You can film while I ask you a few questions."

"Take one," Jay Shepard said with a wink. Siobhán just stared at him. "That's a yes."

—

They ambled down the street. Jay stopped at a storefront window that held artifacts from the Irish Republican Army. An original poster of *The Proclamation of the Republic* was framed center-stage, surrounded by photographs of Michael Collins, as well as photos of other soldiers jailed and executed while fighting for Ireland. She remained silent while he filmed it, then picked up the conversation as they moved along.

"How did you come to be in Peter Mallon's employ?"

Jay kept filming while talking. "Peter found me. Apparently, he'd seen *Dancing Irish*." He nodded to the DVD still in her hand. "You really should see it."

Siobhán wanted to chuck it into the street. Instead she murmured how much she was looking forward to it.

"And when did you hire Hannah Stripes to pretend to be his nurse?"

Jay stopped. He lowered the camera. Then he grinned at her. "You are good."

"When did you hire her?"

"Peter asked me if I knew any young, pretty actresses up for a little game." A worried look shadowed his handsome face. "If I had known he truly was ill, I never would have gone along with it."

"What makes you think he truly was ill?"

"Look at the film footage. He'd become increasingly paranoid and cranky since arriving in Ireland. Obsessed hardly covered it. He even became angry with me filming him. Perhaps if he'd had a real nurse, she would have caught on to his condition before it was too late."

"Even if you're right, are you suggesting that his paranoia is what got him killed?"

"I would have bet the farm that he killed himself."

"He did not. We have the pathologist's findings. It was murder."

Jay sighed. "He must have angered someone. Accused someone of something."

"Such as?"

He shook his head. "I don't have the slightest idea!"

"It seemed like a very *specific* idea to me," Siobhán said.

Jay shrugged. "Hazards of the job. I am a filmmaker, you know."

Siobhán bit her lip. "How could I forget?"

He stopped, stared at her intensely. "You haven't told Tracy about Hannah, have you?"

"Not yet," Siobhán said.

"Don't!" He shouted it, making Siobhán jump. "Sorry," he said. "It's just… well, one of us is a killer. And it isn't me. And it isn't Hannah. I would appreciate it if you didn't give a possible killer the ammunition to go after me or Hannah."

"You think she'd kill you or Hannah, just because Hannah isn't really a nurse?"

"If she's cut out of the will… and blames us? Yes. I think that might just put her over the edge."

"Have you noticed any unusual behavior from Tracy lately?"

"She's been herself," Jay said. "But that's hardly vindicating."

"Why's that?"

"I'm surprised you haven't noticed," Jay said. "Tracy Mallon is a master manipulator. All she's ever cared about is the family fortune." He picked up the camera again. "God help us all if he cut her out of the will."

–

Siobhán had just finished a strenuous jog, when she returned to the bistro to find Macdara waiting for her, his car idling at the curb.

"Hurry," he said.

"If you've got a tip on another horse, I've got a tip for you," Siobhán said. "Ignore it." She wasn't supposed to flirt, but she couldn't help it. This case was wearing on her, and Macdara used to be the one person who could make her feel better, make all the bad feelings go away.

Macdara laughed, and she breathed a sigh of relief. "We're going back to Cork. Greta is waiting for us at a pub in Cork. She claims she's found something of interest."

"I'll be quick," she said, running into the bistro to change. She peeled off her running clothes, pulled off a world-record rinse-off, thanked her lucky stars for deodorant and powder, tucked her hair into a bun, and threw on her uniform. On her way back to the car, she brought the copy of *Dancing Irish* and the journal entry, and set them on the console between them.

"What's that?"

She tapped the DVD. "Jay Shepard's other documentary."

"Anything good?"

She filled him in on her meeting with George Dunne and finding Jay crouching behind a garden shed. Macdara slammed his hand on the steering wheel. "So Greta disobeyed us, and Jay is stalking you." He cursed under his breath.

"There's more." She read the journal entry out loud. After she was finished, Macdara drummed his fingers on the steering wheel before responding.

"I don't like this. Jay Shepard lied to us about Hannah. Now this."

"Agreed. But it does look like the handwriting found in the note in the churchyard. And that one has been authenticated."

"But this is not an original."

"Brandon claimed that when he arrived at the cemetery, all the papers were partially burned. Maybe the killer did take papers with him? Maybe an entire journal belonging to John Mallon? Maybe that's what lured Peter Mallon to the cemetery?"

"Maybe Peter burned them when he realized they were only copies of the original?"

Siobhán shrugged. "I'm more interested in why this was left on Jay's camera bag, and who left it."

"I think we have to equally examine both."

They fell into an uneasy silence. After a few minutes Siobhán felt compelled to break it. "Have you watched the film footage he sent you?"

"Parts of it," Macdara said, keeping his eyes on the road. "And?"

"Nothing startling. Family interviews, shots of their restaurants in Ohio, and some of the gang arriving in Ireland. It's strange to watch Peter Mallon on film. Seeing how excited he was to be in Ireland. No idea what was waiting for them."

"But nothing useful?"

"There's no confession from any of them and nothing sticks out so far. Let's hope Greta found something good."

Chapter 22

The Welcome Inn was situated in Cork City at 24 Parnell Place, across from the bus station. The mural on the building's side featured a horse rearing up, a man below him with his fist raised in triumph (Siobhán didn't know if he was supposed to be a cowboy or just a man who needed to see a man about a horse), and a large MURPHY'S sign. Above it, WELCOME INN was rendered in a dark brown, which popped against the sandstone building.

Siobhán wasn't surprised Greta chose this particular pub for their rendezvous, given that she was into history, and, having been established in 1845, this was one of the oldest pubs in Cork. They entered the comforting dim space (Siobhán loved all the old wood) and found the widow sitting at a corner table, with a stack of papers and a pint of Guinness in front of her. She was wearing her thick glasses and drowning in a navy cardigan. Her eyes, which Siobhán had originally thought were brown, were actually hazel, and tonight she had a bit of a spark about her. After a few minutes Siobhán realized Greta was wearing makeup—some rouge and mascara and a touch of lipstick. *Interesting.* She was also glowing from the aftermath of her research; it was obvious that this family-tree snooping was a passion of the woman's.

"We spoke with Jay," Macdara said. "He said you tricked him."

A sly smile spread across Greta's face. "I work better alone."

Siobhán could feel Macdara tense beside her. Greta had defied his order, and now he perceived her as mocking him. Siobhán didn't think Greta was self-aware enough to be mocking them, and she placed her hand on Macdara's arm to calm him. After a moment she felt him relax. She turned to Greta and gave her a smile that suggested, *"Just us girls."* Had she had a rendezvous with Frank earlier this evening? Could that explain the makeup? "What did you find?"

Greta batted her eyelashes and took off her glasses. Another smile crept across her face. "I know what explosive secret Peter discovered."

"You mean it wasn't the headstone?" Siobhán asked.

Macdara leaned forward. "What is it?"

"I believe it was *this*." She slid a photocopied document across the table. It was a copy of a ship's manifest dated 1853: *J & J Cooke Shipping Agents Records. The* Swan. *From Cork to New York.* Greta had highlighted her discovery. Three passengers were listed in a row:

> *John Mallon*
> *Ann Mallon*
> *Michael Mallon*

Michael Mallon. There it was. A brother. Siobhán couldn't wait to tell Macdara later on that she'd told him so.

"Ellis Island?" Macdara said.

"No," Greta said. "Ellis Island didn't open until 1892. Prior to that there was Castle Garden on the southern tip of Manhattan, later named Castle Clinton. But prior to *that*, as in our case here, ships simply sailed into docks on the east side of Manhattan." Greta turned her attention back to the passenger list and put her finger next to the name of Michael Mallon.

"A child?" Macdara asked, squinting to read the document.

"No," Siobhán said. "A brother." She pointed across the manifest, where the ages of the passengers were listed. Ann was eighteen; John was twenty-five; Michael was twenty.

Siobhán scanned the papers, mulling it over. Michael was five years younger—the same as the discrepancy of the birthdates on the headstones. Oh, this was something, alright. The headstone in Ohio was engraved with Michael's birthdate. Michael Mallon was buried in Ohio. Under the wrong name. A circumstance that would either be very unusual or very deliberate. Siobhán's fingers began to tingle. Even Greta, the great historian, had missed a very important clue.

Cain and Abel…

"A brother," Greta confirmed, eyes flashing with excitement.

"Peter never knew that his great-grandfather had a brother?" Macdara asked. Neither of them seemed to have pieced together the bit about the graves, and Siobhán waited patiently to point out her discovery.

"He did not," Greta said. "There's more." She slid another paper across the table. The document was a copy of a crude passenger arrival list, all written by hand. Two names appeared:

John Mallon
Ann Mallon

"No mention of Michael Mallon," Macdara said. "Did he somehow escape the notice of the clerks documenting the arriving passengers? Human error?"

"I don't think so," Greta said. "After all, even Peter never even knew there was a Michael Mallon." Greta threw up her hands. "It's as if he disappeared from the boat."

And yet he was buried in Dublin, Ohio... under the name John. Siobhán was sure of it.

"A lot of passengers got sick and died," Macdara said. "Terrible journey."

"Exactly," Greta said. "I've searched as many records as I could. The only other official mention of a Michael Mallon is when he and John were boys. Here's the census report." She slid it over. John was twelve and Michael was seven at the time of the report.

Siobhán studied the dates and ages carefully. "Wait," she said. "You said this is the only *official* mention of a Michael Mallon."

Greta began to blink rapidly. "You're good." She slid a piece of paper across the table. Siobhán and Macdara leaned over to read:

> *Michael accused me of making Ann sick. He's not well. He has Da's temper. I hate to say this, hate that the thought has even crossed me mind. I think my brother is in love with my wife.*

"You too?" Macdara said.

It was Greta's turn for a shock. "There are others?"

Something about the way Macdara had exclaimed "You too" was bothering Siobhán, but she pushed it away for a moment and turned to Greta. "Where did you get this?"

Greta pushed her glasses up. Her hands were shaking. "It was slipped under my door this morning. I assumed it was Jay leaving me a note about accompanying me. I didn't want to deal with him, so I just shoved it in my pocket. I didn't even read it until just before the two of you arrived."

Macdara sighed. Siobhán stared at him. He cocked his head. "*You too?*" His words floated back to her, swirled around her mind. *That's it.*

"Et tu, *Brute?*"

Everything was coming together now. She could see how this genealogy research was addicting. She felt as if she were following a treasure map and had just discovered where X marked the spot. It was time to let them in on the excitement. She turned to Greta. "Do you also have a picture of John Mallon's headstone from Dublin, Ohio?"

Greta laughed. "Yes. We all have copies of it on our cell phones." She brought up the photo and handed it to Siobhán. Siobhán brought up her photograph from their churchyard, laid them side by side, then jotted down on one of the photocopied sheets the birth dates of the boys, using their ages in the census report.

"Do you see it?" Siobhán said. She stared at the uncomprehending faces in front of her. "Come on! I expect to hear a few 'Holy Cows!'"

"'Cows'?" Macdara said. "Isn't it just one?"

"Not when you've got something this crazy." She tapped the photos of the headstones, and then pointed to the birth dates on the records Greta provided. "Notice anything?"

Macdara studied it. "The birth dates match the headstones?"

Greta leaned in; then her eyes flicked between documents. "But our John Mallon has Michael's birthdate."

"What are you saying?" Macdara rubbed his eyes in confusion.

Siobhán felt alive with excitement. "Do you have a marriage license for John and Ann?"

"Yes," Greta said, digging through her papers and finding it. "They married in Cork City shortly before they came to America."

"'Explosive' is right," Siobhán said.

"Spill," Macdara said.

"I don't think it's Michael Mallon who didn't get off the boat. It's John."

Greta gasped. "How can that be?"

Macdara frowned. "Just based on the dates?"

"Not just the dates," Siobhán said. "There's the matter of the headstone."

"I don't understand," Greta said.

"We learned something after our meeting at the cemetery," Siobhán explained. "You see we thought 'Out to the field' was some romantic reference to heaven. Instead it's a quote from the Bible."

"Cain and Abel," Macdara said. "On that headstone John Mallon was referencing a brother killing a brother."

"My God," Greta said. "You're saying… one of the brothers killed the other on that boat?"

"Obviously not," Siobhán said. "For we have proof that John Mallon returned to Ireland and went on to live quite a bit longer. But he made a point of accusing his brother of murder on his headstone. *Attempted* murder."

Greta studied the materials in front of her. "You think Michael tried to kill his brother, John."

"Yes. The headstone for *your* John Mallon in Ohio has Michael's birthdate."

Greta's eyes widened. "You're suggesting that Michael Mallon is buried in Ohio in a grave bearing his brother's name?"

"Correct," Siobhán said.

"How on earth could that have happened?"

"I believe Michael Mallon took on his brother's identity when he got off that boat."

Greta, who had just taken a sip of her Guinness, began to choke. Macdara pounded her on the back, then turned to Siobhán. "What are ye on about?"

"Bear with me," Siobhán said. "Let's go back to the headstones. Our John Mallon has John's correct birthdate—we know for sure he was five years older than his brother—and it makes a veiled accusation at his brother with 'Out to the field.' Then there's the bottom portion. I always suspected the last word was 'Ann.' Now I'm pretty sure I know what the other two words are." She brought up her photograph of the headstone:

E_ _u A__

Siobhán filled in the word "Ann":

E_ _u Ann

Greta cocked her head and studied it. "I don't get it."

Siobhán smiled.

"Don't keep us in suspense," Macdara said.

"May I borrow a Biro?" she asked Greta.

Greta frowned. "A what?"

"Sorry. Your pen." Greta handed her the pen. Siobhán filled it in:

224

Macdara let out a low whistle. "He's accusing his wife of betraying him too."

Siobhán nodded. "Because she allowed Michael to pretend he was her husband when they entered America."

"Why on earth would she do that?" Macdara asked.

"Because John didn't make it off that boat. But John and Ann Mallon were married. It was hard enough to make it in a new country as an Irishman back then. But an unmarried Irish woman? The prospect would have been terrifying. I think Michael convinced her to let him pretend to be John."

"Wow!" Greta said. "I'm speechless. But not quite following this. Why did Michael have to pretend to be John? Did John change his mind about America?"

Siobhán couldn't help but feel a flush of pride. "I'll get to that." Maybe she was good at crossword puzzles after all. "'*Et tu*, Ann,'" she said, directing Greta's attention back to the Irish tombstone. "John Mallon is pointing the finger at his wife. Plus there's the portion of the letter we found. 'My Dearest Ann. How could you?'"

Greta straightened up. "What letter?"

Siobhán felt her insides freeze. She'd gotten so excited, she forgot she wasn't supposed to be sharing information. She flashed Macdara a guilty look.

"It's okay," Macdara said. He nodded to Greta. "We found portions of a burned letter at the crime scene. They appear to be from John Mallon to his wife, Ann."

"We couldn't read much of it," Siobhán said. "Just, 'My Dearest Ann. How could you?…'"

"'How could you?'" Greta repeated. "'How could you enter America with my brother?'"

"And allow Michael to steal his identity," Siobhán filled in.

"Cain and Abel," Macdara said.

Siobhán nodded. "Cain and Abel."

Macdara pushed his Biro around his notepad. "You think Michael Mallon tried to kill his brother on the boat."

"Something happened. Perhaps an argument. Michael could have pushed John overboard. Assumed he was dead. Only John survived."

Macdara leaned in. "Must have been a hell of a swimmer. Do you think Michael knew his brother was still alive when he got off that boat?"

"It doesn't seem like it," Siobhán said. "You'd have to be pretty confident to steal a man's identity. Confident that the real man isn't going to come back to claim it."

Macdara picked up the story. "But somehow John Mallon survives. Makes his way to America. Sees that his brother is pretending to be him, and his wife is going along with it."

Siobhán nodded. "He returns to Ireland a jaded and bitter man."

"And starts purging his anger in his journals," Macdara mused.

A journal someone may have used to lure Peter Mallon to his death, a journal that was now being distributed in dribs and drabs.

"I'm not sure I'm convinced," Greta said. "How could they do that?"

"We'll never really know," Macdara said.

"Unless we find John Mallon's entire journal," Siobhán said. She looked at Greta. "I have to ask you something."

"Anything."

"It's very delicate. But it's imperative you tell us the truth."

"Go ahead," Greta said.

"Were there any problems in your marriage? Anything that could have been troubling Peter?"

"Of course not!" Greta said. "We were well-suited. Maybe we weren't head over heels in love, but we were happy."

"I believe you," Siobhán said. If this were true, then all of Peter's comments about "not really knowing someone" had been about Michael and Ann Mallon. Their wonderful love story. Imagine finding out the truth of it.

"*Out to the field…* Et tu, *Ann*?"

Greta was convinced that Peter would have wanted the truth to come out. Siobhán wasn't so sure. Not when the truth was this devastating. Not when one had built his entire family dynasty on the legend of this hero. And not when the hero had fallen so far. Siobhán floated her theory to Greta.

"It was Michael Mallon who created the Mallon family dynasty," Greta said. "He's still a hero."

"A hero who tried to murder his own brother and stole his brother's wife," Siobhán said deadpan.

"Oh," Greta said. She slumped in her booth. "How painful," Greta said, as if reading Siobhán's mind. "Peter must have been crushed."

"Betrayal is always crushing," Siobhán said, her voice thickening. She didn't dare look at Macdara, but she could feel his eagle gaze on her.

"Maybe John was sick. Maybe he got off the boat somewhere else, told them to keep going," Greta said.

"Then why the bitter headstone?" Siobhán said.

Greta chewed her lip. "You're right." She straightened up. "Let's *assume* that you're right," Greta said. "At least some version of it. What does this have to do with Peter's murder?"

"I've been thinking about that," Siobhán said. "Do you think someone could have been extorting Peter? Using this information to get money? Have any large sums gone out of the family account?"

"No," Greta said. "Wait." She paled.

"What is it?" Siobhán leaned in.

"Shortly before the trip Frank and Peter were getting in awful arguments. It wasn't like them. I pressed Peter on it, but all he would say is that it was a financial matter."

"So you think Frank was paying a blackmailer?"

"It's possible. But I hate accusing someone without proof."

"Can you access the financial records?"

Greta shook her head. "Only if I inherit the estate."

"We need to get our hands on Peter's will," Siobhán said.

"I'll call the executor right away," Greta said. "I'll stress the urgency."

"If it doesn't work, have him call me," Macdara said.

Greta let out a frustrated cry. "It still doesn't make sense. Peter would have wanted the truth. No matter what. He wouldn't have paid anyone to keep this secret. You must believe me."

"Maybe that's why he was arguing with Frank," Siobhán said. "Maybe Frank had different ideas about how to deal with this secret."

"Another brother killing a brother?" Greta said. "I can't believe it. I don't want to believe it. Frank is a decent man."

"This documentary business," Siobhán said. "Did it come up before or after this quarrel about the money?"

"After," Greta said. "Definitely after. Why?"

Siobhán felt her excitement growing. "Maybe it was Peter's answer to the blackmailer. Make a documentary that showcased the truth of their family story. Wipe out the ability to be blackmailed by being the first to get the story and the truth out there."

"'Right a great wrong,'" Macdara said.

"'Right a great wrong,'" Siobhán repeated. But the man who said that was supposed to have been a young man. Was the eyewitness simply mistaken?

Or did Jay Shepard know more about this family story than he was letting on? He was just as much of a researcher as Greta. What if he had stumbled upon John Mallon's journal while filming *Dancing Irish?* Then used it not only to get the job as the documentary filmmaker for the Mallons, but to blackmail them as well?

"My God," Greta said. "That's exactly what Peter would have done. Why didn't he tell me?"

Siobhán placed her hand on Greta's arm. "Let us handle this. Please. Not a word to anyone."

"Of course," Greta said.

"She's right," Macdara added. "Not a word. No matter who it is. *Your life* could depend on it."

Chapter 23

It was happy hour and Cork City was buzzing. People streamed in and out of the pubs, the weight of the workday thrown off their shoulders, putting a bounce in their steps. Laughter and music spilled out of the pubs. For a second Siobhán wished she didn't have any commitments. She wished she and Macdara could turn back time and go back into the pub and drink pints of their own and listen to trad music.

"Good work in there," Macdara said. "Imagine. Your first murder probe turns out to be of biblical proportions."

"How long have you been waiting to say that?"

He flashed a grin. "It was painful holding it in."

Siobhán laughed. Then she grew serious. "It couldn't have been Peter who was going around Kilbane saying he was here to 'right a great wrong.'"

"Why not?"

"Because more than one witness said it was a *younger* American he overheard."

Macdara caught on. "Someone younger, but very close to this secret. Someone like Jay Shepard."

"And Jay is making a lot of money making this documentary." They walked in silence for a moment, their boots echoing on the footpath. "He would have also had the skills to research this secretive and explosive family history. He is a storyteller after all."

"My God," Macdara said. "Do you think he staged all of this?"

"It's possible. Maybe while making his documentary *Dancing Irish*, he somehow learned the truth about the Mallon family."

"That seems like a stretch. It took Greta a long time to find all this paperwork, and that was only after we found the headstone. How would Jay have learned about it in the first place?"

That was a valid point. Siobhán thought out loud: "We know that Jay Shepard was in Ireland making his first documentary, *Dancing Irish*. Wouldn't it be just as coincidental that he just happens to get hired by Peter Mallon to work on *their* Irish documentary? Obviously, there's some connection."

"Peter Mallon could have Googled 'Irish document-aries' and found Jay, not the other way around."

"True," Siobhán said. "So let's assume Peter is the one who researched and found Jay. He just wanted a documentary made about his family history. But Jay, being the dedicated filmmaker that he is, could have started to research the story on his own, and voila! He finds out about the tombstone, and Michael Mallon, thus giving him a great twist for the documentary. Or—even more sinister—a reason to blackmail him."

"Jay could have threatened to expose his ancestor as a murderer, instead of a hero." Macdara sighed. "It's imperative that we speak with Frank. If we can prove Frank was paying a blackmailer, we might just solve this case."

"We need to get all our suspects in one place again," Siobhán said. "I'd like to watch them all in action again. Especially Jay."

"That can be arranged," Macdara said.

Siobhán grinned. "It just so happens I know the perfect event."

–

The sun was shining on the day of Ann's camogie game. The last of the snow had melted, revealing shiny green grass beneath it. Siobhán had asked Jay Shepard to film from the sidelines so that he would always be in their line of vision. He was thrilled to take on the assignment, and Siobhán would have no problem keeping him in her sights. She glanced up in the stands where Maria was perched. Maria grinned and waved. Siobhán didn't wave back. Maria frowned. One thing was clear, after the match she was going to get Maria to spill everything she knew about Macdara and Aisling.

When Siobhán joined Macdara in the lower stands, he seemed to pick up on the exchange. "What in the world has gotten into you?" He touched her arm.

She pulled away. "How long can we keep the Americans here?"

"If they fight it, not much longer."

"Do they know that?"

"No one has asked yet," Macdara said. "But they're definitely getting restless and asking when they are free to go."

"We can't just let the killer sail back to America."

"I think they're going to fly."

Siobhán normally would have laughed, and he was waiting for it. But she couldn't. There was a wall between them now and her name was Aisling. She focused on the game, on her beautiful sister showing off her athletic abilities as she weaved down the field with her stick. Life was about moments like this. Living fully and actively. Human beings were here for such a short time. Every minute was precious. And somewhere, maybe even in the very stands where she sat, was a person with no such regard for human life.

"As soon as the game is over, I'll start asking our group another round of questions," Macdara said.

"Don't you mean 'we'?"

"No. *You* should visit with your sister. She's really something."

A lump rose in Siobhán's throat, and she nodded, unable to meet Macdara's eyes.

Ann scored a goal and Siobhán rose to her feet with a cheer. Her eyes flicked to Jay, who had caught it all on film. Was he just an artist, passionate about his work? Why had he really been following her that day? Was it the act of an innocent man, or a killer who was afraid she was starting to get a little too close to the truth?

The crowd stood and cheered. Siobhán looked down to see Ann beaming, standing in front of the goal. Her teammates lifted her up. Ann was grinning, ear to ear, and looked up at Siobhán. Siobhán gave her a thumbs-up, waved, and grinned. Ann had scored the goal. It may not rise to the level of life and death, but it was important. The little things mattered. Her family mattered. Things were going to have to change. Siobhán was going to get better at balancing life and work. But first she had to unmask a killer before he or she boarded a plane and flew away from justice forever. But in order to do that, Siobhán was going to have to get a personal burden off her chest first.

–

Maria did not know what she was walking into when Siobhán invited her to the bistro for dinner. They were closed for business and her siblings were scattered. James and Elise were out on a date, Ciarán and Eoin were playing one of their video games, Ann was having a well-deserved rest, and Gráinne was on a marathon phone call to someone in New York. Siobhán had Maria just where she wanted her. After their supper she topped up their wine, and waited for a gentle lull in the conversation.

"Have you spoken with Aisling lately?"

Maria held her wineglass and gazed into the fire. "Sure," she said. "But not often. She loves Dublin. I don't think she's ever coming back."

Siobhán's fingers tightened around her glass. "Is she still seeing that Scottish guy?"

Maria started biting her lip. "No. They broke up."

Siobhán could already feel herself heating up. She set the wineglass on the table a little too hard, wine splashed from the top. "Is she dating Macdara?"

Maria was startled; she, too, set her wineglass down and sat up straight. "Oh, no," she groaned. She held up her hands. "I am not getting involved."

"Don't say that," Siobhán said. She wanted to cover her ears like a child.

"It's not what you think," Maria said. "Breathe."

"Then what is it?"

"Who told you?"

"That's not what matters here."

Maria shook her head. "They're friends. That's all."

"Friends? Since when are they friends?"

"It's lonely to move to a big city."

"I know." It was also exciting. The independence! So freeing. They must have felt free. Free to do whatever they wanted. Without so much as a gentle heads-up.

Maria stared at her until Siobhán made eye contact. "Why are you freaking out? They've been hanging out in Dublin. It's no big deal."

Siobhán rose from her chair. "If it's no big deal, then why didn't you say anything? Why didn't she?" *Why didn't he?*

"You should talk to Macdara about this. Not me. Not Aisling. *Macdara.*"

Siobhán didn't want to tell her that as her boss Macdara had forbidden her to speak of anything personal. "How often do they hang out? Where do they go? What do they do?"

"I think they just meet for a drink now and then. What does it matter? It's been two years. He's there, and you're here. Are you even trying to have a long-distance relationship with him?"

"It's complicated." Siobhán sighed. "We work together."

"He'll be going back to Dublin soon. Then what?"

"Whose side are you on?"

Maria cocked her head. "Yours, pet. I'm always on your side." She reached over and tugged on Siobhán's hair, like she used to when they were children. "It's not what you think. Talk to him."

"Why don't you just tell me everything?"

"It's not my place." Maria's face softened. She took Siobhán's hand. "You're a good detective," she said. "You need to figure this out."

Maria was right. Siobhán would have to take this up with Macdara. Maybe after the case was solved.

The door opened and James and Elise stomped in. Siobhán sank back into her seat. There was silence in the hallway, followed by what clearly sounded like a heavy make-out session. Seconds later something thumped against the wall.

Wow, Maria mouthed. A grin spread across her face. Siobhán buried her face in her hands as pictures on the wall jiggled. Trigger hid under a chair; Maria howled with laughter.

–

The reading of Peter Mallon's will took place in the Kilbane Library. Ciarán wasn't feeling good and wasn't able for school. Siobhán couldn't cancel the reading, and the rest of her siblings had plans. He tried to argue that he was old enough to stay home on his own, but Siobhán couldn't stomach the thought. Not when there was a killer out there. She was grateful when he agreed to tag along. Magda, the cheerful, plump librarian, volunteered to keep an eye on him. Ciarán rolled his eyes. "Humor her," Siobhán whispered. "She probably wishes she had a lad of her own." He gave a good-natured nod and settled into a comfortable chair in the fantasy section and soon lost himself in a book. Magda stood behind him, hands resting on her belly, smiling over the top of his head. Ciarán threw Siobhán a searing look, and she gave a thumbs-up. He shook his head and went back to the book. Magda was probably going to drive him mental. Siobhán smiled at the sweet librarian, touched Ciarán's forehead, and was relieved to see the headache tablets she'd given him had already taken his fever down. He was right. He wasn't a baby anymore. Siobhán didn't want to admit that. It was partially his fault. There were times he clung to his role as the youngest in the family as well. He was at that awkward in-between age. She pointed to the door leading for the meeting. "I'll be right in there if you need me."

"School would have been less painful," he said with a smirk. "Off with ye. I'll be fine."

"And I'll be right here!" Magda said.

Ciarán rolled his eyes. Siobhán avoided kissing his cheek, patted Magda's shoulder, and headed for the private meeting room in the back. Before she could enter, a hand clasped her wrist tightly. Hannah Stripes was tugging on her, dragging her behind a stack of book-shelves. Siobhán glanced at the section: MYSTERIES. *How apropos.* Before she could scold Hannah or ask her what she thought she was doing, Hannah removed a slip of paper from her purse and shoved it at Siobhán.

"Here."

The lack of provisions on the ship is maddening. The men drink so that the women have more to eat. Michael was delirious with fever. Still, I shan't forgive the things he said. I don't know how much more I can stand.

Anger bubbled up in Siobhán. "Where did you get this?"

"Does it mean anything?"

"Answer the question."

Hannah bit her lip. "It was taped to the outside of my door."

"When?"

"Just now."

The flats above Chris Gordon's shop were accessible by a stairwell in the back of the shop. Anyone who wandered into the store could have taken the stairs and left the note.

But only those who were staying in the room could avoid suspicion for being up there. "Did you see anyone up there who didn't belong?"

Hannah shook her head. It was maddening how these tidbits were being dropped randomly. Siobhán supposed she should be grateful that they were being brought to her attention. Had any of the others received them, but kept them hidden?

Was someone testing the Americans? Seeing who hoarded their secret bread crumbs and who shared? Was it some kind of sick game? Or even, more sinister, a test? If so, how did one "win," and what would happen to the loser?

It was a troubling thought. The longer Siobhán stood staring, the more terrified Hannah looked. Siobhán placed her hand on her shoulder. "You did well. Bringing this to me. Not a word to the others."

Hannah nodded, and the two of them headed to the reading of the will.

–

The conference room was the best part about the Kilbane Library. Siobhán loved the floor-to-ceiling bookshelves, gilded mirror, and roaring fireplace. An oak boardroom table, large enough to accommodate the group, was situated in the middle of the room. A large screen was pulled down, awaiting the executor, who was going to place a video call that would be projected onto the large screen. Greta sat at the opposite end of the table from Brandon and Tracy; Hannah and Jay sat together, as usual; while Frank sat in the middle, stealing more than a few glances at the oblivious Greta.

The poor woman had been so stressed about this will reading that Siobhán was relieved that one way or another it would soon be over. Would everything be left to Tracy and Brandon, or would it all go to Greta? Siobhán had a feeling that Tracy and Brandon were ready to fight the outcome if it didn't go their way. She, for one, could not understand this kind of greed, and was relieved her family hadn't had to deal with it. What money and insurance her parents had was left to the entire family. But if her parents had decided to do anything else with it, donate it, or bequeath it to a stranger, or ask them to fling it off the nearest bridge, Siobhán liked to think they would have respected her parents' decision. It was *their* money. Entitlement should be one of the seven deadly sins.

Then again, it paled in comparison to murder.

The screen crackled and soon a middle-aged man in a suit appeared, smoothing over his comb-over, tugging at the end of a bushy mustache, and adjusting his wire-rimmed glasses. "Hello, hello," he said. "Am I on?"

"You're on," Macdara said.

Siobhán had to look away, so strong was her urge to rip off his mustache.

"Shall we begin?" The man cleared his throat, then stared at the document in front of him. He seemed afraid to look at the group. Siobhán straightened up.

"We're all here and ready," Tracy said.

The man cleared his throat again, pushed up his glasses. "'I, Peter Mallon, being of sound mind and body...'"

Tracy made a noise. A second later she jumped and cried out, then smacked Brandon. Everyone stopped and looked at them.

"You can't say he was of sound mind," Tracy said.

"Shut up," Brandon said.

"I've sent you all copies of the will," the executor said, already looking exasperated. "You can read it for yourselves. This really isn't something I normally do."

"I talked him into it," Jay said. "I thought an actual reading would be much more dramatic." He tipped the camera to the group as if giving a toast.

"We never received our copies," Tracy said.

"I can't control the Irish mail," the executor said, tugging his mustache again.

"Please," Macdara said. "Just give us the overview."

The executor sighed. "Tracy and Brandon are each bequeathed twenty thousand dollars—"

"*What?*" Brandon and Tracy said in unison. Brandon rose from his chair and looked around the room, mouth open. "No. We're supposed to inherit the full estate."

"I told you he was out of his mind," Tracy said as she glared at Greta. She pointed at her. "You did this, didn't you?"

Greta threw a desperate look at Siobhán, shaking her head.

The executor began to speak faster, as if he could outrun the bad news. "Frank Mallon, his brother, twenty thousand dollars. Hannah Stripes, his assistant, twenty thousand dollars—"

That certainly bolstered the theory that Peter Mallon knew she wasn't a nurse.

"Wait," Tracy said. "His nurse? He's giving his nurse the same as his children?" She stopped as if she'd just heard what he said. "'Assistant'? Did you just say his *assistant*?"

Hannah, dressed in a pretty yellow dress, beamed. With her brunette hair piled around her head, she looked like a walking sunflower. She touched her heart. "He was so kind."

"Why did he say 'assistant'?" Tracy persisted.

"You might as well know," Hannah said. "I'm not a nurse. Surprise!"

Tracy gasped. "I knew it." She pointed at Hannah, then glared at Siobhán and Macdara. "Arrest her!"

"Peter knew she wasn't a nurse," Siobhán said. "He hired her to get back at you."

"At *me*? For what?"

"Stop acting innocent," Brandon said. "You were trying to have him declared mentally incompetent."

"Because he was! This is proof!" Tracy sputtered with rage. She looked at Brandon for support. He shrugged. "We're contesting the will," Tracy said. "This will not stand."

"She means this will, will not stand," Brandon corrected.

"What?" Tracy sputtered.

"You weren't making any sense," Brandon said. "You said, 'This will not stand.' People might say, 'What will not stand?' If you say, 'This will, will not stand'—then it's clear. Pretty clear. I think." Tracy stared at him openmouthed. Brandon flushed red and addressed the crowd. "We're contesting the will!"

"You don't even deserve anything!" Frank rose and pointed at Tracy. "You were going behind his back, trying to have him declared mentally unfit, and you..." He pointed at Brandon. "You're gambling again, aren't you?"

"How dare you," Tracy said, turning on her uncle. "Did you have something to do with this?"

"In a way," Frank said.

"What does that mean?" Brandon demanded.

"Your father and I decided it was time to face the truth," Frank said. "I'm afraid we made a very grave mistake."

No pun intended, Siobhán thought. She'd done it once herself. She kept her gob shut.

Frank sank into his chair. Siobhán hadn't been paying much attention to him; but now that she looked at him, Frank Mallon looked awful. His complexion had a greenish tint and he had dark circles under his eyes. "This is my fault," he said. "All my fault."

Macdara and Siobhán exchanged a look.

"What do you mean?" Siobhán asked softly.

"What on earth are you talking about?" Tracy's question was not as gentle.

The executor cleared his throat. "Jay Shepard to receive twenty thousand dollars upon successful completion of the documentary—"

"So kind of him," Jay said. "I'm going to finish it, Peter." He pointed at his video camera on the table. "Recording as we speak."

"Fifty thousand will go to his wife, Greta Mallon."

"What?" Greta said. She slumped, almost in relief. "I'm glad," she said. "I didn't want it all. I really didn't."

"Who gets it?" Tracy asked. "Who gets the estate? The restaurants? The millions?"

The executor cleared his throat again. "You'll find on the next page a list of charities and organizations that will be splitting the estates, including the chain of restaurants—"

Tracy and Brandon cried foul at the same time. "'Charities'?" they cried. "*Charities?*"

"Including quite a few in Ireland," the executor said.

"Well, isn't that just great?" Tracy said, voice dripping with sarcasm.

Brandon pointed at Greta. "Somehow you're behind this."

"Why?" Tracy said. "Why would he do this?"

"Because he wanted us all to be free," Frank said. "Free of generations of secrets and lies."

"What 'lies'?" Tracy said.

Frank hung his head. "It turns out our great-grandfather was no hero."

"That's ridiculous," Brandon said. "Of course he was."

Frank shook his head. "There's proof. We were being blackmailed." He reached under his chair and set a briefcase down on the table. Everyone stared at it as if something horrible was going to leap out the moment he sprung it open.

Macdara shot to his feet. "Hold on," he said to Frank. "Not another word."

"No," Tracy said. "We have to hear this." She lunged for the briefcase.

"Who was blackmailing you?" Brandon demanded. "And why?"

"Don't touch it," Macdara said to Tracy, using his sternest voice. He turned to Frank. "You'll come back to the station with us. The guards will be the first to see this information. The rest of you will have to wait."

"Of course," Frank said. He hung his head. "I should have told you. I've made so many costly mistakes."

Brandon pounded the table. "We still contest this will," Brandon said. "We contest it!"

"You can't just say, 'We contest it,'" Tracy said. "It's a legal process." She glared at Greta. "But we will be contesting it. And we will thoroughly check that one of you isn't behind one of these so-called charities that stand to inherit our fortune."

The screen flickered and went black. The executor had had enough.

"You," Tracy said, advancing on Jay Shepard and pushing his camera away. "Did you know about all of this?"

"No," Jay said. "Peter must have had a flare for surprise. No wonder he was acting so mysterious."

"I'm going home." Tracy stood. "And I mean the United States. I'm booking my ticket now."

"We're still investigating," Macdara said.

"Then arrest us. Because anything short of that and I'm on the next plane back."

"Me too," Brandon said.

"Three," Hannah said.

"But we have a documentary to finish," Jay said.

"Consider it done," Tracy said. She flipped off the camera.

"Come on," Macdara said, standing and turning to Frank. "Let's go." Siobhán was just reaching for her handbag, which she'd placed under her seat, when she heard a sizzling sound, and then the room plunged to black.

Chapter 24

Siobhán immediately thought of Ciarán in the other room and prayed he wasn't afraid. She caught herself. He was probably loving it. That settled it. She was refusing to admit that he was growing up. Still, she'd never stop worrying about him.

"Hey!" someone shouted.

"Nobody move," Macdara said. "Everyone, stay calm."

"The killer!" a woman's voice cried out. "One of us is next." Mass panic ensued and Siobhán could feel people shuffling around her. She heard a thud and then the sound of books pouring off the shelves and tumbling onto the floor. There was a scream, followed by a moan.

"Stay still," Siobhán echoed, but it was no use. Someone elbowed her in the ribs.

"Do you have a torch?" Macdara called out to her.

"There's one on my mobile," she said. "But I can't find my handbag."

"I'll try to find the door," Macdara said. "Call out to the librarian." Just as suddenly the lights came back on.

Books lay piled up on the floor; chairs were upended. The participants were scattered around the room, standing still. Mouths were open, eyes wide with fear. Siobhán scanned the room. Everyone was present.

"My briefcase!" Frank said. Everyone's head jerked to the table, where the briefcase once sat. It was empty.

"Is everyone alright?" Macdara said. Heads began to nod. "Stay where you are, everyone." He turned to Frank. "What was in this briefcase?"

"Evidence," Frank said. "Evidence that Peter and I were being blackmailed."

There were several gasps. "You have to tell us everything," Tracy said. "Right now."

"No," Macdara said. "He'll tell the guards everything. In private. I'm going to have a quick look for this briefcase."

"I'm going to check on Ciarán," Siobhán said. She headed out as Macdara began hunting for the briefcase, picking up the fallen books as he searched. Siobhán found Ciarán asleep in his chair. Relief flooded through her. Magda strode into the room, shaking.

"What happened?" Siobhán said. "Are you alright?"

Magda tucked a stray gray hair behind her ear. "I think someone deliberately flipped the fuse box."

"Did you see anything else?"

She nodded. "Someone slammed into me as they ran past. They had long gray hair." The librarian shuddered and brushed her arm.

"Could it have been a wig?" Siobhán wondered if their mysterious old lady was back.

"It did feel odd," Magda said. "But it was pitch-black."

"Who else was in the library before the lights went out?"

Magda shook her head. "We have brand-new computers and still hardly anyone comes to the library anymore."

"We come," Siobhán said. They did too. Faithfully.

Magda patted Siobhán again. "Besides Ciarán, it was just me. And the person with the long gray hair."

Siobhán headed back to the meeting room. She filled Macdara in on what Magda said.

"Well, it wasn't one of us," Tracy said. "Doesn't that mean we're all in the clear?"

"No," Macdara said. He sidled closer to Siobhán. "The briefcase could be hidden in this room still."

They looked around. It was a large room; there were plenty of places to hide a briefcase. "This is going to take a while," she said.

"Longer than you think," Macdara said. "What if the person slipped outside of the room and hid it somewhere else in the library? Then slipped back in before the lights went back on?"

Siobhán nodded. It was within the realm of possibility. The briefcase could be hidden anywhere in the library. "I'd like to get Ciarán home. He should be resting."

"You go," he said. "I'll call in other guards to help search."

She looked around the room at their suspects, all looking shocked and weary. Most likely, the biggest shock had come from the reading of the will.

"But none of them could have run out and flipped the fuse box," Siobhán pointed out.

Macdara sighed. "You're right. It appears that someone has an accomplice." Macdara and Siobhán locked eyes; no doubt both thinking about the mysterious old lady.

"Someone didn't want us to get our hands on that briefcase," Siobhán said.

The entire group filed out, one by one, leaving Siobhán and Macdara sitting there. He twirled Siobhán's paper on the desk. "That briefcase could have been just the thing we needed."

"To unmask the killer?"

"To keep our suspects from leaving. I have no grounds to hold them here without evidence."

"Then we'd better find something. And quick." Siobhán handed him the portion of the journal from Hannah.

He shook his head. "Someone thinks he's in control."

"Or she," Siobhán added.

"'Or she,'" Macdara agreed. "Isn't equality grand?" He winked as she headed out the door, lips zipped.

-

"I can't believe I slept through it," Ciarán said as they headed home, backpack stuffed with books, thumping as he walked.

"You didn't miss anything," Siobhán lied. "But did you see anyone else in the library before you fell asleep?"

Ciarán shook his head. "Just Magda. The overbearing librarian."

"She means well." Siobhán was relieved. She didn't want her little brother to be a witness. Even if he wasn't so little. She settled him into a chair by the fire, stoked it up, and fixed him a ham-and-cheese toastie and chicken noodle soup.

"Are you going back to work?" He sounded hopeful.

"No," she said. "I'm going to stay with you."

He smiled, bringing her a bit of peace. Everyone needed someone when they were sick. "So," she said, "what are we reading?"

"There's no 'we.' Reading is a solo activity." He pulled out his book. A bookmark fell out. On it was Saint Vincent de Paul. Siobhán turned it over.

KILBANE'S DAY OF GIVING

TIME TO GIVE
A DAY OF FUND-RAISING

It was three days from now. "Are we going this year?" Ciarán asked.

"I'd forgotten all about it," Siobhán said. It was a yearly event. She was sure they had plenty to donate, but she hadn't had time to go through their things. She opened the book to stick it back in, when another piece of paper fell out of the book. "What's this?" She glanced at the familiar handwriting. Another photocopied journal entry.

"I dunno." He reached for it, but Siobhán snapped it up. "Hey!"

"It's nothing," Siobhán said, tucking it behind her back with one hand, ruffling his hair with the other.

He swatted her hand away. "What does it say?"

"Haven't read it."

"Read it now."

Siobhán didn't want him thinking about murders, or attempted murders, no matter how long ago they occurred. "Just something for work."

"How did it get in my book?"

How indeed? When the lights went out. The thought of this person being so close to Ciarán when the rest of them were sequestered in the other room made her blood boil. She left him with his soup and headed into the kitchen to read the note in private:

> *Michael's behavior is troubling. The boat moves so slowly, rocks too violently. Ann is sick. I'm worried. Michael is drinking heavily. I worry about his mental state. It was a mistake to let him come. Something must be done.*

When Siobhán walked into the station the next morning, Macdara was waiting for her. She laid down the most recent journal entry. "This was left in Ciarán's book during the blackout at the library."

Macdara slid open the middle drawer to his desk and slid out another piece of paper. "This was on the windshield of me car this morning."

> *Sang a hearty rendition of "Irish Rover" last night with the crew. Much needed distraction. Michael stayed in his cabin. So many are ill. The smell in the bunks is enough to make you wish you were dead.*

Siobhán clenched her fist. "Someone is toying with us."

"Someone has John Mallon's journal."

Siobhán slumped into Macdara's guest chair, picked up a rubber ball from his desk, and began to bounce it. For a few seconds Siobhán lost herself in the simple rhythm of the ball *thunking* off the wall. "When is Frank due to arrive?"

Macdara glanced at his watch. "Fifteen minutes ago." She let the ball drop and it rolled to her feet. She picked it up and placed it back on Macdara's desk. "Do you think Frank staged the entire bit about the missing briefcase?"

"How could he have done that?"

"Did we look under his chair for it?"

Macdara shook his head. "I think I would have noticed it."

"There was a lot of commotion."

"True." He paused. "But Frank couldn't have cut the lights in the first place."

Siobhán sighed. "I'll be interested in what he has to say for himself."

"Between Frank and Jay, who has the most to gain from Peter's death?"

"Before the will was read, it could have been Frank. Perhaps he thought he was going to inherit more than he did."

"If Frank was paying a blackmailer, as he just claimed, that might have angered Peter."

"Angered him enough to steal a gun?"

Macdara shrugged. "You tell me. I'm an only child. How far can this sibling-rivalry business go?"

"We know it's not unheard of for brother to kill brother, all the way back to biblical days. Still, you're the one who said it was a stretch for Peter to be pointing at that headstone, praying we'd put the whole sordid business together."

"But we did."

"Grand. Let's play it out. Peter finds out Frank has been paying a blackmailer. He's livid. He steals a gun from the museum. Then he pretends he wants to show Frank the headstone."

Macdara picked up the thread. "At the cemetery he confronts Frank with what he knows. Tells him he has to stop paying the blackmailer."

"And what? Frank refuses? Why would Frank want to keep paying?"

"Maybe Peter demanded that Frank get that money back. Demanded to know who was behind the blackmail."

"Why wouldn't Frank just tell him?"

"I don't know. Maybe there was no way he could get the money back. Maybe he saw the gun and there was a struggle. Maybe it was the blackmailer that Peter meant to threaten with the gun. Instead things got out of hand. There was a struggle. Frank gets the gun and shoots Peter."

"Another brother killing a brother."

"History repeating itself."

"So who was the blackmailer?"

"My guess? Jay Shepard."

Siobhán had been thinking the same thing. His presence in their life seemed way too coincidental. Jay wanted to film the documentary and did everything he could to insert himself in their lives. "Let's say that's true. Jay learns that the hero of the family dynasty is a cold-blooded killer."

"How does he learn that?"

"We have yet to figure that out. It must be during his time in Ireland for the other documentary, but stay with me."

"Okay."

"Jay goes to the Mallons to blackmail them. Instead of Peter, he first deals with Frank. Frank starts paying him. On top of that, Jay is getting paid to do the documentary. The point of the Ireland trip is to film the revelation. 'Right a great wrong.' Jay Shepard wanted the shock value of dropping this bombshell on Peter Mallon. But Peter starts making inquiries of his own while here. He finds out about the headstone. He learns of Michael Mallon. He confronts Frank. Frank admits that Jay has been blackmailing them. Peter calls a meeting with Jay at the cemetery. He lets him know there will be no more payments. He says he wants the truth to come out."

Macdara nodded. "There goes Jay's dramatic ending."

"There goes his money, his dramatic ending, and Peter may have even demanded all the money back. Threaten to sue or press charges."

"In this scenario who brings the gun?"

"Jay."

"Jay steals it from the museum?"

"Or his pal George Dunne puts it in a box of socks and places the box outside the museum for Jay to pick up."

"'His pal'?"

"Remember I caught him sneaking around George's property? George had that business card. I got the feeling they were both lying to me about it."

"The old lady?"

"Could be Jay. He's tall enough."

"I don't think he's thin enough."

"The cut of the coat could be slimming him down. And think about it. If the killer was a stranger, there would have been no need to disguise him or herself. The disguise is so that this old lady could follow Peter around without being recognized. It has to be Jay."

"After Peter was murdered, why wouldn't Frank tell us if he knew it was Jay?"

Siobhán sighed. "I don't know."

"And Jay was in the conference room when Magda saw our mysterious old lady with the long gray hair."

"Maybe they're in on it together."

"Jay is still filming this morbid documentary. Artist or no artist—I find that kind of odd."

Siobhán seconded that. "After our meeting with Frank let's go put some pressure on Jay." Macdara's mobile rang. He spoke briefly and turned to Siobhán. "That was Chris Gordon."

"What's wrong?"

"Frank's room appears to have been vandalized and there's no sign of the man."

Chapter 25

The bedroom had indeed been tossed. The closet door was thrown open. A suitcase was in the middle of the floor. Frank's wallet and glasses were sitting in the middle of the bed. The confession was propped up on a small table next to the bed.

> *Dear Family,*
>
> *I'm so sorry. It was an accident. I never meant to kill Peter. He was putting us in danger. I had no choice. I'm going to kill myself. I won't do it here. I have too much respect for someone else's property. Michael Mallon was our great-grandfather. A murderer. I guess it runs in the family. Forgive me.*
>
> *Frank Mallon*

Siobhán didn't like it. "It doesn't make sense."

"Go on."

"Why would Frank toss his own room?"

"Looking for something? The gun perhaps?" He stopped. "Or... he wanted it to look like someone else broke in?"

"Why would he do that, and then go to the trouble of writing a confession and suicide note?"

Macdara eyed her. "Where are you going with this?"

Siobhán scanned the room again. "Maybe he was forced to write it."

"How's that now?"

"Somebody else came in, threatened Frank, tossed the room looking for... whatever evidence Frank had in that briefcase... then forced him to write the confession and kidnapped him."

"You're reaching."

"I disagree. If Frank is *not* the murderer, then the murderer is getting desperate. There must have been something incriminating in that briefcase!"

Macdara shook his head. "We have no proof of that."

"Because suddenly there is no briefcase."

"But there is a note. And a solid confession."

Siobhán threw her arms up. "So is your theory that Frank tossed his own room, looking for the gun? And what? He couldn't remember where he hid it?"

Macdara folded his arms. "That's my guess."

"That means he's out there somewhere with a gun."

"Or he's already taken his own life, and his body is out there somewhere."

"Or he just wants us to think he took his own life and he's on a plane to an exotic island as we speak."

Macdara shook his head. "He wouldn't have time. My guess is he hasn't left Kilbane. We'd better send out the search party."

"*We're* the search party," Siobhán said.

"Then *we* better start looking," Macdara replied.

–

Macdara gathered the rest of the Americans and convinced them to stay in the comic-book store while they searched for Frank. He also got them all to agree to let the guards search their rooms. Siobhán had just started a door-by-door search for Frank Mallon when she felt a hand on her shoulder. She whirled around to see Garda O'Reilly standing behind her. She tried not to stare at his ears.

"Well done," he said.

"We haven't found him yet," Siobhán said, frowning.

"All in due course. But the murderer has been unmasked. We'll all rest a lot safer tonight. Why don't you head back to the station, there's a load of paperwork awaiting you, and I'm sure you'll be wanting to say good-bye to the detective sergeant."

Alarm bells rang loudly in her head. She couldn't process any of it. Especially saying good-bye to Macdara. Besides, there was still a killer out there. "You're closing the case?"

O'Reilly held up a plastic bag. Inside was Frank's confession. "Of course. We have our man."

"He's missing. Macdara..." she caught herself. "Detective Sergeant Flannery and I are about to organize a search."

O'Reilly shook his head. "I have other guards looking for him."

"We don't know for sure that he wrote that note. Frank Mallon could be a victim. And if that's the case, he's in imminent danger."

"The family has verified it's his handwriting. If I have to get in a handwriting expert, I will."

"What if he was forced to write it?"

O'Reilly's face hardened. "I am satisfied that he's our killer."

"I'm not satisfied. Neither is the detective sergeant." She glanced around. Macdara was nowhere to be seen.

O'Reilly shook his finger at her. She wanted to bite it off. "You should be thanking your lucky stars you weren't suspended. You are not in charge here. You follow orders. *My* orders. Do you understand?"

"Of course. But—"

O'Reilly swiftly cut her off. "This investigation is closed. The sooner we get the Americans out of here, the sooner we can go back to business as usual. Either get back to the precinct and start on that paperwork, or go home." He stared at her. "And if you choose the latter, you best not be coming back." He tipped his hat and walked away.

–

Siobhán sat at her desk, fuming. *This case is nowhere near solved. How can he do that? Is Macdara fighting back?*

He wasn't in the office. He hadn't called her; and she was too terrified to step outside the lines, so she hadn't called him either.

Where is Frank Mallon? Is he really the killer? Is he still alive?

She was in the middle of these thoughts when she looked up to find Macdara staring at her. After eye contact he bowed his head. Siobhán rose instinctively.

"He can't do this."

"Keep your voice down," Macdara said softly, with a glance around. The few other guards and employees on duty weren't looking at them, but she knew they were probably straining to listen.

"You can't leave," she said. "I think our killer is still out there."

Macdara shook his head and took another step. "One of the hardest lessons to learn doesn't come from college," he said. "You're not in charge. You must learn to take orders."

"We don't even know where Frank is hiding. Or if he's still alive. Even if it is his handwriting, he could have been coerced to write that letter. Or he's protecting someone. Or, at the very least, we have to find him and get his official confession."

Macdara took off his hat and sighed.

"Don't you outrank O'Reilly?" she implored.

"Yes, but I have superiors. And O'Reilly has already informed the detective superintendent—with much fanfare, I might add—that we've caught the killer. The rest is follow-up and paperwork. I'm to head back to Dublin immediately."

"Fine," she said. "I'll keep digging."

"No," Macdara said. "You won't. Not if you want to be a guard."

"Maybe I don't."

Macdara sat on the edge of her desk and removed his cap. "You're not a quitter."

"Why aren't we opening a new case, then? Frank Mallon is missing."

"There are guards looking for him."

"*We* should be looking for him."

"We're not one-man bands. Life here will go easier if you remember that."

"I had more freedom to catch killers when I was nothing more than a bistro owner."

"You've always been more than a bistro owner." He locked eyes with her.

He was leaving. It was now or never. "I'm sure you're happy to be returning to Dublin." She diverted her gaze to her desk.

"I never said that."

"Say hi to Aisling for me." Pulse thumping along with her throat, she sat down and pretended to be fascinated with the paperwork.

"'Aisling'?" Macdara said. He stood up and hovered over her. "Why would I do that?"

Siobhán was tired of playing games, keeping secrets. "I hear the two of you spend quite a lot of time together."

"I see." He shook his head. "Mystery of what was bothering Siobhán O'Sullivan solved."

"Excuse me?"

"At least that's one down. You could have just asked me."

"It's none of my business."

"No. I suppose it isn't." He stood. Started to walk away. Ignoring her instincts to stay calm, she stood too.

"I would have never hurt you like that," she said to his back.

He turned. "But you did."

She shook her head. "I went to college."

"You made a life-altering decision without even telling me."

"I didn't need your permission. It's my life."

Macdara looked as if she'd slapped him. "Oh, I know. And what a shock it was to realize how small a part I was playing in it."

Is that what happened? Is he right? Did I do that? "That's not fair."

"Isn't it?" He stood close and lowered his voice. "If I had meant anything to you, you would have brought me into your confidence. Shared the news. Not dropped it on me like an atomic bomb." He started to walk away, then returned. "Everyone knows you don't date coworkers.

Any case you work on together could be compromised, or at the very least looked on with suspicion, just by the existence of a romance." The entire station was listening now; it was obvious from the blanket of silence and heads bowed across the station. Macdara jerked his head toward the outdoor patio, and Siobhán followed.

Macdara took a deep breath and faced her. His eyes were swimming with pain. "I just want to know one thing." Siobhán nodded. "Did you discuss it with your brothers and sisters before you decided?" Siobhán's eyes filled with tears. She nodded. Macdara turned his back to her. "Of course I would have supported you. I probably would have put in for a transfer to Cork. So we could try to make both romance and career work for both of us. But you didn't even give me the chance. That's what hurt. Really, really hurt."

Shame started to overwhelm Siobhán, but then her own hurt elbowed its way in. "At least I didn't start dating your best friend behind your back."

"Is that what you really think?" He turned around and looked her in the eyes.

Confusion landed. She frowned. "It's what I heard."

"I didn't ask you what you heard. I asked you what you thought."

She shook her head. "I don't know. Aisling never said a word. Maria never said a word. And you. You forbid me to talk about us."

Macdara bit his lip. It was obvious he was trying to control his temper. Why was he angry? She was the wronged party.

"For a second I thought you were on top of this entire murder investigation," Macdara said. "But you've just delivered a stark and sobering reminder."

"Of what?"

"Your instincts," he said. "They may be good. Some-times even great. But they certainly aren't always right."

She watched, mouth open as he tipped his cap and headed back inside without another word.

--

Tracy was packing when Siobhán entered her room. The woman let out a startled cry and dropped into the suitcase a blouse she had been trying to fold.

"Don't you people knock?"

"I did," Siobhán lied. "You must not have heard me."

Tracy sighed. "I just can't wait to get home."

"How can you leave when your uncle is still missing?"

Tracy turned red. "*Our uncle?* The one who just admitted to killing our father?"

"I'm not convinced the letter is legitimate."

Tracy slammed the lid of her suitcase down. "I feel sorry for you."

"Excuse me?"

"You're obviously obsessed with your job. I know my uncle's handwriting. He wrote that letter."

"What if he was coerced to write it? Or what if he was protecting all of you?"

"You just can't accept this had a simple answer, can you?"

"It doesn't add up." The note didn't even sound like Frank.

"It does to me. Frank was being blackmailed. My father found out. Was furious that Frank kept it from him. Furious that Frank paid God knows how much money. My father told him he was out of the will, out of the family business. Frank shot him."

"So Frank shot him because he was enraged?"

"Yes. A passion kill."

"Who brought the gun?"

"Pardon?"

"Did Frank bring the gun, or did your father?"

"Frank. I'm sure of it."

"That makes it less about passion and more about premeditated murder."

"So?"

"Either Frank killed his brother out of an impulsive rage, as you suggest, or he meticulously planned it. It can't be both."

Tracy threw her arms up. "Rage."

"But the very existence of a prior stolen gun says otherwise."

"Okay, then he planned it." She clicked the locks on her suitcase.

"And who is this blackmailer?"

Tracy sighed. "I suppose Greta must go through the paperwork and try and figure it out."

"Give me five days. Can't you just stay five days if it means finding out the truth? And if your uncle is guilty, don't you want to see him caught?"

"He said he was going to take his own life. Which proves he has the gun. I'm bringing one relative home to bury. If he killed my father, I don't care what happens to him."

"And if he didn't? Do you care then?"

Tracy grabbed her suitcase and stormed past Siobhán. She knocked into her. Her suitcase dropped to the floor and flew open. Photographs spilled over the edge and glided to the floor in a kaleidoscope of memories.

"Look what you did," Tracy said, dropping to her knees to pick them up. "These were supposed to be for the film. Jay wanted to weave family photos throughout the documentary."

"That's nice," Siobhán said as she knelt to help pick them up. She loved family photographs, even if they weren't her own. The poses, the expressions, the moments caught in time. She lifted one, which featured Tracy as a young girl. She was with a group of other girls. They were smiling. Lined up. Posing. And they were all holding rifles.

She slipped the photograph into her pocket before Tracy could see it. She said she had never held a gun, didn't know her way around a gun. Would this photograph be enough to convince Garda O'Reilly that the Americans needed to remain? Just a few more days?

No.

O'Reilly was furious with her, and elated that he could close the case, call it a success. This photograph wouldn't be enough to change his mind. What was she supposed to do now? She slipped the photograph out of her pocket and held it up so Tracy could see.

"That was my 4-H troop," Tracy said. "What? Why are you looking at me like that?"

Siobhán had no idea what a 4-H troop was, but this was hardly the moment for a lesson in American activities. "You told me you'd never even held a gun."

"Oh," Tracy said. "I forgot about that." Her eyes fixed on a spot in a distant corner.

"You forgot that you used to shoot with a rifle?"

"You misunderstand. We were at a barn that was also a gun range. One of the girls thought it would make a good picture if we posed with the rifles. They weren't loaded, and I certainly never shot with it."

So that's the story. O'Reilly wouldn't hold her based on that. And digging into Tracy's past as a teenager was probably a rabbit hole.

"Five days."

"No." Tracy made it to the door.

"Three?"

"What are you, an auctioneer?"

"If I have to be."

"I'm going home."

"I think you're making a big mistake."

"It won't be the first." And with that, Tracy was gone.

–

Brandon was in Paddy Power, eyes glued to the screen in the corner, hands clutching a betting slip. He looked feverish when Siobhán walked in. "I'm free," he said. "I'm out of the will and I can gamble!" He sounded on the verge of hysteria. "I'm losing," he added. "I'm losing and it still feels good."

Siobhán sighed. *The poor lad. He needs serious help.* This was out of her wheelhouse. "I'm sure you're worried about your uncle," she said. "This is how you deal with stress."

"That killer? You think I care what happens to him?"

"So you're convinced he's the murderer?"

"Of course. Wait. You're not?"

"No."

Brandon turned away from the television and studied Siobhán. "Why not?"

"Why confess now? When he'd almost gotten away with it?"

Brandon shrugged. "The guilt was eating him alive?"

"I don't think so. I think he was trying to protect the family."

"From what?"

"The real killer."

"If he knew who the real killer was, why didn't he just tell someone?"

"Why indeed? They might still have some kind of leverage over the family. Frank has already shown that he'll go to great lengths to protect the family name."

"Don't make a martyr out of him," Brandon said. "He wrote the letter. He's guilty."

"Five days. Just give me five days and then you can leave."

"We leave tomorrow morning. Now if you'll excuse me, I'm going to spend every minute of it here."

"I saw a picture of your sister when she was younger," Siobhán said. "She was with a group of girls, holding a rifle."

Brandon laughed. "You're on about the guns again. You can't blame her for lying. You were determined that anyone who had ever held a gun could be the killer."

So she did know how to shoot that rifle. And Siobhán certainly *could* blame her for lying. Her job would be so much easier if everyone just told the truth.

"Your father would want you to stay and finish the documentary," Siobhán said.

Brandon turned to her with a sad smile. "Our father basically cut us out of his will. This was never about the documentary. This was about shaming all of us."

"I'd say you're doing a pretty good job of that on your own," Siobhán said just before she took her leave.

Macdara was loading his car with luggage when she found him. Her stomach flipped and she forced herself to think about anything. Anything other than him leaving. She showed him the picture of Tracy with the gun.

"Well?" she said when he didn't comment. "Do you think this will buy us some time?"

"No," Macdara said.

"Why not?"

"I'll show you." She followed him back into the station. He entered a meeting room with a television mounted in the corner. "Came in this morning. CCTV footage from Cork City the night of the murder." He pushed the PLAY button. A downtown street in Cork came to life. Macdara pointed to a pub on the corner. "Look at the time." It was almost two in the morning. "Watch." She stared at the screen. A few seconds later, and Tracy Mallon came stumbling out.

"Tracy," Siobhán said. "In Cork City an hour after the murder."

"Pretty solid alibi," Macdara said. "I've already confirmed with the publican. She was in from half eleven to two." Siobhán frowned. Macdara studied her. "We've just eliminated another suspect. You should be happy."

"Do we have footage of Brandon getting into the taxi with his father?"

Macdara shook his head. "But I did find this." He played another tape. On the screen was an image of an old woman walking toward the Kilbane Museum. She had long gray hair, a long coat, and a small red hat. And she was stumbling. The camera cut off after a few seconds.

Siobhán leaned in. "What happened?"

"It could have been the wind. These cameras go off all the time."

"That's all we have?"

Macdara nodded. "Yep."

"Play it again."

They watched the old woman stumble down the street once more. "She's obviously drunk," Macdara said.

"Play it again." Macdara did, and Siobhán leaned in closer. "No," she said. "He's just not used to wearing heels."

"'He'? Are you sure?"

"Yes. That is a man."

Macdara played the tape a final time and leaned in closer. "My God, I think you're right. Is this man, dressed as an old lady, our killer?"

"If so, Brandon is eliminated. He's way too short and stocky."

Macdara shut the television off. "We eliminated Brandon when we walked from Butler's to the church-yard. It's just not enough time for him to get into an argument with his father, shoot him, and pick up all the burned papers on the ground before you arrived."

"If this old lady is our killer, we've certainly just narrowed the suspect list."

"Jay or Frank," Macdara said.

"'Jay or Frank,'" Siobhán repeated. "Or someone outside the Mallon family."

"Closer," Macdara said. "But not good enough."

"We can't just let this case go."

Macdara closed his eyes for a second. "Frank Mallon confessed. There's nothing I can do. There will be other cases."

"You've changed." He opened his eyes and stared at her. Then looked away. "I'm not letting this go," she said softly.

"That's a mistake," he said as he brushed past her. "But it's yours to make."

Chapter 26

Siobhán returned to the bistro, weary and furious with just about everyone—except her siblings. God, she missed them. Maybe this was a blessing in disguise. She didn't need the stress of a murder probe. Not all mysteries were meant to be solved. Everyone else was satisfied that Frank Mallon was the killer. Maybe Macdara was right. Maybe her instincts were off. She was all hot to run to the station after discovering a photograph of Tracy as a young girl holding a gun. And CCTV footage proved Tracy wasn't the killer. But Macdara was right about two things: Eliminating suspects meant they were getting closer. And *closer* wasn't good enough.

She hesitated before entering the bistro, wanting first to rid herself of her bad mood, so she stood outside in the cold, under the robin's-egg-blue sign for Naomi's Bistro, and kept chewing on the case.

The fact that no one had found Frank Mallon was a good indication that he hadn't taken his own life, as he claimed. He'd escaped. Those were the actions of a killer.

Then what was bothering her?

Jay Shepard, for one. She knew there was more to that man than met the eye. Was he willing to give up the documentary? Didn't that mean he was going to lose twenty thousand dollars? She hadn't been able to find him, or Hannah, or Greta, in their rooms. Where were they?

The tinkling of the bell as she entered Naomi's was a welcome sound. The fire was crackling and her siblings were sprawled all over the bistro. For once, Elise was nowhere in sight. The relief of being home, coupled with the fact that there was a killer out there who was going to remain unpunished, hit Siobhán at once, and she burst into tears. Trigger was the first by her side, barking excitedly.

"Oh, pet," Ann said. "What's the matter?" Her sister wrapped her arms around her. Gráinne came in from the other side. "Group hug."

Ciarán raced over and piled on.

"Jaysus," James said. "It's a crying lovefest." He went over and rubbed the top of Siobhán's head, a little too hard. "Come on, Eoin," he said. "Make it complete."

"Bollocks," Eoin said. He ambled over and rubbed Siobhán's head.

"Let her breathe," James said. The huddle broke apart. James guided her to one of the chairs by the fire. "Sit here. I can make you one of your magic coffee drinks if you fancy?"

"A mug of tea will be fine," Siobhán said, wiping her tears.

"Thank God," James said with a wink. "That machine is possessed." He ambled into the kitchen to make the tea.

"What's the story?" Ann said.

"They closed my case," Siobhán said.

"Oh," everyone said in unison.

"What?"

"Is Macdara going back to Dublin?" Gráinne asked softly.

"This isn't about that," Siobhán said. "But yes. He's going back."

"Have you told him you wish he would stay?" Ann said.

"We can tell him for you," Ciarán said.

"This isn't about Macdara," Siobhán said. She couldn't even think about him. She had no control over that situation, and thinking otherwise was only going to get her in a world of hurt. "I don't believe Frank Mallon is a killer. I think he's protecting someone."

James entered with the tea. "If you say he's not the killer, then he's not the killer," James said.

One by one, her siblings nodded. "Really?" Siobhán said. "You believe me?"

"I can't say you're the best," Ciarán said. "But you're pretty good." Everyone laughed, including Siobhán.

"What?" Ciarán said, genuinely puzzled. Siobhán ruffled his hair, and he shook her off.

"Tell us the story," Gráinne said. "Tell us what you're thinking."

"Are you sure?" Siobhán said. She couldn't believe how good it felt that they were listening to her.

"Let's use the whiteboard in the kitchen," Eoin said. James reached out his hand, and when Siobhán took it, he pulled her out of the chair. They entered the kitchen and gathered around the whiteboard in the back. She glanced at Ciarán. James punched him lightly on the arm.

"He can handle it."

Ciarán grinned. "And more."

"I know," Siobhán said, sighing.

"Start from the beginning," James said, handing her a marker. "And leave nothing out."

—

She talked until she was out of breath: She told the story of the brothers and the wife coming over to America, the sordid details of brother attacking brother on the boat, and then assuming his identity. She spoke about Ann and Michael Mallon entering America, pretending to be husband and wife, and the dual headstones. There was the cryptic message on the Irish tombstone, a parting shot from brother to brother and wife, and how Peter was found pointing at the grave with his poor, crooked finger. She went over each suspect. Before the reading of the will there were several possible motives—mostly money. But now they knew that none of them stood to inherit the family fortune. If that was why Peter was murdered, the deed had been done in vain.

But what if there was another motive? Everything kept circling back to Jay Shepard and the blackmail.

"What I don't know," Siobhán said, pacing the floor, "is whether the blackmailer and the killer are one and the same—or whether they are two separate individuals." She needed to find the briefcase that went missing during the blackout at the library. She needed to positively identify the blackmailer. She needed to know who had been dressing up as an old woman and why. And dead or alive, she desperately needed to find Frank Mallon.

She wrote it on the board and circled it: *Find Frank Mallon.*

She stopped, looked at her siblings. They were all staring with rapt attention. "Then that's exactly what you'll do," James said.

Siobhán shook her head. "Work has forbidden me to do it."

"That's never stopped you before," Eoin said. He turned his Yankee baseball cap around on his head.

He loved wearing it backward. He caught her staring and winked. He looked more like a man now than a boy. They were all going to grow up and leave.

"The Americans are leaving tomorrow," Siobhán said. "All my suspects, flying away."

"Then you know what you must do first," James said. "Find a way to stop them."

Siobhán felt a renewed energy. "You guys are the best," she said. Eoin rolled his eyes and then fist-bumped her.

"We know," Gráinne said before flouncing out of the room.

Ann patted Siobhán's cheek. Ciarán took her hand. James folded his arms across his chest. "What can I do to help?"

"You already have. More than you know."

"Be careful," he said. "And let us know if you need us."

"Always," she answered; her fingers were crossed behind her back, though. *Almost always.*

–

Chris Gordon was as surprised to see Siobhán standing in front of his shop door in the dark as she was to see him in pajamas dotted with what appeared to be spaceships.

"Tell me you're here because you want me to tell you a bedtime story." He grinned.

She shook her head and tried to look stern. "Have the guards come yet for Frank Mallon's possessions?"

"They've gone through it. Nobody wanted his belongings. I'm going to donate the rest to Kilbane's Day of Giving." Once again Siobhán had forgotten all about that; it was coming up quick. She hadn't had a second to go through their items, but, luckily, the girls were on it. She felt a squeeze of love for her sisters.

"They've sent me for one more look."

Chris eyed her up and down. "In the middle of the night? In your civilian clothes?"

"Of course," she said, answering as if he was being ridiculous.

He sighed, stood aside. "Be my guest."

She stepped in and looked to the stairwell leading to the upper flats. She glanced at Chris and held back a smile. "'Beam me up, Scotty,'" she said.

-

Frank's room had been straightened. His suitcase was lying on the bed. She rummaged through it and found a paperback tucked in between articles of clothing. From the airport. A thriller. He had been telling the truth about that at least. Almost everyone had lied to her in this investigation. She just didn't see Frank Mallon as the killer, and absolutely everyone was abandoning him.

She sighed. What now? Where could he have gone?

A sob broke out in the room. Siobhán jumped. "Who's there?" She heard a sniffling. It was coming from the closet. She opened the door. There, sobbing on the floor of the closet with her knees pulled up to her chest, was Greta Mallon. She was clutching one of Frank's jackets. She was wearing another. And she was crying much harder than she had over her dead husband.

"Why don't you come out of there," Siobhán said.

"It's my fault. It's all my fault."

"We can talk about it out here." Siobhán reached down and pulled Greta out of the closet. Siobhán guided her over to a chair, near the bed. "Sit." Greta slumped in the chair and started to sob again. Siobhán sat on the edge of the bed. "How long have you and Frank been in love?"

Greta stopped crying and her face turned. Instead of a sweet librarian she looked like a rabid dog. "Nothing has ever happened between us. Nothing."

"I believe you," Siobhán said. "But you love each other. Don't you?"

"How can I love a murderer?" The sobs started again.

"You believe what Frank wrote in that letter?"

"Don't you?"

Siobhán stood up. She remembered Macdara's warning about discussing the case and didn't answer Greta's question. "Did you hear anything in the middle of the night?"

Greta shook her head. "Not a thing."

"When was the last time you spoke to Frank?"

"After the reading of the will."

"Did you know he was paying a blackmailer?"

"No. I swear. Those Mallon men. They kept me out of everything."

"It must have been a shock. Being left out of the family fortune."

Greta regarded Siobhán through her red eyes. "I told you. I didn't marry Peter for money. I loved him. I still love him. But Tracy was right. He wasn't mentally well. He hasn't been for a long time."

"How so?"

"*Obsessed*. Peter was so obsessed with the past. He was also starting to forget things. He had mood swings. He just wasn't my Peter."

"And Frank was there for you." Greta simply blinked. Siobhán leaned down. "Stay. Stay and help me find Frank."

"I can't. I just want to get home so I can start putting this all behind me."

"You're all leaving behind a family member," Siobhán said, standing up and moving away. "What would Peter have said about that?" She didn't like manipulating people with guilt, but she just couldn't believe they were all so willing to abandon Frank.

"If you have reason to believe that Frank didn't kill Peter, tell me," Greta pleaded. "Tell me and I'll stay."

"I don't have anything but questions," Siobhán said.

"The note was in his handwriting. Frank was skimming from the company. He and Peter were at each other's throats. I'm afraid it's that simple. And that horrible."

"What were you doing in the closet?"

"Some people are claustrophobic. I'm the opposite. I like small spaces. I just wanted some comfort."

"You were smelling his jacket."

"So?"

"If you think he's a murderer, why do that?"

Greta sighed. "People are complicated," she said. "I'm complicated." Siobhán nodded. She checked the rest of the closet and found it empty.

"I hope you'll consider staying," Siobhán said as she headed for the door. "At least sleep on it."

–

Siobhán was awake long after her siblings went to sleep. She should be asleep too; she should just forget this failure. She was heading upstairs when she stopped, turned around, and threw on her coat. She was outside before she could even begin to talk herself out of it. The snow was all gone, but the air still held the cold bite of winter. She told herself she was just going for an easy stroll, and the fact that she was headed for the cemetery was just a coincidence. But, of course, she knew better. Criminals liked to return to the scene of the crime. Could the killer be hanging around the cemetery? Did the old lady roam the streets at night?

She had her trusty flashlight with her. Father Kearney might be awake, and could possibly see her go into the cemetery. She kept her torch off as she crept in. Silence enveloped her, thick and uncomfortable, like a stranger's hand wrapped around her neck. The headstones looked like hunched creatures in the cloak of darkness, and the statues that were so enchanting in the daylight transformed into menacing figures.

She started humming to herself, thinking pleasant thoughts. She stopped first at her parents' grave and offered up a prayer and a kiss. Then she tread across the soft grass until she made her way back to John Mallon's grave. She almost expected to see Peter Mallon still lying on the ground. Instead the grass was slightly indented. Father Kearney would not be happy. She glanced up at his building. It was dark. She turned her torch beam on low and focused it on the headstone.

There was a small object sitting on top. She moved closer as the hair on her arms stood up. It was an American flag pin—such as the one Peter Mallon had been wearing.

Brandon said that his father took off his pin just before heading to the churchyard.

John Butler confirmed it.

When Peter Mallon entered the cemetery, he was not wearing the pin.

Therefore…

After he or she murdered him, the killer placed another American flag pin on Peter. And now, one was back, sitting on top of the headstone. A respectful token, or a killer's calling card?

Chapter 27

Siobhán continued to stare at the tiny American flag pin sitting on the headstone. She was right. Instinct told her she was right. The killer put the pin on Peter *after* he or she murdered him. But why? So that the guards could identify him? Because they didn't realize Peter had announced he wasn't going to wear it anymore?

She was dying to pick up the pin on the headstone now. Where had it come from? Jay Shepard said he had only given them out to the family members. Was that the truth?

Maybe none of that was important in the moment. *When* had the pin been left? Could she have just missed someone? She turned off her torch and shivered. Then she turned it back to the grass. She could see a swath of grass lying on its side as if recently walked on. She slowly began to walk in the direction of the disturbance. The path led to the opposite end of the cemetery, where, if she remembered correctly, it was possible to exit. She kept the light on the ground, hoping to catch more abnormalities or even objects hidden in the slick blades. If only there was still snow on the ground and she could follow footprints. She reached the stone wall and began to follow it to the exit. After several feet she found it: a gap in the stones where a person could squeeze out, or, if they were so inclined, jump over. She decided to squeeze. Now what? She was facing the back of Saint Mary's. The rising steeple, barely visible in the dark, still offered a bit of comfort. Around the front was the town square, but if she veered left behind it, she would come upon George Dunne's house and Kelly's pub, which had been abandoned forever...

A perfect place for someone to hide.

Had Frank Mallon come to visit, laid the American flag pin on his ancestor's headstone? She began to jog in the direction of Kelly's, trying to keep her breath even. She would just peek in the windows; if anything looked amiss or if it appeared someone was holed up inside, she wouldn't go in. She would call Garda O'Reilly this time. One might even say she was learning her lessons.

–

Siobhán neared the back of Kelly's. The back door was padlocked. The windows dark. She looked for signs that a human had been here recently. But the grass and footpath to the door were pristine.

Not a drop of litter.

Her alarm bells went off. Just the other day she'd noticed litter piled up in the back of the pub. There should be cigarette butts, empty crisp packets, at least a lone bottle of Bulmers. Someone had recently cleaned up every drop of rubbish. It could have been volunteers from the church, given the proximity. But every year Kilbane had a cleanup day, and it was always in the spring. Was Frank Mallon hiding out here? Had he cleaned up first?

But if Frank was inside, he hadn't entered through the back. Besides the padlock, none of the windows were disturbed or broken. She hugged the building, inching her way to the front entrance. Ironically, the Kilbane Gardai Station was only a few blocks away. Wouldn't it be something if Frank Mallon was hiding right underneath their noses? There were only a few street lamps lit nearby. Kelly's was dark, but the nearby lights were enough to see the front windows and door. Like the back, the front door was padlocked. Too many young ones would sneak in if the door was left to their mischievous plans.

Siobhán's current skill set did not include breaking and entering. If she had been on official duty, there would be guards she could call to ram down the door or saw through the padlock, but, of course, she was here simply as a concerned citizen with insomnia.

She reached the front windows, cupped her hands, and peered in. Between smudges on the panes and the darkness inside, she couldn't make out a thing. Her suspicions were rattled once again, for it appeared someone had purposefully smeared the dirt from the inside of the windows to make it harder to see in. She was on full alert. Frank Mallon was either here now or had been here. She was sure of it. She just hoped he hadn't followed through with the threat in his note.

If only Macdara was here. She was sure he would approve an entrance. She started to pace in front of the building. She went back to the window and tapped on it. It was more instinct than anything else. Maybe she would be able to sense movement. Maybe she would startle him and he would cry out. Her actions were met with silence.

There was no outside latch on the windows. It was a squat stone building. How had he entered? She went from pane to pane, trying to see if she could open one. It wasn't until she reached the very last window that she felt it give. Her heart rate tripled as she lifted it open. It stopped after a foot, but it was enough to crawl in. Frank was tall but thin; he could have wriggled through. Before she could talk herself out of it, Siobhán was already shimmying through the window. The front half of her body dangled inside the pub, and her hands searched the dark to find something to hold on to so that she could pull her legs in. Her torch was tucked down her pants—not the brightest move in retrospect. Her hands hit what felt like a bench, so she touched them down and brought her legs in. As she leaned more weight into the bench, a loud creak sounded and the wood beneath her hands caved in, sending her crashing to the floor. She landed with her full weight on top of her hands and cried out from the pain.

She lay still for a few seconds, fully appreciating the mistake of having a torch down her pants. Paying her dues, as they say. At least it hadn't been a long fall.

So much for a stealthy entrance. If Frank Mallon was indeed alive, hiding in here, and asleep, he would probably be awake by now. She clamped her mouth shut, heart beating in her ears, pain roaring through her wrist. *Please don't be broken or sprained.* She lifted herself up a few inches, going slowly, holding her breath. She moved her hands. *Only a little pain.* She brought them up, flexed them, moved them in circles. *Oh, thank you, God.* She stood, blinking, waiting for her eyes to adjust to the pitch-black surroundings.

The pub had been closed for the past five years, but she'd had her very first drink here and she knew the layout well. She didn't want to use her torch, unless she had no choice. It could draw attention from someone outside. If Frank was in here, the killer could be watching. She retrieved the torch and gripped it tightly. In a pinch it could be a formidable weapon.

"Frank?" she called. "I'm here to help you." Shapes were now making sense. Most of the red leather seats and booths remained, as well as the oak bar, with the gilded mirror and shelving behind it, and the heavy lamps hanging from above. Any object that could be carried out had already been spirited away, but what remained was oddly comforting, as if the past was right alongside her, instead of far behind. "Frank? It's Garda *O'Sullivan*. I'm off duty."

Well, that sounded moronic. Too bad the pub was closed, or she could pull up a stool and ask him to join her for a pint. The odor of stale beer hung in the air, a smell she personally found appealing, right up there with the smell of petrol. She began to walk the length of the pub slowly, all senses alert in case someone wanted to sneak up on her from behind. Although guards didn't carry guns, she did receive training in basic self-defense and combative moves. She walked slowly and had the torch on the ready.

She was wrong. No one was here. She finished walking the length of the pub and turned to make her way back. He might have been here at one time, for someone had smeared the windows from the inside, but it was as silent as a tomb. "I don't think you're a killer," she said. "I hope you're okay." She took another few steps, navigating tables and chairs in the middle of the pub. She was about to pass the last round table, but then she saw what appeared to be a figure sitting against the back wall of the pub, knees drawn up, dark eyes, which seemed almost to glow, staring at her. It was a man sitting still, but his eyes were open and he was staring straight at her. She cried out. "Oh! Oh! You're here. You scared me." The man did not move or speak, but continued to stare. It was the creepiest thing she'd ever seen, and she lifted the torch, fighting the urge to run.

"Why aren't you speaking?" She heard a moan, and turned on her torch. She saw thick bands of rope binding Frank Mallon's hands and feet in front of him. A large knot hung just below his chin, as if it had once gagged him, but he'd spit it out.

"Cant. Talk," he said. His voice was hoarse. He must have spent his first few hours in captivity screaming.

"Oh, God." She hurried forward. "I'm here, I'm here," she said. He nodded his head, eyes wild with fear, and then relief. She aimed the flashlight at the rope binding his hands and feet. It was tied tight and in several knots. She couldn't get a single knot undone. "I have to find a knife."

He tried to say something, jerking his head toward the bar. "Good idea." She hurried back to the bar, keeping the torch at high beam. *So much for being the murderer. Surely, Garda O'Reilly would agree that this man couldn't tie himself up.*

She stopped.

But if she untied him and then called the guards, what would happen to her? Would O'Reilly fire her?

Of course he would. He was looking for that very excuse. She couldn't let them know she was in here. She hurried back to Frank and knelt beside him. "Listen to me. Are you listening?"

He nodded his head. "I'm going to call the guards." He jerked his head once again in the direction of the bar.

"Knife," he hissed.

Poor fella. She couldn't blame him. But she also couldn't lose her job. "They can't know I was here. They found your note and shut the books on the murder probe. If I

284

step out of line again, I'm fired. I'm going to leave. And then I'm going to throw a large rock through the window. Don't worry, I'll aim at the windows away from you. Then I'm going to pull the alarm at the gardai station. I'll find a hiding space, but keep a close watch to make sure you're rescued. Will you promise not to mention I was here?"

There was a long pause; then he nodded. "One more thing. Did you murder your brother?" He shook his head again, slower this time. "Did someone force you to write that confession?" His head remained still, his eyes unblinking. She saw terror lurking behind them. "Are you afraid for your family?" He nodded. "Okay. Okay." She swore under her breath. "Will you tell me who did this? Will you help me catch the real killer?"

Tears filled his eyes. He blinked several times. Shook his head.

"He has something over you?" He shook his head again. She had no idea what he was trying to say. They would have to wait until he could talk.

"Does this have anything to do with Greta?" He kept bobbing his head. Her eyes traveled down and that's when she saw it. A piece of paper sticking out of the pocket of his suit jacket. She plucked it out.

I do not like the way my brother looks at my wife…

She stared at Frank. Tears welled and started to run down his cheeks. She tucked the journal entry back in his pocket. "The guards will be here soon. You're going to be okay." She hurried out before she could be persuaded by his desperate moans and pleading eyes.

Chapter 28

Siobhán was helping with the breakfast service when she turned to find Macdara sitting at a table by the window. Time stood still for a brief second. If this had been a few years ago, she'd be approaching with his usual, an Irish breakfast and a mug of Barry's tea.

He gave her a look as she approached. "Frank Mallon was found last night."

"Was he?" Siobhán said, hoping her voice didn't crack.

"The alarm sounded at the gardai station. When that didn't rouse anyone, an anonymous caller tipped off the guards to his location."

"Lovely." There was only one pay phone left in town and she'd probably been the first to use it for its intended purpose in ages. She shuddered to think of all the unintended uses. Going above and beyond the call of duty, she was.

Macdara lasered her with his pretty blue eyes. "Aren't you going to ask me whether he's alive or dead?"

"Of course." She waited.

Macdara shook his head, leaned in, and lowered his voice. "What happened to 'by the book'?"

"I'm going to get you an Irish breakfast and mug of tea," Siobhán said. "I forgot how cranky you can get before you've had your feed." She whirled around and headed for the kitchen, trying to diffuse the huge grin spreading across her face.

–

Frank Mallon had been taken to hospital, although all predictions were that he was going to be released after he was treated for dehydration and a few rope burns. The family had delayed their flights back, and even Hannah remained behind.

"We're sorry we accused you," Tracy was saying to Frank as Siobhán and Macdara entered the hospital room. Frank's eyes flitted to Siobhán and he gave a quick nod, then broke contact. He hadn't said a word about her to the guards. She was grateful.

"He won't tell us what happened," Greta said. "I hope you can get it out of him."

"We will," Macdara said. "In the meantime listen carefully, please. For your own safety we are posting guards at the entrance to your flats. We are also asking that none of you go anywhere alone, and that you are safely inside once it gets dark."

The group, weary and shell-shocked, nodded their heads. Siobhán bit her lip. *Doesn't that mean they'll all be locked in with the killer?*

"Cameras have been set up in the hallways and in all of the rooms," Macdara said. "I'm sorry for the intrusion of privacy."

"But one of us is a killer," Brandon said.

"I don't want to stay there anymore," Hannah said.

"You can stay in my room," Jay said. "I'll sleep on the floor."

"How generous," Tracy said.

"That's enough, all of you," Greta said. "We need to be here for Frank."

"Three days," Tracy said. "And then I'm going home."

"Me too," Brandon said.

"Three for me," Hannah said.

Macdara sighed. "We'll work as fast as we can."

"*Three days*," Tracy said again. "And not a second more."

–

Frank Mallon was ready and eager to tell Siobhán and Macdara his story. "I was in my room," he said. "I must have forgotten to lock the door. Suddenly someone came up behind me. They immediately blindfolded me and stuck a gun up to my cheek. 'Don't move or scream,' they said."

"Was it a male or female voice?"

"It sounded male, but I could tell they were making an effort to disguise their voice." He squinted. "He had an Irish accent too, but it sounded forced. Not natural like yours."

"As if he was pretending to have an Irish accent."

Frank nodded. "That's my guess."

"You didn't recognize his voice?"

"I could barely hear over the beating of my own heart. I didn't think I was so terrified of death, but you don't know for sure until you're that close to the hangman."

"Then what?"

"I heard him place something on the desk in front of me. He told me he was going to remove my blindfold, but if I turned around, I would be shot. I agreed, of course. When the blindfold was removed, I saw what had been placed in front of me. A typed letter. Telling me exactly what to write."

"The confession," Siobhán said.

"Yes. The so-called confession. I was told if I didn't write and sign it, he was going to kill me." He threw up his hands. "What choice did I have?"

"And then?"

"After I wrote and signed the confession, the blindfold was put back on. I was then guided out of the room, down the stairs, and outside. I didn't know it at the time but I was taken to Kelly's pub. Tied up. I was left with food and water. Two days later I was found." He did not look at Siobhán.

"Were you blindfolded the entire time?" Siobhán asked. He was not blindfolded or gagged when she found him.

"No," Frank said, blinking rapidly. "My hands were tied in front of me. He told me I was free to remove my blindfold and gag after he left."

"Did he wear cologne? What did his shoes sound like on the footpath? Are you sure it was a man? Could you sense his height?" Siobhán couldn't help it; the questions came spilling out from her. She felt Macdara's hand on her arm.

Frank held his head as if it hurt. "I was terrified. One never knows until death has you in its jaws how you'll react. I couldn't think, let alone see. I felt him more than anything. I can't possibly guess his height, since I was blindfolded, and I didn't smell him."

He was getting annoyed at the questions.

"Why you?" Siobhán said.

"Perhaps I was an easy target?" he ventured. "History repeating itself? Poetic justice? And everyone believed, didn't they? His plan worked perfectly. Except, of course, he didn't count on me being found." His eyes flicked to Siobhán again, and Macdara glared at her.

Siobhán ignored Macdara. "Why didn't he just kill you?" Frank gasped. "Sorry," Siobhán said. "But it's a question we have to ask." Was the killer toying with Frank? Or was there something he wanted from him before he murdered him? Or did the killer not want to kill again?

"You have to catch him," Frank said. "Or he might come back and finish the job!"

Macdara shifted and looked around, as if trying to pretend they weren't in a hospital. "We still haven't found your briefcase."

"I don't know who took it," Frank said. "But I have something else. It's not much." He reached into his pocket. "The man who tied me up dropped this."

It was Jay's business card. The one with the tree. "Can I see that?" He handed it to Siobhán.

"I miss my brother," Frank said. He started to cry, his shoulders heaved as the sobs increased. "It shouldn't have ended like this. Not like this."

Siobhán studied the business card. In the top right corner she could see a smudge and a little hole. "What happened here?"

Frank sniffed and wiped his eyes. "Jay used to have the American flag pin on his cards," he said. "That one must have fallen off."

Siobhán felt a tingle up her spine. They stayed until a nurse came in and said that Frank needed to rest.

"Wait!" Frank called before they exited. They turned around. His eyes were wide. "I think it was a family member."

Siobhán stepped forward. "What do you mean? Tracy? Brandon?"

"No, no. A descendent of John Mallon. You see, when John Mallon returned to Ireland, he went on to marry. They had a child."

"How do you know this?"

"I started to do some research. My research was in the briefcase too."

"What did you find out?"

"John Mallon married a woman named Lucy. They had a daughter. Her name was Tara. That's as far as I got. I was going to follow the thread to see whom she married and if she had children, but I didn't get that far."

"Did anyone else know you had done this research?" He looked away. "Greta," Siobhán said softly.

He nodded. "I asked for her help. She's good at tracking things down."

"Indeed," Siobhán said.

"It's not what you think. Greta isn't a killer."

"It's not against the law to fall in love," Siobhán said. "Did Peter know?"

"No!" Frank said. "Nothing ever happened between us. I swear. There was nothing *to* know."

"We'll take it from here," Macdara said. "Don't say a word to the others." Frank nodded. "We'll have a guard on you twenty-four/seven."

"Thank you," Frank said. "And Greta? Someone is watching after her too?"

"We're watching everyone," Macdara said.

"One more thing," Siobhán said. "Did you visit John Mallon's grave recently? Did you place anything on the headstone?"

Frank shook his head. "I told you, I was kidnapped and tied up." He narrowed his eyes. "Why?"

"We're here to ask questions, not answer them," Siobhán said. Macdara slipped out the door ahead of her, but not before she caught the smile on his face.

–

Siobhán and Macdara stood outside the hospital. It was situated on a beautiful piece of land, surrounded by rolling hills. The skies this morning were a hopeful shade of blue. Siobhán took a moment to drink in the view. "Spill," he said.

"I went back to the cemetery the other day. Someone had placed an American flag pin on John Mallon's headstone." She held up the business card. "Perhaps it was the one that used to be pinned on here."

"When was this?"

"Just before Frank Mallon was found." She deliberately left the timeline vague.

"And you didn't think to mention this before."

"Let's just say I got distracted."

He squinted at her, then sighed. "Let's go see if it's still there."

–

They stood in front of John Mallon's grave. Even Siobhán was surprised to see that the pin was still resting on top of the tombstone.

"Should we call the guards?" Siobhán said. "Get fingerprints?"

"One of the family members could have left it as a token of respect," Macdara said. "It doesn't necessarily point to our killer." He glanced across the graves and his eyes landed on Kelly's in the distance. "Uh-huh," he said.

Siobhán kept her gob shut.

They started to exit. In the very back corner of the churchyard was a single mausoleum. Usually covered with moss, and tucked away, it wasn't a structure Siobhán had ever taken the time to explore. They were just passing it and Siobhán noticed something odd. She stopped and looked closer. The massive iron door, with a tiny viewing window, was ajar. A padlock and chain hung from the handle. She reached out and grabbed Macdara's arm. "Look!"

"Slowly," he said, putting a finger up to his lips. Siobhán nodded. They started for it, bodies alert, and poised. They positioned themselves on either end of the door. Macdara reached for his torch. "Maybe you should stay out here."

"No way," she said. "I'm right behind you." They stepped into the tomb, torches shining. Their light bounced over a stone crypt, sconces on the walls, dried flowers, ancient mass cards, and numerous Celtic crosses. They shone their lights in the far corners. Cobwebs decorated the ceiling. A damp, musty smell rose up, as if to drive them out. They stepped in farther. A glint of silver in the far corner caught Siobhán's eye.

"There!" She moved forward and Macdara followed. A groan sounded behind them as the iron door clanged and swung shut with a thud. They were sealed in.

"Hey," Siobhán said. They ran to the door. The padlock snapped, and a heavy chain thudded against the door. Siobhán peered out the tiny window. A tall person in a tan coat, long gray hair, and a red cap was running away. "It's the old *lady*." *Definitely a man.*

Macdara edged her out of the way and peered through. "Hey!" he said. "Stop!" Siobhán didn't have to be looking out the window to know that the old lady didn't stop. Macdara pushed on the door, to no avail.

He patted his pockets and brought out his mobile at the same time Siobhán did. She glanced at her screen. "No reception."

"Me either."

Siobhán tried not to panic, despite her worst fears swarming around her mind. How often did anyone ever come in here? "*Never*" was the answer. Nobody ever came in here. Now that the door was closed and locked, nothing would look amiss from the outside. Even if someone was standing near the building, could they be heard shouting? She never thought of herself as claustrophobic, but she felt a clawing desire to get out. "We're going to die in a crypt," she whispered. "If that's not irony, I don't know what is."

"Might as well check it out," Macdara said, taking the torch from her and aiming it at the corner. "My God."

Siobhán edged her way in. There, under the beam of light, was an antique revolver. "The murder weapon." She took a step forward, and Macdara's arm clamped down on hers.

"Best not to touch it."

Siobhán stopped. "Why did the murderer just lock us in here with the murder weapon?"

"They don't think it will matter." Macdara's soft, deep voice was comforting, but his words chilled her to the bone.

"Meaning they don't think we'll be found in time to talk." She inched closer to the revolver. "Shine the light again." Soon the revolver was illuminated. Siobhán saw a white piece of paper sticking out. "It's another journal entry." She crouched down as he kept the light steady. She read it out loud: "'Spoke with Ann. We will part ways with Michael when we arrive in New York. Slip off to Philadelphia. I'm afraid he means me harm.'"

Siobhán sighed. "This may be the last thing we ever read. Why couldn't he have left *War and Peace* and some crisps, and some chocolates?"

"'*War and Peace?*'" Macdara asked.

"It's long," Siobhán. "I'm trying to be an optimist."

"Whiskey," Macdara said. "As soon as I get out of here, I'm having a whiskey." He turned to her and tried to smile. "Someone will come for us."

She shook her head. "Father Kearney never even comes in here. Nobody ever comes in here."

"Just breathe."

"Do you have no sense of smell? I've been holding me breath!"

Macdara shone the light around the inside, carefully going over the place, stone by stone. There were small cracks in the ceiling letting in strips of light. "We'll think of something."

She stepped closer to him and he grabbed her hands. "This doesn't look good, does it?" she whispered.

"Someone will find us."

"We didn't tell anyone where we were going."

He sighed. "We ought to be able to catch rainwater through those cracks."

Siobhán jerked her hands away. "You think we'll be stuck that long?"

"I hope not. I'm just trying to calm you down."

"Try another tactic, because you're doing the exact opposite of calming me down."

"Maybe if we hold our phones closer to the crack in the ceiling, we'll be able to get reception."

"Good idea." They shone their lights on the ceiling. "We'll have to climb on top of the crypt." Siobhán's voiced echoed in the tiny, damp chamber.

Macdara sighed. "I know."

The crypt was lying on a strong stone base. It would hold Siobhán's weight, but she hated stepping on it. "It feels so disrespectful."

Macdara shone the light on the name. "'Daniel Eagan,'" he said. "No disrespect, but we're not quite ready to join you."

Siobhán crossed herself and Macdara followed suit. "I'll lift you up. Hold your mobile close to the cracks and see if you can get a signal."

He lifted her up onto the crypt and she steadied herself before standing up and stretching toward the ceiling. When she had a grip on her balance, she lifted her mobile toward the crack. She watched as it went from no signal to one bar. Then two. It stopped there.

"Two bars."

"Try 999."

She dialed. The call immediately cut off. "Not enough of a signal."

"Try a text." She stared at the phone. "Well?"

"I don't know who to text."

"Who's the one person you'd text if you were really in trouble?"

Is he serious? "You," she said softly.

"I deserved that."

You deserve a lot more. "I'll try all my siblings." She started with James, although she knew he was lazy about checking his phone unless he was separated from Elise:

> Help. Locked in crypt in churchyard. Call
> guards or Father Kearney.

He was probably going to think it was a joke. "I didn't get an error message. Hopefully, it went through."

"Good, good."

"I'll keep texting everyone I know."

"Do you have Garda O'Reilly's number?"

"Are you kidding? He hates me."

"I have it in my phone. I'll toss it to you. Are you ready?"

"Yes." He tossed his mobile and she managed to catch it without falling off.

"Good catch."

"Thanks." She turned his phone over.

"Wait," he said in a shout, panic in his voice.

It gave her a jolt and she almost lost her footing. "Don't do that."

"Just toss my phone back."

But she didn't. She looked at the screen. Staring back at her was a photograph of herself. At her graduation ceremony from Templemore Garda College. A lump immediately formed in her throat. "You were there?" she asked. Macdara cursed softly under his breath. Silence echoed through the crypt. "Dara?" She hadn't used the shortened version of his name since they'd been together.

"You weren't supposed to see that."

"Where did you get this? Were you there?"

"Just text O'Reilly."

"Answer me. Please."

He sighed. "Of course I was there." Anger and hurt poured from him. "Do you think I would miss it?" In addition to the lump in her throat, tears were welling in her eyes. She was grateful for the dark. "And if you must know, my meetings with Aisling were all about you. She was giving me progress reports, since I'm not on Facebook."

"You should really be on Facebook." Her attempt at humor was undercut by the tremor in her voice.

"I am never going to be on Facebook. If someone wants to see my face, it's easy enough to do in person."

She was pondering whether or not to tell him how much she loved his handsome face, when her phone dinged, startling her. It was a text from Ciarán: *Ha ha*.

She let out an exasperated cry. "It's Ciarán. He says, 'Ha ha.'"

"At least it went through. Tell him."

Not joking. Call 999 and Father Kearney.

On my way.

No! Stay in school. Just make the calls.

Already thrown out for texting during class.

Siobhán sighed and repeated the conversation to Macdara. His soft chuckle filled the space. "I'm afraid we'll have to forgive him for this one."

Siobhán crouched down and within seconds Macdara was there to help her down, his arms secure around her as he helped her to the floor. When she landed, he didn't break away.

"I'm sorry," he said softly.

Tears welled in her eyes. "Me too."

"I'm proud of you."

She nodded, barely trusting her voice. "Back at ye." She launched herself into his arms, holding him tightly in case she never got the chance again, and soon she felt his arms encircle her.

"There's something I'd want more than whiskey if I was facing the end of my life," he said.

"What?"

"This." Before she could respond, his lips were over hers. She sank into the kiss, and kissed him back, as years of wanting him came rushing into this moment. And it may have been two years since she'd been kissed, and she was no expert, but it seemed even better than before. He certainly hadn't forgotten how to make her nerve endings sing. When they finally pulled away, she could hear the pounding of their hearts. She could have kept shifting him forever. At least until she really had to pee. Which was pretty much right now.

Voices rang out, calling their names. They parted and ran for the door.

"Macdara? Siobhán?" It was Father Kearney.

"In here!" they said in stereo.

"It's padlocked," Father Kearney said. "Who did this?"

"We didn't see," Macdara said. "Just get us out!"

"I'll have to call the volunteer fire department."

"Understood," Macdara said.

"I'll be back."

"Hurry," Siobhán said.

"Don't want to be stuck with me any longer?" Macdara said. "Guess I'm the one who should be nervous. Locked up with you and a loaded gun."

"Don't take it so personally," Siobhán said. "I drank three cappuccinos this morning."

Hearty laughter rang out. "So what should we chat about?" he said, mischief dancing in his voice. "Water-falls?"

Chapter 29

"Now?" Macdara said. "You have to go for a run right now?" The guards had come to retrieve the murder weapon. Ballistics and fingerprints would take some time to come back. Siobhán wasn't hopeful, chances were good that the killer had worn gloves.

"Yes," Siobhán said. "I have to go for a run right now."

"It's not your lunch hour."

"I have to go for a run right now."

"Why?"

"Because there's something rattling around in my brain and running helps me think."

"Something to do with the business card?"

So he still had it, his annoying ability to read her mind. "Please. Just let me go for a run."

"I'm coming with you."

"I'm going to run far and I'm going to run fast," she said.

Macdara sucked in his stomach. Then sighed and let it out. "I'll do me best to keep up," he said.

–

There was satisfaction in hearing Macdara strain beside her. Siobhán started the run in her usual way. Down Sarsfield Street, then past the museum and out to the field, where the abbey stood. Over the bridge, through the field to the abbey, and around it. This time, just because he was starting to breathe hard, Siobhán entered the abbey. She sprinted up the steps leading to the bell tower, then flew back down, passing Macdara, who stood at the bottom of the steps with his hands on his hips and a frown on his face.

She bypassed him and sprinted out, back to the field, and instead of heading back to the roads, she wound her way up to the medieval fence and settled into a slower pace as she jogged along it. She cleared her mind and focused solely on her breath and the sound of her trainers hitting the ground. She had never imagined she'd be able to reach this state when she first started jogging. The runner's high she supposed. Where you melted into your body and quieted down. Where nothing mattered but the feel of the wind, and the push of the muscles. Macdara must have entered a similar state, for he was no longer laboring beside her, but keeping up in a comfortable rhythm. She had never run with Macdara before and she was startled how comfortable it was, how easy.

They headed in the direction of what used to be Sheedy's cycle shop, now abandoned, circled the property, and headed downhill. Siobhán stopped at the bottom of the hill, put her hands on her knees, and breathed in and out.

"You've upped your game," Macdara said. "You're fast."

"Thank you."

"Did you solve the case?" Siobhán met his grin with a glare. "Can we unwind my way now?"

"What did you have in mind?"

Maria's broad smile greeted Siobhán and Macdara as they stepped into O'Rourke's, sat at the counter, and ordered pints.

"This isn't my normal cooldown," Siobhán said, lifting her pint.

"I think we've earned it," Macdara said, clinking her glass. "*Sláinte.*"

"Cheers." They sipped in silence for a moment.

"Start talking."

"The killer didn't want to kill again. Don't you find that strange?"

"You mean they didn't kill Frank."

"And," Siobhán said, "they didn't kill us."

"Tells us he or she may not be as cold-blooded as we thought. Perhaps they didn't want to kill Peter. Only threaten him."

"I believe that Peter's response to the family's secret being unearthed enraged the killer."

"How do you mean?"

"First came the blackmail. They blackmailed Frank. He cooperated and was paying. But when Peter learns of the blackmail, the payments stop."

"Maybe that's why they didn't kill Frank."

"I think so too. But there's something bothering me. According to Greta, Peter would have wanted the truth to come out."

"Go on."

"Frank was behaving in a way that was predicted. It's all building up to their arrival in Ireland and the documentary. I think the killer wanted to hold all the cards, and play them at his or her discretion. Possibly use the documentary to do so."

"But Peter started nosing around." Macdara finished his pint. Siobhán gawked. She'd only taken a few sips of hers. "We've been through all this."

"But we've learned something new. The killer feels remorse. So much so that he or she puts the American flag pin back on Peter's coat as he lies there in the snow. A killer who didn't know that Peter had announced to his wife that he wasn't going to wear it anymore."

"Are you saying Greta is no longer a suspect because she wouldn't have put the pin back on him?"

"Not necessarily."

Macdara sighed. "You're losing me."

"Greta made sure to mention it. 'He must have changed his mind.' That's what she first said. I asked what she meant. Maybe she was hoping that we would eliminate her. Come to this very conclusion and say, 'Why would she put the pin back on when she knew he stopped wearing it? Why else would anyone care to put a pin back on a dead man?'"

"Why indeed," Macdara said. "But once again you're suggesting that she did all this hoping we'd catch these little clues. It's a bit far-fetched. And she doesn't inherit the bulk of the fortune."

"She didn't know that at the time. And we still haven't thoroughly checked all the so-called charities that do inherit the bulk of the estate."

"True."

"And she definitely wouldn't have killed Frank Mallon."

"Interesting," Macdara said. "Greta somewhat clears herself by distracting us with the bit about the American pin. And Frank clears himself by confessing, then being found nearby, tied up, and claiming it was a false confession."

"Making us clear both of them for the murder."

"My God," Macdara said. "If they're behind this, it's quite genius."

"I thought you said it was far-fetched."

Macdara looked at Siobhán. "Do you think it's them? Did Greta and Frank set this up?"

"No," Siobhán said. "I just think that somebody wants us to think that. Somebody with knowledge of the past, a grudge against it, and a flair for the dramatic."

Macdara nudged his empty pint glass toward the bar. "What aren't you telling me?"

Siobhán looked away. She had feelings, not enough to amount to a theory, and she wasn't ready to commit to them. And even if her feelings turned into a solid theory, she still didn't have any hard evidence. "I have a few more things to look into."

He pointed at her. "You aren't supposed to go rogue."

"It's nothing dangerous. I want to finish researching John Mallon's descendents."

"Oh," Macdara said, relief lighting up his eyes. "Yes, you can do that all by yourself."

"Gee, thanks."

"But ring me if it unveils anything. Anything at all."

–

Siobhán had just reached the bistro when she heard someone running behind her. Brandon was on her heels, sweating profusely. She turned around and he came to an abrupt stop in front of her.

"I just thought of something." He paused to catch his breath, then stepped closer.

Siobhán wanted to back up, but didn't want to signal weakness, so she forced herself to endure his invasion of her space. "What?"

"Something's been bothering me."

"I'm listening."

"My father was left-handed."

"Okay," she said. "So?"

"Why was he pointing with his right finger?"

"Maybe his left was occupied. Or maybe his arthritis was flaring up."

"Arthritis?"

"Yes. His index finger was crooked."

Brandon shook his head. "I don't know anything about that. I didn't even know he had arthritis."

"Happens to all of us when we age."

Brandon's face darkened. "I still think he would have pointed with his dominant hand."

"I'll keep that in mind. See if anything occurs to me," Siobhán said.

-

She put the DVD into the player. *Dancing Irish.* Most of it was centered on the talented and adorable little girl. She watched the entire thing. Nothing seemed to relate to the current case. She sighed, then made herself a cappuccino. The door banged open and Ann came in, dragging her camogie bag. She dropped it in the hall and entered the bistro with Gráinne.

"It was right in front of her face!" Ann said. "How can you not hit a ball when it's right in front of your face?"

"Ah, don't let your pride get the best of ye," Gráinne said. She was wearing high heels and a short skirt. She kicked the heels off. "How do women walk in these things? My feet are killing me."

"I told ye," Ann said. "You look ridiculous in them too."

"Do you want to say that again, to my fist?"

"You mean to my face."

"No. To my fist." Gráinne made a fist. Ann stuck out her tongue. Siobhán stared at the heels on the floor.

Right in front of my face.

—

The Kilbane Museum had a copy of Jay Shepard's documentary *Dancing Irish*. Siobhán assumed Jay Shepard had dropped the documentary off recently. On *this* visit to Kilbane. But when she'd told him George Dunne had found a copy of the DVD in the museum, he was browned off. Annoyed that someone dared to donate his precious documentary. So if he didn't donate it recently, how long had it been at the Kilbane Museum? Siobhán threw on her coat and headed over.

Pio was behind the counter, plucking strings on his guitar. Siobhán asked about the DVD. "I told you, I don't know what happened to our copy."

"I just want to know when you received it."

"When?"

"Do you keep a log of donations?"

"Hold on." He leaned under the counter and came up with a notebook. He flipped through it. Turned the records around to Siobhán. Six months ago. The DVD had been donated to the museum six months ago. No name was attached to the donation. But it didn't matter. It was the timing that interested Siobhán. She took a photo of the page. "Keep this book safe. The guards might be asking for it soon."

Pio's eyebrow shot up. "Why?"

"Official business. Not a word to anyone."

Pio mimed zipping his lips. "Must be some documentary," he said. She stared at the space under the counter, where he'd retrieved the donation book. An image of the counter in Kelly's flashed into her mind. The mirror was a secret door. It opened into a safe. Mike Kelly used to hide valuables in there. She'd forgotten all about that. Had the guards checked behind the mirror? Probably not, she hadn't even thought of it until now.

She had an appointment in Limerick to check into more records of John Mallon. Cork County didn't have a marriage license or any records of his children, so she was going to check Limerick. But that would have to wait. On the way out she noticed a flyer for Kilbane's Day of Giving hanging by the door. It was coming up. She thought back to the charities to which Peter Mallon had left the bulk of his estate, including ones in Ireland. Something else that warranted more research. She could feel the clues gathering around her like storm clouds, hovering and threatening. She was close. There were a few more dots left to connect, and then she needed to prove it.

-

Siobhán was hurrying back to Kelly's when Macdara popped up in front of her. "Where are you going?"

"Kelly's. I think the briefcase could be there."

"We searched the pub."

"We forgot a hiding place."

"Let's go."

She was so close to solving this that there was part of her ego that didn't want to share. She understood Jay Shepard a little more, his desire to launch a big surprise, a dramatic reveal. But she was a member of a group now, a tribe. She told him about her visit to the museum and how the DVD was donated six months prior.

"What are you thinking?" he said. "That Jay Shepard was visiting Kilbane six months ago?"

"It's worth checking out. But not necessarily. The documentary could have easily been purchased by someone in Kilbane, and when they were done watching it, they donated it to the museum."

"Right," he said. "I guess we can check into travel records for Jay Shepard, or ask him about it."

He wasn't quite putting the pieces together the way she was. And yet he wouldn't be able to accuse her of not sharing. She then told him about Brandon's declaration that his father was left-handed.

"I think a person could easily point with either hand, don't you?" Macdara asked.

"I'm right-handed," Siobhán said. "I would not point with my left."

"He'd just been shot," Macdara said. "Hardly a time to think, let alone worry, about which hand was which."

Siobhán disagreed. She had been mulling it over and she agreed with Brandon. Instinct would have kicked in. Reflex. His left hand was lying by his side, not occupied, as she'd suggested to Brandon earlier. So why did he point with his nondominant hand? It bothered her. They reached the pub. This time they could walk in the front door. For a moment she and Macdara stood, taking it in.

"You had your first pint here," Macdara said softly, as he took in the pub.

Siobhán was shocked. She was instantly back to her eighteenth birthday. Her parents had given her a new blouse, the prettiest shade of blue-green she had ever seen. "You were right," her da said to her mam when Siobhán walked down the stairs in her new blouse. "It makes her eyes glow."

Siobhán turned to Macdara. "How did you know?"

He laughed. "Never mind."

"Tell me."

A flush crept into his cheeks. "I bought it for you."

"Bought what?"

"Your first pint."

"You did not."

"I did. I just didn't want you to know."

"You were here?"

He pointed to a stool in the back corner of the pub. "I sat right there. You walked in, big grin on your face, your hair on fire from a ray of sun that seemed to follow you, wearing a blue blouse. The color of a summer sky." Siobhán was, maybe for the first time in her life, speechless. She was jammed up by the competing feelings running through her. "Moving on," he said. "I don't think we missed any spots." The guards had indeed gone through the pub. Cabinets were open, drawers searched.

Siobhán walked behind the bar. She stood in front of the mirror. "I forgot all about this until Pio fetched the donation register from under the counter."

She pulled it open.

"A secret hiding space?" Macdara said.

"Mike Kelly used to keep the expensive liquor in here." The hiding space was the size of a small closet. Inside she saw a cardboard box and a briefcase. "Bingo," she said.

"Well, I'll be," Macdara said. "Don't touch them. We have to call this in."

Siobhán sighed. Her hands were twitching. Macdara laughed behind her. "What?" she said. It came out testier than she intended.

"Some people just don't play well with others," he said.

"When the guards get here, do you think they'll let me go through the box first?"

"No," he said. "Definitely not."

—

Siobhán gathered in the gardai station with several other guards, Macdara, and O'Reilly. Two cardboard boxes were recovered from the hiding place. The first held letters, photos, and a journal kept by John Mallon. Siobhán couldn't wait until she was allowed to read them. The second box held a wig, high heels, a tan coat, and a red hat. Underneath everything they found Peter's wallet and mobile phone. They were going to examine the phone straightaway to see if Peter placed or received any calls on the night of the murder.

O'Reilly wheeled around and pointed at Siobhán. "How did you know they were there?"

Siobhán met his gaze. "I didn't know for sure. I remembered the hiding place and I thought it was worth checking out."

"I didn't approve of the mission," O'Reilly said.

Macdara stepped up. "I did."

"Oh," O'Reilly said. "Very well. Good work."

"Garda O'Sullivan should get the credit," Macdara said.

O'Reilly cleared his throat. Siobhán didn't need his approval. "Will we be able to get fingerprints off the high heels?"

"We'll send them out and see," O'Reilly said.

"We could go around the village and ask old ladies to try them on," one of the guards joked.

"They are rather large," Siobhán said. "It fits my theory that they were worn by a man."

"And what theory is that?" O'Reilly said. He couldn't hide his disdain. Macdara tensed.

"I believe a man was dressed as the old lady."

"Please tell us all about your theory."

Siobhán blinked. "I just did," she said slowly.

"A theory I second," Macdara said.

"The woman was described as over six feet tall. No woman I know would wear high heels in a churchyard. And the indentations in the ground that so disturbed Father Kearney suggests this person was stumbling around because *he* was not used to walking in heels." She pointed to the wig in the box. "And then there's that."

O'Reilly pursed his lips. "Anything else?"

"Yes," Siobhán said. There were no wig shops in Kilbane. She could only think of one place where a person could have obtained that wig in Kilbane. "I think we should check with the Kilbane Players. See if the wig is one of their props. If it is theirs, they may be able to help us ascertain who took it."

"Great idea," Macdara said.

"Why don't you do that?" O'Reilly said.

"I'll do it," Macdara said. "Siobhán was going to check on some genealogical records."

"Thank you," she said once they were outside.

"Ring me as soon as you find anything."

"Yes, boss."

Chapter 30

The clerk at the Limerick Courthouse was a studious young lad with thick black glasses. He agreed to search for any records related to the Mallon name, but warned her it was just going to take some time. Siobhán didn't mind, one of her favorite chippers was in Limerick and it was a grand excuse to get a basket of curried chips. She was headed out the door, when the clerk called after her. "Are you related to the fellow who was in here a while back asking for these same records?" he asked.

Peter Mallon certainly had gotten around in the short time he was here. "No," Siobhán said. "No relation."

"Limerick man, wasn't he?"

Siobhán nodded. "They set sail from Cork, but he was believed to be a Limerick man."

"Who?"

"The man he was researching," Siobhán said. "His great-grandfather."

"I was on about the fella who came in. He was the Limerick man."

"Right," Siobhán said. "His ancestors, anyway."

"No," the clerk said, frowning. "I'm pretty sure *he* was a Limerick man." Siobhán sighed. Irish pride was strong, especially within the counties. She was surprised the clerk even cared where an American was from, but maybe that wasn't very generous of her.

By the time she arrived at Donkey Ford's, and was sitting in front of a basket of curried chips, she started putting the clues together, rearranging them, testing them out. After she ate, she walked the path along the River Shannon. It always calmed her down to be near water. Finally it was time to go back to the courthouse.

As soon as she walked in, the young clerk nodded and slid documents across the counter. He'd found two birth certificates and another marriage certificate. "Hope this helps," he said, pushing up his glasses with his index finger. Siobhán looked at the first birth certificate: *Tara Mallon*. She looked at the marriage certificate. Tara Mallon married a man named Danny. Her eyes landed on his full name: *Danny Dunne*. A slight shock rippled through her. She looked at the last birth certificate, although she already knew what she would find.

George Dunne. John Mallon's great-grandson was George Dunne.

She stared at the clerk. His face mirrored her concern. "Everything alright?"

"The Limerick man you mentioned. He was an American, right?"

The clerk scrunched up his nose. "How could an American be a Limerick man?"

"I thought you were talking about his ancestors."

The clerk shook his head. "I think I can tell an Irishman from an American, t'ank you very much."

"An old man? Kind of crabby?"

The clerk grinned. "That's the one."

—

Magda was standing outside the library, locking the doors, when Siobhán caught up to her.

"How ya?" Magda said with a smile.

"Grand, grand, you?"

"Not a bother."

"I need to ask you about your computers."

Magda glanced at her watch. "They're lovely. But I'm afraid we're closed."

"You said brand-new ones were donated."

"That's right."

"How long ago?"

Magda looked up and to the right. "Ah, let's see. Four months, I'd say. Yes, four months it would be, alright."

"Who donated them?"

She clasped her hands in delight. "It was an anonymous gift, can you believe it? Men arrived, took the old computers, and replaced them with the new ones." She looked toward the heavens. "Someone is looking out for us, I'd say. An angel."

"You don't have any idea who donated them? Not even a guess?"

Magda shook her head. "But they did come with a lovely card. Would you like to see it?"

"Yes."

Magda unlocked the door and they slipped in. She went to the counter, where the card was proudly displayed. "Here it is." On the front was a rendering of Saint Vincent de Paul.

–

Siobhán burst into Macdara's office, and caught him sitting at his desk in front of a basket of curried chips. She gasped. For some reason it never occurred to her that he was eating them without her.

316

A guilty look stole across his face; then he covered the chips with a napkin and stood. "Wait until you hear what was in the second box," he said.

He isn't even going to offer me a chip?

Macdara snapped his fingers. "My eyes are up here."

"I found something," Siobhán said. "A few things actually."

"Same as," Macdara said. "We found George Dunne's box of woolies, and Declan O'Rourke positively identified Jay Shepard as the man who announced he had come to Ireland to 'right a great wrong.'"

The second news stopped her. "Declan? You've got to be kidding me."

"I have his statement right here." Siobhán couldn't believe it. She'd spent all of her time questioning Maria. She'd missed another opportunity that had been right in front of her face. "That means Jay Shepard knew Peter was being blackmailed, and he knew they were going to use the documentary to tell the truth."

"Or," Macdara said, "it means Jay Shepard was the killer."

"What great wrong would Jay be righting by murdering Peter?"

Macdara threw his arms open. "I haven't worked it all out yet." He stole a glance at his basket of chips. "There's more."

"Go on."

"Jay admitted he was the one who had been leaving journal entries."

"Jay had the journal?"

"Well," Macdara said, "Jay claimed he only had copies of the journal. It was part of the blackmail material that had been sent to Peter."

"Was the original journal in the box recovered from Kelly's?"

"Yes," Macdara said. "But Jay could have put it there."

"What about the box of wooly socks? Where did you find them?"

He brightened. "C'mere." She followed him through a maze of desks to the evidence room. They put on gloves, signed the checkout sheet, and were buzzed into the evidence locker. Macdara headed straight to the back. The cardboard boxes were set upon a table, the evidence laid out. Piles of socks dominated one corner. They were bursting at the seams. "Is that...?" Siobhán stepped closer and peered at the socks.

"Cash," Macdara said. "They're stuffed with cash. Now we know why he was so desperate to get his socks back."

Cash he received from blackmailing the Mallons. Maybe George truly thought he'd donated another box to the museum, but he soon realized his mistake. He returned to the museum, stole the gun, and hid it in the box of socks. He returned once more as the old lady to retrieve it. Money and guns. And George Dunne's gnarled toes and fingers. It all made sense now. Who would have guessed that the cranky old man from Limerick was a blackmailer, not to mention a cold-blooded killer? Siobhán turned to Macdara. "George Dunne's mother's name was Tara," she said.

"Okay."

"Tara Mallon."

Macdara whistled. "What exactly are you saying?"

"Shortly after the murder I was summoned to George Dunne's house."

Macdara nodded. "The case of the missing socks."

"Exactly. At the house I noticed a few things. I didn't realize the significance at the time."

"Go on."

"First of all, his feet were beyond disgusting."

"What do his feet have to do with anything?"

"They were gnarled and bruised."

"Do I really need to picture this?"

"High heels."

"'High heels'?"

"George's feet were gnarled and abused from stabbing around Father Kearney's churchyard in high heels."

Macdara's face stilled. "Go on."

"He also had an old computer sitting on a chair. Not plugged in. And a poster of Saint Vincent de Paul, and in addition to his gnarled feet, he has a crooked finger. A crooked *right* finger."

Macdara was listening intently. "Start with the computer."

"Two months ago the library got a donation of brand-new computers. From an anonymous donor."

"Not a crime."

Siobhan nodded her agreement. "The donation was left with a card featuring Saint Vincent de Paul."

"He's a common saint, the saint of charities."

"Charities. Peter Mallon's fortune went to charities." Siobhán stared at Macdara. Didn't he see?

"You're saying the computer in George's house?"

"One of the old library computers. I believe George had been using them to research the Mallon family. Research he started conducting after he discovered and read his great-grandfather's journal. You see, he had been preparing a box to take to the museum. But he never did donate the items. Because suddenly they were worth a lot more."

Macdara pointed at her. "Blackmail material."

Siobhán nodded. "And then he finds a copy of *Dancing Irish*. I assumed it was left by Jay Shepard. I checked with the museum, it was donated six months ago. George Dunne admitted to taking the DVD from the museum. Then Peter Mallon mysteriously receives a copy of the DVD, as well as a suggestion that he should make his family story into a documentary—along with the bombshell."

"That his great-grandfather was Michael Mallon."

"Indeed."

"A murderer." Macdara's voice was low and ominous.

"Correct. Well, a would-be murderer anyway. Had his brother not survived." It was so frustrating that they would never know the nitty-gritty of what happened. How exactly Michael tried to kill his brother. How John managed to survive. Did he get back on the boat right away and hide, or did he make it to shore another way? What did Michael tell Ann after the dastardly deed was done? Did she believe whatever tale he spun? Or was she too frightened of a new land to question him? Why didn't John catch up to them and confront Michael? Siobhán imagined the pain of seeing his wife Ann with his brother, pretending as if he were John, had been too big of a blow. Instead of retaliating, he made his way back home, an embattled and bitter man. If only they'd had Facebook back then. No paper trail in the world would give her the answers she craved, no amount of research would recreate the scene. At least they had the diary, but only snippets from John's perspective. Oh, it was like having a soap opera chopped off mid-story! She could only imagine what really happened.

A terrible fight. Michael pushes John overboard. He tells a frightened Ann that John accidentally fell? A drunken accident?

Why on earth would Ann go along with it? Was she just that naive?

The story went that a friend of the family was expecting John and Ann Mallon in America, had promised to help them set up a pub and restaurant. Did Michael assume his brother's identity to make sure the deal would still go through? To protect Ann from the stigma of widowhood? Or was he just aware that a single woman in Ireland was vulnerable to all kinds of shenanigans? The Irish faced so much prejudice in those days, they certainly weren't always welcome. Ann would have been greiving and frightened. Easily manipulated.

It seemed Michael was ashamed of what he'd done. So ashamed he never went back to his real name. Instead he kept his brother's identity. Perhaps tried to make up for his sins by feeding the hungry—

Oh this is why she could never be a historian. It wasn't facts she wanted, it was truths. The truths behind the names and the dates, and the places.

"Earth to Siobhán." Macdara snapped his fingers.

"Sorry. Just pondering it all."

"Can you ponder out loud?"

Siobhán laughed. "Where were we?"

"George Dunne and the documentary."

"Yes. He enticed Peter Mallon with the idea. Hoping to lure him out here and blackmail him."

"So George Dunne never expected the documentary to be made? It was all a ruse?"

Siobhán nodded. "That's what I believe."

Macdara began to pace. "Frank Mallon intercepts the material and starts paying George Dunne."

"Yes. It all goes swimmingly. Until Peter Mallon decides he does want a documentary, he wants the truth to come out."

"He hires Jay."

"To 'right a great wrong.'"

"Not the reaction George Dunne wanted?"

Siobhán shook her head. "Quite the opposite. He's Irish. Prideful. Old-fashioned. Wouldn't dream of his family history being splashed all over telly."

"He must have been surprised when Peter Mallon showed up in Ireland."

"Shocked. Frightened. He started stalking the cemetery, waiting to see if Peter would discover the grave. Dressed up as an old lady."

"Why?"

Siobhán knew that Macdara was following her train of thought, yet inviting her to expand, think it through. He was a good mentor. "He lives right next door to the churchyard. I'm sure he was afraid Father Kearney would recognize him."

"And he was at the museum when the revolver was stolen."

"Donating his own box of socks, which he later picked up, dressed as the old lady."

"And the revolver was inside."

"That's my guess."

"It's all circumstantial," Macdara said.

"But there's a lot of it. He's the only one who would have tried to burn the journal to keep Peter from using it in his documentary. He was the only one who couldn't

322

have realized Peter Mallon stopped wearing his American flag pin."

"Why would George Dunne put the pin on him?"

"He probably assumed it came off during the struggle. He couldn't have realized Peter had just given it to Brandon. George had an extra pin—from the business card Peter had left at his house. George would have noticed Peter wearing it then."

"You're saying Peter Mallon visited George at his house?"

"Yes," Siobhán said.

Macdara shook his head. "I can only imagine how that family reunion went down."

Siobhán nodded. "Peter probably insisted he was going to go ahead with the documentary. That's when George knew he had to stop him. On the day he donated his box to the museum, he used the donation boxes to block the gun case and steal the revolver. Then he used the journal as bait to entice Peter to the cemetery."

"We've no hard proof."

"Poor Peter tried to give us a clue."

"What?"

"His finger. His *nondominant* hand. It was pointing, yes, but it was also crooked. I thought the poor man had arthritis."

"My God," Macdara said. "He was imitating George's finger."

"That's my guess."

"It's still not proof. We need hard evidence."

"I have an idea," she said. "But it might not exactly be by the book."

"How far afield are we talking?"

"I want to stir the pot."

"'Stir'? Or knock it over?"

"Just a little stir."

Macdara sat on the edge of the table and rubbed his chin. "I'm listening."

Chapter 31

Siobhán knocked on George Dunne's door once again, but louder this time. When he finally opened it, he was glaring. His eyes narrowed when he saw Siobhán standing there. "Did you find my wooly socks?"

"You donated them to the museum, remember?"

"Why would the museum want my wooly socks?"

"They didn't. They threw them out."

George Dunne shook his fist. "I'll sue!"

Siobhán pinched the bridge of her nose. She wasn't sure if he was truly this forgetful or if it was an act. "Did Peter Mallon visit you? Perhaps leave this card with you?" Once again she showed him Jay Shepard's business card. The one with the family tree. The one he made especially for Peter Mallon.

"I can't read that," George Dunne said, waving her away with his hand. "I don't have my glasses."

"Why did Peter Mallon visit you?"

"Poor fella," George said. "Who did it?"

"Why did he visit you?"

George leaned against his door frame and exhaled. "He wanted to know about me mam, if you must know."

She shoved the marriage certificate at him. "Your mom was a Mallon."

"I just told ye that."

"No, you didn't. I found the records at the courthouse in Limerick. Tara Mallon."

"So?"

"John Mallon is your great-grandfather. You didn't think of mentioning this?"

He grinned. "I had no idea she had rich relatives in America." He leaned in, his breath bad enough to be a murder weapon. "Have they read the will yet? Am I in it?"

"Did Peter Mallon pay you a visit?"

George sighed. "Yep, yep. I told him too. That's *my* great-grandfather."

"What did he say?"

"He tried to argue with me." George shrugged. "I told him he had the wrong end of the stick."

"He was using the legend of your great-grandfather to build a family dynasty," Siobhán said.

"Imagine," George said, "Americans lying about their Irish ancestry. Shocking."

"Did Peter Mallon believe you?"

"I didn't ask him."

"Did he say anything else?"

George blinked. "Like what?"

"Anything." Siobhán knew it was a virtue to be kind to the elderly, but she wanted to throttle George Dunne. And force-feed mouthwash into him. "Why didn't you tell me this when I visited you before?"

"I thought you were calling on me to report my theft."

"I asked you if you saw any Americans in town."

"Did ye? I don't recall."

Siobhán bit her lip and curled her fists. Just one little punch. What would the punishment be for that? "Do you have anything of your mother's? Any information on the Mallon line?"

"I took a box of her stuff to the museum." They locked eyes.

"How many boxes did you take to the museum?"

"Just the one."

"Before they went missing, where did you store your wooly socks?"

"In a box." Finally the light switch flipped. "Wait a minute. I think I took the wrong box to the museum."

"*You think?*"

He squinted as if trying to figure out whether or not she was being sarcastic. She sighed. "May I see the other box now?"

"What other box?"

"The one you were going to take to the museum, but didn't, because you took your wooly socks instead."

"Oh," he said. He shook his head. "Right. No."

Siobhán was flummoxed. "No what?"

"No, you can't have the box."

"Why not?"

"Because I already gave it to the filmmaker."

"Jay Shepard?"

"That's the name." He pointed to the business card in her hand. "That's the fella."

"When did you give him the box?"

"When he visited me and asked for it."

"When was that? Before the murder? After?"

"I don't recall."

Siobhán curled her fists. "Do you keep a calendar?"

"What for?"

"Activities, dates, things you want to remember?"

"No."

She gritted her teeth. "You should."

"I don't need to."

"If you had, it might help us with our investigation." She knew she should let it go, but he was so maddening. "If Jay Shepard has already taken and paid for the box, then what was he doing back here?"

George paled. "What do you mean?" His brash demeanor was gone. He seemed truly upset.

"When I visited you the other day, I found him crouching behind your shed."

George grabbed her. "He came here to kill me!"

"What?"

"I'm the witness. The sole heir."

"You're the sole heir."

"Aren't I?"

"Are you saying you're Peter Mallon's long-lost brother?"

"No." He waved his arms. "Some kind of cousin, I suppose. Many, many times removed."

"Then you're not an heir."

"He came to kill me. I know it!"

"Why? Why would he kill you?"

"Because if John Mallon is my great-grandfather, that means they've been lying about theirs. Making him into a hero with this documentary business. Their entire movie is based on the legend of John Mallon!"

"It sounds like you talked extensively with Peter Mallon."

"It's a disgrace! In my day you didn't tell tales out of school."

"Jay Shepard was bragging about town that he had come to Ireland to 'right a great wrong.'"

George started to stammer. Then he grabbed Siobhán with both arms. "He's c-cleaning house. I'm a witness. Are you going to protect me?"

This was Siobhán's chance to really get something out of him. She hated to manipulate him, but fear was a great motivator. "I'll try. But you have to help me. What was in that box?"

George crossed his arms. "Photographs, a few letters. My great-grandfather's journal. Nothing that was going to pay my bills. I don't care much for family. Dead or alive."

She knew exactly what was in that box, because the guards had it. "In other words, blackmail material."

George gasped. "That's why he paid me so well for it."

"Who?"

"That filmmaker!"

"How much did he pay you?"

"Five hundred euro. For a few photographs and a journal. He fooled me!"

"What did the journal say? Did you read it?" The guards weren't letting her read it yet; she was dying to.

George shook his head. "My eyesight isn't any good. I wish I had read it. I just wanted the money."

"I'll talk to Macdara. We'll make sure the guards keep an eye out for you. Keep your door locked."

"That's it? That's all you're going to do?"

"I didn't see Jay Shepard with a weapon, and he told me he knocked on your door and you wouldn't let him in."

"He did not. I'm telling you *he did not.*"

"I'll look into it. I promise."

George shook his fist at her, spit flying. "If he comes back to kill me, my blood is on your hands." And with that, the old curmudgeon slammed the door.

She hurried out of the yard, and met Macdara at the end of it.

"How did it go?"

"He's blaming Jay Shepard. For the blackmail and the murder. He said he sold the box of his mother's belonging to Jay for the film."

"Let's go," Macdara said. They hurried off to find Jay Shepard.

–

Siobhán and Macdara found him filming outside the churchyard.

"Hey," he said. He flashed a smile devoid of any real warmth. He wasn't only a director and filmmaker, but an actor too. Siobhán had an urge to tell him not to bother, he was too transparent. He glanced around the churchyard. "Even the cemeteries are nicer here," he said. "They have character and charm. You're very lucky."

Macdara glanced around. "I'm sure there are a few in here who would disagree with ye if they could."

"I suppose you're right." Jay flashed another hollow smile. "I don't suppose you're here to chat about head-stones?"

"We just spoke with George Dunne," Macdara said. Technically, Siobhán had just spoken with George, but she wasn't going to nitpick.

"Hope you had better luck than I did," Jay said.

"I'd say," Siobhán said. "We discovered you're a liar." Siobhán hoped her voice was loud enough to carry across the churchyard. She took a few steps away from Macdara in case he wanted to kick her. She couldn't help it, but she was getting fed up with these Americans.

He lowered the camera and gazed at Siobhán. "Pardon?" This time he didn't try to sound friendly, and although his tone was polite, it was guarded, and tinged with venom.

"He told us you bought a box of letters and photographs and a particular journal from him."

"He's lying." Jay's eyes darted right and left as if he was considering making a run for it.

"Why would he lie?" Siobhán asked. She stepped closer to Jay. "If I were you, I would be nothing right now if not very, very cooperative."

Jay threw his arms open. "I gave you all my footage, I've remained here filming, despite the fact that my client was murdered, and the family certainly doesn't seem to care if I finish the project—"

"What were you really doing hiding behind George Dunne's shed?" Siobhán asked.

"Following you."

"Stalking a police officer is a serious offense," Macdara said.

Jay shook his head. "I was just getting B-roll. For the film. Siobhán is very photogenic."

"That's Garda O'Sullivan to you," Macdara said.

Siobhán nodded. "George Dunne thinks you came to his house to kill him."

Jay looked startled.

"Did you hear me?" Siobhán said. "He told us you're the killer."

Jay cried out. "It's not me. I swear." He started pacing.

"Why were you passing out the journal entries?"

"They were copies of the blackmail material Peter had. He'd shared them with me. I was trying to draw out the killer. I wanted to see who would report finding the journal entries and who would keep it a secret." He threw up his hands. "But they all reported it!"

"Quite a twist," Macdara said. "Turning the documentary into a murder mystery."

"I would never do that," Jay said.

"'Never'?" Siobhán said.

"Okay, okay, I was caught up in the drama. As a filmmaker. But the only reason I've continued filming is to tell the truth. To unmask Peter's killer. *I swear.*"

Macdara took off his handcuffs. "Turn around."

"What are you doing?" Jay's voice was laced with pure panic.

Siobhán glanced toward George Dunne's house. Sure enough, he was in his yard, watching. She hoped he had a clear view of Detective Sergeant Macdara Flannery leading the filmmaker away in handcuffs.

Chapter 32

The Mallons gathered around the churchyard. Siobhán wanted them all in one place, and occupied. Guards were hiding in Kelly's, ready to alert Macdara and Siobhán if anyone entered. "Go ahead," Siobhán said to Frank.

Frank cleared his throat and addressed the group. "John Mallon was not our great-grandfather," he said. "This was brought to my attention six months ago. An anonymous package was delivered. It contained a ship's manifest, photographs, the tombstone in Kilbane, and copies of letters written in the late 1800s from John Mallon to his wife, Ann. The letters chronicle everything that happened on the ship. Michael Mallon physically assaulted John, then threw him overboard. Believing he had killed his brother, he claimed his identity and his wife, and made his way to Dublin, Ohio, to start the restaurants. The blackmailer said that the story would be made into a documentary, and then it would go to the American media, and our restaurants would be finished."

Siobhán carefully watched the Mallons react to Frank's confession.

"It's true," Greta said. "I've examined all of it."

"*Believed* he killed his brother," Brandon said. "But John Mallon lived. The tombstone in Kilbane."

"Yes," Siobhán said. "'Out to the field' is a reference to Cain and Abel. And '*Et tu*, Ann' is pointing a finger at his wife."

"This is crazy," Tracy said. "Who was this blackmailer? Is he also the killer?"

Frank took a step forward. "We never knew who the blackmailer was. And I never saw my kidnapper's face. Peter was furious with me for going along with the blackmailer. His entire purpose for coming here was to let the truth come out. He wanted to make the documentary himself. In fact that's how he found out about Jay Shepard—from the blackmailer!"

"Why on earth would he want to do that?" Tracy said. "Blacken our good name?"

"He didn't see it like that," Frank said. "He wanted to be free. Free of the blackmailer, and free from the lies our legacy was built on."

"Speaking of which," Brandon said, looking around, "where's Jay?"

Siobhán's radio crackled, followed by Macdara's. "Stay here," Macdara told the group. She and Macdara ran for Kelly's.

They entered through the back, having secretly cleared the door earlier for entrance. They crept toward the center of the pub. George Dunne was halfway in the safe, hauling out the cardboard box that the guards had placed back inside.

"Does that belong to you?" Macdara said.

George whirled around. "It's an abandoned p-pub," he stammered. "I use it as storage."

Siobhán stepped forward. "I was surprised when I first visited your house to see a poster of Saint Vincent de Paul," she said, "the patron saint of charities."

"You shouldn't have been," George said. "I'm a very charitable man."

"I also noticed your finger," Siobhán said, pointing to it.

George held up his gnarled finger. "What about it?"

"Peter was left-handed," Siobhán said.

"So?"

"He was pointing with his right hand. We thought he was pointing at the headstone."

"He was. What else?"

"He was trying to tell us who his killer was by pointing out your most distinctive feature," Siobhán said. "*Your finger.*"

George Dunne's face flooded with red. "That's nonsense!" He looked around. "It's the filmmaker! I saw you arrest him!"

"Yes, we arrested him," Macdara said. "Knowing you would run straight here and try to clear out the evidence."

"Lies," George said. "All lies!"

"The DVD of *Dancing Irish* was donated to the museum six months ago," Siobhán continued.

"So?"

"It had Jay's card attached to it. That's what gave you the idea to make the documentary."

"What is this?" George yelled. "A trick?"

"I spoke with the costume department at the theatre," Macdara said. "We have you on CCTV stealing the gray wig, red cap, tan coat, and high heels."

"They really kill your feet, don't they?" Siobhán said.

George began to back up. "There's no law saying I can't dress up!"

"You were the only person *not* in the library when the lights went out."

"All circumstantial!"

Siobhán continued. "You volunteered at the museum around the time the gun went missing. You donated your own box of wooly socks, then hid the gun inside, and returned for it dressed as the old woman."

"Then reported your socks missing, just in case," Macdara said.

"W-where's the proof?" George sputtered.

"You sent blackmail material to Frank Mallon," Siobhán said. "We recovered it."

"You did not!"

"Check the boxes," Siobhán said. "They're empty." George couldn't help it. He looked. When he looked back up, his face was beet-red. "Your great-grandfather's journal, which is how you learned about Michael Mallon in the first place, along with Peter's wallet and mobile."

"Anyone could have taken those."

"We're checking the pub for fingerprints. My guess is we'll find yours on the mirror." He glanced at George's hand.

George glared at Siobhán and Macdara. "You should have been on my side!"

"We'll check bank records too," Siobhán said.

"You won't find any bank records!"

"Because the money is in the socks?" Siobhán said. "Oh, wait. The money *was* in the socks. The guards have it now."

"That's my money!"

"Received through blackmail," Macdara said.

George clamped his mouth shut. "You can't prove anything."

"Why?" Greta cried. "Why did you have to kill him?" Siobhán and Macdara whirled around.

"Get back," Macdara said. "Stay out."

George started to shake. "It's *his* fault. Peter wanted it his way! It was *my* movie."

"He wanted the truth to come out," Greta said.

"Greta," Siobhán said, "do as you were told. We're handling this."

"Why?" Greta shouted. "Tell me why!"

"I didn't want my family's dirty laundry spread all over Ireland!" George shouted. He shook his head, spit flying. He picked up an empty bottle. "I just wanted my share. Hadn't John Mallon been humiliated enough?" George hurled the bottle across the room. It shattered on the wall. Everyone ducked.

"Hands on the counter," Macdara said. "You're under arrest."

"I was trying to stop the documentary. He wouldn't hear of it. I gave him chance after chance. He kept insisting the documentary would be made. I had no choice. Besides, all the money was going back to Ireland. Every single penny to charity!"

"You killed him for his honesty," Greta said.

"I was protecting my family's name!"

"You killed him because he wanted to tell the truth."

George's hand trembled. He reached under the counter. "Stop!" Siobhán yelled. "Hands where we can see them."

He brought his hands up. He was holding a gun. He smiled. "A man has to have a backup. This is my trusty hunting weapon. I renew it every three years. Never hunted a thing with it. Until now. This one isn't antique. It'll shoot just fine."

"If you had that gun, why steal the antique one?" Siobhán just wanted to keep him talking.

"Now why would I use my own gun as the murder weapon?" He tapped his own head. "Think! Anyone could have stolen the antique gun. Plus I liked the optics. Ancient gun to settle an ancient feud." George's eyes swam with pride.

"Well you're in plain view of two guards right now," Macdara said. "So why don't you just put the gun down before you make a bad situation worse?"

"I'll fight to the bitter end," George said. "I've nothing more to lose."

"What do you know of your great-grandfather?" Siobhán asked. "What happened on that boat? Were there any family stories?" If anyone knew what happened, it had to be George.

George jerked his head. "John Mallon was a surviver. That's the only story that matters."

"I'm sure it was quite the tale," Siobhán said. "I guess you don't know. I guess no one will ever know."

George's face contorted. "I know! Of course I know!" He took the bait and let the story spill. "Just before the *Swan* reached the shores of America, John told his brother Michael that he thought they should part ways. Told him he didn't like his erratic behavior, didn't appreciate how he looked at his wife. His drunken fool of a brother was enraged. A fight ensued. Michael managed to corner John against the side of the boat, then pushed him over. Always a hothead that one. Michael thought John went into the ocean, assumed he drowned. But John Mallon was saved by a porthole. That's the story. Just enough to get a grip. John never went into the ocean. He clung to the side of the boat. Crawled back up. He probably would have killed Michael. Should have killed Michael. But then he saw his wife in his brother's embrace. That sinful woman fell for Michael's lies. He told her John was the one that tried to attack him. Told her he only fought back in self-defense. Even said he tried to save John but it was too late. He said John was drunk and enraged and Michael had no choice. She swallowed it all. He convinced her the friend waiting for them in America might not help if he heard about what happened to her real husband. John Mallon waited for her to scream at Michael, accuse him of murder. Waited for her to say she was going to report this to the ship's captain. But she didn't. She didn't even walk to the side of the boat to look for him in the murky depths below. That's a woman for you. My great-grandfather was the real hero. He should have killed them both. Instead, he let them go. Watched his brother walk off that boat arm-in-arm with his wife." He glared at Siobhán. "After that he just wanted to go home. He just wanted to go home."

Silence filled the pub. "I'm sorry," Siobhán said. "I can see why you're still so angry." It was true. George spoke as if it had happened to him. For him, it wasn't a long ago. It was right here, right now.

"God didn't even punish them. Let them go on to be rich. That sniveling bastard pretended to be my great-grandfather the rest of his life. Even on his tombstone they carved his brother's name. That's the kind of coward he was. My great-grandfather was the hero!"

"It's over now," Siobhán said. "It's over."

"It's not over until I'm free," George said. "I didn't ask for this. I didn't ask for any of this."

"We have guards surrounding the building," Macdara said. "There's nowhere to go. It's time for you to be the hero now. It's time for you to face up to what you've done."

George jerked his gun to the front door. "I'm going to walk out that door." He came out from behind the counter. "She's going with me." He grabbed Siobhán's arm.

"Don't be a fool," Macdara said. He was trying to be strong, but Siobhán could hear the terror in his voice.

"It's okay," Siobhán said. "I'll go." It was better to have just one hostage than many.

"No," Macdara said.

"This isn't a negotiation," George said. He shoved Siobhán. "Keep moving."

-

Macdara radioed for the guards to stand down. George marched her out the door and down Sarsfield Street. Muttering the entire way. He hadn't thought this plan through. That was to Siobhán's advantage. "My keys are in the bistro," she said when they were near Naomi's. Her siblings were all at Kilbane's Day of Giving.

He narrowed his eyes. "Keys to what?"

"My scooter."

"That pink thing?"

"Yes."

"What about it?"

"How else are you going to get away?"

"*Me?* Ride a pink scooter out of town? Are ye mad?"

"Unless you want to steal a guard car. But that's back the other direction."

George chewed on this. Then nodded. "No funny business." He steered her to the bistro.

-

"I don't want you coming in," she said when they reached Naomi's. He was an ornery type, the kind who would do the exact opposite of anything one asked.

"Too bad." His hands were shaking. He was afraid. And his fear, more than anything, worried her the most. She wanted to keep him talking.

"I understand why you didn't want the truth to come out. We're Irish. We're proud. The Americans don't get that."

"Don't try to sweet-talk me. Inside. Get the keys. Now."

Siobhán opened the door to the bistro. She passed the keys hanging on the coatrack. Maybe if she could lead him into the kitchen, she could get ahold of a frying pan. Hit him over the head with it. They had to step over Ann's camogie bag.

"Where are the keys?" he demanded.

"In the kitchen."

He shoved her. "Move."

She passed the window just in time to see Ann's pretty face coming home. Siobhán quickly turned and began backing up into the rear dining room, near the garden. She held up her hands. "I lied. I'm sorry. The key is in the garden." She tried to catch Ann's eye, to warn her, to wave her away. There wasn't any time. Ann would come through that door any minute.

"Listen," Siobhán said. "This is between us. Nobody else knows you're a killer."

"What in the world are ye on about?" George Dunne began walking toward Siobhán. His back was now to the front dining room.

"Be careful with that gun," Siobhán said. "Why don't you put it down?"

"Get the key."

"Is it really loaded?"

"You want to take the chance?" George asked.

"Put down the gun." She pointed at a nearby table. "Put it right there. If I try anything funny, you'll be able to reach it before me." He frowned. "Put it down or shoot me." She made sure her voice was loud and clear.

"That's a stupid thing to say."

"I'm not getting the key unless you put that gun down. You don't want to kill me. You only killed Peter because you had no choice."

"He left me no choice."

"Well, now you have a choice. I don't want any trouble. Just put the gun down."

"Is this some kind of a trick?"

"Guns make me nervous."

"You're a guard."

"Now, you know we don't carry them, and I'm new on the job. *Please*."

"You'd better not be trying something funny."

"I'm not. I swear. And you're wasting time. You know the guards are on the way."

He glared at her, then put the gun down on the nearest table.

"Now!" Siobhán yelled. "Not the head!"

"What?" George's frown deepened, and it took him a minute to turn around. When he did, it was just as Ann's hurling stick was coming straight for him. Ann aimed it at his side, bringing him down with one whack. Siobhán lunged for the gun as George Dunne moaned on the floor.

"Good hit," Siobhán said when she caught her breath.

"Thank you," Ann said, beaming. "Aren't you glad I leave my sticks and balls lying around, now?"

Chapter 33

The Americans had their last meal—their last Irish meal, that is—at Naomi's Bistro. Siobhán cooked bacon and cabbage, and veg, with a lemon meringue pie for dessert. A fire crackled, and traditional Irish music played in the background. For those who wished to imbibe, there were pints of Guinness rolled over in a keg by Declan O'Rourke, and for those abstaining, there was Barry's tea or minerals. Her siblings helped prepare the meal, and then watched from the back portion of the dining room as if it were a show on telly. Siobhán had grown fond of the quirky Yanks, faults and all, especially since it turned out that none of them were cold-blooded murderers. She hoped she hadn't been too hard on any of them. The least she could do was fill their bellies one last time.

"I told you it wasn't one of us," Tracy said when they were all too bloated to move from the table.

"You did indeed," Siobhán said. "You did indeed."

"We can hardly blame her," Brandon said. "Seeing as how Siobhán was brand-new to the job and all."

Siobhán glanced at Macdara, who was sitting by the window in front of his second slice of pie, and rolled her eyes. He gave her a wink and a nod.

"Poor Father," Tracy said. "I'm going to forgive him for cutting us out of the will."

"You aren't going to fight it?" Greta asked.

"No," Brandon said. "We discussed it, and we just want this to be over. Start our lives anew."

They weren't *entirely* cut out of the will, but Siobhán kept her gob shut, and raised a pint. "To your da. May his legacy continue."

"Which one?" Hannah asked.

First everyone looked at her sharply; then Brandon broke it by laughing; soon everyone joined in. "The good parts, my dear," Brandon said. "We'll carry on the good."

Tracy raised her pint. "He'll be thrilled that we're going to carry on with the documentary."

"It's going to be a huge hit," Jay said. "So many twists." He stared at Siobhán with a smile. "Good thing you have Netflix."

Siobhán's head snapped up. "I thought you were all leaving in the morning?" She hadn't grown *that* fond of them.

"We're going to continue with the documentary in the States," Greta said. "Peter died wanting the truth to come out."

"Why don't you come with us?" Jay said. "I'd love to have you play your character."

Siobhán was starting to feel a tummyache coming on. "My 'character'?"

"The feisty, gorgeous redhead?" Jay said. "She'll be the star."

"I told her it wasn't one of us," Tracy stated again. "You'd better put *that* in the documentary."

"She stayed on the case until it was solved," Jay said, leering at her. Siobhán wished he'd stop talking about her; then she wished he'd stop talking altogether.

"However," Frank said, with a worried glance around the room, "we wouldn't want to rile up any more Irish folk, so please don't worry about the documentary."

"No one is worried," Siobhán said. "Except George Dunne. And where he's going, he won't have Netflix." She returned Jay's sarcastic smile.

Siobhán glanced at Greta and Frank, and wondered what would become of the pair. At the thought her eyes drifted back to Macdara, who was gazing toward the kitchen as if willing a third slice of lemon meringue pie to come sailing out the door and land in front of him. She also wondered what would become of him and her. Maybe some mysteries were best left unsolved.

Siobhán saw the Americans to the door. "I'll send you a copy of the documentary when it's finished," Jay said, winking at Siobhán.

"Please do," she said.

"Just do me a favor. Don't donate it to the museum."

Siobhán laughed. "I wouldn't dream of it." She watched as they headed down the street, wondering if one day, half a century, or a century from now, their ancestors would go to the same lengths to learn about *them*. There was something special about that, a bond of blood that neither time nor distance could break. She looked toward the sky and gave a quick good-bye to Peter Mallon, and silently wished them all well. The bell tinkled on her way back into the bistro, the comforting jingle that always reminded her she was home.

–

They stood in the Shannon airport, a clump of crying O'Sullivans, and a heap of overweight luggage. Elise looked somewhat perplexed at their public show of emotion. Gráinne wailed louder than all of them.

"You'll come visit me in New York, wont ye?" she said, wiping her tears.

"Of course, pet," Siobhán said, wiping the tears from her own eyes. "And you can come home anytime. For a visit, or forever."

Gráinne sniffed. "I wish you'd all move out with me."

"Do you have room for us?" Eoin asked.

"Not in the same flat, like," Gráinne said. "You can live in Brooklyn."

"But you're in Queens," Eoin said.

"Exactly," Gráinne said.

"How about the Bronx?" Eoin grinned, tapping his Yankee cap.

Siobhán grabbed Eoin and held on. "Let's just say good-bye to one at a time." He laughed and gave her a gentle shove.

"I hope you have a very nice time," Elise said. "Lucky I'm here to fill in the gap!"

"Mind the gap," Ann said under her breath.

James grinned at Elise; everyone else attempted a smile and failed.

"Send me loads of postcards," Ann said.

"Postcards are for tourists," Gráinne said.

"You'll always be a tourist," Siobhán said. "This is home." That started a fresh round of tears.

"Enough," James said. He shoved Gráinne forward. "Off with ye."

"T'anks," Gráinne said. She heaved her luggage onto a cart and pushed off. The O'Sullivans watched her until she was a speck in the distance.

"Come on," James said, looping an arm around Siobhán. "Let's get you some curried chips."

—

Siobhán stood in her tiny office, with her single cardboard box. She hadn't been in this office more than ten days, and here she was, packing up.

"Ready?" Macdara stood in the doorway. She turned, then smiled.

"Ready." He led her to the larger office. Next to his.

He watched as she unpacked her few items.

"I'm glad you're staying," she said.

"There's nowhere else I'd rather be," he said.

"I'm going to learn a lot from you."

"Ditto."

She met his eyes. "It's not going to be easy to follow all the rules."

"Oh, I know," he said. "But until we figure this out, we'll have to try."

"Are we talking about the same thing?"

"I've no doubt." He winked. "Are you going to take all day, or are we going to pop into the chipper for a basket of curried chips?"

"Yes, please," she said.

"Let's go then."

"What will the others say?"

He glanced at the guards in the outer room, milling around, pretending not to listen. A grin spread over his face. "They'll say what a cheap bastard I am, rewarding the guard who solved the murder with a cheap basket of curried chips." She laughed. "So what do you say, Garda O'Sullivan?" He tipped his garda cap and flashed her his lopsided grin.

"As long as you're buying," Siobhán said as the image of that sweet, sweet curried basket of chips filled her soul.

"Yes, boss," Macdara said with a tip of his cap and a wink.

Acknowledgments

First, thank you to the usual suspects: my editor, John Scognamiglio, my agent, Evan Marshall, my publicist, Morgan Elwell, director of social media & digital sales Alexandra Nicolajsen, production editor Robin Cook, and all the other Kensington staff who work so hard to help and inspire their authors. It takes a village to raise a book! Thank you to my Irish friends: James and Annmarie Sheedy, Fiona Curley, Bridget and Seamus Collins, Eileen Collins, and Kevin Collins.